AN EMPRESS OF AIR & CHAOS

By Noelle Rayne

First Paperback Edition August 2021
First Hardback Edition August 2021
First eBook Edition August 2021

ISBN: 978-1-9196109-0-0 (Paperback)
ISBN: 978-1-9196109-2-4 (Hardback)
ISBN: 978-1-9196109-1-7 (eBook)

www.NoelleRayne.com

A dedication

To my grandmother, who always taught me to believe in imagination. Who taught me to search for the magic in adventure and myth. My Faerie Angel.

CALEDORNA
Mountains of the N
The Waterfall of Uttara
Helmsbrook City
The Fairlands
So
Solden Coal Mine
Huntswood City
Ashdale Forest
The River of Vanadey

The Temple of the Gods
orth
The Lake of Rhiannon
SKYELIR
Tolsah Bay
Crimson Dock
The Broken Sea of Thorin
lden Diamond Mine
Mossgrave
N
W
E
S

CHAPTER ONE

The air was crisp enough for the hairs to stand up on the back of Emara's neck. She brushed her hand over them as a command to stand down. They reappeared within a second. The air was changing. Rolling her neck, she turned her gaze to the burnt orange moon that lit the night's sky. The Blood Moon was entering the waxing gibbous stage of its cycle, coming close to its fullest strength. A full moon happened twelve times a year, but the Blood Moon—a celestial event that took place once every year—was one that her grandmother was always uneasy about. For whatever sacred reason she had that linked to the ancient Gods of Caledorna.

A feeling of unease spread over Emara's skin and she folded her arms in efforts to calm the growing unrest that had been brewing in her stomach all day. Nothing in particular had happened today that could have stirred up the strange sensation igniting in the pits of Emara's belly, but regardless, it swirled.

"Emara!" her name vibrated through the glass doors to where she stood on the balcony facing the surrounding forest of fir trees. "Emara Clearwater, come inside at once."

She threw a glance over her shoulder to spy her grandmother standing in her room. Her slender finger pointed at her and then motioned to come inside.

A bitter shiver snaked up Emara's spine as she turned her back on the moon and ventured into her room. Tugging at her white nightgown, she wrapped the loose material around her body as if it would defend her from the chilling night air and tiptoed from the humble wooden terrace. She slid open the glass door that gave entrance to her room and rubbed her feet on the thick, woven rug that offered instant heat. Feeling the warmth niggle into her toes again, she inhaled deeply.

"What on earth are you doing outside, child?" her grandmother asked, her unsmiling eyes meeting hers at last. "By the Gods, you must be freezing standing out there."

"Grandmother, I am not a child. There is no need to lecture me on what temperature I should keep my body." She smiled warmly. "I was just fine."

A small corner of her grandmother's lips turned up. "Regardless of your age, one can still catch a chill."

Emara wanted to roll her eyes, but thought better of it and just smiled. "Were there any interesting clientele at the gallery today?" she asked as she rubbed her arms to gather heat.

Her grandmother swept a paint-stained hand over her brow and raised her chin. "My darling, when you work with art, your clientele is always interesting," Theodora Clearwater declared as she looked around the room. Emara knew exactly *who* she was scanning the space for. "Speaking of interesting individuals, where is Miss Greymore?" Her grandmother's lips pursed together in the way that one's did before a poised person lost their temper.

Emara's nose wrinkled. "She still appears to be out at the moment."

Theodora Clearwater's dark blue eyes narrowed in on Emara's face. "I can see that. Does Callyn Greymore believe that she lives above the rules of my household?" Her structured face straightened, but a glimmer of amusement rang through in her voice. "She knows that curfew is before dusk in the lead up to a full moon, yet she always seems to think she can bend the rules."

Dusk had fallen onto the earth an hour ago and that meant Callyn had missed curfew—again. It was a condition that her grandmother was unfaltering on, even as they matured into young women.

Emara sighed internally and cursed at whatever quarrels her grandmother had with the full moon before hearing a noise from downstairs. "Ah, I think I can hear her now," she announced, her heart beating a little faster. "That must be her." She gathered from the creaking wood that moved on the staircase.

Theodora Clearwater turned towards the door slowly, awaiting the arrival of Emara's best friend.

Emara let out a nervous exhale. Just as her swirling breath disappeared, she heard a clicking of familiar shoes as footsteps made their way through the hallway. Before she could move towards the door to warn her that her grandmother was in the room, Callyn Greymore burst through the threshold of the bedroom, looking glamorous.

As always.

"Sorry, I am late. I have wine—" Callyn halted, her fashionable footwear skidding on the wooden floor. "Mrs. Clearwater!" Callyn's eyes widened, and her spine straightened as she observed Theodora, standing cross-armed before her. She drew a dazzling smile across her face to hide the fact she knew she had been busted. "I thought you might still have been working," she gulped. "You know…late."

Emara stifled a laugh at how, even after living with them for most of her life, Callyn still called her grandmother "Mrs Clearwater."

Theodora pulled in her cheeks tight and took a step towards her before saying, "Callyn, in case you haven't noticed, it is dark outside." Her hand broke through the regal, cerulean cloak she had gathered around her shoulders and gestured to the night outside.

Callyn nodded, her light-as-sand hair lay curling around her shoulders, immediately brightening up the room with its golden shine.

"And it is rather cold," Theodora said, taking in Callyn's attire. "You should be wearing a lot more than what you have on."

Her ensemble certainly wasn't made to keep out the cold, as the soft fabric of her cerise pink dress hugged her thin curves, exposing her bare arms and most of her long legs.

Immediately, Emara knew Callyn had made the garment. Probably in the last day or two. The village of Mossgrave only had one seamstress and she certainly wasn't the one responsible for making that dress. Not in a million moons.

Since having ambitions in women's fashion, Callyn had been pushing every boundary there was in hem height, tight fabrics, and suggestive cuts, and the sleepy, traditional village of Mossgrave had never seen anything as scandalous as Callyn Greymore's style since they day the Gods put life on the world. She, of course, had picked up the newest fashion trends from the elite she styled, who often had travelled to cities or more exotic places outside Mossgrave.

"I am terribly sorry, Mrs. Clearwater," Callyn announced with an angelic smile. "But I had a job to finish up. You know what clients can be like." She flicked a look in Emara's direction.

"That I do." Theodora said before turning to Emara. "Very well. Have a good night, girls."

Relief filled Cally's face as Theodora moved towards the door to exit the room, but halted midway.

She peeked over her shoulder and said, "And just before I leave," she turned back to Callyn, who had gone rigid again. "Whatever is clinking away in that bag of yours"— her suspicious eyes trailed over the leather haversack that was completely out of place on Callyn's shoulder—"please do not drink it *all* in one go."

Theodora eyed both girls in warning and then left the room, her cloak sweeping behind her graciously like a soft, blue wave.

"Phew." Callyn's shoulders sagged as the door closed. "I thought I was done for there. She almost always knows when I am up to no good. It's like she has super-powers." She chuckled, placing the bag on the floor carefully.

Emara let out a hearty laugh. "She can see right through you, Cally."

Cally.

A nickname she preferred. She always said Callyn was way too formal for her.

"However, what I do want to know is what sort of *no good* you were getting up to this time." Emara eyed her best friend before making her way over to the fireplace to check the wood. "Because I know you were not working until this hour. The elite never have dress fittings at night."

Cally's light blue eyes twinkled. "I may or may not have met someone to trade some fabrics that they will not sell to me in Mossgrave."

"Oh?" Emara popped an eyebrow. "And who exactly are you meeting to do a dodgy deal of forbidden fabrics with?"

A devilish smile formed on her face, highlighting her curved cheek bones. "Well, there is this *guy*—he's very handsome and he works at the farm, up past the village centre. You will know it. Rosemill farm?" She bit into her pink lips as naughty look flashed in her eyes. "He has connections."

A barking laugh escaped Emara's throat, "What kind of connections? Do I even want to know?" she asked hesitantly as she poked the dead firewood with the pit shovel. The motion sent ashes flying up into the air and she stepped back to look at her best friend.

Cally's hands flew up. "Okay, you start the fire, and I will get the alcohol prepared before I tell you."

Emara rolled her eyes and snorted. *Typical Cally!*

Callyn Greymore was more like a sister to Emara than a friend. Having met when they were just ten years old outside the village bakers, it seemed even then that Cally had a knack for getting herself into situations she shouldn't be in. Whenever trouble would be caught red-handed, Cally would be the one with the paint.

The day Emara first met Cally, she was being dragged out of a bakery shop by the hair, kicking and screaming like a wild animal.

She had been screaming, *"I don't want your shitty bread anyway, I don't even like it. There are maggots in it. You heard it here, folks. MAGGOTS! Maggots in the baker's bread. Don't feed this to your children. They might die!"*

Cally had bellowed and cursed at the shop owner for ten minutes as he emptied her pockets in the main street of the village. Five different kinds of confectionery had dropped out of her coat and fallen into the muddy road. The human traffic went by, gawking at the young girl with the face of an angel and the actions and mouth of a feral heathen.

In that very moment, Emara couldn't help but feel drawn to her. Entertained by her. Something about Cally was freeing and alluring, even though she had just stolen from the only baker in the village and got herself branded a thief, she found her *unique.*

Emara, who had nipped 'round to the baker's from her grandmother's art gallery, was compelled to strike up a conversation, just desperate to speak to another child her age, even if she was abrasive. In the village, you didn't tend to have many kids your own age, let alone someone as thrilling as Callyn Greymore.

From that day, she and Cally were inseparable. However, the recollection of her first time speaking with Cally had been overshadowed with her thoughts on why Callyn would have to steal. How hungry had she been that she had to steal bread to eat? To survive?

Due to Theodora finding out about Cally's turbulent family life at the orphanage, and the inseparable bond they had made so quickly, her grandmother had signed for her adoption papers a year after they had met and moved her into their home. It wasn't in her grandmother's nature to have maternal instincts, but Theodora took Cally in like she was her own child. And Cally had come willingly, with few belongings.

A smile almost broke past her lips at the memory of how their friendship had begun as Emara made her way over to the unit beside her bed for the matches that lit the fire.

Pushing her thoughts of the past aside, Emara plucked the matches from her favourite storage box that was encrusted with stones of bright jade, flushed pink, glowing-sun yellow, and sapphire that wove around an ancient mandala design on the pale wood. It always sat atop her bedside table, keeping a few things like notes, some coins, and hair pins inside.

It had been a gift from her grandmother on her ninth birthday and it was by far the most sentimental and valuable gift she had ever been given because it was once her mother's.

Emara had gone to stay with her grandmother when her parents had been killed. She had just turned three years old when a fire ripped through her family home, devouring everything—including her parents. She didn't remember them or even the fire. And her grandmother had, oddly, made sure to keep it that way. She never spoke of the day that took her only daughter to the other side, leaving behind her only grandchild. Information on her mother was something Emara never pushed for because she saw the pain it caused her grandmother to talk about. So, through the years, she welcomed any forthcoming stories that Theodora would offer on her own accord, but never asked for more.

Emara ran her fingertips along the pattern of the box.

"This box now belongs to you, keep it safe and always remember your mother when you open it."

She had kept it safe; she had opened it a thousand times and always expected something to appear inside it—as if her mother could gift her something from the other side to remember her by. But nothing ever came.

Just before she could feel that usual pang in her chest when she thought of her parents or even the longing to know them, Cally dragged a bristle brush through her hair, giving her a decent tug back to reality.

"Remember before you start giving me all sorts of horrible looks, you promised that I could give you a makeover tonight." She said it with a flat confidence like, that was a good thing. "A Cally-style makeover. Which fits in perfectly with the new garments I need modelled."

With a groan of disapproval, Emara heaved herself away from Cally's evil bristle brush and threw a lit match into the fire before she made her way over to her four-poster bed. "Do we *really* need to do this tonight?"

Cally heaved the leather bag, stacked full of all sorts of trickery, onto the bed and then unbuttoned it. "Yes. What else are we going to do now that we are stuck in here for a few nights?"

True, Emara thought.

Cally opened the bag wide with dramatic flair that was fit for a theatre performance and revealed her newest fashions.

"What in the mother of Gods?" Emara's eyes widened, her cheeks flushing crimson as she took in what she saw in the bag.

"Em, hear me out!" She placed out a hand to stop Emara from objecting. "I need a model to try these on and it must be you." Cally chuckled. "You have no idea what I had to do to get my hands on these garments; and, as much as I would like to see them on myself, I need to see them on someone else first. I think it could change fashion as we know it. For women, of course."

"Cally, no way! I am not wearing any of this stuff." She dipped her hand into the bag and picked up a pink lace corset that had shimmering, intricate detail in all the places it needed to be. She had never seen anything like it. Certainly not in this house. Her cheeks blushed at the sight of it, even though it was beautiful.

"Oh, wow, Cally, where do you even get this stuff?" She flashed her best friend a look of concern before she surveyed the contents of the bag. There was no store in the village that would dare to dream of a front window that displayed or sold garments like this. The villagers would have a heart attack, or a brain aneurysm.

Or both.

Emara doubted any of the women in Mossgrave had seen attire like this, let alone owned any. "No, seriously, where did you get these?" Curiosity coated her tone.

"Well, you know that *farm guy?*" She patted down the lace that had peeked out the bag.

Cally never called a guy by his actual name. It was always, *milk carton guy,* or *handsome welder guy,* or there was even a handsome man who sold sugar at a stall in the village, so she had referred to him as *sugar lips guy...*

But never by their actual names.

"Uh-huh," Emara confirmed, acknowledging that she was following which man Cally was referring to.

"He has family in *Huntswood city!*" she almost squealed. "And he takes trips up there and they have those markets there..."

"Yeah, yeah, yeah, we all know what kind of *markets* there are in Huntswood city," Emara said, flustered, pushing the pink lace back into the bag.

The Huntswood markets were notorious for selling all sorts of black-market items you would never find in the fluffy village of Mossgrave—or anywhere else in Caledorna, in fact. Cally talked about them religiously.

Even in her sleep. She was obsessed!

But you couldn't just wander into markets like that, you had to either know someone or *be* someone to be able to gain entry to them. And two small-time village girls weren't exactly anyone special enough to gain that kind access.

"This *stuff* came from Huntswood city?" Emara almost sounded impressed.

"Yes," Cally beamed. "Well, now you know that *farm guy* could be a great asset to keep around." She walked over to the other side of the bed and swung around one of the four poster bed poles like she was dancing for someone special. "To be fair, I have heard all the boys from Huntswood City are great assets to have. They are hot and *dangerous. City boys. Their* sex appeal is unnatural. Off the charts. I have laid eyes on a few in the homes of the elite, their guards are often from the city and they do not disappoint." She raised her eyebrow and a smile tugged at the corner of her mouth as she flopped onto the bed. "It's a shame we have to stay in for the next couple of nights because of this lousy moon shit, or I could really be seeing what good-looking *farm guy* was all about." She puffed out a dramatic sigh. "Grandma Clearwater needs to update her rules, Gods damn it. She is to blame for all your superstitious malarkey." She flung a hand in Emara's direction.

Emara blew out a breath and ignored any digs Cally took at her grandmother's rules and said, "You don't even know the guy's real name and you have him bringing you all this...*underwear.*" She gestured to the display of feathers and lace and revealing bodices sticking out from the bag.

Cally rolled onto her stomach. "See it as a little preview for him." Her azure eyes danced with wicked delight. As Cally giggled, the moonlight streamed through the window just a little bit brighter than before, casting a glittering light through her hair. "If he plays his cards right."

"You heathen!" Emara laughed as she flung a few of the items that had been left out of the bag at Cally's face. But she was quick and caught them with one hand.

"A girl's gotta do what a girl's gotta do to have some entertainment in this suffocatingly small village," she said in a dismissive tone as she lounged back with her hands tucked behind her glorious crown of golden hair. Emara would bet the most expensive artwork in the gallery that Cally would move to the city if she could.

Callyn sat bolt upright. "I have the perfect garment for you to start with." She scrambled onto her knees and caught hold of the bag before bringing out a black, lacey bralette that had sheer material dripping from the hem—and the undergarments to match.

Emara blinked.

Oh, Holy Gods above.

"Try it on. Please, please, *pretty* please with icing sugar on top." Cally batted her eyelashes like snow was falling on them and she was trying to get it off. "It's the most subtle one I have, and it has more coverage. It's tasteful," she tried to negotiate. Emara looked over the garment in Cally's hand, and she had to admit that she had seen worse come out of the bag a moment ago.

Cally, in the interim, had formed a petted lip and moved her eyes to convey what could only be described as that of a puppy begging for a bone.

For the love of the Gods…

"Okay, fine." Emara rolled her eyes. "But only if you stop making that face at me." She pointed. "If I try this *thing* on, will you leave me alone? No more digging the brush into my scalp. No more black lines drawn on my face, making me look like I have bird wings coming out of my eye. No more creams or glitters or perfumes… If I try on this black undergarment, will you agree to *nothing* else tonight?" She raised her eyebrows uncompromisingly.

A squeal left Cally's mouth as she clapped her hands together. "Yes! Em, of course. Deal. I can't wait!" She squealed again, like an over-excited child. "You are going to look amazing, I can just tell!" Cally seemed accomplished with her fashion suggestion as she looked it over before handing it to Emara.

Emara took it, feeling the delicate, intricate fabric in her hand and sighed.

After all, what else was there to do in the boring town of Mossgrave before a full moon?

CHAPTER TWO

Before Cally could negotiate another item to try on that barely covered any skin, Emara dragged herself to the bathing chamber with the lacey underwear balled up in her fist. She closed the door, flung the undergarment onto the cabinet - where the sink lay low in a white ceramic bowl - and scowled at herself in the mirror.

As she looked at herself, her mother's eyes stared back.

They were very unusual, changing frequently depending on her mood; sometimes they were green that would morph into blue, sometimes hazel, on occasion they looked grey. They had rarely even been as dark as black oil. But they were a peculiar mixture of her very own.

Her grandmother had described her mother's eyes during bedtime stories as a child, making them sound like beautiful magic mood stones that flickered and changed into different colours and hues depending on how she felt. For Emara, this had normalised the fact that, growing up, she had never seen anyone's eyes change colour.

Not like hers.

She took some comfort to know that her mothers had too. That someone was like her. The lighting in the bathroom was so dull it almost made them look closer to a dreary grey than blue tonight.

Anxious? They were usually greyish when she worried.

She shook off that thought. There was no reason to be anxious.

Her skin was a tan colour, which was another standout point on her body. The locals of Mossgrave were typically pale with light-coloured hair and fair features, totally contrasting with her own. She'd hated standing out in the village as a child, and she often dreamed of having hair and skin like Cally's, pale like homemade vanilla ice cream, with gleaming light hair and forever sea blue eyes. Callyn was a true picture of sunshine and warmth.

She couldn't change her tanned skin or her straight, midnight dark hair that draped down her back, or her unusual eyes that changed like the weather. She was stuck with it all.

And not to forget the curves that rounded her body, making her a little more self-conscious than she would like to be. She knew Cally was thin, but she couldn't help but compare her muscular legs to hers or the fact that her rear was rounder.

And bigger.

How could she not compare herself to the only close friend she had ever had?

She sighed.

Fed up with scrutinizing herself and picking herself apart in front of the mirror, she braced the lace.

As she walked back through to her room, she noticed Cally had unloaded a couple of bottles of dark wine from her bag and was lazing along the bed reading a journal.

Emara waited until her *traitorous* best friend sipped the dark liquid from her glass before shouting, "Callyn Greymore, that better not be my diary!"

Startled, Cally choked on the ruby liquid that had filled her mouth, as if she hadn't been expecting to hear a voice for some time yet. Swallowing the remainder of the wine that hadn't spilled from her mouth to the bed, she sat up, tossing the diary to the side.

"Oh, Emara, look at you!" Her mouth fell open wide. "You look sensational. Taymir Solden would be crawling on his knees at the sight of you in that garment," Cally continued before pouring out another glass of wine for each of them. She handed one to Emara and the silence settled into the room as she drank from her glass.

Taymir Solden.

The Solden Dynasty.

Emara chewed her lip as the blush from Cally's compliment died on her skin.

"Actually, I'm not going to be seeing Taymir anymore," she said softly, looking out the window to avoid making eye contact with Cally. "It's not what I want. I don't feel like it's going anywhere. So, I ended things with him."

"Emara?" She paused, searching over her face with her questioning eyes. "He's drop-dead gorgeous, incredibly rich, and he treats you…*nice-ish*. He could give you a good life, you know." She took a swig of wine. "Village girls don't always get the opportunity to socialise with an elite man, let alone have one swoon over her. Think about your rich little children, running around in silk diapers," she entertained, swirling the liquid around in her glass like a scarlet whirlpool. "Think about the diamonds, the dresses, the fabrics…"

"I don't care about what material things he can provide, Callyn." Emara's tone was a little shorter than she had meant it to be. She cleared her throat. "We don't want the same things."

"What do you mean?" Cally rolled onto her side, obviously noticing the tone in Emara's voice.

"I can't stand the thought of it all." Emara wrapped an arm around her bare midriff. "I don't want to be a little elite wife, stuck inside a *massive* mansion house with no one to talk to but the maid or the butler who is probably too scared to even look at me the wrong way. I am just a girl from the village. Not a girl who is going to be married to someone whose coin practically runs the kingdom. Do you know how close he is to all of the powerful men that make the important decisions of the continent?"

It wasn't the idea of being married to someone powerful that didn't sit well with her. She had heard stories about the wives of the elite. They weren't viewed as important, and they certainly weren't treated that way, either. Their words were not valid or respected.

The males of the elite society dominated the world with wealth, greed, and trade. The Minister of Coin, a generation of old money financiers, were a consortium of individuals who oversaw public affairs as well as finances for the kingdom. And they had run the kingdom that way since the Great War, seeing no benefit of a monarchy or dictator.

And the wives of these men? Well, they were merely a trophy or an act to please the Gods, to produce heirs for their fortune and to ensure they carried on the family name. Or more like keeping the old money of Caledorna with the rich.

The women in the elite homes were certainly not viewed as equal to the men and it had always boiled Emara's blood. But, then again, as a normal resident of Mossgrave, she probably wasn't viewed as an equal— and not because she was a woman. That's why her relationship with Taymir would never work.

"I'm not..." She huffed before speaking again, taking precaution in what she said, "He would expect more from me at some point. He does expect more..." She pushed Cally over and she slumped onto the bed. She looked down at the wine in her glass before admitting, "He asked me to marry him, Cally."

Her brows arched over to support her frown, and she flung her head onto one of the goose feather pillows that lay at the top of the bed, white and plump. Cally almost spat out her wine for the second time this evening as she registered what was said—but she would never waste a good red.

"He *what?*" Her eyes bulged from her head, a hand coming up to save any of the liquor that had, indeed, escaped from her mouth this time.

"You heard me." Emara sighed.

"Since I don't see a big, obnoxious Solden diamond on your finger, I am guessing you said no?"

Emara nodded.

"Why didn't you tell me?" Cally also flung herself back onto the pillow next to Emara, keeping the glass of wine in the upright position.

Another skill that Cally had clearly conquered with excellence.

"I didn't want to make a big fuss over it, nor did I want to relive it." She let out a sigh that lasted longer than it should have, allowing her chest to feel a little lighter. "It was awful, Cally."

"He will get over it." She shrugged. "I'm sure he has already."

"I hope so," Emara admitted at the recollection of his face, not quite sure which emotion he had conveyed in the moment she had refused him. "I felt so guilty afterwards."

Cally sat up and retrieved the bottle of wine from the other bedside cabinet before resting back on her elbow. She looked sincerely at her best friend and said, "Open your mouth."

"What? No, what the—" Emara tried to protest.

"Open your Gods-damned mouth and stop being such a wet blanket."

Cally held up the bottle of wine like it was a magic potion for stripping away the guilt and sorrow inside someone's heart after a breakup. Like wine was the answer to everything. No words of advice or sympathy. Just actions. Well, actions of alcohol.

It was very Cally.

As she started to pour, Emara ducked her head under the bottle just in time to catch the burgundy beverage in her mouth.

Pushing the bottle upright with one hand, she wiped her face with the other before glugging down what had been poured. Eyes wide with shock, she said, "Are you mad? My grandmother would kill me if you got red wine on the white sheets."

Cally's wide grin was infectious as it spread across her oval face. "Not to worry. *darling;* if you frown over a man again, there's plenty more where that came from".

"You are the devil, Callyn Greymore!" Emara felt a light laugh burst from her lips.

Cally shimmied off the bed and corked another bottle of red wine. "I know!"

CHAPTER THREE

A sharp pain blistered into Emara's ears. She peeled open her eyes and sat upright in her bed. The noise sounded again.

Was that screaming?

No, wait, breaking glass?

Both? She shook her head, trying to think straight.

Another scream.

"Cally, get up, do you hear tha—"

She silenced when she realised Cally wasn't in the bed next to her. Panic flooded her whole body. Her eyes flickered to the glass windows—the moon was still exploring her kingdom from above in a dusky haze.

Cally had drunk two bottles of wine before bed, passing out almost immediately once the second one was drained. Emara had had four glasses, which had left her head feeling a little buzzed and almost relaxed. Cally had absolutely been in her bed when she'd fallen asleep. So where was she now?

Another crash came from outside and a blood-curdling scream breached the air.

A woman's scream.

"Cally," Emara breathed as she leapt from her bed. She flung one of Cally's silk overgarments around her shoulders as quickly as she could, realising she had forgotten to get dressed from the black two-piece she'd tried on earlier this evening. Fumbling to tie a knot on the band around her midriff, she heard voices that sounded like they were coming from the kitchenette. A lightning bolt of dread struck through her as she slowly walked out into the hallway. She curled her hands up tight, digging her nails into her palms, and made her way through the dark.

As she took the first step on the stairs, she knew exactly where to place her feet to not give herself away. Her grandmother's house was an old wooden structure right in the middle of the private estate and the aged wood often creaked and groaned when walking anywhere in the house.

Sometimes when she was little, Emara would sneak downstairs and listen to her grandmother sing while she painted. It had given her comfort from the nightmares as a child and reminded her that she was safe here. She was always safe with her grandmother.

"I don't have it!" The voice of her grandmother was stern and solid. There were no pleasantries in her tone as she spoke.

Is she arguing with someone? Emara thought as she stilled on the step.

An animal-like noise, almost like a hissing sound, interrupted her. The goosebumps from earlier returned over her neck and spread all over her body, standing her every sense to attention. This time she didn't dare move to command her goosebumps to stand down.

"Do not lie to us," the voice hissed back. "We will burn this village to the ground. The longer you let this lie live, the more people will die. Trusted sources say it could be in your possession. Help us and he will reward you by not sentencing you to death."

The unusual voice ripped at Emara's ear drums and sent shooting pains through her head. She scrunched her eyes and her mouth fell wide at the pain it caused.

Who was that?

What was that?

The voice couldn't have been human. It was agonizingly disturbing. Unnatural.

Undiluted fear coursed through her, making her skin both icy and inflamed.

Something wasn't right. Why wasn't her grandmother running? Was she acquainted with the person who spoke in an ancient, acidic voice?

A horrible thought crossed her mind.

If her grandmother was in the kitchen, then where was Cally?

Another sharp pain invaded her head as the person spoke again, "The king will be glad to know that we have finally found you and what is his. Give it to me, Theodora." The person spat her grandmother's name with venom. "It is time to stop running. It won't only be you that will suffer the consequences if you don't. You know we can't touch her, on the king's orders; but we can rip out the living from this kingdom until we find what we have come for."

King? Emara's brows pulled down in confusion. *There was no king of Caledorna.* It was governed by the elite. The Minister of Coin. The kingdom had voted against a king.

"She"—her grandmother's voice was tart and quick—"is innocent in all of this. She doesn't know about your *king* and it will remain that way. So, leave and tell your trusted sources that they were wrong. I don't have it."

Emara's features twisted as she tried to think of what or whom her grandmother was referring to. Confusion and tiredness didn't go together. Gently, she put one foot out onto the next step, which allowed her to see through the staircase spindles. Who would threaten to kill everyone in the kingdom of Caledorna for something her grandmother had?

Or didn't have.

Although she was shaking, she slowly lowered her body into a crouching position and peered through the space. Theodora was standing in her loose nightgown. Her greyish-brown hair was tied up at the top of her head, rolled around a pin which held it in place. She had an expression on her face that Emara had never witnessed before. She couldn't place it. Was it fear, or determination? Possibly repulsion?

Whatever the expression, it aged her grandmother's face terribly. Her grandmother had fared extremely well for her age. But tonight she looked like she was in her eighth decade of living.

Another scream pierced through the air, coming from the estate outside, and the muscles in Emara's legs pinched tighter to keep her from jumping. Her heartbeat so quickly that she felt faint.

What was happening out there?

Theodora gritted her teeth together, hearing the scream too. She shifted uncomfortably.

Emara had been so concerned with her grand-mother's expression that she hadn't noticed the figure that stood like an ancient rock in the middle of the room below. Her breathing caught as she took in the enor-mous size of the man that towered head and shoulders above her grandmother. Power radiated from him, power she had only read about in story books or old traditional folklore. Power which comes from nothing good—or human.

Emara glared at the figure dressed in what could only be described as battle attire; it looked completely out of place for this world. He had black boots that laced halfway up his shins, metal pads over the vital spots, and awkwardly big shoulders that were covered in steel. His hair was as black as the tunnel to hell and lay slick with moisture, tied at the nape of his strong neck.

Her grandmother's eyes flickered to her on the staircase for a brief second and then re-focused back on the intruder.

She had spotted Emara and, for whatever rea-son, she got the feeling her grandmother didn't want to bring any attention to the fact that she was there.

Oh, Gods, I'm in trouble.

Fear ran thick down every vein in Emara's body. This wasn't just a robbery or an argument from an angry art aficionado. This person was an undeniable threat. This man was death.

What should she do?

Think! Think! Oh, Gods, think!

She tried to command her brain to come up with some sort of plan, but fear paralysed her.

"I don't have what you are looking for," Theodora warned, never again looking up to the staircase. "It's long *gone,* with the ancestors before my time. I think it's best you go back from where you come and tell your king that you failed him again."

Just then, the male figure moved quickly—inhumanly fast—and struck her grandmother over the face with his gigantic fist. Emara covered her mouth with her hand, trying not to scream.

"You reek of lies. I can smell them. Tell me where it is!" the creature roared at her, his voice penetrating through the skulls of the village. Emara had to blink a couple of times to regain vision as she held onto the spindles of the staircase.

It was the only thing stopping her from falling over.

"Putting barriers in place won't stop us, Theodora. It will only delay the inevitable. We know your daughter had it. Where is it, you insignificant witch?"

Theodora held her face from the punch for a second longer and then straightened. "If I was insignificant, you wouldn't be here, begging me for something your *k*ing will *never* have." Theodora spat at him. "I will never tell you anything. You will never get what you are looking for—the Gods will protect it. I will die to protect it. To protect her."

Suddenly, out of nowhere, the figure pulled out a blade from his belt and plunged it into the side of her neck.

Her grandmother's neck!

A shriek escaped Emara's mouth before she could control herself, her body pinning itself against the wall behind her. The figure spun to stare her right in the face. Their eyes locked, glued together.

She had been right, that "man" wasn't human—not with the burning crimson eyes that had spied her on the staircase.

Before she could even think about what had just happened, her grandmother choked out, "Run, Emara, and don't stop," as blood spilled from her neck and mouth.

Emara tried to stand, but wobbled enough to hit against the wooden beams of the banister. Her face was wet with tears. She hadn't realised she was crying until her vision started to blur, almost blinding her. She blinked the tears out of the way, unable to use her hands to wipe them.

Move!

She had to move.

She had to get away from that—that *thing*. Before her brain could catch up with her body, her legs were carrying her up three stairs at a time, grabbing every spindle the staircase offered to hoist her up quicker. She heard a roar from the kitchen that had her tumbling over herself. It had come from that beast of a creature. That unnatural being. Another roar shot through her mind like she had been impaled by his sharpened blade.

But she had to keep moving.

Keep climbing the stairs, she swore to herself. *Push! Push, push!*

She flew through the hall, wiping her tear-covered face frantically to explore her options. She swung around a corner, her body stumbling out of control, bumping into her grandmother's décor as she moved. Paintings and ornaments smashed and shattered behind her as she hurled through the hallway. She flung herself into the main bathing chamber, rounding the door at a speed she didn't think was possible and slamming it shut. Her heart thundered against her ribs, vibrating against everything inside her, and she pushed her hands against the door until she could see the white straining in her fingers.

"Emara?" a voice croaked.

She spun to face the bathtub to see who was in the room with her.

Cally stood alone, shaking, tears dripping down her face. Her pale hair was now flat and lifeless on her head, her eyes awake with fear.

"Cal—" She couldn't even get the words out as she flung one arm around her best friend. "I didn't know where you were! When I got up, you were gone—I—I—my grandmother…" She couldn't think straight. She closed her eyes as she heard her grandmother's blood-filled throat warn her to run and to keep running. Reopening her eyes, she said, "We need to get out of here, Cally!"

"I went to the bathroom and when I came back, you were gone," Cally explained. "And—and then I heard all the screaming from outside and I ran to the window. I saw the Fortfox estate house on fire. There are bodies scattered on the ground, Emara. It was Mr. and Mrs. Fortfox." She sobbed, finding it hard to swallow. "And then—I saw it!" She covered her mouth in horror to stop a scream from curling in her throat.

Emara looked at her best friend in confirmation and nodded. "I know what you saw! One is downstairs right now. It—it just attacked my grandmother."

Cally's face paled even further, draining her completely of colour.

A hissing sound entered the hall and Cally sprung back against the wall as Emara put one finger to her lips to silence her. A single tear rolled down Cally's cheek, dragging along with it a black charcoal droplet.

"What are they?" Cally whimpered, gripping her skull in anguish. "Why does my head hurt?"

The hissing sound grew louder as it made its way down the hallway, in a slow, deepened buzz. The pain intensified as the creature walked closer to the bathroom. Emara remembered how fast it had moved in the kitchen; it was clear that it was taunting them now. She had seen how it *really* moved. It was building up their fear, moving slowly, to enjoy this kill.

It was a predator—and Emara had just become its prey.

Emara's throat bobbed as she looked at her best friend in the realisation that they weren't going to make it out of this bathroom alive.

She felt the power from the creature creeping in from underneath the bathroom door like a dark mist that oozed from an ancient world, long forgotten. Stumbling back a few steps, she let out a whimper.

He was outside!

That murdering bastard stood outside the bathroom where she and Cally were taking shelter.

What was he looking for? If she could work that out, if she could find it and give it to him, would he let them live?

Emara tried to think of the conversation he had had with her grandmother, but fear took over every other emotion. If he had just come to kill her, then why did he ask her grandmother for something? Something that, if her grandmother had, she certainly wasn't going to hand it over.

She'd died to protect.

"Emara," he hissed from outside of the door. Her name snarled from his lips a second time and she wanted to scream or plead with him or lash out.

Why was he taunting her?

Cally's eyes darted to Emara's face.

Fear. Pure fear.

Emara mouthed *"I love you"* to her best friend for the last time as the door broke open with one burst of power released from the creature that stalked outside. Emara flung up her hands to shield her face as she was thrown against the sink unit. Her skull cracked against the solid wood.

A dizzying darkness quickly folded in around her and everything went black.

CHAPTER
FOUR

The sound of Cally's screaming pulled Emara back from the darkness. She cradled her head in her hands as every cell in her body pulsed with pain. As she looked up through blurred vision to find Cally, nothing formed right.

Scrambling to get to her knees, a sharp ache in her arm caught her attention.

She was bleeding.

Really bleeding.

Raw flesh was peeled back on her arm like the power from the blast had evaporated her skin. She swallowed the vomit that tracked up her throat as she looked down at it, swaying on her knees.

Cally's scream sliced through the night as the creature grabbed her by the throat. His crimson eyes glaring at her, his strong jaw contracted.

"Please, please don't hurt me," she begged.

The creature ran a hand over Cally's pale face which made her look as white as a chalk.

The minute Emara spotted the creature's hands, she knew for certain that he wasn't human. They were claw-like as he dragged a pointed nail over Cally's lips. His laugh broke into the air; the most hideous sound she had ever heard.

She flinched.

"I would like to taste you before I slaughter you," he said as he drove a malignant smile onto his face.

Cally let out a whimper and her eyes pleaded for Emara not to watch, to turn away, but Emara could do nothing but freeze.

She couldn't move.

The fear set in about her body like concrete, cementing her to the ground. She watched as the creature licked Cally's face, his long tongue retracting as he shoved her against the wall. The gesture alone brought out an anger from within Emara that she had never felt before.

Rising to her feet on shaky legs, she looked around. She needed to do something. She needed to act. She couldn't just freeze and do nothing—Cally was all she had left. She snatched the vase that was sitting on the unit beside the sink. Just as she was about to smash it over the creature's head, he whirled to face her, grabbing her neck with one clawed hand that stopped the air from flowing. Burning filled her lungs like someone had poured boiling hot water into them. Struggling, she smashed the vase over his head, but his steel grip didn't waver. Smithereens of glass littered the floor around them. The man's head titled, taking in her attempt to fight him off almost like it had amused him. Suddenly, the iron grip loosened around her throat and she took a desperate inhale of breath.

Emara moved, backing up, leading him away from Cally. As he stalked towards her, the grinding of the glass on the floor underneath his enormous boots sent shivers up her spine. He eyed the wound on her arm.

For a second, she had forgotten all about the pain in her arm. A glint of dark malice pebbled in his eye as he inhaled the scent of her blood, that was pouring down her skin.

Too many ludicrous thoughts crashed into her mind all at once.

Was he a vampire? Was he looking for her blood?

That was preposterous; vampires were something of old folklore, used to scare children. Vampires were not real. But when his dead eyes met hers...he displayed the most terrible smile that a creature could ever muster—and she thought that he might be.

He was pure evil. An evil that was so sickeningly destructive that every part of her soul screamed in retaliation at the sight of it.

Suddenly, he flashed in front of her. She gasped at how quickly he had moved. Emara cursed, realising that she had backed herself against the wall on the other side of the room. There was nowhere else to go. She was stuck. This was it...

"Run, Cally!" she cried, still looking at the creature who was studying her. If Callyn could get out, if she could just run... "What is it that you want?" She pulled her lip over her teeth. Very quickly, she realised, she was not going to go down without a fight. She might die tonight. In fact, there was every possibility. But Cally would get out.

"Right now,"—the monster purred, tipping his head to the side like a predator assessing his prey— "you."

She lunged for the door that was now a gaping hole in the wall, but the creature clutched her by her long, midnight black hair and swung her into him. Her body collided with his, slamming the little air she had gathered out of her lungs.

"I am not allowed to kill you, sweet Emara, but that doesn't mean I can't enjoy you," he sniggered.

The creature was so caught up in Emara that he hadn't noticed Cally's approach. She swung a rolled-up fist into the side of his head. Cally cried out in pain as the impact of his solid form shot through her hand. The creature didn't so much as move his repugnant stare from Emara's face. With one swing of an arm, he batted Cally away like she weighed nothing, a mere fly on a summer's day. Her body flew through the room and cracked against the bathtub. Her head rolled to the side and she lay limp on the floor.

"Cally! Callyn!" Emara screeched, her eyes wild, searching for some proof that she was alive.

There wasn't any.

The man moved again sharply and pinned her against the wall with one hand.

Emara tried to struggle but she couldn't free any part of herself to make an impact. His odour was toxic, filling her nostrils and mouth with a scent that could only be related to death and destruction. The malevolent scent made it hard to keep the wine she had drunk in her stomach.

The beast lowered his face so close to hers that she could see the reflection of herself in his crimson eyes. Dirt, blood, and desperation coated her face. She was a pathetic picture of morality in comparison to whatever he was.

He trickled a long, black nail down her face. Instead of whimpering, she bared her teeth, gnashing them together, begging herself not to show any more fear than she already had.

She would be strong, like her grandmother had been for her. She had shown no fear in the kitchen.

Or ever.

She would be just like her, until the end.

He continued to lower his nail until it grazed over her wounded arm. She nearly buckled with the pain that jolted through her limb, her legs almost collapsing beneath her. She stifled a scream.

Stay strong, she chanted. *Stay strong!*

Blood flowed from her arm and he let it drip into his nail like he was filling up a glass of wine. He raised the nail to his lips and drank her blood, licking every last drop. The man flung his head back in ecstasy, his eyes dazzling like rubies, like the impact of her blood had been the biggest high he had ever had.

"If only I was permitted to drink every drop." The creature toyed with the idea. His black hair sprayed across his face was the only sign of the struggle she had put up.

Evil oozed from his solid core; she could feel it festering in the air. His eyes changed and in that moment, she knew he wasn't going to stop. She knew she was going to die. There would be no stopping him.

He attacked, driven wild by the taste of her blood. She pushed and punched at him, but it wasn't enough. She wasn't strong enough. So, she screamed and prayed that it would be quick. She also prayed it would be quick for Cally, when her time came—if it hadn't already.

Muffled voices broke through her prayers and a bright gleam of light swung past her face.

Was it the blade that the creature had stabbed into her grandmother's neck not long before? Would she get the same death?

She closed her eyes, clenched her jaw tight and let death sweep her to the other side.

She would be reunited with loved ones who had passed. She would finally be reunited with her parents.

She heard cutting sounds like steel slicing through bone and flesh, but didn't feel any pain. The Gods that her grandmother so often made her pray to as a child had clearly spared her from any more pain until it was over.

Her only miracle in this nightmare.

A man's voice broke her thoughts, but it was not the creature's...

Were there more like him?

She sprung her eyes open to see another man standing over the body of the creature that had attacked her—its head now detached from its body.

She let out a scream and pressed herself harder into the wall. She flinched as she felt the cold plaster touch base with her spine.

Another man appeared at the doorway. "Dead?"

"The one in here is," the closest one to her replied.

She couldn't concentrate on any faces or take in if they had the same eyes as the other man because she couldn't stop staring at the head of the creature—looking up at her, still promising her death.

Bile rose in her throat and she hurled herself over, spewing the contents of her stomach. The man who had taken the creature's head off, the one with the sword, walked over to Cally.

"Don't you dare touch her," she managed to warn, struggling to breathe through the burn in her throat. "Kill me instead." Her voice was stern and authoritative, a trait she had picked up from her grandmother. "Leave her!"

"She's feisty, I like that!" the man said casually to the other, turning his attention back to Cally. "Relax, she's alive," he said in a nonchalant way, like he saw this sort of thing happen all year round. "For now. We need to move out."

He wasn't like the creature; he didn't have dead, crimson eyes. They were ocean blue.

Maybe they were part of the elite's guards. Maybe they had heard the screams?

Before she could decipher anything, she felt an unusual cold consume her body.

"Gideon, she's going into shock," the blue-eyed man said.

Emara brushed her hands over her upper arms to protect herself from the freezing stiffness and a searing pain jolted down her left arm. The agony surged through her body and she fell to her knees. She hadn't realised just how open the wound was when the adrenaline of the last few moments had taken over her, but when she looked at it now…

She glanced around the room, her head now spinning and throbbing. When she closed her eyes to compose herself, all she saw was her grandmother's face, splattered with blood.

It's too much.

This was all too much.

She couldn't breathe. She couldn't feel her body. She was…

She plunged into darkness, like she had fallen into the sea in the dead of night. She could hear voices around her, but she didn't care. She didn't want to listen anymore. Someone hollered for help.

Help?

She still wasn't sure if they were here to help or if they were going to rip her to shreds like the other creature had planned to.

Before she could think any more about creatures, blood, and crimson eyes, the dark sea swallowed her body whole and drank her to the bottom of the blackest pit.

CHAPTER FIVE

Blood red eyes, skin thick like leather, talons as sharp as a razor, and the smell of sulphur.
Gideon Blacksteel confirmed the demon was dead. It had taken his brother one swift swing of his sword to behead the demon that had attacked this home. Quick and easy.

The element of surprise seemed to have been on their side this time. The demon looked like a high demon, a powerful one, but it had been too distracted by the girl's blood to notice them. Higher demons normally put up a better fight than a lesser demon, but tonight it has been painless. For them.

As he assessed the room, he held his bow upright in case there were any more vile creatures that needed to be slain in here. It was unclear how many had come to Mossgrave but the clan wouldn't be long in finding out. Looking around, it looked clean, apart from the two victims.

He lowered his weapon of choice, taking a breath. Down the dirt track leading into the estate, the

Blacksteel hunting clan—an army of demon hunters—was completing the same tasks given to them by their commander.

Get into Mossgrave, save as many humans as possible, kill every demon, get out.

Normalcy.

He knew it was coming. Only on a night like this when the apex of the moon was so strong could demons gather enough magic to portal from the underworld to the human lands. It was always worse in the lead up to a full moon...

Gideon was a member of the Blacksteel hunting clan, by blood and by oath. Being the son of the commander of the clan meant that he had been thrust into the world of demon hunting since he could walk. He was a warrior; this was his purpose by blood right, and he knew how to do his job efficiently and effectively, alongside his brethren.

To his father's delight, his mother had borne three boys. Torin was the eldest of the three. He was as tall and broad shouldered as any warrior should be, which made it easy for him to toss around his favourite swords like they weighed nothing. He had the crystal blue eyes of their mother, but that was all. His father's sharp features dominated his face, making him look like he was a younger version of the commander and older than his age of twenty-two.

Gideon was the middle child of the Blacksteel boys; he was fairer and had softer features than Torin. He came in just shorter and slimmer, being a year younger. What he lacked in strength in comparison to his older brother, he made up for in speed and agility.

His father, Viktir Blacksteel, never allowed for weakness. Gideon had taken the lucid green eyes of his father, piercing and oval like a cat's. His bow was like a second limb to him, having been trained in weaponry since he could walk or hold the damn thing.

The youngest of the brothers was Kellen—*the baby*. For being over six feet tall at the age of sixteen, Gideon struggled to see why his mother still called him that. For a child he was not. Kellen was a mixture of both parents—a split right down the middle; his face held one emerald eye and one sapphire.

Where Gideon was from in the kingdom of Caledorna (Huntswood City), the healers would tell tales of those with different eyes born from magic blood, calling them special ones or ones that could bring hope to the world. However, Kellen had never shown any signs of magic other than his Hunting blood. And that was a good thing in this father's eyes.

Kellen was just old enough to finish training and he had completed the selection—a grisly and extensive process that every hunting-blooded man had to endure—a few moons back. Therefore, he was ready to hunt with the clan.

His mother, on the other hand, had done everything she could not to have him involved in the blood battles and direct fighting. She had tried to find him another role more suited to his disposition, like a treasurer or an office bearer. But Viktir Blacksteel had seen this as a direct weakness of the clan and forced Kellen to train harder. Just shortly after the Selection, Viktir removed their mother from the tower, advising it was necessary for the unit to be stronger.

Gideon tensed as he allowed himself to think of her—his beautiful, kind, and adoring mother—before he turned his attention back to the job at hand. He glanced at the girl on the floor, sprawled out over a mixture of her own vomit and blood.

His nose crinkled.

It wasn't the worst thing he had ever seen or smelled. Torin was one step ahead and had already lifted the blonde girl into his arms, her body still limp as he left the room.

Gideon assessed the injury on the arm of the girl with the raven-coloured hair.

He drew a breath through his teeth. "That's a deep one," he muttered to himself as he positioned her to lift her up. He gently scooped her into his arms without hurting the injury.

No human infirmary would be able to heal a wound that was triggered by demon magic. He would need to get her to the infirmary at the hunting tower where a healer could look over her. A healer of his world. One with magic.

As he walked through her home with the girl in his arms, he turned his thoughts back to what he had seen as he entered the threshold of the bathing chamber. He had been surprised that the girl had still been upright when he and Torin found them. They had heard their screams even before getting into the house.

Their awful, heart-wrenching screams.

No matter how many times he had heard them from humans who were attacked, it never got easier.

When he had gotten to the room, right before Torin had sliced the head from the demon's neck, he had seen her. It was never easy to see someone look like they had accepted their death, but she had. Her head had been against the wall, eyes shut, welcoming the angel of demise. She had clearly put up an impressive fight beforehand, given the state of the house, but a human like her couldn't kill a demon. Not one of higher class.

And then she had passed out, once seeing what his brother had done to the demon and noting her wounded arm. The demon wound had probably taken its toll on her human body. She had lost a lot of blood and Gideon now feared she had poison seeping into her bloodstream. He had to act fast to make sure she survived. She didn't have blood from the Gods running through her veins like he did. Although he looked human, he wasn't.

Catching up to his brother in no time, taking long and precise strides along the hallway, he tried to keep his rough hands from marking the girl's delicate skin. Even after everything she had endured tonight, she was still glowing—the complexion of her skin was remarkable. Her hair tumbled over his arm like black silk woven from the black widow witch herself, and he couldn't help but acknowledge that she was wearing practically nothing.

He swallowed down the frog in his throat and looked ahead. Undergarments as black as her hair covered what it needed to, and to avoid her being completely exposed, a dark, thin overdress was fashioned around her shoulders and tied at her waist.

A command that had been given at tonight's briefing from his father had been controversial. Before dawn, for the first time in Gideon's existence, they were commanded to bring any humans that remained alive back to the tower. It was a command that not every hunter agreed with, but the instruction had come from the prime. And if the instruction was rolled out from the prime, then it was law. Final.

As they neared the hunting wagon, Kellen approached. "I killed four," he said, his unusual eyes lighting up as he searched for a reaction from Torin.

In true warrior fashion, not much impressed Torin—maybe the occasional sparring fight, or an expensive bottle of rum. His mood could be...*temperamental.*

"That's what you're supposed to do, Kellen," Torin huffed. "I would be worried if you had come here just to watch us do the work." He placed the blonde girl into the wagon carefully, completely dismissing Kellen as he jumped back down and strolled past him.

The excitement on Kellen's face fell and disappointment broke across his adolescent features.

Gideon placed the dark-haired girl into the wagon and called for some supplies and a healer to mend her arm as best as they could until he got her to the infirmary.

"Hey," he shouted towards Kellen, who had turned his back to walk away. "Good job tonight." He patted his little brother on the shoulder. "I knew you had it in you. It was great to see you out there, mirroring Marcus, on the hunt tonight. I bet he showed you a trick or two." Gideon flashed a great smile. Marcus had trained him in combat and weaponry from a young age;

he was well and truly part of the family, if only by oath. Blacksteel blood did not run through Marcus' veins.

Kellen smiled in response to Gideon, but said nothing before making his way to the front of the wagon.

"Line up the dead!" Torin yelled from a few yards down the road.

Gideon could still smell burning wood from the pillaging the demons had done as he turned to face the second-in-command. "Bring anyone who is alive to the tower. That is a direct order from your commander. Tomorrow marks a change in everything we have ever known. It might seem out of the ordinary, but regardless of how we have done things before, this is the new protocol. Marcus, oversee that the dead are taken care of," he finished, very matter-of-fact. Although Gideon knew that some part of Torin's humanity would have struggled with the latter command.

Torin's eyes met Gideon's.

His brother would be commander one day, and when the time came, Gideon would fall underneath him. He would take direct orders from Torin, even if he didn't agree. Even if it cost him his life, he would obey the commander of the clan, because that is what hunters did. That was part of their oath.

No one from the human world had ever been let into the tower, only ones of importance who came to talk politics with Viktir. However, as more and more humans died at the hands of the Dark King's army on their mission for the Stones, something had to change.

And that was telling the humans the truth.

It was getting harder to cover up all the slaughtering's. Only so many villages could burn before people started to talk, and the hunters had been covering up demon tracks for centuries.

But they were done doing it.

"Let's move out," Torin bellowed the command to the other hunters. "Let's go. Round it up."

Crunching gravel under heavy boots could be heard as the clan took instruction.

As Gideon looked up to the sky, smoke and death lingered in the air, but he could have sworn that the moon, with her bright glow and tinge of orange around the outside, winked at him.

He closed the door of the wagon with a shudder, shutting her out. He knew it wasn't over. The Blood Moon hadn't arrived yet.

It was only getting started…

CHAPTER
SIX

Emara felt the heat on her face and smiled. It was over. She was on the other side. She was found worthy enough to be granted access to the other side, a spiritual realm her grandmother believed in. She would be able to see her mother again—possibly even her father.

Her heart stumbled a few beats.

Even though her grandmother never talked ill of her father, she hadn't thought greatly of him when he was alive—otherwise there would have been more stories of him, or at least more to remember him by. Emara often felt a sinking feeling when she thought of him. She had no drawings or paintings of him other than the one she had stolen from her grandmother's chest of drawers back when she was a child.

The painting wasn't of great quality, but what the artist had captured was her father saying something to make her mother laugh so hard. She had always wondered what it might have been or what he might have said that had produced so much happiness. Sometimes she would lie in bed at night and think of phrases or memories that her father would have told her mother to make her laugh that way. Her mother's beautiful smile had gleamed wide from one side of her face to the other. Her dad's head was buried in her long, honey brown hair that was a couple of inches shorter than Emara's. Her father's hair, what she could see of it, was inky black, thick, and glossy. Just like hers.

Anytime Emara ever mentioned her father, her grandmother would either shut her down or not even respond at all. So after some time, Emara had stopped asking about him.

But she never stopped wondering.

Movement brought her back to this world and she tilted her head to the side, sluggishly blinking her eyes open. A large window fixed from ceiling to floor allowed daylight to flitter through the room. Blinded by the rays at first, she blinked again to adjust her eyes. Through the window, a vast hillside could be seen, imprinted with small houses the size of a fingernail in the distance and greenery extending right out across the land.

Where was she?

She twitched her legs, scrunching her toes and then her hands. This is not what she had pictured the spirit realm to look like. She'd visualised the other side, where souls went to rest, to be cloudy and mesmerising, illuminated by the light of the Gods. She hadn't expected it to look like a town or city embedded within the trees of a forest. She was high above the landscape, that's for sure.

Scary high!

Realising that she lay on a soft bed, she tried to move her body up the mattress, groggily drawing her eyes over the room.

Not her room or her house, in fact, but a room she had never encountered before. There was a grey brick fireplace lined with brass metals. The dull stone walls were relatively bare, only displaying a few art pieces that appeared to be in a different language. The room was spacious, yet it had enough furniture to meet someone's storage requirements.

She placed a shaky hand up to her forehead as her brain hammered against her skull.

Is this what the afterlife feels like?

Surely not.

Surely you weren't supposed to feel pain in the afterlife. That's why her grandmother always prayed to the Gods. Maybe she had prayed to the wrong one. Maybe she should have paid more attention to her grandmother's lessons.

"Welcome back," a soft voice drifted over to her from the corner of the room.

Startled, her soul leapt out of her skin and she met a pair of emerald-green eyes, fanned with thick, black lashes. A man sat in the corner with his elbows on his knees, his back arched over, leaning forward. His hands were placed together calmly, and his strong chin rested on the top of his fingers. He didn't look harmful according to his stance, but she knew by the belt of weapons around his waistline that he had to be.

She pushed back into the bed, looking for an exit, but he was closer to the door than she was. Her head ached, forcing her eyes to shut momentarily. Panic set in.

She was not in the afterlife, she realised.

"Don't worry, you're safe here." His soft voice warmed up to an almost velvet tone as he spoke to her.

She blinked but said nothing. She couldn't find any words, just a pounding in her head.

"We managed to save you from your home last night."

Utter fear scuttled through her as he spoke.

As if sensing that, the stranger said, "I'm not going to harm you." He put his hands out in front of himself.

She looked down at his waist again to where steel had been forged and crafted into fighting knives and daggers. He studied her face through those glittering eyes before saying, "I promise."

He was strong, she could tell by the muscles in his arms and legs, but his face was gentle and charming. It was such an interesting contrast, she had to remember to breathe.

Was she hallucinating?

A crashing ton of vague memories flashed like still paintings in her mind. Paintings of crimson eyes and bloodshed. Her mouth opened but her tongue couldn't form the words she wanted to say.

Broken memories of last night all merged together to create one horrifying art piece.

She swallowed.

"Am I alive?" Emara croaked, feeling ridiculous even asking such a question. She lowered her eyes to her hands, looking down at the blood that still stained them.

"Yes," he said softly and then paused. "You did extremely well last night to remain alive. You went through a lot." Something in his voice made her look up at him again. He had dark eyebrows that framed his face, darker than the hair that lay wildly on his head, curling around his ears. She turned her attention to his mouth. Full lips covered a set of perfectly white teeth as they parted like he was attempting to speak, but didn't. His jaw was square and strong, and his skin was golden like he had caught the sun.

He was extremely handsome.

Handsome enough for her to question what she currently looked like.

Dreadful, she imagined.

She felt a spasm of guilt for even thinking about her appearance given the fact that she didn't even know where she was.

"Where am I?" she whispered, afraid to hear the answer.

The green-eyed stranger stood, not moving his stare from hers.

Gods, he's tall, she noticed. She had to raise her chin to keep the eye contact engaged.

"I'm Gideon," he said, his voice a little deeper than before. "This is my home—well, training facility. This is the tower." He paused, trying to gauge her reaction. But she had no clue what he was referring to. "You are at the tower that separates Huntswood and Mossgrave," he said.

She pulled her stare away from him to look back out the window, mapping in her mind where she was located. It was early daytime, and the winter sun was low enough to split the trees as she gaped out at the landscape.

"You might know it as the old Huntswood infirmary for healers," he added.

She winced as the sunlight tunnelled into the room, burning her eyes.

"Be careful" he advised as he moved a step closer. "You lost a lot of blood last night and hit your head real hard—a couple of times, by the looks of it." He offered her a sympathetic smile. "You're a little banged up, but the healer said you will survive." He offered her a friendly smile.

She couldn't smile back even if she tried hard. "Are you a guard for the Minister of Coin?" She looked at his waist again.

"Something like that." He laughed a little.

"Can you take me home?" She tried to move, to get out of the bed, but agonising aches gathered in every cell of her body, causing her to flinch.

"Easy," Gideon warned. She saw his soft features harden for a second, but they relaxed immediately.

"Why am I here?" she asked reluctantly.

Abruptly, thoughts and memories of last night started pouring through her mind, exploding into her thoughts. They were no longer broken pictures, but real memories.

They were real!

She tried inhaling and exhaling rapidly to calm herself, panic gripping tightly in her chest. She pulled off the blankets that were suddenly too heavy for her body. Lowering her eyes to her legs, which were covered in bruises and scrapes, she tried to move them.

"I'm sorry, but we can't let you go out just yet. Not like that, anyway." He gestured to her lying on the bed. "A healer will be around to check on that wound any minute now." His eyes locked onto her arm. "She has been here every hour to check on you." His voice was fond and light, like he appreciated the work the healer had done. He trusted her. "In case you have forgotten, you were blasted with demon magic last night. Your arm took a pretty bad hit."

She blinked.

"No, wait, sorry." She touched her temple again to steady her waves of dizziness. "Did you just say demon magic?" Her tone changed along with the feeling in her stomach. "Demon magic?" she repeated. If she had enough energy to scoff at him, she would have.

"There is a lot that you need to learn, and shortly you will learn all of it. My commander will tell you everything you need to know, but for now—"

"I think I deserve an explanation of what is going on, don't you?" The sharpness in her tone reminded her of her grandmother.

"Demons attacked your village last night," Gideon stated, very matter of fact. "They burned your homes; they murdered the people of your village..." he trailed off.

Emara's eyes were stinging with tears that lay waiting to fall down her face. "Something killed my grandmother last night."

"That something has a name." He paused, shifting on his feet. "It was a demon. It was a higher demon, to be exact. They appear as human as possible. Although some others don't bother taking a human form at all. But I won't go into that now. More will be explained to you later once you have rested." He faltered, seeing the shock on her face. "That demon would have killed you and your friend if we had gotten there a second later." He palmed his closest knife as if out of instinct and her eyes trailed to it before they went back to his face.

"You expect me to believe that *thing* last night was a demon?" The memory of his face, his hands, and his smell overwhelmed her.

To be truthful with herself, she knew it wasn't human. She knew it deep in her gut when it had attacked her grandmother. Its unearthly eyes, its powerful radiation, its brute strength as it batted Cally away—

Cally. Oh, Gods! Cally!

With whatever strength she had left, she wrestled to remove the covers entirely, pushed up from the bed, and got to her feet in a matter of seconds. Pain like a hundred stabbing needles punctured up through her feet and into her shins.

Gideon's eyes moved with her as if trained to anticipate sharp movements. His face showed a little shock, but he bent his knees, ready for her next move.

He was prepared to stop her.

"My friend." She stuttered over her words, "Sh-she was with me last night; you must go back for her. You need to help her," she begged.

"Don't worry, she's here too," he said. "Take it easy."

Utter relief washed over her that Cally was here. "We lifted her from the same bathroom we found you in. She's banged up, but she wasn't affected by the demon magic like you. She's okay."

Cally was not only here alive, but she wasn't badly hurt. Emara's legs gave out and she braced herself for the impact of her knees hitting the floor.

Gideon moved faster than lightning and appeared at her side from the other end of the room in a second. He swept her up into his arms before she could crash to the ground.

At first she felt dazed, as if she couldn't quite comprehend how quickly he had moved. But overwhelming emotion took over her, pushing out any curiosity about how he'd done it.

Cally was alive and she was here. A lightness in this dark. Her heart burst with relief and delight and Emara covered her face to shield her tears from Gideon, her stomach contracting as she cried. She couldn't control it anymore. Emara let her sobs take over as everything raced through her mind like flash cards, pinning all the broken pieces together.

The demon. Her grandmother's words as she took her last breath. Cally's limp body lying beside the bathtub. The darkness. The blood. The pain.

She cried harder than she ever had.

Shockingly, Gideon didn't put her down. Instead he held her, pulling her into his chest. Before she could stop herself, she realised she was holding him back, tucking her face into the nape of his neck. She hadn't known she needed to be held. It wasn't something she was used to, but she needed the support. She needed the comfort, even if he was a stranger…

Minutes passed by; as her weeping slowed, Gideon ran a hand through her hair, calming her. She let out a huff of embarrassment and the emotion sunk into her cheeks, a rose-pink colour. Exhausted, Emara wiped both sides of her face with one hand.

What am I doing? she thought as the emotional breakdown passed. *I don't even know this guy.*

Weirdly, her thoughts turned to Taymir; she realized that she had been dating him for over a year but she had never been consoled by him like this. She had never even opened up to him emotionally.

Had he survived the demon attack?

Her breathing hitched as dread coiled up into a tight knot in her stomach again. She stole a quick look at Gideon, who was still looking at her, patiently.

Instead of rose-pink, her cheeks flushed bright red; she was certain now that he wasn't going to hurt her after crying into his ear for the last ten minutes. As if reading her mind or *embarrassment,* Gideon slowly lowered her onto her feet—so smoothly. He placed his strong hands around her shoulders to steady her and a muscle contracted in his jaw as he let her go.

Is he scared to hurt me?

He examined her again as she stood in front of him—she assumed it was to make sure she wasn't going to collapse into a big mess on the floor.

"You good?" he said, his eyebrows rising in concern.

Emara gathered herself, unable to really look at him, and said, "Take me to Cally." Her request was authoritative but came out sharper than she had intended. "Please," she added.

Gideon gave a single nod and faced the door. "I'll bring her to you if she is awake, but it's still extremely early." He turned to face her again. "Please, for my own peace of mind, stay in bed until she comes in to see you. I am currently responsible for ensuring that you are okay, and we don't need you to contract anymore injuries. Stay in bed."

Emara forced a small, gracious smile. "Thank you."

Gideon nodded and left the room politely, leaving Emara to sift through her darkest thoughts.

CHAPTER SEVEN

Gideon left the infirmary room, took two steps down the corridor, and paused.

She's awake.

He ran a hand over his face and shook his fluffy hair. He needed a shower. He hadn't left her infirmary room until now. The healer had confirmed that she would survive in the early hours of the morning after abstracting all the poison from her wound, but he had waited to see it for himself. And the sun had come up, granting her a new day to live.

To see another sunrise at dawn is to count another blessing. His mother would tell her boys that every morning as they got up for a gruelling training session.

As he'd waited for her to wake up, dusky beams of light had pushed through the window onto the bed where she lay, highlighting her face and the dark threads of her hair. Her face had been still, her lips parted in a way that made them pout. He could see where the tears of the night's terrors had marked her face, leaving tracks on her skin. Her high cheekbones had been swollen with the impact of a fist—or worse.

He stiffened in the corridor, rage running through his veins.

Demon scum!

He crossed his arms to hide the fact that anger had crept into his hands and he balled his fists. Just then he saw the healer returning to Emara's room, coming down the corridor. She paused as if sensing something was wrong.

He was just standing there in the middle of a corridor, after all, probably looking like he could punch something.

He smiled gently. "What's the damage, Rhea?"

She put a hand on Gideon's forearm, and he instantly felt the anger draining from him, like someone opened the drain to his bathtub of fury and unease.

Rhea, he realised. She had touched him on purpose. *Her gift.*

He smiled gratefully and said, "I'm okay. I'm asking you about the girl." He nodded his head in the direction of the door.

Rhea spoke so very gently, "The girl will recover with some days' rest. I shall check on her every hour to apply the lavenderbane to her wound." Lavenderbane was a natural remedy used by witches to heal wounds quickly, especially ones that had come from the battlefield. "There is no debris of dark magic in her wound. It is clean and should heal quickly with my salve."

"You don't have to do that; I can do that for you, Rhea. You've been up all-night taking care of the casualties within these walls. I can apply the lavender-bane." He made it sound like it was no big deal, like he knew the skill it took to make the remedy and apply it correctly.

Which, of course, he didn't. He just wanted Rhea to rest.

A smile tugged at her lips as she let go of his arm. "I didn't realise you had become a healer over-night," she said before setting both hands on her tray of equipment and heading to another door. "I will see to her in another hour, *you* should get some rest," she said. She gave him a look over her shoulder as if to say, "*Go to bed, Gideon Blacksteel.*"

So, he had.

For a whole fifteen minutes. He hadn't even taken off his boots while lying on his bed, fully clothed. Wide awake and nowhere near slumber, he had to fight the urge to go up to the infirmary at the top of the tower just to make sure she was okay.

He didn't know her name, but he would find it out as soon as he went back up to get her friend when it was a respectable time of day. He wondered for a minute or two what her name might be, trying to think about what she looked like.

After a few moments, he couldn't think of a name pretty enough. Instead, he tried to count the number of knives in the weapon room, hoping that sleep would find him before he could reach the figure, but he failed.

Damn it! He exhaled as he moved from his bed in pursuit of the infirmary. He climbed the stairs sheepishly, hoping not to run into Rhea.

Since sleep was Gideon's new enemy, the best he could do was deliver the girl's friend to her. He would take some comfort that she would be with someone and then he could try to rest. He hadn't been able to relax since the mission.

As he made his way down the corridor, he knocked the room that the blonde girl had been assessed in last night.

"You can come in."

As he entered, he noticed that she was sprawled along the bed like she had stayed here for weeks.

"Hi, I am Gideon Blacksteel," he said softly. Her face was also beautiful, the kind of beautiful you would see dancing in a tavern and be tempted to spend every coin you had on her.

Not quite my type, he thought to himself.

"Hi," she said, raising her chin with confidence, and Gideon wondered if Torin had made acquaintances with her yet.

At that moment, a knock sounded on the door and Torin glided into the room.

He stilled and Gideon could tell he was shocked to see him standing there.

"Some say that if you think of the devil, he shall appear." Gideon's brows raised.

"Gideon," Torin said, smiling off the taunt. He sounded a lot cheerier than he had last night as he made his way into the room. "Did you beat me to asking this gorgeous girl her name?" A charming smirk appeared across his face.

Here we go.

Gideon sighed.

"Not exactly," he muttered.

Torin grinned back, displaying his *"show time"* smile, his blue eyes dancing with the opportunity of something new.

From his waist down, he still wore his fighting leathers, which led Gideon to believe that he had just made it home from the city's taverns. His fresh shirt was open a little, allowing his muscled chest to be on display.

"Father said I was on blondie duty." Torin grinned. "I was to make sure she was comfortable enough to settle into the tower, you know; let her know where everything is situated and all those pleasantries."

Pleasantries, Gideon snorted internally.

"Did you bring her up to speed?"

"I will." Torin's shoulders relaxed.

"My name is Cally, by the way," the blonde girl announced. There was a little hesitance that coated her voice, but she was confident. Sitting upright in her bed, wearing the clothes she had come here in, she stared at both brothers.

Gideon looked away instantly, realising that she too was in some sort of undergarment made for fantasies. And she wasn't keen to hide it. She owned it.

Fuck! was Gideon's first thought.

And the second was how stupid was his father? The commander of the Blacksteel clan had ordered *Torin* down here to focus and be professional. Gideon was about to witness the epitome of unprofessional. Torin would be in his element. The one thing he loved more than swinging a sword into a demon's skull and drinking rum was women. Women who he could dance with, flirt with, and drink shots out of navels with. Torin never slept with a woman more than once or twice; he wasn't interested in forming any attachments. He had always alleged it was better for him that way, and so Gideon never challenged him. That was his prerogative.

Torin walked around her bed and sat in a wooden chair near the fireplace with a causal but confident grace. Cally watched him as he walked, her eyes burning through his body, already giving him *the look.*

Gideon knew that look.

He'd seen it on the faces of many women when they headed to the tavern or the streets of the Huntswood markets. Or even when he felt like he needed a little something more than demons or bows and arrows.

"Sorry to interrupt, but your friend is awake, and she is asking for you," Gideon coughed towards the blonde.

Cally's eyes lit up and she bounced off the bed. "Oh, my Gods. Can you take me to her?"

Gideon pushed out a hand. "Okay, you need to get dressed before you go anywhere." He looked down so that he didn't need to make any eye contact with her. "Torin, if you will, please see to it that Cally has something that covers her up before leaving this room. The underage hunters will have a meltdown if they see her walking around the tower like that and we need them sharp for training."

It was exceedingly rare for any hunter who hadn't gone through the selection to have the time to be in the presence of a female. Let alone a half-naked one. So, when the opportunity arose…

"You should have something leftover from one of your *sleepovers* that should fit," he threw a verbal jab at his brother.

He knew it had been a low blow, but he understood how to dig his brother out without going too far. It was also a warning shot to Cally. Maybe she wouldn't be stupid enough to fall for Torin's charms. Although, judging by the look on her face, Gideon wasn't hopeful.

Torin shot him back a look as if to say, *"Nice try, brother."*

Bidding them both farewell, he spun on his heels quickly and darted down the corridor to leave Torin to it.

Arriving at his room, Gideon ripped off his tunic and leathers and kicked off his boots quicker than he had left Torin with Cally. What he really craved right now was a steaming hot shower to burn off the night, cleanse his soul, and straighten out his mind. A grumble wiggled free from his stomach and he realised he hadn't eaten in about ten hours. He hadn't even thought about food last night; other things had taken priority when he'd returned from the mission.

He pushed her face to the back of his mind.

Instead, he thought about what he could have to eat as he soaked himself in a piping hot shower that turned his skin pink. Musk and lemon filled the shower room as he lathered himself with soap. As he looked down he could see the trail of blood, dirt, and demon gunge run down the drain for good.

CHAPTER EIGHT

She couldn't believe she had cried the way she did. Emara had let her emotions pour from her—in a stranger's arms, of all places—and she couldn't stop it. She shook her head, staring at the trees below her as she stood against the bay window. Her grandmother had always instructed her how to control her emotions; she had always insisted that in every lesson.

The minute you let your head get the better of you, you are defeated.

Her grandmother had home-schooled her since she could talk, delivering lessons in art, literature, cookery, and fitness. She would endure lessons about the Gods and deities that had created the worlds and all the ancient history that came with it. Her grandmother also tried to instil lessons in etiquette and politics, but Cally (who had also attended the classes) had vowed them outdated and voted for new topics such as textiles and sewing. Her Grandmother had been impressed by her negotiation skills, but also saw the requirement for her to learn about ancient history.

So, with a little bit of persuasion from the girls, Theodora had added textiles and sewing to the lesson plan. Everything her grandmother did, she had done to build her into the young woman she was today.

An unimaginable pain tightened in her chest. Emara couldn't help but wonder if she had been preparing her for this. For her inevitable death. She'd known that she would lose her one day, but she hadn't thought that day would come so soon. Her heart cracked open a little more and she pressed her hand against her chest, desperate to keep it from breaking entirely.

The heavy mahogany door to her room opened and Cally's face peered around as if she was making sure that Emara was in the room before bursting through it. She wiped away the wetness on her face.

"Hi, you," she said tenderly. Cally walked slower than she normally did, wearing a white, baggy shirt that was three sizes too big for her. She had a slight limp, but she would never show that she was in pain. After all, she was used to walking around dirt roads in the highest heeled shoes she could get her hands on, somehow never managing to break an ankle.

"Hi," Emara mouthed back. She gave a small smile as it was all she had the strength to do, holding back the inevitable wave of grief that threatened to crush her.

Cally crawled onto the bed in the middle of the room and gestured for her to sit down beside her.

As Emara walked over, she let the tears roll from her eyes and snuggled in beside her best friend.

Cally took it upon herself to wrap around Emara like a human shield, and they sat like that for the longest time.

Letting out a long sigh, she whispered, "I am so sorry about your grandmamma, Em! She was like a mother to me, too." Emara thought she heard a crack in Cally's throat. "I just can't believe it."

Control your emotions, Emara coached herself. She turned onto her back and looked at the ceiling, taking in the design on the brickwork to distract herself from the ache in her chest. "I know she was," she managed to say back.

Silence settled in amongst them on the bed for a few moments as they lay together.

"Do you believe what they are saying?" Cally broke the silence. Her eyes were wide as she also looked for nothing on the ceiling. Her expression was unreadable.

"What other option do we have?" replied Emara.

"I think—I don't know. I think I believe…"

"I always have believed," Emara said quickly. "I have always believed in spirits and angels, I mean. From a young age, I prayed to the Gods with my grandmother, always believing in a higher power and the other side—and if you prayed to Gods, they would look after you. But demons?" Emara trailed off. "My grandmother's books never did mention anything about demons."

"If anything, what we must believe in is luck." Cally turned her head to look at her. "Because I believe that luck is the only thing that kept us alive last night."

Emara's throat swelled. "Do you remember everything?"

Cally was silent for a minute before answering, "Yes." She grabbed Emara's hand and squeezed it. "And that is why we must believe in luck. Not everyone made it out of the estate alive, but we did."

"I can't even bear to think who is still left," Emara admitted, feeling that horrid pain in her heart.

"You don't have to bear what happened alone." Cally's eyes welled up a little. "You have me. You will always have me."

"I know, and that is why I will continue to pray to the Gods and thank them that you are alive."

The heavy door swung open with a little more force than it had before. Both girls jumped, not expecting any other person to be alive in the world other than them. For a few moments, it had felt like it was just them.

"Oh, good, you found her." An exceedingly tall man walked through the door. His body radiated strength as he walked into the room. "Aren't you good with directions?" he said, aiming his words at Cally. He then slid his ocean blue eyes to Emara. "You look a little better than you did a couple of hours ago." His glittering eyes lingered on her face.

Cally's breathing hitched a little beside her and Emara suspected he knew exactly what he was doing with those baby blue, smouldering eyes as he dragged them from her face and back to her best friend. Cally was a sucker for a guy who had the confidence of a king and the swagger of a pirate.

And this guy had tons of both.

"I'm Torin, by the way," he said casually as he walked further into the room.

Cally returned a deviant smile and then focused on Emara's face as if waiting for her to say something.

She didn't.

"How are you feeling?" the man asked Emara, his eyes darting to the bandage around her arm.

However, she said nothing again. Something about the way he had strolled into the room irritated her.

"Okay, silence it is, then," he said, raising one eyebrow. He crossed his bulky arms over his toned torso and smiled. "I don't mind silence."

Cally laughed.

His cheeks pulled in, like he was doing his very best for his grin not to broaden across his lips. "This is normally where you would say, 'Hi Torin, thank you for saving me last night,' or something to that effect." He held out a hand as his cool demeanour batted away the silence. "I will also accept thank you lined with the phrases such as 'devilishly handsome, captivatingly beautiful, sexually sensual—'"

"They are the same thing," Emara cut him off, meeting his stare.

His face was still overflowing with confidence before it fell slightly. "So, you do speak." A corner of his mouth pulled up slightly in amusement.

Cally chuckled and bit her lip.

Did Cally find this funny? Did she find *him* funny? Emara didn't know if she was just overtired or if the pain in her body had taken its toll on her tolerance levels, but she could feel the heat building up inside of her and it was boiling.

She was livid.

How dare he waltz into this room after what she had just gone through and expect her to thank him? And call him handsome?

The heat rushed up past her ears, washing through her face, and her hands balled into fists. She ignored the pain in her arm and focused on the anger that consumed her. "First of all, how dare you insinuate that I am not capable of speaking just because I didn't answer you. You are just about to find out how *capable* of speaking I really am. Secondly, I didn't ask for you to save me. So, leave your macho ego at the door. Thirdly, I don't care who you are, and I certainly don't care who thinks you're *handsome*! I don't give a flying fu—"

"Woah, woah! Em, calm down!" Cally interrupted before Emara could continue. She caught Emara's hand and squeezed hard, trying to calm her. "It was just a joke, it's no big deal. He didn't mean anything by it. I am sure he was just trying to lighten the mood."

Something inside Emara snapped.

"Do you really think I want to be joking right now?" she fired at her best friend. The anger turned to something else entirely, "Do I look like I am someone to mess around right now?" She flicked her gaze over to Torin, who had gone utterly still.

His eyes narrowed and the smugness left his face.

"To be taken somewhere without even asking my permission, leaving my dead—" She stopped herself. She couldn't say it out loud. "—lying on the floor? I haven't even said goodbye and—and I have been taken from her!"

The only remaining heartstring she had left intact snapped, disconnecting her from every rational emotion she had tried desperately to hold on to. She opened her mouth and let out a scream.

Torin Blacksteel couldn't make out the next few words that came out of the girl's mouth. She started screaming and shrieking. It was a shrieking that Torin had never heard before and he could have sworn a cold wind drafted through the room at the sounds of it.

In the selection, he had been schooled about the levels of grief and how to shut it all out. As a Hunter, he would lose people. He had lost people to the hunt. Torin had heard men roaring for help as they died, and he had even heard the bellows of men who had lost a brother or friend—or maybe even a wife or child—to the dark army.

He knew loss.

He had even heard the rumbling roars of a demon right before he'd hacked it to pieces or severed its head. But this girl's screams shot through him in a way he had trained emotion not too.

He ran a hand through his hair and gathered himself. Torin approached her, the screams still vibrating in his ear drums, and held her arms tight. Tight enough for the pain in her arm to send shock signals to her brain and cease the panic. She was in the wave of an aftershock of loss, and he had triggered it. Torin felt a niggle where his heart used to be.

"Hey!" he yelled a little louder than he meant too. Fuck. He wasn't good at this shit.

She looked him dead in the eye and her mouth shut immediately.

"I am sorry for what happened to you." He was uncompromisingly direct as he spoke. "I understand you are in shock, but you must control your emotions better than this." He could see the surprise in her eyes, but he didn't stop. "You must gain control of yourself. You can overcome this. Do *not* let this drown you."

He didn't care if the other girl was watching as he said, "Sorrow can take you under, down and down until you cannot breathe anymore." He gripped her tighter. "*Do not let this own you. The world is bigger than your grief.*"

He took a moment, realising that he had been harsh.

Again.

This time, he controlled the softness in his voice. "That is a cruel way of putting it, but it is the truth. And that is what brought you here. The truth. What is about to happen to this world is much bigger than your grief."

He let her go of her arms, realising he had been gripping her a little too tight. The bandage on her arm began to seep a reddish orange colour and she opened her mouth, but no words left her.

He stepped back again in disbelief at his words and how emotion had escaped him. He looked over at her. She hadn't moved an inch since he had held her. Her lips remained parted, her hands shaking.

Fuck, he hissed internally.

He hadn't meant for it to come out like that; he only wanted to calm her, but clearly he had done the opposite. Her unusual eyes were unruly with a dam of emotion that threatened to burst at any moment. But she held it in.

Were her eyes changing, turning black? He could have sworn they were hazel before.

He had to be imagining it.

He blinked.

The girl's hair lay around her like a blanket of ink, spilling around her shoulders and down past her undergarments. Her cheekbones lay high in her oval face that was still smeared with dirt and blood.

But through all the filth, she was intriguing to look at.

Consumed by the girl's face, he hadn't fully digested that, for the first time in forever, he had lost control of his own emotions. He never showed depth to anyone.

And she had held her own with him using her snappy tongue, which was even more interesting. Never before had a woman spoken to him in that manner. He took another step back so that his spine was against the wall.

This girl had unlocked emotions that he kept in a crypt, in the deepest part of his soul. He didn't let *any* feelings venture out.

Whatever that outburst was, he knew it had been a mistake. Emotional outbursts were always a mistake. He looked over to the blonde—Cally—and her stare gave off a stunned look too.

Unable to find any more words, Torin left the room without looking back, closing the door on his emotional depth, too.

CHAPTER NINE

Viktir Blacksteel stood like a monarch at the front of the briefing room, dressed in all black leather. Gideon listened as his father, the commander, went through the briefing in fine detail of how last night's mission had gone. The commander always gave a breakdown on where improvements could be made or what he would like done differently.

Demon hunters dated back millennia, traced back to the bloodline of Thorin, the God of the Sun and War. The Blacksteel hunting clan were a relatively tight clan; small in comparison to others, having around thirty to forty hunters across the Huntswood territory and some more in other parts of the kingdom. Although they were one of the smaller clans, they were notorious throughout the kingdom of Caledorna for their ferocity and unyielding devotion to the hunt. Much like their larger brethren in the west, the Stryker hunting clan.

No matter their size, it was still their oath of devotion to this world to protect Caledorna's humans and other magical factions. The tower was located between Huntswood and Mossgrave and had been in the Blacksteel family name for centuries. They lived there to ensure that the people of the city were protected from anything that surfaced from the underworld. Huntswood was a city in the heart of the kingdom, well known for its spike in individual fashions and infamous for its markets. It was surrounded by forests on the southern half of the territory and buildings from the city on the northern half. It was a city birthed by nature, the best of both worlds.

"The four quarters still remain under control; the wards haven't been compromised by the Dark Army," Viktir assured his men. "Although we believe they are making attempts to bring them down."

Most of the hunting buildings were protected by magical wards that acted as a shield against demons. However, you required elemental magic to raise the wards, and a strong witch or her coven to keep the wards bound to whatever you were protecting.

Viktir's chin raised and his eyes narrowed to the back of the room. Gideon's gaze followed, to find his oldest brother. Torin looked like he had sent his mind off to a different realm. His blue eyes glared at the desk he sat beside, his thoughts elsewhere. His father's booming voice brought Gideon back to attention.

"I have advised the prime of how many we have staying under the tower's roof and that we plan on telling the residents of Mossgrave in the next few days about the truths of the Dark Army." Viktir took a moment to breathe. "The witches of the north have informed us that they have had a few unsettling incidents among their humans in the mountains."

Gideon's ears perked up, knowing that "a few unsettling incidents" meant something else entirely. Human slaughtering. And probably multiple.

Viktir continued, "Maradia will be keeping us informed if any more demons slip through the portals close to the House of Air Quarters."

Being the Empress of Air and the leader of her house, Maradia often aligned herself and her coven along with the hunters, keen to keep a good relationship should she need their protection or guardianship. There were no hunting clans based in the north, only a few hunters that stood in as guards to important witches, so they had to monitor what happened up north.

His father raised his voice a notch. "The clans have tightened their units across the kingdom and will be doubling their patrols." He took a breath and refocused himself on Torin. "We will be doing the same." His jaw tightened. "I have notified the shifter leaders in Huntswood and Ashdale; therefore, it will be down to them to communicate the news to their packs to patrol their territory. I have sent word to Skyelir, too, informing the fae. When the prime sends word, I will inform you all." Pausing, his eyes hardened. "Keep your senses alert. Do not lose focus this close to the Blood Moon. Your lives depend on it." He nodded, his hands placed firmly behind his back. "Torin, Gideon, and Kellen, stay behind. The rest of you are free to go to the training rooms and start patrols."

The men took their command and headed out of the briefing room doorway. Torin had gotten rid of whatever had taken up space in his mind and now his eyes were on his father. They were both twisting their features in the same way, sharpening them, ruling them even more alike.

"Kellen," Viktir announced his youngest's name. His father's voice was so worryingly upbeat that it made Gideon flinch. "Congratulations! Marcus informed me that you were the only Blacksteel that made it to your combat session this morning."

Ah, shit!

Gideon had been so distracted that he had forgotten that he was training for combat at dawn.

He hadn't missed a session in years.

"Torin." Viktir took in a small breath and then released it slowly as he turned to face him directly. His nostrils flared. "I heard about your little *incident* with one of the human girls in the infirmary."

Gideon's head snapped towards Torin.

He could have sworn he saw Torin's back straighten and embarrassment gush onto his face; but he must have imagined it, because Torin wasn't one to get embarrassed easily. So, what exactly had happened when he'd left him with Cally? Surely, he couldn't have caused that much damage.

"An assistant healer informed me that Rhea has had to rebandage the girl's arm," Viktir snarled. "Apparently, she is still in shock and hasn't spoken a single word since you left."

Gideon tried to locate the bandage on Cally's arm, but he couldn't remember the blonde having a wound on her arm.

And then something awful clicked in his mind. His father wasn't referring to Cally, was he? He was referring to the raven-haired girl. The girl who had spent more time kicking around his thoughts than he had liked her to. His fingers curled around the desk.

What did Torin do?

"Rhea is with her now, giving her a calming ritual. Hopefully the shock of you invading her personal space will have died down by the time the healer is done. I cannot stress this enough: We can't have human guests screaming in the tower because of one of my Gods-damned sons." Viktir's lips pulled back over his teeth tautly and he glared.

Gideon's eyes narrowed on Torin's face. Curiosity was killing him from the inside out, but Torin gave nothing away. Gideon straightened in his chair, something protective rising in his instincts.

"Emara Clearwater is *not* to be touched, do I make myself clear?" his father spat.

Emara Clearwater.

Gideon said her name a few times over in his head. He inhaled deeply and flashed a look at Torin who had gone rigid in his chair. Torin feared nothing—no man or beast—but he wouldn't dare cross his father's orders even if he really wanted to. It had been part of his training to obey the commander at all costs. Even if it wasn't in his personality to obey anything or anyone at all, he had to obey his commander. He'd taken the oath.

"Do I make myself clear?" his father's voice was rugged with masculinity as he raised it again. "That goes out to you all!" His dark green eyes pinned them all to their seats.

Torin held his father's gaze, his strong jaw pushing out defiantly, challenging him the only way he could. It was always a fight to see who could out-alpha whom. His mother had always been pulling them apart as Torin grew older and stronger.

But Viktir Blacksteel was getting older, too, and the more Gideon thought about it, Torin would probably have a good chance at winning should they go head-to-head without weaponry. But it would be a direct insult to the clan and the oath if he did.

"Understood." Torin dragged out every letter in the word. He shot to his feet, his strong legs holding the weight of his broad stance. Gideon, too, was on his feet, pulling him back by the shirt as he passed him.

Torin turned. "Get your hand off me!" he seethed, squaring up with Gideon.

Gideon didn't back down as Torin's head pushed down atop his. He had never backed down and he wasn't about to start. Torin was older by a year but looked about three or four years older than Gideon due to sheer width and height.

"What did you do to her?" Gideon growled, looking his brother directly in the eye.

Torin pushed his shoulder back with no clear intent of hurting him, but to eject him from his peripheral space. He clearly wasn't in the mood for a fight this morning, which was very un-Torin-like. He would normally throw a punch first and ask questions later.

"Gideon, in case you haven't noticed, I'm not in the mood. Stand down." He paused as he let a snarl curl in his lip. "Brother!"

Gideon looked at Kellen who had turned to stone, watching in trepidation. Kellen didn't have the same relationship as Gideon and Torin had. He hadn't grown up fighting with them, sparring together, fishing, or learning the art of the hunt like they had. He was the baby; his mother mollycoddled the life out of him. Something that frustrated all three other men and brought the "steel" in the name Blacksteel.

Tough, loyal, relentless.

The Blacksteel moto.

Gideon's fear was that Kellen was too soft for the hunt; not in the way of strength or power, but mentally.

He knew his father often wondered that too.

"Enough," Viktir ordered. "If you are going to fight, don't stand around here bitching like the wives of the elite. I'm sure the sparring room would like a visit since you both missed this morning's session." He rolled his tongue up to comb his front teeth. "Once you are done bitching, Gideon, you are needed in the infirmary. Rhea has instructions. I think it's best if you sit this one out, Torin." The commander dragged his sharp eyes from his eldest son.

"Follow me, Kellen. We have work to do." Viktir stalked out of the room with Kellen at his heels.

"What did you do in the infirmary, Torin?" Gideon asked again.

"Honestly, Gideon, if it were *any* other day, I would be happy to answer your stupid questions and then smash your face right into the mats of the sparring room to wipe that dazed look off your face. Lucky for you, I am not in the mood." Torin sneered.

Gideon blinked; he wasn't expecting him to say that. He didn't think anyone had noticed that he couldn't shake the daze he had been in. But he wasn't about to let his brother best him. "What's wrong, Torin? Did Father ruffle a few of your feathers and now you're not in the mood for a good spar? Have you gone soft?" he taunted.

Torin turned, his eyes blazing with that icy fire of his. "Oh, I am going to enjoy every moment of this," he said coolly as he rolled up his sleeves.

Gideon wasn't quick enough to even rustle up a response before Torin was gone. And he knew exactly where he was headed.

Before he headed to the sparring room to throw a few punches, he let her name float through his mind one last time.

Emara Clearwater.

CHAPTER TEN

The water was warm on her skin, her lengthy hair lay like a tangled rope on her bruised back. She still hadn't spoken a word, unable to. Cally assisted Rhea in the bathing chamber, heating towels, preparing bandages, and warming a collection of oils. Mint, sage, jasmine, and rose perfumed the air, burning in small bowls around the bathtub. Emara clasped her arms around her legs.

"Pass me the second oil from the left; it should say eucalyptus," requested Rhea, nodding her head in thanks as she received it. The warm oil trickled onto Emara's scalp and ran down her hair like a thick honey. The lilac perfume from another oil that she had dropped into the warm water met the other aromas in the room and she inhaled it all into her lungs.

Between the steam and the aromatic oils, she could breathe clearer than before. The horrible tightening in her chest, easing a little. She pressed out her breath loudly, allowing the air to fall from her mouth like Rhea had instructed.

"That's it, sweetheart," Rhea encouraged. "Breathe them in; take them into your lungs and slowly breathe out. Imagine the air of your breath hugging your lungs. Hugging your muscles. Relaxing them." Her soft voice filtered through the room, echoing as she lifted the jug of warm water over Emara's head and poured it gently onto her hair. She did as she was told, following the instructions from the healer. The fog and pain in her mind started to dissolve. Even the terrorizing images from the night before evaporated with the steam, leaving room for calm in her mind.

Rhea rubbed another balm into her temples and then onto her wrists. She had heard of a calming balm that could be bought at the Huntswood markets. She wouldn't have dreamed of trying such a thing, as they were often used recreationally by some people in her village to get high, but today, she would try anything to pacify her anxiety.

Anything to dull the pain.

After a while, Cally mouthed "thank you" to Rhea. She pulled against the bathtub to heave herself up and walked to the door. "I'm just down the corridor to your left, Em, if you need me. I love you."

Emara didn't turn to see if she had left, but she assumed she did.

Rhea handed her an iridescent vial of liquid and whispered gently, "For the pain. It helps to soften your muscles. You're pretty bruised."

Emara took the vial and held it in her good hand, she studied it for a moment noticing the shimmer, swimming around inside glass like a mermaid's lagoon.

That would be the next thing they would tell her was real. It wouldn't hurt to feel relaxed, though, would it? She tilted her head back and let the liquid slide down her throat. Instantly, she felt a comforting heat brush over her skin; it swirled around her bones and melted them as if it was hot lava. Not the kind of lava that incinerated, but the kind that held your insides in a toasty hammock. Rhea lay a white, fluffy towel over her shoulders; it was soft and warm and helped her rise to the ledge of the tub.

She wrapped the towel around her body like a dress that *just* covered her modesty, and she reapplied a new dressing to her arm. Rhea ushered someone to come through the door, hushing them as they entered, but Emara didn't even care that she was naked under the towel. Without this enchanting bath, six different calming oils and balms, and a mermaid shot, she would never have allowed anyone to see her this naked. No one ever had.

Strong arms withdrew her from the water fully and she gasped a little. She felt giddy as the warm water ran off her skin and the cool air kissed where it had been.

Kissed.

Her head was light, the lightest it had been in months and her chest even lighter.

Wow, the healer was absolutely wonderful at her work. Emara wondered how much coin Rhea would earn for a post like this. How did she get wrapped up in this world? She was so delicate, soft, and kind.

Emara opened her eyes as she felt skin to skin contact. The room was still bright as she looked at the muscled, tanned chest carrying her, a little trail of hair curled at his sternum. She toyed with the idea of tracing one finger down the line of hair.

"How are you feeling?" Gideon's deep voice entered her ears, tingling around her earlobe.

She didn't answer him. She couldn't. Instead, she looked at him—really looked at him—as they walked through the threshold of the bathing chamber to an open corridor. Her face inches from his, she could see how immaculate his complexion appeared. His eyes stayed ahead, focused on the task of getting her from the bathing chamber to the infirmary room. She dragged her top teeth over her bottom lip as she studied his face. His skin was flushed and a bead of sweat rolled from his hairline down his face. She giggled like an adolescent girl.

"Are you struggling to carry me, *Mr. I Like to Show Off My Muscles?"* She chucked her head back and laughed hard.

Gideon let a confused expression cross his face, but he kept his gaze ahead as he walked effortlessly, holding her. "If you are referring to this"—he gestured to the bead of sweat that rolled onto his cheek—"I missed my training this morning and my brother needed an ass kicking. So I killed two birds with one stone before I came up. He ripped the tunic I was wearing." His hair lay flat to his face, held down by perspiration. "Didn't have time to get a replacement."

Gideon had been fighting?

Warmth swept over her as she thought of him sparring in the training room. Shirtless and fierce. Strong shoulders bulked with muscles, defined abs working their way down into a v shape, hugged by his loose, black bottoms.

She yanked herself back to the present, shaking her thoughts away.

No one looked that good when they worked out, she reminded herself. Only in her colourful imagination.

She noted that his sculpted torso was currently pressing against one side of her body as he carried her, his strong arms embracing her close against him.

On second thought, she gulped, *maybe he would.*

"Why is it that every time I see you, you have no clothes on?" His stare finally met hers and a smile pulled his full lips up to reveal his gleaming white teeth. His eyes were even more beautiful than she remembered. Green like the richest grass, and his smile…well, you didn't see smiles like that in Mossgrave. His eyes sparkled with anticipation of her answer. Was he flirting with her? Had she flirted with him? What was in that elixir?

"Clearly, you have impeccable timing," she battled back, offering him a gradual smile.

He huffed a laugh.

Her body was still heavy, but she managed to move a hand across his chest to hold onto his neck as he carried her.

Just to support him, she told herself.

She could have sworn she felt his body stiffen in response to her movement.

Closing her eyes, Emara took in how euphoric she felt. She felt like she lay amongst the floating clouds above the kingdom, warm and safe. This is how she'd expected to feel when she woke up this morning—on the other side.

Gideon pulled a breath in through his teeth and she opened her eyes; his gaze moved from her face quickly. He looked directly ahead, focusing on the corridor once again. She noticed his eyes strain before he let out a barely audible sigh.

"Am I too heavy? You can put me down. I am sure I can walk..." Her voice didn't sound like hers. It sounded lower, huskier.

"I have wielded swords heavier than you. I don't think it will be a problem to carry you through a corridor or two." He allowed for a polite smile to form on his face.

They entered the infirmary room where she had been before. Gideon laid her down on the bed and gestured to the clothing that was neatly displayed there. "These are for you. Rhea picked them out," he said.

She looked down at herself in nothing but a towel. If she hadn't been so calm, her cheeks would have been flushing red by now.

Gideon turned slowly on his heels and faced the wall. "I have to stay put until you are in decent clothing," he teased. "Healer's orders."

"I am glad my outfit choices amuse you," she replied, keeping her eyes on the back of his head. His back muscles flexed as he crossed his arms over his chest. *Waiting.* Her mouth parted, hypnotized by the leanness of his frame.

Get dressed, the sensible voice in her head fought back. She reached for the clothes that were pre-laid on her bed. A baggy shirt and a pair of tight training trousers. Easy enough garments to get on her jelly like limbs. *Right?*

Feeling a little drunk, she tried to place one leg into the material—no, not even drunk. High. She was high! But she was determined to get this new attire on.

She gasped out loud.

"What? What is it? Are you okay? Can I turn around?"

"If I had any other choice, I would say no…but, um, I am kind of stuck." She giggled, almost snorting.

Gideon whirled around in panic to see her laughing, half in half out of her shirt. Her injured arm, still not willing to cooperate. Well, at least she had managed her trousers on.

It could have been worse.

"I've got you," he said as he slowly brought her shirt over her arm. She didn't care that he could see her bare midriff—Gods, he had seen most of her by now. Parts of her that Taymir hadn't seen, despite their relationship. What was a bare stomach in comparison?

For a second their eyes flickered to each other's, connecting. His gaze dropped to her lips and he drank them in. He was beautifully dangerous but oddly caring—a unique combination. His hair dangled over his brows, messy and wild, and her stomach flickered like a candle in the breeze as his scent circulated the air between them.

Lemon and musk.

His large hand brushed away a stray hair that had started to dry and fall into place over her face. A tingle danced on her cheek where his fingertips brushed her skin.

She had no idea why, but she felt herself gravitate towards his lips like a magnetic pull. Unexpectedly, she felt her heartbeat again, thudding against her ribs.

A siren sent shock waves through her and blasted into her ears.

Gideon jumped. "I have to go," he announced obediently.

She couldn't help but feel a sting of disappointment. Searching his eyes with her own to see if she could read why his face had changed, she asked, "Where are you going?"

While the burn of lust had been in his eyes before the alarm sounded, it was now gone.

A hardness had taken its place—a focus.

"Hunting," he confirmed.

He turned without a goodbye and was sprinting out of the room. She watched the doorway for a couple of moments after he was gone, as if he would return. But he didn't. Her head was still light and cloudy. She replayed his words over and over in her mind.

Hunting.

She felt a tightening in her chest, and a second later her buzz died along with the alarm that rang through the tower.

Gideon raced from the infirmary room, his heart slamming against his chest.

Not from the sound of the alarm that resounded through the tower which meant there had been a demon spotting, but from her. *Emara Clearwater.* Everything about her. Her smile, her hair, her eyes. The way she had smiled at him had made his heart pound. Her full, red lips that pouted when they rested. The way her eyes had changed as she explored his body. The curves of her figure as she lay in his arms, her hand on his chest…

Stop! He protested to himself internally as he entered the weapon room. He was about to go on a mission. He could *not* afford to be distracted at all, let alone be thinking about a *girl*. If his father knew he was distracted by a girl, he would nail him to the wall.

He pulled down his bow from the hanger and loaded arrows into a quiver that was strapped over his back. He hauled open the giant wooden drawer to an array of knife choices. Grabbing two throwing knives, a large dagger, and a small sword, he stacked them into his weapon belt and fastened the buckle around his midriff.

Weapons secured, he would let himself think of her when the mission was complete.

And if he couldn't stop thinking about her...well, then he was in deep shit.

CHAPTER ELEVEN

A while had passed as Emara lay on the bed, replaying what she could remember of the last couple of hours. The elixir was starting to wear off, her bones hardening again and her bruises pulsing. She brushed a hand over her wounded arm that was still wrapped in bandages.

The wound was going to leave a scar, that was for sure. Suddenly, she thought of Gideon. How many scars did he have?

Hunting, he had said. Did that mean Gideon was out hunting demons? Creatures that roamed in the dark?

Too many thoughts came to her at once.

What did they look like? Were they all like the one that attacked her home? Was he fighting alone? Was he scared? How long did a hunt take?

Worry twisted in her stomach. It wasn't an occupation she had come across before, but she assumed it was his, given the fact that he had been part of her rescue mission. She wondered how close she had ever been to a Hunter before or if any of them stayed in Mossgrave.

Were Hunters hiding in plain sight?

Agitated, she sat up after tossing and turning over every thought possible.

All signs of the sunlight that had shone through the floor-to-ceiling window had now been chased away by the night's shadows. The only light now in her room was an oil lamp. Emara didn't dare look to see if the moon was in the sky. The Blood Moon must be only a few days away now and she couldn't help but wonder if maybe—just maybe—everything was connected somehow.

She swept the mass of her dark hair 'round one shoulder and constructed a messy braid that tumbled down her side. A rumble from her stomach reminded her that she had turned down all the food that Rhea had brought to her.

Instant regret flooded her.

She needed food and she needed it now.

It hadn't occurred to her if she could just walk around the tower to find the kitchen. Did she have to wait on them to bring food to her? Was she confined to these four walls?

The setup of the tower confused her; she should have asked Gideon all these questions instead of wasting her time, semi-flirting, high off her face.

She sighed.

The tower wasn't a prison, but she didn't know if she could wander freely. Well, she would soon find out.

Her legs, stronger than before, carried her up from the bed and out of the room, taking a left as soon as she exited. The corridors were built up with grey brick, shadows cast up them by candlelight that flickered against the dark. The ceilings were high and the hallways long, with similar doors on each side. Every step she took outside the infirmary felt like she was doing something wrong.

I'm just down the corridor—to the left, Em. I love you.

As she made her way along the corridor, she arrived at a door that had "Callyn Greymore" marked in white chalk on black slate. She knocked once and opened the door.

A pleasured moan halted her steps.

Cally's head arched back in rapture as dark hair kissed at her neck. Two bodies knotted together, her hand tangled in the man's now-messy hair.

"Oh my—I'm sorry, I didn't mean to—I didn't know you would be…" she trailed off, her cheeks blooming red as the blood rushed to her face.

Torin Blacksteel's sapphire gaze met hers as he looked up through his dark lashes. His smile was sensual for a moment before he moved to the side of her best friend. Emara shifted awkwardly, not knowing where to avert her eyes to.

Cally's eyes widened with embarrassment, but she laughed and combed a hand through her hair. "Sorry, I—"

"I can leave. I was just—" Emara backed to the door, stumbling over a piece of clothing that lay on the ground. She kicked it off her bare foot and made a small gagging noise. She refused to look down to confirm what she'd stepped on, but she could hazard a solid guess.

She turned to leave.

"Don't!" Cally called out sharply. "I don't want you to leave."

Emara paused, heat beginning to burn in her face as Torin rolled from the position beside Cally. Clearly, she had killed the moment for him.

Good! She thought. She didn't feel guilty in the slightest about that. He buttoned his leather trousers and threw on a black shirt that had been lying on the ground. As he tugged the material over his head with one hand, she couldn't help but take in the structure of his muscles. Her mouth fell open slightly.

Did everyone around here have abs that looked like they had been carved by the Gods?

Cally devoured his body with her eyes, too, running a finger across her lips.

Emara looked away, wishing she had gone in search of the kitchen instead of Cally's room. But here she was, interrupting her best friend's sex life instead of finding the nutrients to survive.

Gods, give me strength.

Torin strode towards the doorway—which Emara realised she was blocking—with a casual swagger that made her eyes narrow in irritation. He was in no rush. She stepped to her right to let the warrior-like male past...

Awkwardly, he moved the same direction. Their eyes met for a brief second and she drove her gaze to the floor as he smiled at her through dazzling, pearl-white teeth. He was intimidatingly tall and solid. Raw masculinity poured from him as well—as the sweet smell of liquor. It was sweet, yet spiced. His jaw-line arched perfectly from his ear to his chin, sharp like a sword. His nose was thin and symmetrical on his face, and he had one scar that scored a white line between his thick, dark eyebrows, making him look a little more menacing than he already did.

"Don't miss me too much." He turned, winking at Cally, and stalked through the door, making the space feel bigger in his absence.

Cally almost combusted where she sat, her eyes filled with excitement to tell Emara all the juicy details of what had just happened.

She let a few seconds of silence pass between them, gathering her breath, before she spoke, "What in the world was that, Callyn Greymore?" She made her way across the room to sit beside the blonde who was already adjusting her undergarments. She fixed the sheets around her bottom half, confirming that what Emara had stepped on was, indeed, her underwear.

With no fear, she said, "That, my friend, is Torin Blacksteel." She grinned from ear to ear, her eyes wide with desire. "Or, as I would call him, *'Insanely Handsome Hunter guy.'*"

More like just insane.

"Oh, I am aware of who he is." She raised an eyebrow. "But what I want to know is how he ended up here. In your bed."

"He was just making sure I have everything I need."

"You can say that again," Emara huffed.

"Don't judge," Callyn cut in quickly. "After all, I *always* say the best distractions come in man-like packages." Her eyelids fluttered. "He knocked on the door after he returned from that *hunting thingy* that he does, clearly looking for a distraction of his own." She ran her fingers through her messy, golden hair. "I swear, it must be my pheromones or something. Guys just flock to me."

"Your pheromones." Emara rolled her eyes. "That's your excuse?" She paused, dipping her chin. "Again?"

"It is not an excuse, Emara!" Her lips parted. "I live with an incurable disease; I am irresistible to men." She flicked her messy hair over her shoulder. "He just knocked on the door and kissed me straight away. Like, grabbed me and smacked his lips to mine. It was—" She swooned, letting out a sigh. "I needed the distraction."

Emara knew the feeling. "Me, too." She bit into her cheek.

Secretly, she had always wanted to swoon like that after a kiss—the way a girl did in a great romance novel when the man's kiss is just…everything.

Sadly, the kisses that had been placed on her lips had never given her that feeling. Or what did Cally call it again?

Oh, yes: *Fluttering.*

"And I think I could get pretty distracted," Cally said, breaking free from her daydream to catch Emara's eye.

Emara offered her a giggle and then she paused. "Do you think it's a good idea to be messing around with him? I mean, guys like him don't belong in the real world. We will be going home soon."

Her thoughts flashed to Gideon's face that had been so close to hers and asked herself the same question internally.

"You know I don't like to feel."

"You can't shut it out forever." She had lost everything, too.

"I can try." Cally gave her best friend a half smile that didn't quite reach her eyes. "I want to have fun, Em, and these Huntswood boys know how to do that. I need something to take my mind off what just happened, and the city is perfect to get lost in. We have never been to the city, Emara." She grabbed her hand, "Who would I be if I didn't dip my toes into the Huntswood pool of distractions?" She looked at her best friend with a sincerity that made Emara want to laugh.

Rolling her eyes, she considered that they were vastly different people. And they would deal with what had happened differently. Heal in their own ways. Plus, she didn't have the strength to lecture Cally for the nine millionth time on who she slept with. She always did as she pleased, anyway, so Emara opted for a change in conversation.

"Please tell me you kept some food in here; I am starving," Emara practically begged, looking around.

Cally hopped from the bed, dragging the covers with her, and returned with a tray of sandwiches, cakes, and pastries that had been sitting on a table in the corner. Emara's mouth watered. They smelled divine.

They both tucked into the tray of treats, Cally chatting and Emara listening. It was *almost* a normal night for them. Cally stopped for breath now and then and to make sure that Emara was okay; it was comforting to know that Callyn brought some normality to an incomprehensible time. She was thankful to the Gods to have her.

After talking and eating for an hour or more, exhaustion overtook them both and they snuggled into the same bed. Emara was grateful that whenever she was pulled from the nightmares of her sleep, Cally lay beside her.

CHAPTER TWELVE

Emara had been woken out of her slumber by one of the infirmary maids who brought fresh clothes, towels, and bed sheets. She blinked one eye open to watch as the maid offered her a smile.

"Please read the note left by the towels" the maid stated timidly before leaving.

Cally, who had clearly been awake, rolled out of bed, walked over to where the note had been left, and brought it over to Emara. "You read it," she said.

"Have you gone blind?" She stole the note from Cally's hands and proceeded to read aloud, "'Dress in the clothes provided. Be at the sparring room in the east wing after breakfast. Eat light. –Viktir Blacksteel.'"

"Are we missing something?" Cally grabbed the card from Emara's hand and read it to herself, looking totally confused.

"Eat light? Sparring room? Sounds ominous." Emara's forehead creased.

"If it involves anything endangering my face, I am out," Cally said, sashaying her way over to where the maid had laid out the towels and clothes. She held up the black, skin-tight clothes bearing the label "combat gear."

She raised an eyebrow. "Combat gear? They expect me to dress in *combat gear?*" Cally's voice squeaked. "What is this? A war camp? Do I look like I wear leggings?"

"Well, I guess you do today," Emara laughed, getting out of bed. "Gideon said the commander would want to speak to us at some point. So, let's go and get it over with. And wear the Gods-damned leggings."

Cally let out an over-exaggerated scoff and strode to her bathing chamber.

After breakfast, they strolled along to the east wing of the tower to find the sparring room. Emara was dressed in a pair of long, tight bottoms that stopped just shy of her ankles, and a black, long-sleeved top that clung to her curves. She had taken out her messy braid and tied her long hair into a swishing ponytail. Cally looked incredible with her hair pulled into a gracious bun that sat tightly at the top of her head. She was dressed in a black shirt that fit tightly that she had crafted with a pair of infirmary scissors to have a little fringing at the bottom, and leggings which she had, of course, cut shorter.

It was impressive what she could do in half an hour with a pair of scissors.

Walking into a massive gymnasium, Emara noticed it was well-lit, considering it didn't have windows. Panelled bars of metal that could be used for climbing framed the bottom section of the space. She also noticed them above her, too; tilting her head back, she could see the ropes that dangled from the ceiling. She noticed a small brass bell at the top and wondered how people actually reached it.

All of the hunters, probably.

Weights were neatly stacked at one side of the room. Weights that Emara knew she would never in her wildest dreams be able to lift. Canvases of art were plastered around the walls like a form of motivation, the paintings showing warriors and battles.

Gods against monsters. Good versus evil.

She looked around the room, searching for familiar faces that would assure her that the families of Mossgrave were safe, and she saw a few.

Her heart lifted a notch.

She might also have been looking for Gideon, too. She hadn't seen him since he left her room in a hurry last night and she wanted to apologise for how spaced out she had been.

Cally flashed a flirtatious smile across the room and Emara turned her head to find Torin standing in similar clothes to what he had worn last night, but a little more relaxed. He met her gaze and she averted her eyes quickly to avoid any awkward glances.

After all, he was intimidatingly attractive.

The kind of attractive that made your cheeks gush red after two seconds of eye contact. But he knew it, and that annoyed her.

Looking away, she studied the people in the room; it was a mixing pot of age, height, and gender. Although she could tell straight away which of them were the hunters and which were ordinary villagers. She didn't stop exploring the room, looking out for—

"He's not here yet," a deep voice spoke from behind her. She turned as Torin offered her a mocking grin. She folded one arm across her chest, ready to say something snarky, when Cally cut in before her.

"Hey, you," she said, trying to compose her face so as not to reveal how much she was smiling on the inside at Torin being here.

"Excuse me," Emara said politely to both of them.

Wandering away, she left them to strike up a conversation without her. A conversation she was *sure* she didn't want to listen to. Looking over her shoulder, she was shocked to see that Torin was still watching her.

Emara swallowed down the tension.

As a distraction, she turned her gaze to the artwork. One stunning painting caught her eye. It hung in a solid gold frame. He was a God of some sort—she was sure of it by his mighty crown and monumental body. Reading the scripture on the golden plaque, the words formed *Thorin, God of the Sun and War.*

She had heard of Thorin before, in the stories and lessons her grandmother used to tell. But did the Hunters know of the same Gods as she did? Did they celebrate the same holidays? Have the same beliefs?

A hush mellowed across the room and she turned to face the entrance. An older gentleman walked into the sparring room, and immediately she could sense his authority. His presence radiated around the room. His features were familiar, yet very much his own. He must have been in his fiftieth year of life, but his authority could have been mistaken for someone who had owned the kingdom of Caledorna for a thousand years. She knew instantly that he had been the one to send the note.

He was the commander.

She narrowed her eyes to get a better look, and then she saw him.

Gideon.

He stood beside the commander. Other men flanked the outside of him, but they kept to one step behind. The ensemble of hunters made their way to the front of the room and the villagers watched in silence as they parted. Emara noticed that Torin had now joined the men at the front of the room, standing shoulder to shoulder with the commander. Emara couldn't help but gawk at the strong similarities between them.

Her eyes found Gideon again and she offered him a smile that died when his eyes pulled away from hers quickly, his mouth tightening. She tried to hide the disappointment in her face by shifting her weight from one foot to the other and looking down at her new boots.

Was she stupid? Of course he wasn't going to offer her a smile. This was his duty.

"Great gene pool, huh?" Cally whispered, looking at the three men. She had made her way across the mats to stand beside Emara.

Gideon and Torin are related?

"The Blacksteel brothers," Cally confirmed. She continued to say something about a third brother, but Emara couldn't stop staring between the two men.

Brothers. Torin and Gideon. One fire and one ice. Gideon was warm and golden. Torin was dark and intense. A mesmerizing combination for both.

Although, she could see some similarities in the way they stood together at the front, she found it difficult to wrap her mind around the fact they came from the same family. Gideon seemed so gentle and Torin, well – he was something else entirely.

"Thank you for coming," the commander started. "I am Viktir Blacksteel, leader and commander of the Blacksteel hunting clan." He was strong in the delivery of his words, his voice commanding the room like an enchanted spell. "You were brought here two nights ago in the efforts to save your lives."

His stern eye coasted over the faces of the villagers. "I can only imagine what it feels like to be brought here with no understanding of what goes on in our world and what you must have witnessed that night. But the time has come for us to expose what we are up against. We must reveal what secretly goes on under the noses of the human world. I know it's hard to believe what I am about to say, but you need to understand what we are—and what we deal with."

He paused and scanned the crowd again. "We are not a human hunting clan that hunts animals for sport or labour; please do not get us mixed up or compare us. We are a breed much more skilful and efficient. We are deadly to our enemy, and we do not hunt animals, so to speak." He paused. "We are a hunting clan bound in an oath of blood and honour to the ancient Gods of Caledorna to protect these lands, and we have been warriors of this world since life was born."

Emara's heart thundered quickly as she knew what was about to be confirmed. It already had been by Gideon.

"We hunt demons and all demonic presences; we kill them before they kill you."

A woman to the left of Emara wept quietly into her hands, breaking her attention from the commander's dark green eyes. Tears merged in hers too as she dragged her gaze back to Viktir.

"But most of you here have already witnessed such evil." Viktir rolled his neck and continued. "And I am sure the clan member I have assigned to you will make sure of your comfort while you are here. If they have not already informed you of our truth, I will. But before you can fully understand, we must take you back…to the beginning of our time."

CHAPTER THIRTEEN

In the ancient world, a world that we have long forgotten, there lived the first God." Viktir Blacksteel
moved closer to the circle of villagers who were
desperate to understand him, by the looks on their
faces. They were desperate for this all to make sense.
For their nightmares to feel like nightmares instead of
reality.

"The ancient manuscripts that belong to the
temple of the Gods often refer to her as the Mother God
or the Three-Faced God. For having three faces allowed
her to be all at once the maiden, the mother, and the
crone." He spoke with passion.

Emara took a quick side glance at Cally, who,
to her credit, looked like she was engaged in the story
of their history.

Viktir continued, "She had existed alone for an
eternity, for a time unthinkable to us here. As the
mother of the world, she longed for something more.
Something *maternal* stirred. Something which would
never grow within her womb, but within the womb of

the world. She wanted to love something more than the vast, dark void of her existence. She wanted to be the mother of life.

"The Mother God plucked from the simplest of magic that lay fruitful in her world and created the first of her children. She pulled from the brightest light she could and gathered energy from the strongest fire she could find and birthed a son. She named him Thorin of the Sun and War, Protector of the Lands." Viktir squared his shoulders, standing tall as he looked over to the painting of the God that hung on the wall.

Emara confirmed, in that moment, that Hunters did believe in the same Gods as mortals like herself.

"And when night fell, she then pulled from the rawness of the moon's light to create her first daughter. She named her Rhiannon of the Moon and Dreams. For her third child, she drew from the stars of that same night, and before dawn broke she created Uttara of Stars and Dawn.

"For a while, the Mother God was happy with the life she had created, but to be *truly happy,* she wanted more children. Therefore, pulling on the magic of all living things; she extracted magic from the trees in the forest and the rivers that ran from the mountains. She pulled from the plants, the critters, and the soil, combining them all into one—and she named her Vanadey of Life and Beauty."

Cally, as if sensing Emara's unease, placed her hand into hers and squeezed. She squeezed back.

"But the Mother God longed for another son, as she had not created one since Thorin and she had three daughters. She decided to complete her family and create one last God of the world. As the Mother God tried to create life, she realised that her magic was fragile. Weak. She had wrenched from too many sources of magic—from every element she knew to be good and pure—to create her family." Viktir paused and closed his eyes. "But she couldn't pull from any more light. The sun turned her down, the moon shunned her, and the landscapes could not offer her magic without the sun and the moon. They refused to give light. So, in her darkness—in her terrible and desperate despair—she pulled magic from the only thing she could: Her darkness. Her inner chaos. In her utter despair, she created her fifth and final child. She named him Veles of Darkness."

Silence swallowed the entire room.

Emara pulled at the rim of her shirt, trying to adjust the neckline, her breathing feeling thick and tight in her throat. Viktir looked over his crowd—a sea of silence, stunned looks, and pale faces looked back.

In the human version of the Gods' manuscripts, there was no mention of the Dark God, only the Light. Her grandmother had never included Veles in her lessons.

Viktir continued, "The Mother God placed all of her children in the ancient world to live freely and, of course, create lives of their own. Therefore, with their powers, Thorin, Rhiannon, Uttara, and Vanadey created life.

"After time, the deities fell in love with humans from the ancient world. And mated. This sparked the first creations of the magic wielders we know today.

Anyone born from Rhiannon's line seemed to manifest magic from the elements of the world—fire, earth, air, water, and spirit. And anyone from Thorin's bloodline was strong and fierce. The first clan of men born from his bloodline took an oath in his name as protectors of the land, the blood of a warrior God running in their veins.

"Anyone of Uttara's bloodline seemed to have powers of Light, but they were different from the witches. They called themselves the Faeries; unique creatures with powerful warrior-like tendencies and subtle magic. Life meant something different to Vanadey; she created creatures big and small to live in her forests and rivers and amongst her mountains. After a few thousand years of being at one with nature, she finally found herself seeking something more. A mate. From her magic, she allowed her creatures to change and shift into a human form, finally finding her mate in a wolf."

Emara blinked. All of those creatures lived here? In Caledorna? In Huntswood?

"But the Mother God noticed that her son, Veles, was incapable of love, emotion, or compassion. Therefore, she forbade him from ever creating life or finding a mate in fear of what he would do—what he could create. In a blind rage at what his mother had forbidden, Veles killed his creator, the mother of life. Outraged and struck with grief, Thorin declared war against his brother for his act. But Veles had become too powerful, not wasting a drop of magic in creating other lives; he was whole and strong." Viktir shifted himself. It was the first time Emara noticed him wince.

"So, with the help of his sisters, they created a cage for Veles— the underworld—because they were unable to kill him at his full strength. Whilst in the cage of his very own realm, Veles pulled from his own darkness, just like his mother had, and created."

A sob sounded through the room from a woman who held two young babies in her arms. Emara's throat closed and she struggled to hold back her emotion.

"However, these *creations* of his were not human, nor were they animal. What he created was an army. An army of demons. His very own subjects to help him storm the ancient world and destroy everything that his family had created." Viktir spat out the last of his sentence with pure venom, like he had witnessed the events of the ancient world.

"Rhiannon knew her brother wouldn't stay caged for long and forged a plan. With her magic, she decided to create four magical stones. One, for each deity of the light. The Protection Stone, the Resurrection Stone, the Immortality Gem, and the Dark Crystal. Each of them took one for protection, should Veles try to slaughter them. The magical relics were created to ensure their survival."

Someone in the crowd stirred, causing everyone to turn. An older village woman had hit the ground. Emara noticed Rhea rush to her aid. Clearly, all of this was too much for her.

Viktir didn't acknowledge the woman as he drove home the final part of this story. "And they were right to do so, as Veles did come. I will not bore you with the details of the Great War—but what I can tell you is that it was the worst violence that the ancient world had ever seen. Women and children were murdered and men were slaughtered fighting to protect them. Not seeing any end, Thorin slammed his stone—the Dark Crystal—into the ground, causing a shift so great it broke the ancient world in half. The sea gushed in and wiped out most of Veles' army, helping Thorin and the Hunters defeat the rest. But Veles didn't get lost in the depths of the broken sea. He found his sister Uttara and stole the Immortality Stone from her before returning to the underworld—and he was never to be seen again. But his demons were."

Torin spoke next, catching Emara off guard, "The ancient manuscripts have never given us a reason as to why Veles was never seen again. Some believe the Gods caged him again, some believe him dead. We know the latter to be untrue, otherwise his faithful army of demons wouldn't still enter this world for vengeance." He flicked his gaze over the villagers and then to his father. "But I am sure you have had enough history of our ancient world for one day."

Torin placed a large hand onto his father's shoulder. "Our old commander likes to get himself carried away in his stories." He winked at a woman in the crowd and she almost swayed.

Viktir's jaw hardened.

Cally smiled.

Torin cocked up his chin. "So, let's tell you why you are really here, shall we?"

CHAPTER FOURTEEN

The commander drew his eyes from Torin's slowly, but his eldest son took no notice.

"The demon king has a few close missionaries. They are what we call the Knights of the underworld—leaders in the dark battalion, his trusted disciples. They have been spotted on these lands leading demons to destroy homes, families—everything you know and love." Torin's ocean blue eyes swept the crowd. "We believe they are combing the kingdom for the ancient relics that were lost as the deities left the ancient world." He paused, looking at Emara. "And last night, the Blacksteel hunting clan was victorious in slaying one of these missionaries."

Had the man last night—that *creature*—been one of Veles' missionaries?

Emara wanted to cover her ears and pretend that this was all just a lie. But looking around the room at the hunters and the severity on their faces, she knew it to be true. Something deep in her gut told her it was the truth. They had no reason to lie, and the clan had saved people in her village—including her.

"It is our job to hunt and kill them all. Eradicate them from this world if they step foot in it. It is what we were born to do. It is what we live and breathe," Torin stated. "They are not caged like their Dark God and they seek to free him using the relics." His biceps flexed impressively as he placed his hands behind his back.

"The battle between the light of the world and the parasites that feast upon us is inevitable. Our bloodlines have fought for millennia to ensure the safety of humans and we will continue to do that. We will not stop until the Dark Army ceases to exist."

Emara flickered her eyes over Gideon; his hands were clasped behind his back too, shoulders squared off and powerful. His eyes looked ahead—narrow and focused.

Her heart skipped a beat.

Or a few.

Torin stepped forward. "We saved who we could from the village of Mossgrave and we have opened our tower to the survivors of this brutal attack. The demons will attack again. We are expecting the next attack when the Blood Moon hits its full peak in the sky. It's when their portals from the underworld are at their strongest." He paused as a few cries could be heard. He swallowed, drinking down the trepidation of the room, and continued, "Make no mistake—they will return."

A shiver exploded over Emara's body, leaving her cold and rigid. The room was unsettled with whispers and grieving cries as the villagers processed the world they lived in. A sharp pain shot up her arm. The same arm that had been wounded by the Dark Army. She held it tight, eyes on the Blacksteel brother.

"Today, you have been brought here to learn how to fight and defend yourself in these dark times. Gone are the days when Hunters wouldn't accept the help from humans. If we are going to win this war, we need everyone on our side," Viktir announced. "And that means you. The ones who have witnessed these evils. We need you to cooperate with us."

Gideon stepped forward, aligning him with his father and brother, and spoke clearly to his audience. "Today, we offer you to train with us and learn the fundamentals of what Hunters learn in their early stages of training, giving you skills to aid your survival during a demon attack. We will be opening our sparring room for two sessions a day for as long as it takes for you to learn how to defend yourself." He took a breath. "We will not hold you here against your will. You are not our prisoners. You are free to go should you not want to learn these skills."

Torin's dark eyebrows knitted together on his forehead. "But if I were you," he said, "I would stay and learn what we are offering. It might be the difference in your survival."

A woman from the crowd asked, "Are the women going to learn too?" Horror filled out in her voice.

"Even the women." Torin's deep voice filled the room. "Demons do not care what you are."

Viktir Blacksteel nodded in agreement. "This is the time for you to leave if you don't want to stay and train alongside my hunters. If you don't want to fight, we won't make you. Once you are healed, you are free to return to your homes—those of you that have homes left. But hear this: You will have a better chance of survival when demons enter our world and pillage your village. You will at least understand how to kill our greatest enemy. Your greatest enemy."

Cally looked at Emara. Emara stared back.

There was no way she wasn't staying to learn how to fight, even if it was just the basics. There was no question about it, she was staying. She nodded to Cally and she nodded back.

Understanding, she faced the front again, their hands still interlocked.

Surprisingly, no one left the room.

"Well, then,"—Viktir's voice changed, a little slice of surprise lingering in his tone—"let the training commence. First up, blocking—learning self-defence. Hunters, take a partner and find a space on the mats. Take it easy on the wounded."

The hunters dispersed, each of them making their way to a villager and introducing themselves. A few of the village people went with them willingly to the mats, others held back.

"Ponytail?" a husky voice said close to her ear. "Follow me." She peered over her shoulder to meet metallic blue eyes laced with mischief.

Oh, great! Emara sighed.

Her partner must be Torin Blacksteel.

CHAPTER FIFTEEN

Gideon watched his brother stride over to Emara Clearwater and claim her for his partner. His jaw ticked. With his observations, she didn't look pleased at that, either. She rolled her eyes and followed him onto the mats. A smirk appeared on Gideon's face at her attitude.

Pulling his attention away from her, he walked over to Cally who was standing alone, arms folded, her face bubbling with upset and her eyes on Torin.

"Callyn, I know we are already acquainted." He gestured to the mats. "Let's get started."

"Cally." She dragged her eyes away from Torin and walked across the space. "Call me Cally."

"Cally it is" Gideon smiled.

"Does Torin have anyone…special?" Cally prompted as she looked across the room.

The dreaded question.

If Gideon had a gold coin for every time he was asked that, he wouldn't need to take a wage from his huntings. How did he tell Cally that Torin had a new "someone special" every week?

He cleared his throat. "I'm not really sure Torin's into special things. He's more into special…" Gideon tried to find a word that would let Cally down with ease.

"Flings?" Her pretty face pulled up at the one side and she chewed on the corner of her cheek.

She knew his type then.

"You're too good for him anyway." He offered her a friendly smile and she presented a deflated one back.

"I know," she responded. There was no confidence in her delivery, but Gideon gave her credit for her strong front.

"Shall we?" Gideon motioned to the mats where people had commenced warming up.

She let out a small huff. "If we must," Cally smiled. "But do not, and I repeat, *do not* mess up my face. The Gods will be angry at you."

"I won't," Gideon laughed.

"Okay, now lift your left arm higher. Your good arm," Torin advised. "You need to be able to block my fist. You won't be able to do that with your arm as low as it is now."

"Block your fist? How can I block something the size of a giant boulder coming towards my face?"

Emara shot back. There was no way she stood a chance defending herself against the size of his hands. They were weapons on their own accord.

"Let me ask you this, do you like your face?" He studied her as he awaited her answer.

"Well, I would like it to remain intact, if that's what you mean."

"All the more reason not to let the 'giant boulder fist' smash into your face." He touched her temple with his index finger and flashed her an icy grin. Emara rolled her eyes and raised her arm, awaiting impact. They had battled back and forth on the mat for about an hour or so. Torin talking about the art of balance and core strength and Emara struggling to keep her breathing as normal as possible. Torin hadn't even moved a hair out of place.

Unlike Gideon's, his hair was tidy and shorter. *Darker*. So dark, she could see traces of glossy blue threaded through it.

"She wanted you to pick her, you know," Emara affirmed, getting ready for the next attack from Torin. Something she had learned already— always expect an attack. *Be ready.*

"I know she did." Torin didn't let any emotion cross his face as he pretended to deliver a direct blow to Emara's stomach. "When you are not concentrating, you can make fatal mistakes. Focus."

Suddenly, Emara saw another fist coming towards her and this time it was her face that was about to receive the impact. She raised her arm like she had been coached to block it. His fist crashed against her arm, causing a shooting pain to travel all the way up to her shoulder joint.

But she didn't let the pain stop her.

She was on the move, ducking under his bicep and pushing back, creating space. Like he had shown her.

Stunned, Torin struck again, moving forward at a serious pace. This time she darted to her left, ducking low as he swung.

He smiled. "Good." He let the smile drop off quicker than it had appeared. "You are a quick learner when you don't talk."

"Why did you not pick her?" she asked, not caring if he had just taken a verbal dig at her ability in concentration. "If you knew she wanted you to, why not just pick her?" Emara knew already that to keep Torin talking, she would need to keep training. Moving. Torin wasn't the kind of guy to stop mid-way through a training session for girly gossip.

So, she advanced on him this time. Not that she was supposed to, but maybe just to see if she could get herself a sneaky jab anywhere on his body.

"Be unpredictable, ponytail. Life is more fun when you live on the wild side." For a second he allowed recklessness to rule his eyes. "You should try it." He raised his eyebrows as he corrected his stance, keeping his legs wide and his knees bent.

"All I am asking is that you don't play games with her, Torin." She glared at him, dropping her hands that guarded her face. "I don't care who you are, just don't lead her on."

When he said nothing, she just bit down on her lip, awaiting the backlash.

"That's twice now you have said you don't care who I am." A slight dimple appeared in amusement.

"I am serious, don't you dare hurt her."

It was a warning that, somehow, had made it out through gritted teeth. She had just given a warning to someone who killed for a living and was built like an ancient deity.

Maybe madness had slipped into her mind.

"Are you threatening me?" he asked, his eyes narrowed and his thick brows furrowed in jest. A wicked smile threatened to grace his lips, but he held it together. The only noise that could be heard was the sparring of everyone in the room.

And the pulse in her ears from her heartbeat, as it quickened.

A siren—different from the one before—rang through the room and Torin stretched his arms.

"Lunch time." He smiled a real smile. One that she suspected he didn't use very often. "Follow me, ponytail."

The dining hall wasn't what she expected. It was light and airy, and it reminded her of her favourite café just outside of Mossgrave where she would sit and read. Parlour palm plants sat on the middle of every table, adding a little colour to the room, and it smelled like bread.

As she sipped her freshly squeezed orange juice, the spot next to her at the table filled up.

"You are fully dressed, I can't quite believe it." Gideon laughed as he kindly mocked her.

"Believe it." she gestured to her new attire.

"Nice." Gideon chuckled. "You look good in training gear."

Emara gave a small giggle. "You must be bored at the sight of my bare skin." She grabbed the straw in her drink with her teeth and finished off the rest of her juice.

"I wouldn't use the term 'bored.'" His eyes tore from her face to his food, and he tucked in. "So, how did you find your blocking partner?" he teased, changing the subject.

"Not nearly as interesting as Cally does." Her head nodded over to the lunch line where Cally and Torin looked to be flirting. "I walked in on your brother and Cally having a party for two last night." She grimaced at the memory.

"Ouch! That could not have been good for the eyes." He pretended to shudder and ripped a piece of bread off with his teeth, his eyes drifting back to hers.

"I fear they may never recover," she joked. He laughed warmly and she looked away. Gods, he was handsome. "I don't know about you, but I am just dreading the aftermath of the break-up when Cally gets bored or—"

"There won't be a break-up." Gideon swallowed down the bread and twisted in his seat to face her. "Torin doesn't do relationships, he's more like…I don't know…all about the chase, I suppose? Cat and mouse, you know? He doesn't get attached to anything or anyone."

"That's good. Cally is the same." She found herself jumping to her best friend's defence.

They both turned their attention to Cally and Torin, who were standing in the corner next to the line for food. Torin looked like he had just uttered something smutty to Cally because her eyes were on his belt and she bit into her lip.

"Ugh!" Emara rolled her eyes. *Again.*

Gideon stifled a laugh. "What? Is Torin not your type? He's usually every girl's type." Gideon looked like he might be studying her face for a reaction.

"I don't have a type," she challenged, sweeping her eyes over his lips. "So, he's not *every* girl's type."

Torin probably was *every* girl in the kingdom's type, but Emara would never admit that. Not when he knew it.

Gideon's chin leaned forward. "Yeah? I have a type. I'm a sucker for—"

"Hey, block partner." Cally's plate hit the table hard, and she sat across from them both, a smile gleaming from ear to ear. "What are you guys talking about? Looks *intense.* Fill me in."

Emara's heart thundered against her chest as she dragged her eyes from Gideon's. "Not as intense as what looked to be going on over there, Callyn Greymore," she said in full spirit, although she meant every word. She couldn't help but raise her eyebrow like her grandmother used to when she was checking her behaviour.

A pain crunched in her heart. She would never see her do that expression again.

"I can't help it, *Emara Clearwater;* he is just the most attractive guy I have ever laid eyes on," she enthused. "No offence, Gideon," she said, putting her hand up. "You're obviously handsome, too."

"None taken." He laughed as he continued to rip apart a half loaf of bread with his teeth.

Emara's eyes drifted over the dining hall as Cally spoke about Torin for an hour, asking any questions Gideon would entertain. Torin sat at the other side of the room with a man who had a shaved head. He was older looking than him, yet not quite his father's age. She recognised him from this morning's session.

As if feeling her gaze burning into him, Torin looked up. Flustered at being caught, gawking, she began playing with the fork in her hand. He had seen her looking. Oh, Gods! How embarrassing.

She needed a distraction.

She placed her fork down, "So, Gideon, do you have a partner in the next session? We could partner up if you don't."

Oh, holy mother of all Gods, why did that just come out my mouth?

She tried to hide her embarrassment with false confidence, sitting straight in her seat. She needed a distraction, not a rejection!

Cally shot her a look of interest as if to say, "We shall talk about this later."

Gideon's eyes changed from relaxed to entertained. "Do you really think you could handle it?" He placed down his fork too.

She had to get out of this dining hall before the burning in her cheeks set fire to the place. Emara lifted her tray to leave before her false confidence gave way to the raging embarrassment under her skin and said, "Sure. Show me what you can do in the next training session."

She turned and left, her heart stammering in her chest.

"I look forward to seeing what you have got," Gideon challenged, but she did not dare look back to see him. She could feel the radiation from his smile burn into the back of her skull. Or was it the heat from her burning cheeks?

At least she had a little time to herself before the next session started.

CHAPTER SIXTEEN

The man who had been sitting next to Torin in the dining room led the next session, which was a tour of the whole tower. He introduced himself as Marcus Coldwell, a hunter who had joined the Blacksteel clan from another hunting clan years ago.

Marcus led them through corridor after corridor until they stopped at a weapons room. Emara's mouth fell open at their artillery, taking in an array of spears, swords, knives, axes, and crossbows that were displayed along shelves, all in order of size and weight. It seemed that anything that could be used to end a demon's existence lay within this room.

"The minute the hunting siren is sounded, we know we need to make it to this room. We need to stock up for our hunt and do it quickly." He gave a tug at the belt that lay on his waist. Just like Gideon's.

Torin nodded once as he fastened a scabbard across his chest, strapping a sword to his back. Emara noticed how relaxed he looked in this room—which was unsettling when all she could see was instruments created to ensure sheer annihilation.

As Marcus talked, her gaze found Gideon; he was caressing a finger over an arrow as he assessed the sharpness of the point.

"Miss Clearwater." Her attention snapped back to Marcus. "What weapon do you gravitate towards? If you were to choose a weapon, which one would it be? Go to them, see how it feels in your hands." He picked up a sword. "Feel how it responds to you."

Emara looked at him and nodded. Everyone in the group started to move around, doing the same, admiring the weapons they were drawn to. She ran her hand over an axe and lifted it. Eyes going wide, she couldn't believe how heavy it was. She placed it back on the rack with two hands, using every muscle in her arms to do so. Next, she moved across to the swords which looked like they had been handcrafted by the Gods themselves.

Maybe they had. They did look antique.

She tried to pull one of the swords from the casing, but had no luck. The sword was even heavier than the axe.

"Why not try something lighter?" Gideon's voice stroked the back of her neck like soft velvet. "Someone your size should try something with less weight."

"We are not training with weapons, are we?"

"No," Gideon smiled. "You are not ready for that." His voice floated through the air softly, like he didn't want to offend her. "But it's good to know which one calls to you."

He leaned forward, brushing past her to the spears. He lifted one out the stand and studied it thoroughly. It was a long golden pole with a beautiful emerald encrusted in the middle of the spear; it had two sharp edges.

Double the danger!

The emerald stone winked under the lights of the oil lamps as Gideon moved it gracefully through his hands.

"This is beautiful," Emara admired, taking hold of the weapon. She slid her finger along the metal, up and down. It felt heavier in her hands than it looked, but it was something that she could work with. Something that, if she were allowed, she might like to train with. "I didn't realise something so destructive could be so beautiful."

She looked up, meeting Gideon's gaze.

He smiled at her like she had said something profound.

Her cheeks flushed as her heart picked up pace.

He took the spear from her grip and said, "The most beautiful things in the world are always the most destructive."

When coming back into the sparring room for round two of training, Marcus had advised that they must bow in the direction of the painting of Thorin, the God of the Sun and War. He advised that superstitions believed it was disrespectful not to bow, and it would cause misfortune in the next hunt if they didn't.

So, she had. Emara didn't need any more misfortune or bad luck.

"Please gather around the mats. Do not enter the mats at any time, unless instructed. Do not even have your foot placed on there because I am not responsible for what might happen to it," Marcus shouted to the crowd.

Emara watched as both Blacksteel brothers formed a mischievous smile. When doing the tour, Marcus had stopped in at the weapon room for one reason, she realised. And that reason was for the hunters to stock up on weapons for the next session.

"Okay, clan, I am looking for some volunteers to demonstrate to the villagers how we use a weapon in combat," Marcus said openly. "This should show a thing or two of what we can do when in full battle mode." A small smile curled at the corner of his lip.

Torin boldly stepped up to the mat. Followed by Gideon and another hunter. Another clan member with reddish brown hair moved forward. And another. And another. Torin's smile was wicked with confidence as he surveyed his potential opponents. Gideon's was unreadable as he kept a straightforward focus, waiting to be chosen.

"Well," Marcus spoke to his audience. "As you can see, we have a few volunteers, but as I do love a good brother-to-brother combat...Blacksteels, you are up." He turned to the crowd. "You guys are in for a treat." He dazzled them with a smile. "Try to keep up."

Emara's stomach flipped a few times and then Marcus blew his whistle.

Torin and Gideon strode forward and positioned themselves at either side of the mat. All too quickly, they were no longer normal men, but warriors in battle. Torin had strapped a sword across his back, and Gideon had done the same.

They bowed before each other before drawing their weapons and another blow of a whistle sounded through the air. With one flash of movement, Torin was in front of Gideon. A clash of metal clanged through the room and both brothers stood with swords raised above their heads, grinning at each other.

"Don't worry," Marcus said. "What they are wielding are training swords. Blunt. We only sometimes train with real swords."

Sometimes. Emara gulped.

Gideon moved to his right, ducking low, and sliced out his sword.

He missed.

Torin's moves were almost identical in his pursuit of him. A real game of cat and mouse had commenced. But with weapons.

She watched them dance across the mats. Their feet never tripping, their arms never faltering in a blur of movement as they either attacked or defended.

Torin spun around and brought his sword above his head, then lowered it towards Gideon with extreme force. The crowd gasped in horror as the sword almost sliced down his skull, but Gideon swung up to defend himself just in time. Steel smashed against steel, causing the watching crowd to recoil. Emara remembered how heavy the swords had been in the weapon room and instantly admired the way the brothers effortlessly threw the steel weapons around like a feather quill.

No wonder they both had heavy-set shoulders, bulky arms, and a mass of muscle fathered on their abs.

And thighs.

And backs.

She gulped again.

"A little slow there, brother," Torin taunted. "Is your mind elsewhere in the room?"

"I was just testing your attack, *brother*. My mind is on the mat."

Gideon took the next swipe at Torin. He pushed forward, finally gaining on him. But his older brother had set him a trap. Tricking him with some fancy footwork, Torin swung his sword at Gideon's with the strength of a god and sent it swirling into the air. The gleam from the sword was all too familiar as it flew past Emara's face and clattered to the floor.

She rolled her shoulders, shaking off the weight of the memory from her bathroom and inhaled. She tried her best to steady her breathing.

Torin was not done.

But Gideon suspected so.

Anticipating Torin's move, he pivoted on his left foot and swung a punch into Torin's stomach. Emara flinched and Cally let out a squeak but she couldn't look away. They glided over the mats in a perfect synchronisation, punching and swinging, pivoting and circling, blocking and shattering, before Torin finally managed to back Gideon into the corner of the mat.

"Are you scared to put that sword down, Tor? In case I am too quick for you?" Gideon's eyes winked in taunt. He was quicker than Torin just due to his build, but he clearly wasn't foolish enough to underestimate Torin's power.

He was buying himself time, Emara realised.

"Come on, Torin, are you scared to fight me with just your fists?"

Torin dropped the sword and slowly walked towards him. "Haven't you had enough of my fists in the last few days?"

"I guess not, brother."

"Is there something bothering you, Gid? If so, just say it." Torin's face contorted fiercely as they locked into battle. Gideon dodged two lightning-quick hooks from Torin's fist of destruction. "There is no need to taunt me. I will happily drop my sword and use my fists."

"Sometimes strength doesn't win," Gideon enticed, provoking his opponent.

Torin stepped forward and Gideon sprung into the air, turning and bringing his leg out to kick him in the chest. Torin took the blow to his chest and stumbled back. Emara couldn't believe that he was still standing. Torin dived towards Gideon, tackling him to the ground, his face turning red. He sat up and delivered a single punch, pinning Gideon to the mat. Torin lifted his fist into the air again and Emara closed her eyes.

Cally let out a small yelp.

The whistle blew again three times in short, sharp blows and just like that the brothers both tore apart. They were no longer each other's opponents.

Gideon got to his feet quickly and spat blood onto the mat.

"If you bleed on the mat, you clean the mat," Marcus pointed, as he repeated the rules.

Torin flashed his victorious smile. He wasn't bleeding. But Gideon was.

Brute!

For the rest of the afternoon, Gideon taught Emara the art of balance. He also taught her core skills in defence and techniques on breathing. After that, Gideon instructed that she must start running with a weight—which she found ridiculous, but he insisted on it for strength and endurance.

After the run around the sparring room, carrying the weight for half of the time, the skin began to wear on her hands from the heaviness of the iron plate. Calling it a day, Emara noticed that blisters were forming on the pads of her hands; with no healer in sight, she strode across the mats to the black box which was labelled "medical supplies." She searched for material or some form of plaster that would protect her newly formed wounds.

"I saw you looking at the spears," a warm, husky voice drifted down to where she kneeled. "In the weapon room."

She looked up.

"Good choice for you." Ice blue eyes that twinkled with mischief stared down at her, his dark hair still sitting perfectly. Torin was standing with one hand wrapped in a bandage. Taking in the red stains that seeped through the material, her eyes met his again, a little wider than before.

"Let's just say my partner wanted to train with a weapon and isn't very good with knives." A smile tugged at his lips.

Emara stood, holding his gaze. "You let Cally train with a knife?"

"Why not?" His lip tugged upwards.

Gideon had told her that they couldn't train with weapons, but she found herself laughing anyway. "And here's me, thinking Cally would go easy on you."

"Where would be the fun in that?" His eyes smouldered through her skin as if she were transparent. She let out a breathy laugh and rolled her eyes.

Thinking back to what Torin had said yesterday in the infirmary, she took a minute to let herself look at him. She had thought about what he'd said a lot since then and maybe she *had* overreacted at him trying to lighten the mood. *Just a little.*

"I wanted to say thank you," Emara said gently. "To you."

Surprise and confusion hovered across Torin's face.

"I know it was you, um, in the bathroom...who killed that demon," she fumbled.

Torin blinked.

"I didn't mean to get so upset the other day in the infirmary and I feel—I feel embarrassed that I acted the way I did. So, I just wanted to tell you that I am sorry." She expected Torin to laugh it off or make a funny joke to break the tension in the air, but there was nothing else in his eyes. "I shouldn't have snapped at you the way I did."

She searched his face for something other than silence, heat filling her cheeks.

He drew a bandaged hand over his face and then met her stare. "It's my duty. No big deal," was all he said, and his body brushed past hers, leaving her alone.

As she stared at the empty space where Torin had been standing, she wondered, *Did I say something wrong?* Emara's mouth twisted and her eyes squinted, trying to process what she had said.

She had apologised.

Confused, she spun on her heels to search for Torin, but instead slammed into Marcus.

"I am so sorry, I didn't—"

"Don't worry about it." Marcus' eyes were kind, and a gentle smile warmed his lips. "We are going to send you home for an hour to collect a few things. Only essentials. Don't bring anything unnecessary into the tower." He nodded.

Home.

Her stomach squeezed tightly.

Emara didn't know how to feel about going back to the place where her grandmother had been killed and she had almost died. It was her home, but it was tainted.

"Your girl, Cally, she said she's not coming and that she will get everything she needs another way— whatever that means," Marcus advised.

Emara dreaded to think what Cally had planned, or how she could get her things—her essentials—but she was too consumed by the trauma of going home to question it.

"Emara," his gentle voice gave warning. "She's not going to be there when you go back. We had to take care of her body that night. We never leave them lying."

Take care of her body?

Her grandmother's body. That's what he was referring to.

A shiver broke over her skin.

"Where is she?" Emara drove her eyes to the scuffed floors of the sparring room, unable to look up as tears swam into her eyes. She gritted her teeth, fighting them back. All this training had distracted her for a few hours. It had taken her mind from the pain of her heart. And she needed that distraction again—soon.

"She's gone." Marcus placed a hand on her shoulder. "To a better world than we live in now." Another shoulder brushed past her, leaving her alone.

She fought hard to control her emotions. She would never have a burial or a service for her grandmother's passing. There would be no resting place for her body where she could visit or pay tribute to her. Her heart scrunched up painfully. Her grandmother had deserved so much better than to be "taken care of."

With a shape inhale of breath, she held her head high and walked out of the room, fighting with the overwhelming pain in her chest. That night, she didn't head down to the dining hall like she had been instructed to. She didn't even have the notion to see where Cally was or what trouble she was getting herself involved in. She just wanted to be alone until she had to face the space where her grandmother took her last breath. Until she was sent for, she prepared herself to go home.

To a home that she knew, deep down, was no longer her *home*.

CHAPTER SEVENTEEN

Emara stepped down from the hunting wagon that had taken her back to Mossgrave. It was a rickety thing, rather large and based in a metal that she wasn't familiar with. She didn't see very many wagons in Mossgrave. She had only heard of them in the city.

Facing her home, she swallowed.

Her grandmother's house. A sanctuary of happy memories, tarnished with blood and evil. The giant fir trees that surrounded the backdrop of her home bristled in the wind, their branches feral, sending pine needles in all directions. Her hair whipped wildly around her face and against her shoulders, making it hard for her to see.

But she couldn't feel the cold.

"You have one hour. Essentials only," the short haired man instructed. "Someone will wait for you outside and will bring you back to the tower when the hour is up."

Emara didn't look back at the hunter who spoke. She simply nodded and the wagon pulled away, the gravel crunching under the weight of its wheels.

She walked up the dark stone steps and halted midway. Looking up, she could see where her grandmother's room watched over the front garden. She would look out the window and watch Emara play when she was a child. That hideous crack in her heart burst open again as she dipped her head down and climbed the remainder of the stairs. Opening the door, she couldn't face going to the kitchen where her grandmother had been in the final moments of her life. So, she raced past it and flew up a set of stairs.

The word "essentials" hummed through her mind, keeping her focused on her task. She walked quickly to her room at the back of the house and when she entered, her room was cold—almost too cold—and she pulled the dark cloak that Marcus had given her a little tighter around her shoulders. Her bedsheets were wrinkled; they hadn't been touched since she had slept there the night of the attack.

It was clear, even just from the sheets, that her grandmother's presence was no longer inside the house. The sheets were not made-up like Theodora had her do religiously every morning. She moved across her room like it was a foreign place, not wanting to touch anything.

Essentials. Get in and get out.

She pulled out her case from underneath the bed and launched it wide onto the mattress. Dust flew up from the case into the air and fell again like thick snow. She coughed, a hand covering her mouth, a few times before running her fingertips across the case, the soft leather embracing her touch. She picked out some practical clothes and laid them neatly into the case. Hovering over her bedside table, she pulled out her mother's box. That was an essential; it held more than just her coin…

She opened the box with a tiny piece of hope and thought of them both, her mother and her grandmother. Her hands clutched the box fiercely as she whispered a goodbye, an unsaid message to her grandmother. A message that she hoped so dearly would reach the other side.

Disturbed by an unsettling noise, she looked up, hearing footsteps on creaking wood. No one should be in here but her. Lightning panic struck through her core.

"Emara?"

The call of her name sent her heart into a frenzy. The box tumbled out of her hands and crashed to the hard floor. The hunters weren't due back, that she knew. It couldn't be one of them who called her.

"Emara?" the voice called for her.

Should she hide? Run? Fight?

She scoped up the box and flung it into the case before taking a step closer to the door.

What if it's a demon? She was too late to run. She had to fight.

Anything can be used as a weapon, Torin Blacksteel's voice entered her mind from her first training session. *Anything.*

She ran across to the standalone fireplace and grabbed the fire iron that leaned against the brick. She braced herself as heavy footsteps ran through the corridor towards her door. She parted her feet and made sure to bend her knees. Another lesson she had taken onboard. The fire iron was gripped in her hand, ready to swing.

The door burst open.

"Emara!" Taymir Solden ran through the door and wrapped her up in his arms, spinning her around. It was absolutely the last person she'd thought of.

"I thought you might be dead." He let her slip down through his arms and placed her feet on the ground. His brown eyes were bright with relief. With hope. His fair hair that was normally pristine, lay wildly on his head.

She dropped her weapon and it thudded against the wooden beams.

"Taymir, what are you doing here? How did you know I was here?" She stepped back, trying to make sense of her emotions. It was a mixture of relief, yet it was also foreboding.

Stay calm, you have a task to do.

Although she was glad to see him alive, she had wanted to be alone for just an hour in her home. She didn't know if she would ever come back.

"I've been going crazy, Emara! I thought I had lost you. I've had my grandfather's watchmen surveying the house in case you returned." He pushed a hand through her hair, trying to hold on to her waist. Emara pulled away, rubbing a hand over the back of her neck. Inching some space between them, she tried to force a smile to replace the rejection of his gesture.

An uncomfortable feeling spread over her.

"It's good to see you," she half-lied. "But I am sorry, I can't do this right now, Taymir. I have to pack." Her hand gestured to the case on her bed. "It's not safe for me here."

"Just hear me out! I have gone days—*days*—not knowing if you were alive or dead!" His facial expressions were melodramatic.

Another reason they didn't fit together was his ability to be overwhelmingly false. Like most of the elite. It irritated every part of who she was.

"I put out a search party after the attack, but we couldn't find you. I've been going crazy! I wanted to keep searching, but grandfather said the hunters would have cleared everything up." His lips thinned. "You were right about one thing: You shouldn't stay here. It's not safe. Pack and come with me!"

Emara tensed. "Wait! Hold on." Her eyes narrowed. "You mentioned Hunters? What do you know of the Hunters?" she demanded. Back before the attack, Emara hadn't known anything about the kind of world that involved demon hunters.

But evidently, Taymir did.

The look on his face gave away that he wasn't supposed to reveal that information. "That doesn't matter, Emara. Darling, I can protect you from it all. Just come back to the Solden manor with me."

The way he said "darling" made her feel ill. It was cold and demeaning. There was no warmth.

"You didn't answer my question, Taymir. How do you know about the hunters?" Her voice raised in irritation.

How long has he known? What else did he know?

"Emara, it's nothing. Now, come on; pack up and come with me."

"Why are you avoiding the question if it is nothing?" She searched his pale face. "What are you not telling me?"

"Oh, Emara! Why do you insist on acting like a dog with a bone?" He closed his eyes as if running out of patience with her and huffed.

She flinched. The fact that he referred to her as a dog sent sparks of fire through her body. "A dog?"

"Can't you for once not question everything—like a *normal* woman?"

Emara balled her hands into fists and pressed her nails into her palms so hard it pierced through skin. *Like a dog. Like a normal woman.* The thought of even considering an acceptance of engagement to him made her stomach flip. "If you find yourself too superior to answer a woman's questions, then I think it's best that you leave." She crossed her arms over herself, keeping in mind where her wound lay.

Tamir's jaw tightened. "The Hunters and the Soldens go back generations. The elite have an understanding with them. They won't speak of what they do—what they hunt—if they do a few things in return."

Emara winced at the thought of what "service" the Hunters would provide for the Soldens. Or any other elite family. Surely it wasn't polishing their silver.

"Listen," he tried reasoning with her. He reached out to run a hand through her hair again, but she pulled back. A flash of frustration lingered on his face. "I am not entirely sure about the boring details and you shouldn't be either. Don't worry about them." He paused. "I know we've already had this discussion and you weren't sure *then,* but things have changed. Your circumstances are a *little* different since I last saw you." His tone turned even more contemptuous. "I can guarantee your security now; finances and stability."

Rage boiled in her blood, turning it to molten lava. He wasn't here to make sure she was alive and well, but to see if his *arrangements* were still in place. He was here for him. The last time she'd seen him she couldn't have made it any clearer on the status of their relationship.

"Coin? Is that what you think I want?" Emara ground her teeth together.

"Isn't that what is attractive to a woman? A secure life, with things provided for them—"

"I think you have a very cavalier view of what a woman wants." Emara's voice almost fractured with frustration. "I don't want your *money;* I don't want your houses—I can't be bought! If you took the time to get to know me instead of thinking about yourself, you would know that." Her breathing came out short and taut.

Taymir was of the age that to secure social acceptability and status, he needed a wife. And an heir to his fortune. However, Emara was not going to provide either one.

"I can give you what you want, Emara—what every woman needs. I don't understand what you don't find appealing." His features screwed up, causing all the tension in his bone structure to cast dark shadows on his face.

"Your wealth does not seduce me, Taymir, nor will it ever be something that impresses me."

He dusted the cuff of his sleeve. "Every young woman needs a husband. I could at least give you a better lifestyle than this." He gestured to her room. *Her room.* The only room she could remember having.

Her voice broke through the room, sharp and dominant, "You think that's what every woman wants?" She scoffed. "How dare your pretentiousness assume that because I have just lost my grandmother that you can take advantage of that. My grief doesn't need a knight in an expensive tunic to rescue me. It needs *time!* Not *money* or lavish dinners or evening balls where my gown would cut off my air supply." She took a needed breath. "I need time to deal with what I have just gone through." She exhaled and didn't stop. "Just because you are of an elite bloodline doesn't mean I am going to run into your arms."

I'd rather train with swords and spears every day for the rest of my life than have a button for a mouth and a pretty dress, she thought. The tower was starting to look like the best deal in the kingdom compared to Taymir. She would take a million blistered hands over an engagement to an elite family.

His face changed, his mouth pinched into a tight pout. "What is wrong with you?" His tone exposed his disbelief. "Most girls would jump at what I can offer them. They would jump at the chance of being with me!" His temper started to boil from the rejection.

"If you could be with anyone, then why are you here? Be with someone else. Anyone else."

"I can't…" He paused, contemplating his approach. "I don't want anyone else, Emara." His voice was filled with refusal and desperation.

His blatant lack of respect for her almost had steam blowing from her ears.

"Listen to what I am saying, and I will try and make this as clear as possible. I can't be who you want me to be. No, wait. Let me rephrase that—I *won't* be who you want me to be." She closed the gap between them, desperate for him to see the sincerity in her eyes. She softened her tone. "The answer is no, Taymir. As it always has been. Nothing has changed."

A darkened rage flashed across Taymir's face. His full body started to shake.

Emara backed up a few steps. "I tried; I did. It is my choice, Taymir, you can't take that away from me," she challenged softly.

Almost begging him not to.

"I can take what I want, Emara." His voice changed to something more menacing. "Soldens always do." His eyes darkened. "Do you know what I think's amusing? How you think you are in control of what your future holds." He rolled his tongue over his teeth, his chest heaving in fury. "I could take everything that means something to you and ruin every part of it." His eyes mad, he took a step towards her.

Emara's heart was beating so fast, her eardrums were ringing. She pushed down the thoughts that were crossing her mind.

"You need to leave. Get out of my house. Now!" Emara yelled, but Taymir's body only moved towards her. He was going nowhere.

"There's always one thing in particular that I was very patient with you about." His eyes lowered to her curves and he traced them all over. "I told myself, *'Be patient, Taymir. You will get her underneath you someday…'*" A crazed laugh burst from his mouth in mimic of himself. Emara's skin wanted to turn inside out at the sound of it. "You always liked to play hard to get; teasing me, but never giving me it *all. Or any of it, as a matter-of-fact.*" He tilted his head to the side to survey her body underneath the cloak.

Emara stilled with fear.

Coming closer, he slowly weaved a hand around her neck. She batted it away, but he held her still. "I'm done waiting for you to realise what I am, who I will be, and how grateful you should be to have me between your legs." He grabbed her wrist and dragged her into him, his face so close it was almost touching hers as he strengthened the grip on her neck.

Furious, she hurled spit right into his face. "I don't care what blood runs through your veins, you were never good enough to get any part of me." She pulled back and he released her in shock. Not taking her eyes off him, her steps fumbled back, her stomach convulsing.

He laughed callously as he wiped his face and his eyes changed forever. "Let's play more games, shall we? Since you like to play games…" His tone was intimidatingly low as he tilted his head to the side, taking a step towards her. "Let's play the game where you see what it's like to become a Solden whore! I can take *that* from you and ruin your name in this village."

"Fuck you!" she roared, trying to create more distance between them, her heart wedged in her throat.

He sprung forwards and grabbed her by the hair. He swung her onto her bed and she crashed into her case. Emara threw a fist and punched into his face, but his body was already on top of her, pinning her to the mattress. She punched again.

"You can't take anything from me, everything I have is *gone!*" Emotion burst through her throat as she scrambled up the bed. He kicked her case off with his shoe, allowing him more space to lower his body onto hers. He grabbed her by the face and pushed his lips to hers. Her stomach heaved as she dug her nails into his wrists, trying to remove his grip.

"You will be my whore, my wife, and you will do as I say." He released her face as he took one hand and ran it to her waist, pulling at her shirt underneath the heavy cloak material. "You don't have the social class or the power to say otherwise. In fact, you don't have anyone anymore."

She heard a rip of material and her cloak came apart at the neck.

"I will never do anything for you, you are filth!" She tried to punch again, but his arms pushed her down further into the mattress.

No, no, no! *Not like this*. Her virtue was all she had left in this world. Something that she had kept for her. For her to decide—when the time came—when it happened and with whom.

"Now, now, *Emara,* the wife of a Solden doesn't say such things." His smile was a sickening slit on his cruel face. "A Solden wife simply nods her head and does as she is told without speaking a single word."

"Go to hell," she cried.

He pulled back, sitting above her, and slapped his hand across her face. The sting blasted into her check and she couldn't help but let out a scream.

"You won't be speaking to me like that from now on," he said. "In fact, you won't speak at all."

"Get. The. Fuck. Off. Her!" a booming voice sounded from the doorway.

Taymir turned in surprise.

Even though the stars from the slap across her face dizzied her, Emara could still see him. Gideon Blacksteel stood in the entrance, bow and arrow pointing straight at Taymir's heart.

"I am going to count to three and if you haven't taken your hands off her, I will shoot this arrow into your heart and then rip out your throat with my bare hands." His voice was unnervingly sincere.

Rattling.

Taymir also sensed the promise of his threat and dismounted her. Emara sucked in a breath of hope, but didn't move. Her full body flooded with reprieve as she saw messy, chocolate brown hair standing in the doorway. Arms that had once cradled her now tense with a bow and arrow ready to deliver a fatal blow.

"Stand by the door." Gideon gestured to the sliding doors that led to her porch with his readied arrow.

Taymir moved slowly.

"Don't even look at her." His voice was feral with wrath. He took a step into the room and his jaw ticked. His eyes slid to Emara, inspecting her face. Noticing the mark made by the impact of Taymir's hand, his nose wrinkled. He swung his arrow back to Taymir, lowered it, and released the string within an unexpected second. An arrow soared through the room and stabbed into Taymir's leg.

The elite screamed out in pain, his hands out in a surrendering pose as he leaned down to touch his new injury. The arrow protruded out of his leg and he screamed in agony again.

Emara jolted up right and scrambled off the bed, putting a hand to her mouth.

"Get your things, now." Gideon lowered his voice to a soft, yet demanding tone, never taking his eyes from Taymir.

Emara didn't hesitate. Her head was still dizzy from the clattering hand that had slapped her. She tried to gather her things through blinking eyes.

"You shot me!" Taymir screamed in pain. "Do you know who I am?"

"No, but now you know who I am. Gideon Blacksteel!" He ground his teeth. "Touch her again, speak to her again, even *think* about her again, and I will deliver an arrow right through your throat," he promised. Taymir didn't speak, eyes wide with terror.

"Now get the fuck out of her house and be thankful I am letting you live."

Emara watched as Taymir went to take a step to head to the door Gideon's frame blocked.

"I don't think so." The Hunter smiled, his eyes darker than before. "That way." He gestured to the sliding doors on the porch again.

"Are you mad? We are a storey or two up with no way of getting down without jumping." Taymir's voice broke in pain as he tried to stop the bleeding in his leg.

"Well, then, let's hope it's only your legs that you break when you make the jump." No emotion crossed Gideon's face.

Taymir turned to Emara. "Look, Emara, I am sorry. I didn't mean to—I just got so angry. I am under a kind of pressure you will never understand."

Emara couldn't respond. She couldn't find the words. There were so many spinning around in her head. She looked to Gideon, whose eyes were still on Taymir.

"Did I not just tell you *never* to say her name again?" He pulled another arrow from his quiver and slid it into the bow, arching the thread—ready to release. "Or speak to her." His nose wrinkled in anger. His scowl was deathly.

"Look, Hunter, I am *sorry,* okay?" Taymir cried as he backed up to the door quickly. "Emara, tell him to stop."

Gideon released another arrow and it sunk right into Taymir's shoulder. He let out another scream and Gideon lifted his jaw to assess his shot. "The next one goes straight through your heart, and don't think that it won't." Gideon reloaded the bow and pulled back the string. "One, two…"

Taymir's face was no longer smug. He let out a shout that was a mixture of frustration and pain.

Emara's body jumped in response.

"You're going to fucking pay for this, Blacksteel." He looked at Emara, loathing where she stood. "And you."

Taymir turned, struggling to open the door with one hand, and entered the porch with a limp. Looking over his arrow-penetrated shoulder, he shot a glance back at Emara, his teeth pulled back over his lips.

A spidering sensation crawled up her spine.

She placed a hand over her mouth as he heaved himself over the wooden railing and jumped from the banister.

CHAPTER EIGHTEEN

Gideon lowered his bow and strung it over his back. He now palmed two fighting knives, thinking about what he had witnessed and wishing he could go after that man and end him. His blood raged through his veins, his temper still seething through his body from his head right through to his toes. Thank Thorin he had come into Mossgrave on the wagon with the other villagers to help gather their things. He had only wanted to check in on Emara, knowing that Cally had stayed behind at the tower. His eyes flickered to Emara's; her face was hollow.

"Do you have everything you need?" he questioned, straining to keep the anger contained. Her eyes curved up at the side to showcase her long lashes as she looked back at him. One cheekbone was now swollen.

He tightened his grip on the knives.

She was still so beautiful.

"Even if I don't have everything, get me out of here," she said softly, looking down at the floor.

He closed the space between them carefully, taking his time, tucking the knives into his belt. Something about her face and how she looked at him made him want to end anyone who hurt her.

He had always been protective,—it was his duty—but he had never felt the urge to defend someone like he had with her. Something changed inside him when he saw her fighting the man off. Something instinctive…

"Look at me," he said softly. Her jaw pushed up as she gathered the strength to look at someone in the eye. Their eyes met momentarily, before she averted them to her hands. "You didn't do anything wrong," he protested quietly. "He should never have done that to you. Are you okay?" he asked.

She said nothing.

"I can go back down there and—"

"It's fine." She spoke without looking at him, cutting him off.

He took a breath. It wasn't fine. It really, *really* wasn't fine. "Emara, you did nothing wrong." He paused. "Some people think they own the world because they have coin, but they don't."

"I know I did nothing wrong," she said. Turning her back to him, she put a few items into her case and fastened it shut. "He doesn't own me."

He shifted on his feet. "You don't ever have to feel fear when you are with me—us" he added. *Us.* The Hunters, he assured himself. Gideon walked around to her side and placed a hand over hers. She didn't look up. "I promise you, I won't let anyone hurt you."

She let out a sigh, allowing her body to relax a little more as she looked out at the wooden terrace. "I'm not scared, I just want to get out of here," her voice was faint, but she spoke with certainty.

All Gideon wanted to do was cradle her in his arms. He wanted to tell her that everything was going to be okay. But he was on duty and affection was not one of a hunter's dispositions.

He removed his hand from hers as he said, "Let's get out of here."

She didn't move as if frozen there.

He placed a hand in the middle of her back and gently guided her towards the door. She followed, case in hand, sniffing back her tears. He watched as one single tear rolled down her cheek.

In that moment, he didn't care that he was on duty; he could feel human instincts and act on them without feeling guilty about it. Even the Gods had some humanity.

He stopped and turned to face her. Slowly, he pulled her into his chest with one hand and embraced her with the other. She let him welcome her as she wrapped her arms around his back, leaning her head against his chest. He didn't really know how to handle the tears of a girl, but like the last time, he was willing to try. "Please, don't be upset. He doesn't deserve your tears for one second."

She pulled back after a few flashes of blissful silence between them, her shadowy, long hair curtaining her shoulders. "My tears are not for him, but for this moment."

Gideon understood. She was saying goodbye to her old life. A life which she could no longer safely live. The bump on her face was starting to take further colour and he forced himself to take the first step away. "Your eyes have changed colour," Gideon realised.

"I know, they do it all the time," she replied, looking at her case. "I can't help it."

Gideon had an awful feeling that she wanted to shield them away. They were so stunningly rare that she probably felt ashamed of them. But she shouldn't. Her eyes watered and she wiped the single tear that broke away.

"Let's get back to the tower," he said firmly, and she nodded sheepishly. "I can get that for you." He tried to take her case.

"I have got it," she said sharply and walked out the room.

Gideon watched as Emara walked away from her home with another darkened memory of it. He hoped he would see Taymir Solden again, and he prayed to the God Thorin that he would see him soon.

The journey to the tower had been a silent one. He watched as she unloaded her case from the wagon and proceeded through the gardens without her cloak, her midnight hair wafting behind her as the ice-cold wind tore at it. Admirably, she didn't shiver; keeping her back straight, she continued through the cutting wind, her thoughts elsewhere. Gideon shook off the cold as he followed her up the path, staying one step behind her.

Marcus, who had clearly been on guard duty, swung open the door to the foyer, his eyes warm with welcoming. "Welcome back. You have a combat session with the clan in half an hour. No weapons," he advised Gideon, keeping the door open for the other returning villagers who were making their way through the gardens.

Gideon bowed his head in acknowledgement and mouthed, "See you there." He would fill Marcus in about what had happened back at Emara's home when they were in the training room and he took a mental note to brief his father, too.

As he walked with Emara to her room, fearing that she might fall apart any second, he calmed himself from wanting to kill Taymir. Dumping her case as she walked in the door, she went straight over to the window. Her arm wrapped around her waist, the other arm rested on top, as her hand came up close to her mouth. The thoughts in her head troubled her face as she sifted through them, chewing on a nail.

It didn't take a genius to presume what she was thinking about. Thank the Gods above it had been him who found her and not Torin, or the Hunters would have found themselves in a civil war with the elite humans for slaughtering an heir to one of the wealthiest families in the kingdom. And every faction of the prime knew wealth meant power. However, there was no doubt about it that Torin would have ripped Taymir limb from limb for what he had done. He would have parcelled up his remains and sent them back to his family with a smile on his face and Gideon would now be prepping for a war against the mortal men. The Hunters couldn't afford to war against the elite—they paid them handsomely for their protection—but they wouldn't take their bullshit, either.

Of course, Gideon had known who Taymir Solden was when he had seen him—an old money elite that produced earthy materials never went unnoticed. Old money went a long way in Huntswood, and having an elite as an alliance certainly could help with a thing or two. Especially if they were tied to the Minister of Coin.

Gideon had heard rumours of Brahmon Solden (Taymir's father) paying Hunting Clans in the east a pretty coin to wipe out a rival diamond mine family. And some Hunters would do it for a bit of coin without blinking an eyelid. It wasn't unheard of for Hunters to do dirty work for the elite. He just hadn't expected to find a *Solden* in Emara's room…forcing himself on her.

He focused through the anger as it started to peak again.

Were they together? Had they just broken up? Is that why Taymir had gotten so angry?

The questions that ran through his head didn't matter now. Taymir wouldn't be bothering Emara again if he had any sense.

"I will come back later," he said softly to her. "To make sure you're okay. But right now, I have got to go to the training room. Is there anything I can do before I go?"

She shook her head once, her eyes not meeting his. He turned, taking his cue to leave, wishing he had something else to say to her.

"Gideon," Emara was quick with his name on her lips. It sounded so sweet. "In fact, I do. When you return, can you bring some of the fresh orange juice from lunch?"

He let out a barking laugh, not really expecting her to say that. "Sure, anything you want."

Emara walked towards the brown leather case that she had filled with things she couldn't even remember. She had avoided opening it for about an hour. Its contents represented her bedroom which was now tainted with unpleasant memories that had been turning over and over in her mind. After Gideon left, she had headed to the bathing chamber to scrub off the recollections of her bedroom, letting the roasting hot bath melt away this afternoon's happenings.

After getting out of the tub, she had stood in the room, staring at the case that held her belongings as the cool air cupped her skin. Unbuttoning the case with one hand, holding the towel she wore with the other, she pulled out some clothing items that she could relax in before the sparkle of her encrusted box caught her eye.

As Emara lifted the box, she noticed that the drop to the floor had damaged the lid. Lowering herself onto the bed, she pondered how she could fix it. Examining the hinges, she brushed her fingertips along the inside of the lid. It wobbled from the inside.

What was that?

The wood from the top of the lid was broken, dented inwards. *Great!* Holding up the box, she pushed the lid with her finger, forcing one end to cave in and the other to pop out at the side. She heard a sliding noise and a smallish stone fell into her lap.

What in the Gods' name was that?

Picking up the unusual stone, she held it in her palm. The light from the window frolicked around the precious stone, sending out glistening lights of turquoise, lime, and violet. She could feel the supremacy of it burning into her palm and she dropped it.

"What is that?" she hissed to herself.

Looking at her hand, she studied the mark it had left. *It had burned her.*

She kissed the mark better like a mother would kiss a child's wound for comfort and picked it back up. It was a strange little thing, and again, it burned the two fingers she held it in. It didn't feel hot to touch, but the longer it touched her skin, the more it singed.

A knock on her door startled her, causing her to stand. Quickly, she put the stone back into the broken box and shoved it under the clothes in her case. She ran over to the door, feeling her damp hair caress her back, and opened it up.

"Freshly-squeezed orange juice, as requested." Gideon stood in all black, holding a jug of pure orange. His smile was infectious, and it slipped onto her face too, knocking the false one off. As the muscles in her face moved, an ache on her cheekbone and lip niggled, reminding her of the slap Taymir had delivered.

She flinched.

The curve of his jaw tightened as he looked at her and she knew instantly that he was checking her all over for injuries, which ultimately made her feel like a fourteen-year-old girl. Heat rushed to her face, causing her to avert her eyes from his.

"I can see we are back in the towel dress." He offered her a polite smile and she looked down before her cheeks turned scarlet. "I am not complaining." He raised an eyebrow that met his brown hair. "I just didn't expect you to be wearing that as I delivered your request. I thought you wore *hunting* attire now." A subtle laugh escaped his lips.

She ignored the fact he highlighted her towel dress. "I didn't think you would remember my request after a long, hard training session with the clan." She managed a small smile back. "That's what you call each other, right? The clan?" She gestured for Gideon to enter the room, trying to distract him from the redness in her cheeks.

If she hadn't been so distracted with that stone, she would have had clothes on by now. He laughed as he lazily entered the room. He placed the jug on the table beside the door and put down the two glasses. One for him, she noticed. He planned to stay long enough to have a drink.

Was he worried about her?

He lifted the jug and poured, still managing to look at her without spilling a single drop. "That is what we call each other *sometimes.*" He extended his arm and held out a glass full of orange juice. She walked over to him, moving her hair that lay irritatingly around her neck, flipping it over her shoulder as she reached out for it.

"Thank you for bringing it to me." Even though it was something as little as juice, she appreciated it. He didn't have to do that.

"It was no problem at all," Gideon said.

"My grandmother always used to make orange juice," she admitted as she sipped it.

Gideon was in relaxed training gear. Loose bottoms and a tight, black tunic. With this look, he could have passed as a normal human if he wasn't tiered with rope-like muscle underneath his clothing. She swallowed, suddenly finding it a little bit warmer in the room than before.

"Getting unpacked, I see." He gestured to the messy case, lying sprawled out on her bed.

Embarrassed, she walked over and flipped the lid closed. "Not quite unpacked," she said before sipping on more of her juice to hide behind the glass. "I don't know how long I will be here."

"You can stay for as long as you need to."

"Thank you" she muttered, knowing that she had no other plan to go elsewhere yet.

"So, a little birdy has informed me that Cally has somehow talked my brother into taking her to the Huntswood markets for seamstress supplies." He raised his eyebrow. "She's starting over, apparently."

"Of course she has." Emara found her lips twitching upwards. It would be Cally's dream come true to start a fresh life, buying everything from the city with her coin. "Even us village girls down in Mossgrave know about the markets in Huntswood." She mirrored his eyebrow raise. "They are a hot topic there amongst the younger generation. And a scandal to the elders."

He laughed, taking a sip of juice. "I think they are famous throughout the kingdom of Caledorna."

"I would probably use the term infamous…" she replied.

"Well, in that case, if you, too, are planning to go to the *infamous* Huntswood city markets"—he paused, placing the glass on the unit he stood against— "I can escort you. I don't want you going down there with just them."

His unsaid words were heard loud and clear. Going down there without protection was reckless.

Dangerous.

Her heartbeat quickened.

"Thank you for the offer, but I don't need a bodyguard. I am fine."

"I am not referring to *that*. The truth is, I think you could use a break—a distraction—and the markets can be fun. But they are also dangerous. You can get anything you want there and that's not always a good thing. All sorts roam the markets in search for things you can't buy locally. From knives to exotic animals to illegal substances."

Emara's ears perked. Her thoughts turned to the hidden stone in her box. If there was anywhere in the world that she could find out peculiar information, it was the Huntswood markets.

Maybe someone could inspect the stone and let her know what it was. Maybe there was a reason why it had been tucked away in a box of her mother's. Maybe it was special? And maybe they could let her know why it burned her skin like a branding iron.

"I will go with you," the words spilled from her mouth quicker than she could think them over.

Gideon shot her a smile that lit up his eyes before he moved closer and paused just in front of her.

She took a deep breath.

He was much taller than her and she had to look up at him to see his face. She could feel the heat from his body radiating towards her, gravitating. His pine green irises glided over her face and he lifted his hand to cup her jaw. She took in that now-familiar scent of lemon and musk, breathing it into her lungs as he turned her face from side to side. His thumb brushed over the mark on her cheek and then lip as rage returned to his eyes, his shoulders tensing.

"Don't look at it," she asked of him. Emara didn't want him studying the result of what she had just endured. She didn't want him to feel sorry for her, nor did she want to remember it. Not when she felt the way she did around him. She wanted to forget it happened altogether.

He didn't move his gaze. "It's starting to bruise." His eyes narrowed.

"I told you not to look at it." She removed his hand from her cheek and took a step back.

"Even with a purple bruise forming," he said lightly, "you're still beautiful, you know."

His words swirled around in her head and her heart glitched. She had been called beautiful before, but she hadn't felt the depth in someone's voice like when Gideon had said it. A small laugh broke from her throat and she was glad of it. She needed to inhale air as she quite frequently forgot to breathe when she was around him.

"Maybe we should get Rhea to look at it," he said, still studying her face from cheekbone to lip.

"It will heal on its own." She rejected the idea of Rhea working on her again. The poor healer needed a break; she knew she hadn't had any time off since the attack.

"Okay, you're the boss." He shot her a surrendered look. "No healer."

A shooting pain entered her cheek as she smiled, but she tried her best to hide it from Gideon.

Something within her shifted and changed, the pain reminding her of her weakness. It was a shooting pain that she never wanted to have to hide again. Emara knew, in that moment, she had to find a way to protect herself. She couldn't let herself be a victim again…

"Train me," she said, meeting his gaze. "*Fully*. Not just the basics like everyone else. If I am going to be here indefinitely, I should train." She placed the glass down on the unit next to her bed. "I want to learn it all. I don't want to just learn defence; I don't want to feel fear every time I see a man or a shadow in the dark. Never again do I want to be"—she paused, swallowing the frog in her throat—"helpless." She looked up. "Show me how to wield a weapon properly. Train me how to throw an axe or a knife or something." Her eyes explored his face.

He crossed his arms over his chest. "Emara, you are not ready to throw an axe before you can throw a punch. I don't want you to run before you can walk with this stuff."

"I don't care how I learn, I just want to learn it." She paused. "I will put in more training sessions to learn. Someone can train me."

"You don't have to. We can protect you here. Girls don't usually ask for much more."

"Gideon, please do not insult me because I am a *woman." Not a girl.* She made that clear in her tone. "I don't care if the girls before me didn't want to learn. I do."

He ran a hand through his hair, shaking it a little. "I understand where you are coming from; it's natural when someone has gone through what you have to want to learn how to fight. But there is more to it than just a few training sessions."

"I know that, Gideon. I know you weren't born looking like that." She went silent, feeling the embarrassment of her words crawl into her cheeks. "I just don't want to be weak anymore."

He raised an eyebrow. "Are you sure you want to do this? You will be putting yourself at risk, pushing your body and mind to its limits. Not to mention, I shouldn't really be doing it."

"I am positive." As she stepped closer to him, her eyes dazzled with the hunger to learn. "Learning defence isn't enough. I can handle it."

He lifted his hand and ran a thumb over her plump lip and she closed her eyes, exhaling. "You could get hurt. Really hurt," he said, the stubbornness of his tone beginning to deplete.

"That's a risk I am willing to take."

A long moment passed between them as he looked down at her. His hand fell from her face. "Okay. I will train you," he agreed.

Emara felt an overwhelming rush sweep over her heart and a tightness in her chest lifted. "Thank you," she whispered.

He nodded. "It won't be easy."

"It might be easier than how I am feeling right now."

Their gazes met and something like sympathy spilled into his eyes before she looked away. The energy between them was so natural, so organic, yet she barely knew him at all. But she felt like she had known him for a long time. She felt safe with him.

"Are you sure you are okay?" Gideon asked softly. "After what happened today?"

She looked over at him and the wall that she had built around herself collapsed. "No." She shook her head. "I don't know if I will ever be."

He offered a melancholy look before it turned to something else entirely. "I could have killed him," he admitted.

His voice was so sharp, Emara lifted her gaze to his furious face. "And then his blood would have been on your hands—and like you said, he is not worth it."

"I am not so sure anymore."

"He's just an entitled brat," she gritted out.

"That doesn't make what he did okay."

"I know. I am just trying to rationalise everything." She placed a hand on her stomach, trying not to think of it too much.

Gideon stepped closer. "Look at me."

She did.

"There is nothing to rationalise. You did nothing wrong. What he did was disgraceful, and I should have shot my arrow through his heart."

A charge of vibrant energy surged through her as he placed a hand on her shoulder. It was reassuring.

"Thank you," she said, reaching up to touch his hand. "Thank you for being there. I don't know what would have happened if you hadn't been—" her voice cracked.

"Come here," he gently moved closer, pulling her into him. "I promise you I won't let anything happen to you."

She let him embrace her, feeling comforted enough to rest her head on his chest.

"We can train together. I will train you so you do not need to fear men like him."

"You have no idea how much I needed to hear that," she muttered, leaning into his embrace further.

"Sorry to break up this little love fest," a deep, husky voice entered the room.

They broke apart and she looked to the side of Gideon's shoulder as he went utterly still.

Torin Blacksteel stood in the doorway, palming a dagger. She hadn't even heard the door open. Gideon moved directly in front of her as if to protect her from prying eyes.

Her shield.

"Torin," was all he responded. Emara studied his back muscles. He was tensing, hard.

"Are you two lovebirds going to be joining our crusade to the markets?" His brother's voice drifted over to her, gilded in trouble.

She peeked around Gideon's shoulder again to see Torin's ocean eyes vivaciously awaiting a response.

"We will be there," the words rolled from Emara's tongue quicker than she expected.

Torin smiled and kicked his foot off the door-frame, propelling himself into an upright position. The dagger gleamed, catching the light—but not as brightly as his smile. "That's what I like to hear." He looked his brother in the eye. "It can get wild down there, especially this close to a full moon. It should be a good time."

"How long were you standing there?" Gideon demanded to know.

"Long enough to put me in the mood for a good night." Torin winked. "You should wear that dress to the markets." He tossed his head towards Emara. "It's daring. I like it," he purred coolly.

She looked down at herself.

Shit! She was still in her Gods-damned towel. A towel that barely fit around her body. A towel that was slightly loose from embracing Gideon. Mortified didn't cover it. But when she looked back up, Torin was gone from the doorway.

Tonight was certainly going to be interesting…

CHAPTER NINETEEN

"We're here," Torin called as he jumped from the wagon with ease. Gideon followed, tapping the driver on the shoulder. The brothers had dressed down for the occasion, no longer sporting their combat gear.

Well, they may as well have; it wasn't much different. Gideon was dressed in a deep burgundy shirt and leathers and Torin was in all black, his shirt long-sleeved. Although they didn't wear their weapon belts, Emara assumed that they had some hidden steel stashed somewhere on their attire.

Out of sight, but not out of mind.

"You have no idea how excited I am to finally be here!" Cally grabbed Emara's hand with a squeal. "I have heard about these markets since I was a little girl and I've tried to swindle my way into them since. But now I am here!"

Unlike the Blacksteels, she had dressed up for the occasion in a lilac dress that climbed right up her thigh and a pair of even higher shoes. She had painted her lips to match her accessories, and of course her hair was bouncy and gleaming on her shoulders.

"Just be careful," Gideon warned. "Stay vigilant. Don't buy anything without asking us and do not go into the back of any stalls, okay?"

Cally's eyes glistened at the danger in Gideon's words, and she turned her head to wink at Emara.

"I saw that, blondey," Gideon scowled.

Emara chuckled.

"Relax, brother." Torin struck Gideon over the back in a masculine embrace. "Learn how to be off duty," he smiled.

"A hunter is never off duty, you know that." Gideon shot him a dangerous look as they started to walk.

"Are you in the tower? No. Are you on duty to the clan tonight? Also no." Torin strode forward. "Loosen up, Gid. Let's show the girls what it's like to have a good time in the markets." Torin's eyes were reflective of mischievous memories.

Oddly, his features were more relaxed than Emara had seen them, and he almost didn't look menacing. Two men stood at the entrance of the gate; Emara assumed they were guards of the market's admission, given the fact they were armed. They both looked at Torin and Gideon and allowed access immediately. Torin give a small nod and Gideon gestured a thank you.

"The girls are with us," Torin advised as the guards parted and let everyone through.

"Do you always come to the markets when you are off duty?" Cally questioned both hunters, hands on her hips as she strutted down the path, past the entrance.

"Yes" and "No" came at once.

Emara laughed at the differences in their response, not having to guess who said what.

"Torin has more time to be off duty," Gideon said with a diplomatic smile. "Being the second-in-command, he schedules it."

"Don't be jealous, little brother; someone needs to fill Viktir's shoes one day. Just call it networking in the city," Torin replied. "I am simply working the crowd out here, getting information on what's happening in the magic world."

"I don't think that's all you're getting," Gideon said under his breath, but it was loud enough for Emara to hear. "Networking is not drinking the market taverns dry of rum."

Emara noticed the fun in Gideon's tone as he spoke this time, but Torin only lifted one eyebrow, unfazed.

"Enough chit chat," Torin commanded. "We are eating into happy hour." He pushed power into his steps and walked ahead, into the belly of the Huntswood markets.

Emara's eyes were wide as she viewed the bustling life of the markets. Stalls upon stalls of clothing, herbs, potions, weapons, and more were all lined up next to each other. The vibrant colours of the stalls were like nothing Emara had ever witnessed. Materials of silk, cotton, velvet, lace, and satin were displayed on hanging reels. Knives, swords, bows, and other death devices that she couldn't place were stacked in rows, exhibiting their lethal power.

To one side, battle armour was being welded, and to the other, jars of unexplainable origin were stacked high. As she passed one stall, she could have sworn she saw what looked like a human eye floating in a pickling liquid.

All different herbs and spices swirled around the air of the market; stalls were cooking foods that she had never tasted before, smelling both sweet and savoury. Rows and rows of gorgeously handcrafted trinkets sat glistening as the sun reached the earth, its warm, dewy glow tinting the backdrop of the stalls. Shadows were starting to appear on the dusty ground, but it was light enough to see everything in its rawest glory.

Music from different tents drifted through the market like a summer bee. Some beats pounded, some were enchanting, some seeking and alluring—they could only be made by magic. There was no way an instrument could form those sounds.

Fluorescent light glowed in tubes of water that formed signs outside the taverns and tattoo parlours that *should* have seemed out of place, but they didn't. Not here. Magic must have burned bright in the tubes in order for it to shine the way they did.

Masses of people crowded each stall in search for a unique item or literally just for the experience.

Emara noticed the Hunters straight away, identifying them by their combat gear, weapon belts, and physiques. Although most of them were lingering near the weaponry stalls, in deep chats or testing out the merchandise.

"Are the rest of the people around here human?" Emara quietly asked Gideon.

He laughed. "No, most are not human at all. The guards only let a few humans through. These people? Some are witches. Some are fae, some are shifters. Some could be of vampire origin."

Emara stilled at Gideon's words. *Witches. Fae. Shifters.* "Vampires?" she said, feeling her eyes bulge from their sockets. She blinked, trying to see any hints that these people walking around the markets—so human-like—could be anything like what Gideon mentioned.

"I know it's a lot to process." He chuckled. "But the likelihood is that the magical creatures that were fantasied or demonised in your story books as a child are our magic-wielders and they are walking around this market."

"Aren't you a magic-wielder?" Emara asked.

"We fall under the magic world, yes. We have magic in our blood, but we are not like the witches or the fae. We are the protectors. Our powers are in our ability to fight. To hunt. We are the demon slayers. Or from time to time, if anything gets out of control in the other factions, we are ordered by the prime to step in and sort it out."

Emara's forehead wrinkled in confusion, "What is the prime, exactly? I heard your father mention it before in the sparring room."

"The prime is made up of each magical faction known in Caledorna and it even branches out to the Island of Skyelir. Hunters, shifters, fae, witches, and humans come together to regulate the kingdom."

Emara's eyes widened. "And here I thought it was just the Minster of Coin who governed the kingdom," she breathed out loud.

"You are not wrong," Gideon advised. "He governs the human faction, and for so long it has been believed by the humans that he is the *only* faction in the mortal world."

"But he's not? He's the one who governs the *humans* from the hierarchy of the elite?"

"Correct. He is the Minister of Coin, after all. He oversees every financial affair in the kingdom. Even in the magical world—and that gives him a lot of power."

Understanding, Emara nodded her head. "But what of the other factions? Is your father the head of the Hunters?"

Gideon laughed. "Ha! No. Even if he would like to be, he still has a chief commander. The chief commander of the Hunters has a seat in the prime." He looked over at her. "As do the king and queen of the fae. Faeries have a soft spot for monarchy." He flashed a dazzling smile as he steered them around an iris-coloured tent. "Most of them relocated to the Island of Skyelir after the Great War, where the broken sea parted the continent, so the prime allowed them a king and queen. The Hunters were never one to wear a crown," he laughed.

"And the shifters?" she asked.

He raised his dark brows. "Shifters come in many forms. But currently, their Alpha is a wolf. The Blacksteel Clan have an extraordinarily strong relationship with them. The Alpha stays in the Ashdale forest just next to the tower."

Emara took a moment before speaking again, "It all seems very cordial."

Gideon huffed a laugh. "It hasn't always been this way."

Emara only looked at him for a few seconds before Gideon continued, "For example, if a pack of shifters get out of control, sometimes the prime will order the Hunters to step in and that doesn't go down well." He looked her over in a way that made her lips part. "We try our best to keep the peace between all the magic factions." Gideon skated in and out of the market stalls, following Torin. "But that is politics you don't need to worry about."

Emara had to walk at twice the pace to keep up with Gideon. And as usual, Cally lagged behind, allured by all the sparkling material. Emara was so distracted by all the information that was booming around in her head to fully look at the stalls.

One thing was clear, The Minister of Coin knew about the magic world. A man that was not a king, nor was he a born successor to the kingdom, but someone who controlled the coin. That's why the elite held so much power over the human faction. The Minister of

Coin came from an elite family. Old money. They controlled the kingdom as part of a secret authority. And at this point, Emara thought that her kingdom had freedom of reign. A kingdom run by the people. Freed from any ruler, dictator, or king. But that wasn't the case. Not underground.

Emara walked a few steps before asking her next question, "So, witches? They can use magic?" Emara felt ashamed to ask but she was too curious not too. "Like real magic?"

"Gods, you are getting really into this, aren't you?" he laughed.

"Knowledge is a powerful thing," she shot back at him.

"Of course it is." He grinned, revealing all of his teeth. Her heart flipped. "There are all different types of witches that belong to different covens and territories. Just like the hunting clans do. And just like the fae. And, of course, the shifters." He tossed some glances around himself before continuing, "The Hunters work closely with the Forest Witch, who is often referred to as the Green Witch. Or as you might know her, the Healer." He smiled fondly.

Rhea.

"Anyone who practises green magic or healing belongs to the House of Earth." His tone found a different path as he continued. "There are witches who have the ability to move things, manipulate objects with the element of wind and air and they belong to the House of Air. They can stop the air entering your lungs by just looking at your throat. We have kept a good relationship with that coven. It may have taken us centuries to do so, but we now have a good alliance.

"The fire-bearing witches belong to the House of Fire. I know of a fire-bearing girl so powerful, she could incinerate you in the blink of an eye. Dangerous little creatures," he mused as he steered Emara around another stall. "The House of Water are majestic beings. Witches who can breathe underwater and work with that element. Almost mermaid-like. It has been said that they could gather up enough strength to create a massive wave that would wipe out most of the population if you made the coven angry enough. You mostly find them close to the ocean or lakes, but they also stay on land amongst other witches. Everyone is free to roam as long as no trouble is caused."

Emara couldn't take her eyes off Gideon as he ran through the specifics of the Witching Houses. She felt a tingling in her bones as she processed the information, her brain weaving through all the new possibilities that were out in the world.

"And don't forget my *favourite* kind of witch." Torin spun around. He had clearly been listening in on the conversation. "The Divination Witch who belongs to the House of Spirit. They are like cosmic goddesses who can switch between living and dead worlds—and note to all, they are the most sensual of the witching houses. Super kinky. They like to *express* themselves." Torin was now walking backwards, his full attention on Emara's reaction. She forced herself not to roll her eyes into next week. "They can even bring back the dead with the right tools." He added, lifting an impressed eyebrow.

"Adding in a more accurate note," Gideon corrected. "The Spirit Witch will most likely tell futures and fortunes; you can even find them here in the market. They are popular down here with the tourism and can make a quick coin. It has been said that a powerful Spirit Witch can resurrect the dead,"—he flung a glare towards Torin—"but as usual, my brother likes to get carried away with himself." Gideon flashed another mocking smile.

Emara searched for Cally to see her reaction to the learnings, but she was heavily distracted by everything the markets had to offer and Emara was sure she had heard absolutely nothing of her new revelations about the magic world. She pulled her eyes from Cally who had just picked up a book titled *Sex Potions*. Emara was fairly certain that Cally thought the title was *Sex Positions* and was flicking through the pages. But she didn't interrupt; she would soon work it out.

"Most witches have little beacons of each elemental power, but they have a *dominant* element." Gideon continued. "That is how they are divided into each coven. Some are born into the coven and bear that coven's magical element, but some don't. Witches are discarded from their elemental house for showing dominant signs of another house." He turned to her. "For example, if you were born into the House of Fire and you had dominant healing powers over fire-bearing, you would probably be forced to leave the coven and join the House of Earth. They see it as a weakness.

Sometimes as a disgrace. But the witches don't like their internal affairs to be known out with their kind."

"Their family just rejects them?" Emara was stunned. "Because one element is stronger than the other?"

"Yes, it doesn't serve their house purpose. They can be competitive." He walked a little closer to her. "Witches are strongest when they are around other witches with the same elemental strain as them. That's why there are always rising tensions among the covens. There is a head of each coven, their empress. They call the shots within each house and most witches *want* to become the empress. But it normally comes from the bloodline. And that's not to forget the almighty witch. The queen of the witches is the supreme. She's a member of the prime. Just like our chief commander."

"Rumour has it that the witches believe that the current supreme is dying," Torin casually cut in. He seemed bored of the topic now that they had moved into politics and not the aesthetic of the witches. "And that the new Supreme Witch is emerging. But it's probably just a rumour. The current one isn't old enough. Normally a new one arises every four decades or so. Maybe Five."

"As the new supreme rises, the current supreme falls—it's very poetic." Gideon's passion on the topic was splattered across his face. "It is predicted by the House of Spirit. The new supreme will arise soon and it has them all on edge."

"I bet my favourite throwing knives that the House of Fire takes the supreme title again," Torin challenged Gideon. "They have the most Supremes in history to come from any House."

"Oh, I don't know, Tor—I think the House of Air could take this win; they have some strong contenders up in the mountains of the north. And they had the title before the House of Fire took it." Gideon's eyes focused on Torin's. "They need the win. Their reign was cut short due to illness of their supreme, leaving Fire to take the crown."

"Wow!" Emara laughed. "I can't believe how human you just made me feel." She rubbed her arm close to where her bandage still rested against her skin, a little pain forming. It was still weaker than before, but Rhea had done an amazing job in healing her.

Gideon chuckled. "It's going to take some time to get used to all of this. You'll get the hang of it." Gideon stopped, bringing Emara to a halt too. "You are in our world now."

A ghost wind blew through the gap where they both stood looking at each other.

"Ah, there *she* is," Torin sighed in pleasure.

Emara followed his gaze to a tavern that was named in blue: La Luna.

"Oh, a tavern. This is promising." Cally's attention finally returned to the group. "Please tell me they sell shots of hard liquor."

"Would you expect me to bring you to a tavern that didn't?" With a grin on his face, Torin entered through the door of La Luna.

CHAPTER TWENTY

As they made their way through the packed tavern, Emara noticed that its interior didn't match the exterior. The outside looked rundown and neglected, but the inside was the complete opposite. Beams of coloured tubes glowed around the bar, changing colour to the pulsing beat of the music—a sound she had never heard before. It had to be some form of magical enchantment. The floor twinkled underneath her feet, changing from white stars to black. The walls were coated in purple and gold panels and flashing tubes above turned everyone's skin into a tanned violet, illuminating their teeth brilliant white. Emara could feel the magic pressing against her skin, her ears, her face. In regard to what kind of magic it was, she had no idea. It just felt...exhilarating.

Figures on the dance floor writhed against one another, glistening with sweat. Their bodies relaxed as they connected with each other through the height of intoxication and rhythm. Cally was like a kid in a candy store, her eyes wide as she took in the sights.

Torin led the group to the bar area, pushing his way through the crowd like he owned the place. Or maybe the crowd parted for him.

"Breighly, my favourite girl," Torin greeted the barmaid with his charmingly warm smile. As she noticed him approach, her smile grew. She was beautifully dark blonde with glitter through her middle part, which trickled down her bouncy locks, sitting above her shoulders. Her fingernails were long and red, matching her lips.

"There he is," she shouted over the music, her eyes flirting with his smile. She was already pouring a drink into a crystal glass for him. "I haven't seen you in a few weeks, Torin Blacksteel. Hey, Gid." She tossed a glance at Gideon, who hadn't yet approached the bar. "Long time no see."

Gideon smiled and nodded.

"You know how I like it." Torin lowered his torso against the bar, his muscled back bulging under his tight, black shirt and watched the drinks being poured.

Gideon gave a quick wave to Breighly and shouted over the music to Emara, "I will get us a table." Cally was already dancing, her hips swaying from side to side watching the dance floor, eager to be amid it all. She seemed enticed by the gorgeous men that littered around the bar, quickly forgetting Torin existed. Clearly magic ran through their veins too; you didn't look like that if it didn't.

Fae or shifter? Emara thought.

"Emara," Torin's voice broke over the music. She closed the distance between them to hear. "What do you want to drink?" His eyes focused on her face, trying to read her lips.

So many to choose from…

"I will surprise you," he shouted, his mouth twisting into a dangerous smile.

"Nothing too strong," she shouted over the music, waving her hands.

"You want something strong?" His face was so close to her ear that as she pulled back, their cheeks brushed. She didn't try to hear him again as she hurried to divide the space between them, looking up at the drink menu for the second time.

"Don't worry, I got you," he mouthed with a grin so sinful it should be illegal.

Her stomach flipped.

As she walked away from the bar, Gideon sat with his arms on the table, his shirt wrapping around his biceps neatly and his chin resting on his hands. Emara had witnessed Gideon swing swords and shoot her ex with arrows in total ease—but this environment made him look uncomfortable.

Cally sat next to him mouthing, "I love it here" as she rolled her body to the beat.

Emara slid into the chair beside Cally and mouthed, "I need to tell you something." A shockwave hit her heart as she thought about what had happened in her home. If she was honest, she had somehow managed to stuff the incident with Taymir into a dark hole to forget about. Until now…

She looked at Cally who finally had that twinkle back in her eye and closed her lips. "In fact, I will tell you about it later, I don't want to ruin your night."

"Don't be silly, Emara. You won't ruin my night. What happened?"

It wasn't exactly Cally's night she wanted to ruin talking about it. Conveniently, Torin returned from the bar with a tray full of liquid that distracted her.

"Anything clear, mix it. Anything coloured, put something clear in it. Anything that glitters and looks like it could be unicorn's blood—shoot it," Torin instructed.

Cally lifted one of the shots that sparkled in the lights and put the glass to her lips. She flung her head back and downed the liquid. She raised the glass into the air and slammed it onto the table. Her eyes flickered over the lipstick mark that was smudged onto Torin's cheek and her body tensed as her hand found another glass. She downed that one too.

Great! He was only in the tavern for two seconds and he already had the outline of another girl's mouth on his face. Emara picked up a shot, braced the glass against her lips, and sank the liquid. In fact, she took a drink for every crazy thing she tried to process.

Witches. Demons. Supremes. Houses. Covens. Hunters. Fae. Shifters. Taymir Solden.

Emara picked up a crystal glass that was lined at the bottom with clear liquid. The smell of the liquor flowed up her nostrils, making her eyes water slightly. She sank that glass, too. The alcohol burned as it flushed down her throat and lay heavy in her stomach. She felt a heat wash over her. The beat of the music carried the warmth from her toes, spreading it through her calves, pushing its way up through her chest and into her head, making her feel giddy and soft.

Cally's eyes studied her and a smile broke out over her mouth. Emara knew by the look on Cally's face that she had the same feeling.

Oh, Gods, the alcohol was clearly stronger in the markets. Much stronger…

"Wanna dance?" Cally was already on her feet, her tight dress hugging her perfect curves as she pulled it down a little. Her hair was messy but with sheer, effortless style and her hands were above her head as she pranced along to the floor to meet the crowd which swallowed her whole.

"I am heading to the dancefloor," Emara mouthed to Gideon. She didn't want her best friend out there alone. "Wanna come?"

Gideon shook his head in protest and sipped his drink. "I don't dance."

"Are you sure? It could be fun…"

"I will sit this one out," he smiled. "Go, dance. Have fun."

With a disheartened smile that she tried to hide, Emara lifted her glass and took off in search of Cally. She pushed her way through the crowd as the bass of the song thrummed through her body, her bones vibrating. Cally's blonde hair swung as she spun and pushed her hands into the air.

"Let go," she shouted to Emara, flinging her hands out to reach her. "Just let go."

Emara laughed and took another swig of her drink, reaching out to join their hands together. She merged with Cally as the buzz of the alcohol married the song and the lights on the grinding bodies of the floor. She couldn't help but move her body. It felt good to let go. Let go of everything that was tight in her heart…

Not to be outdone by Torin's kissing affair with the barmaid or whoever it was, Cally pulled a guy from the crowd beside her and spoke into his ear. They both laughed and carried on dancing together, her body getting closer to his.

He was beautiful, blond, and tall.

Emara closed her eyes and lost herself in the sway of the crowd, letting her body feel the beat, knowing she was not alone. Here, she was not in her mind. She let the tension from her body disappear into the crowd as she danced, sipping on her drink, not thoughtful about anything. Her hips swayed, allowing her spine to move like a snake, feeling the momentum of the music taking her higher…

She felt a hand on her waist, and she smiled, turning to step into Gideon's arms. He had followed her.

Turquoise blue eyes met her stare instead of pine green. She pulled back, realising that it was Torin behind her, his hand still on her waist. If she had been sober, red heat would have flushed her face in embarrassment, but she stood still.

"You don't have to stop dancing." Torin towered over her, making her feel tiny.

"Where's Gideon?" she demanded.

"Over there talking to Breighly." Torin pointed to the stunning blonde barmaid and a twang of jealousy spiked through her chest as she watched them. He laughed at the barmaid with a familiarity. Their bodies were close. Too close.

"Dance with me," he said. Dominance lined Torin's voice, bringing her attention back to him.

He's serious, she realised as she looked at his face. Her heart hammered into her ribcage. She punched the image of Gideon and the barmaid to the back of her mind. Torin removed the glass from her hand, brushing her skin as he took it, and led her into the heart of the dance floor.

He gripped onto her hand, soft but firm, and she felt the calluses on his fingers graze over hers. He spun her out and around, raising one arm into the air and moving to the beat. For a moment she was going to refuse him, but she heard a small voice say, *Just let go.* She moved her hips to the beat and laughed.

Let go…

She was allowed this. She was allowed to let go of all her worry and fear. She was allowed to enjoy tonight. His hand slid down her arm, his movements surprisingly rhythmic for someone of his size. She was free, with no more weight of an impending engagement looming over her.

She was free. And clearly, so was Gideon.

Torin smiled as he moved, his face relaxed. His fierce features were gone, but his eyes were still dangerously intense. For a moment, she couldn't break her eyes away from his. Beautiful pools of crystal clear water glazed with glittering ice.

His grin turned deviant as he noticed her watching. "You know, rumour has it that if you look into a

Blacksteel's eyes for more than ten seconds, you fall in love with them."

"Don't be so cocky, you're not my type." Her eyes held his stare, her chin pulled up proudly. She swished her long hair around her shoulder and turned around, moving her body to the music. Torin caught her hand and spun her back to face him and moved closer to her. He was so graceful, she could hardly believe it.

"I thought you didn't have a type?" he challenged, his forehead crinkling as his eyebrows lifted.

How did he know that?

"I have spies everywhere in the tower; they tell me *all* the secrets." His full lips parted to make way for a wicked grin.

The movement of the crowd forced them closer together, but he stood strong against them as the beat picked up, blocking anyone from touching her.

"It's a good thing I don't have any secrets," she said, her hair splashing across her face.

"Everyone has secrets." His playful charm surprised her. He took her functioning arm and swung her out and in and Emara laughed at the thought.

I bet the tower is full of secrets.

She moved her hips to the beat as if she were the only one in the tavern, as if the music played for only her. Her hands moved up her body and into the air as she flung her head back. She smiled as the alcohol twirled in her veins and freedom was light in her chest.

"Am I going to see your wild side tonight, Emara Clearwater?" Torin smirked, amusement crossed his face.

"I don't think I have a wild side, Torin Black-steel." Her smile expanded on her face as the endorphins from her dance floated around her body.

Happy! She was happy for the first time in days. Was she even allowed to steal a moment of happiness in her grief?

"I think you do." Torin lowered his eyes to her lips. "From the minute I saw you, I thought as much." His hand brushed a black strand of hair from her face.

She couldn't breathe.

You know, rumour has it that if you look into a Blacksteel's eyes for more than ten seconds, you fall in love with them.

His words played through her mind.

His head leaned into hers…

Someone from the crowd knocked her from behind, sending her flying into Torin's chest. She braced herself as she put her hands out and he caught her in rock solid arms. She hauled herself upright as she met the intensity of his gaze once more.

The crowd was too much. This wasn't right. She couldn't look at Torin like that! Maybe she wasn't allowed happiness yet. Especially not with Torin, of all people.

She whirled around to find the exit, a space she could move through, but Torin caught her arm in protest. "Where are you going?" he yelled over the music.

"Don't!" She yanked her arm back. "Don't touch me!"

Torin's face went straight with concern. He took a step back, honouring her space.

Whatever *this* was? It wasn't right!

She knew Cally was into Torin and that it wasn't fair to be doing this. Even if Cally was dancing with someone else and clearly moving on.

She shook her head as she shoved through the crowd. Locating the table where Gideon had been sitting, dread hit her with a smack. He was no longer there. And there was no sign of the blonde barmaid, either. Her stomach swirled all the consumed liquid around like a whirlpool of intoxication.

She needed air, now.

Her eyes ran over the tavern, searching for the door which led to the street.

There! She darted across the space, smacking into anyone and everyone, and pushed the door open with two hands. Fresh air hit her face, cold and hard, and she took in the smell of smoke and alcohol coming from the people standing outside. Inhaling a large breath, filling her lungs she tried to clear her mind.

And for the first time all night, Emara felt the stone burn into the back of her trouser pocket—reminding her why she had come to the markets in the first place.

CHAPTER
TWENTY-ONE

The markets looked completely different from when Emara had first walked through them. The stalls were murkier and seedier now that she was alone. She pulled her arms tighter to her torso and a tremor ran down her spine, causing her shoulders to pull in. The people of the markets were weaving in and out, some drunk, some working, and some killing time.

A female voice called seductively from her left, "Hey, honey, are you looking for love tonight?"

Caught off guard, Emara looked up to the podium that she had just passed. A red-haired female winked and gestured a crooked finger for her to come closer, her eyes dark with glamourous coal. Trying not to be rude, Emara raised a hand to offer a polite "No, thank you." It was the first time a girl had ever tried to make a move on her. She kept her face forward, trying not to make eye contact with a large man who was sitting behind a stall with fighting knives. The man's face was covered in tattoos, and a scar ran right through his mouth. The markets were boldly different without the security of the Blacksteels.

She didn't know where to begin her search for someone who could give her information on the mysterious stone with so many alley paths leading to different stalls. It was a maze of tents.

Walking along, her concentration turned to the circumstances of the tavern: Cally had secured a guy in the efforts to make Torin jealous, Gideon had clearly been flirting with a girl who he maybe had history with, given what she had seen. He'd looked comfortable enough to have had something with her. To still have something with her.

She tried to brush down the niggling feeling in her chest of unrequired jealousy. She had no right to be jealous. And as for Torin? Had he attempted to kiss her? Charm her? She tried to replay the scene over in her head, the drinks, the crowd, the dancing.

Dance with me.

His intense eyes, his dangerous smile. His God-like frame which held mountains of muscle…

Stop! The command screamed through her head and she halted in the middle of the street.

The glowing winter sun was now lost in the darkness of the night and a sudden draft of cold made her shiver.

"Emara," her name barked through the markets.

She turned to see Torin running through the crowd, unapologetically moving people out of his path. He halted as she turned to face him fully.

"Leave me alone." She turned and continued to walk down the path she had chosen by a spice stall.

"Emara," he called again as he powered into a light jog.

She wasn't sure if she could look back at him without seeing him running a hand over her face, almost brushing her lips. And, well, truthfully, she didn't know where to place those feelings. The guilt of hurting Cally ate at her, even though nothing had happened.

"Wait!" he called again, his voice gruff but smooth at the same time, like two tones challenging each other. This time she could hear his feet pounding the path behind her before she could see him.

"I said wait!" His voice deepened with a hint of temper.

Emara stopped dead.

As he caught up with her, he swivelled in front, putting out his hands. "What happened back there?" He searched her face for answers.

"It...I don't know. It felt wrong." She folded her arms. The heat of the stone still burned in her pocket.

"I don't want you to feel *wrong, "* he said it like he truly meant it. "We were just having fun. It didn't mean anything," he spoke quietly, his eyes puzzled.

"Yeah? Well, it might not have to you, but it would maybe mean something to Cally."

And Gideon. *Maybe.*

Emara met his stare, forcing herself not to look away.

Was she overthinking it?

She had never felt so small in comparison to someone's height or strength before. And maybe she felt intimidated by his striking attractiveness as she stood in front of him. His face was so ruggedly handsome. But she would never admit that.

Daring and inviting, yet off limits.

Emara vowed to herself, in that moment, that she would never admit her thoughts to another living soul. He knew how handsome he was, and he was the kind of guy that used that to his advantage. Torin Blacksteel did not need to hear from one more girl that he was *attractive*.

His head was big enough.

"Emara, we were just dancing. It didn't mean anything." Torin's voice was firm.

"Yeah, it didn't mean anything. You've said that already." She swallowed as she shook her head and looked in the opposite direction. "It didn't mean anything to me either."

Torin's eyes darted around the markets, assessing if anyone was watching. "It's not like I kissed you."

He folded his arms over his chest and relaxed, his mouth turning into a buoyant smile.

Cocky!

He wanted a reaction from her. She knew his game before he even started playing. He wanted to know how she felt about that, if he *had* kissed her.

Smug ass! Clearly, he liked to test his limits.

Abruptly, she wanted to test her limits by punching him in the face. Maybe that would wipe that smart ass grin off his face.

"I didn't even *try* to kiss you, did I?" he said with a smile that was antagonistic. It was so antagonistically charming, she couldn't help but bite.

"I don't know *why* you are so smug when all you have is two lines of seduction," she mocked. "It's boring." She pushed her jaw out. "I have never met anyone so cocky in all my life. And can I just add that I don't think it's attractive or clever to be acting the way you do? I told you not to mess my friend around, but you can't help yourself, can you?" She ground her teeth and balled her hands into fists at her side. "You didn't have to dance with me. You could have danced with her."

Torin stepped into her space, his head bowing down close to hers.

She gulped as he pressed his lips into a thin smile and then rolled them like he was toying with a terribly naughty thought in his mind.

Maybe she just pushed her limit…

"I have told you this before, I didn't want to pick her. I picked you."

"Well, maybe I don't want you to pick me."

He tried to hide his smile. "And here I was, thinking we were becoming friends. You wound me." He placed a hand over his heart.

She snarled back at it, rolling her eyes.

"Has anyone ever told you that you are so sexy when you're feisty?"

She could have punched him in the face, there and then. She should have punched him. He was pushing her buttons and he knew it. His face was so impeccably masculine with his tight jawline and his stupidly perfect hair. Why did he get under her skin so much?

"Do you realise how much of a dick you are or, are you just oblivious to everything else around you?"

She flung her hand out. "I bet you think you can just buy a girl a drink and she will jump straight into bed with you." Her face twisted.

"I don't normally have to buy them a drink," Torin casually replied.

"Ugh, you are such a pig. It's disgusting. I don't even want to be around you!" Her hand gestured up to him.

"Then don't be. Go! Walk around the markets yourself this close to the Blood Moon and see what becomes of you." His tone was so flat it haunted her, and she swallowed down the fear of being truly alone out here. "Or you could stop being dramatic and just come back to the tavern with me."

She scoffed at the word "*dramatic*." She was not being dramatic. He was dramatic! She saw his face switch from playful and cocky to a warrior with no emotion in a split second.

"Besides, my father would arrange my execution if I let something happen to you..." he trailed off.

"What is that supposed to mean?" Emara disputed.

"Never mind. Let's go back..." He turned on his heels, just expecting her to follow suit.

"No," she protested.

"Emara, I'm not playing games anymore." His voice was low and danger crept into his tone.

"Neither am I," she said, standing up tall.

He shifted. "As if I am going to let a woman roam the markets alone."

"There are plenty of women roaming the markets themselves..."

"Yeah, well they are not with me. You are."

Something about what he said stuck in her throat. He probably wasn't used to anyone challenging him, let alone a female, but she wouldn't do as he told her, even if she wanted to go back with him.

Stubborn, she realised. She was being so awkwardly stubborn with him, just to prove a point.

"I came here because I wanted…I wanted information on…on something," she said finally. His eyes narrowed onto her face and his ears perked up. "You are the last person that I want to ask for help, but it's not looking like I have much of a choice right now."

Since Gideon's not here, she wanted to add, but thought better of it. She didn't let herself think of where he might be or what he might be doing.

Torin's lips parted as if he were about to say something snarky, but she quickly added, "And don't say something sarcastic or sexual or I will walk away, and I will go alone."

His lips shut into a tight smile as his chest puffed out in a sigh. "What is it?" he demanded, thinking better of his snarky comment.

"I need to find someone who can help me understand what a stone means...or what it even is." She looked up.

Confusion crossed Torin's features. "You are not making any sense Emara. What stone?"

She reached into the back pocket of her trousers and pulled out the stone she had found earlier. She held it in her palm, presenting it to Torin. The stone looked like a different colour under the darkness of night.

Darker. More powerful. The colours that had sparkled before were gone.

She winced as it burned further into her skin. "I don't know why it hurts to hold it, but it does. It's clearly magical," she added. "I knew the minute I saw it."

"Give it here." Torin took the stone from her hand and evaluated every inch of it. He looked around himself again. "We need to go!" he commanded, his face grave. He tucked the stone into his dark leathers and tugged on Emara's arm.

"Wait! What? I—" Emara tried to dig her feet into the dirt path, but Torin was on the move.

"For once, don't question me and just trust me. We need to get out of the main avenues of the markets." His jawline hardened as he scanned around the market again for a third time. He was back in full hunting mode.

Emara, for once, didn't argue back, clamping down hard on her lips. Her legs tried to keep up with his strides, but his movements were rapid. She tugged her hand back, receiving a glare from Torin. But he let it slide.

"Where are we going?" Emara tried to say through staggered breath.

"To see an old friend."

CHAPTER
TWENTY-TWO

Emara ducked underneath a low arch that was crowned with herbs and flowers hanging from brown string, into the back of a stall. Torin's face was hard, his body prepared for anything as he stood in front of her. Unease sailed into her stomach as she placed a hand over her navel in efforts to cease the nausea. The room was cluttered in trinkets, crystals, candles, salt lamps, and obscure symbols. The lighting was dull, casting an eerie atmospheric glow over the room. Sage and salt swirled into her nose as she looked around for a sign of this so-called "friend" of Torin's.

A five-pointed star was featured on the wall in front of her. She realised the star was made from all different types of crystals, enriching the star's frame. Red and orange crystals outlined the section that had *Fire* written in metallic paint. Green and brown gems indicated *Earth.* An array of blue and light purple stones represented *Water.* Misty-coloured stones and transparent crystals embodied *Air,* and dark purple and black stones headed the star to represent *Spirit.*

All houses of the witching covens joined by one symbol.

A five-pointed star.

Torin stepped forward, his dark hair sleek under the light that painted it an inky blue colour. He slipped a hand into his waistband and pulled out a medium-sized dagger that curved into a fatal tip.

"Melione," Torin's voice was soft and seeking as he called. "It's Torin, we need to chat."

He knew her *well.* Emara could tell by the way he called her name.

A hand appeared around hanging fabric that was sectioned into long strips, forming a colourful, flowing door. A woman's face peered through the fabric, parting it as she made her way through the entryway.

He placed the knife back into his waistline, determining her not a threat.

A seductive smile caressed her lips and she slowly walked over to Torin. But not too close.

"You just can't resist me, can you, Torin Blacksteel?" she purred.

"Actually, it's not that *kind* of visit," Torin announced, a slow, seductive smile pushing its way onto his lips.

He couldn't help himself, could he? He had dragged her all this way down into the pits of the market to flirt with an old flame. Emara shifted onto one leg, popping her hip out to the side and crossing her arms. This time, she couldn't hide the eye roll. Or the sigh.

Melione's piercing eyes darted to Emara. She looked her up and down from head to toe, judging every inch of her. Melione dragged her sharp indigo fingernails through her hair.

"Who is she?" she asked, her voice inquisitive.

Melione held incredible beauty, her hair of moonlight silver and her eyes dark brown, framed with dark lashes. Her lips were painted a dark mauve colour and her features contrasted together to make something magnificent.

"It doesn't matter who she is," Torin replied sharply.

"Charming," Emara muttered.

He heard her and he stiffened, but he didn't look to where Emara was standing, his face focused on Melione. No wonder he couldn't stop looking at her. She was stunning. Her long gown hugged her cinched waist tightly as the material flowed to the floor in a dark shimmering purple. The gown's neckline plunged down into the curves of her breasts, making anyone who looked at her instantly drawn there. Male or female.

Emara noticed a small tattoo on her collarbone, a singular circle in thick, black ink.

"Oh, but it does matter who she is," Melione said, her face unreadable, as if she knew exactly who she was. "Follow me." Her tone changed to something more ominous.

Emara's stomach flipped, but she obeyed.

Once through the makeshift drape, Emara couldn't miss the centrepiece of the room. A table lined with black, sparkling fabric held a deck of cards and a large ball sat in the middle, made of the purest crystal. Little crackles of energy swam through the transparent centre like tadpoles in a pond, making it enchanting to look at.

"Take a seat." Melione gestured to the two chairs.

Torin pulled out the chair and looked at Emara as a command to sit.

She did, apprehensively.

"Blacksteel, your fate has not changed since I last looked through the crystal ball. I can cleanse the air and check to see if anything has altered, but—"

"That's not why we are here," Torin dismissed.

Emara's head shot around to study him.

Your fate has not changed since the last time…

She couldn't help but find herself wondering what he had been told.

"Then why have you come? You know I cannot change your fate, but only guide you—"

Torin jumped in again; this time he wasn't dismissing her, but changing the subject, "Melione, can you confirm to me what this stone is?" He pulled out the stone and placed it on the table.

Melione glanced down and pushed back from the table, gasping.

Emara's soul squirmed as she saw the instant fear that crossed the fortune teller's face. *A witch that belongs to the House of Spirit,* she recalled from the information session earlier. Now understanding the symbol that lay on her collarbone, she traced over it again with her eyes.

The symbol of *spirit.*

"How did you acquire this stone, Torin Blacksteel?" Her long nail pointed at the stone that lay on the table.

"Is it what I think it is?" Torin urged, his voice low.

Emara looked between them, both locked in a bull-strong stare.

"The resurrection stone," the witch whispered, as if scared to say it out loud.

"It can't be." Torin closed his eyes for a second and then he leaned forward. "This stone has been lost for centuries—millennia. How can it turn up in some *human's* belongings?"

Melione intercepted, "She is no human." Her mouth curved in amusement. "But you suspected that."

He knew what?

"Otherwise, you would not have brought her to me." The spirit witch's eyes twinkled with a beacon of light.

Emara wanted to look in Torin's direction for clarification. For clarification on what she was missing. But she couldn't pull her eyes from the witch as she continued to speak.

"I can feel your power bubbling beneath the surface," Melione played with the idea as she wiggled her fingers. Her hands were covered in rings that all had different meanings. Melione's dark eyes pierced through Emara. "But *you* don't know what you are, do you?"

Speechless, Emara's body had turned to stone. Her lips parted, but was incapable of drawing in air. She shook her head as dark hair fell over her shoulders.

"Place your hands onto the crystal ball." She gestured to the centrepiece.

As if entranced, Emara leaned forward in her chair.

"If you are not willing, I will not make you. You don't have to, but the spirits are pushing their way forward to speak to you. One in particular has a message that you need to see." Her hand orbited her crystal ball as bangles dangled down to meet the bone in her wrist.

"You can communicate with spirits?" Emara's voice was small as she thought over the possibility of receiving a message from her grandmother.

Anything at all.

"She can connect and communicate with spirits as well as seek out your fate from the Gods," Torin encouraged.

Emara locked eyes with Torin for a moment longer than she would have liked.

This is *not* how she'd thought the night was going to go. She leaned into the crystal ball and placed her fingertips onto the glass and then allowed her palms to gently follow.

At first, nothing happened. She waited to feel something, see something. A gentle breeze blew into the room, causing the candle lights to flicker. She looked to see if the wind had come through an open window or door, but there were none.

"Do not move your hands from the ball until the spirits are done with you," Melione commanded, as she placed her hands on top of Emara's.

A gust of air swarmed the room and the candle lights died as Melione chanted unknown words in a soft rhythm. She couldn't see Torin, but she imagined he would be alert and ready to take on any danger should it present itself.

A surge of energy flowed through Emara's hands, forcing its way past her elbow and into her shoulder. She let out a gasp as it travelled up her neck, around her ears, and into her mind.

Close your eyes, a voice whispered. A voice that was so ancient it had no accent.

The electric current of energy formed into a ball of light that moved like an orb around her mind. Faintly, she heard a woman's voice.

Focus and you shall see, the ancient voice whispered.

And so, she did.

The voice grew louder and louder until she could hear what was being said. The orb's light burst into colour in her mind and expanded into a thousand different pigments. The energy shook through Emara's body, but she clutched onto the ball, not letting go.

At that point, she was transported into a new world, a home she didn't know. Looking around, she saw her grandmother, yet she was younger, her eyes less wrinkled and her frown lines non-existent. Her honey hair, long and weaving down her back. Her grandmother's voice broke through the silence. Her face spoke a hundred words.

"You will not marry him, Sereia." Her mouth twisted around her teeth, making her snarl.

Emara turned to see her mother standing in front of her, her face wet with tears. Emara's legs weakened in this world and they wanted to give way, but the ancient voice coached her to stay strong.

"I love him, Mother," Sereia pleaded, her voice almost non-existent. "You can't change that."

"Love makes you weak," her grandmother spat. "And weak is what you are for declaring your love for *him.*"

Emara flinched at the fierceness in her grandmother's face. Although her grandmother could be harsh with her, she had never seen the ferocity that now lay within the plains of her face. "If not weak, then downright foolish. You are destined to be the Empress of Air. You are the daughter of the supreme. You are to ascend in just a short number of days, the coven needs you." Her grandmother's chin raised. "Marriages are an alliance for women like us. Marriages bring us protection. *He* will not be your husband; he offers no real protection. What he offers is war. Your fate was sealed long before you fell in love with the enemy, Sereia."

"I will not have *that* fate. He is not the enemy. Mother, please, I am begging you. Let me slip into the night with him or let me go to the prime and beg for us to be together. Let them grant us the grace of the law…"

"The daughter of the supreme does not beseech *anyone* to change a witching law, nor will she marry anyone beneath her."

"I will run, Mother! I will go with him." Sereia's voice broke with a threat she didn't want to resort to. "I don't want to be the empress of a coven that I don't belong to. I don't want to be an empress at all."

Her grandmother flew across the room and slapped her daughter across the face.

Sereia's head snapped to the side, causing her to lose balance.

"You belong to the House of Air, don't let me hear words escape your mouth that determine otherwise. No daughter of mine will be a disgrace. No one else knows that you are a dominant fire-bearer, and it will stay that way, you foolish girl." Her grandmother's eyes turned black with rage. "You are next in line to be the reigning supreme of the witches. As you rise, I will fall. That is what the prophecy states. If the fire-bearers knew that you were dominant in fire, they would claim you for their own. The House of Air will not accept that, and I will not allow it. The House of Air cannot lose your alliance—"

"I don't care about the hunter alliance. I won't be the supreme, I will refuse to ascend to empress."

Her grandmother's hand flew out and Emara braced herself as her mother squealed. Instead of her hand making impact with her face, she stretched out her fingers and the air from her mother's throat was vacuumed out of her lungs. Emara watched as her mother struggled to breathe, clutching at her throat.

"Stop!" Emara tried to scream, but it was no use. They couldn't hear her. "Stop! Stop! Grandmother, stop!"

Sereia flung out her own hand in a desperate attempt to blindside her grandmother and a flame of fire seared from her palm. Speedily, Theodora Clearwater ducked to the side.

Another blast of fire sparked out of her mother's hands as she screamed but Theodora tossed an arm around in a circle motion, casting a shield of water that put out the attacking fire. Damp ashes fell to the ground.

Emara couldn't breathe as her grandmother's airy mist wormed its way around Sereia's waist.

"Stop! Please stop!" Sereia screeched. "I am pregnant. I am with child," she cried, trying to catch her breath. The water from her grandmother's shield splashed to the ground and her mist fell, too. "There's nothing you can do now," she panted, gasping for air. "I will be with *him* and that will have to serve as my fate to the Gods. The prophecy was wrong, Mother."

Air blew through the scene, wiping away everything Emara could see in a misty haze. A surge of power jerked Emara back in her seat, to the present. Her head whipped back and strong hands were on her shoulders, pinning her as if to prevent herself from an injury.

She blinked open her eyes.

Her hands ripped away from the ball, tearing away from Melione's grasp. By the look on her face, she too, had saw the vision. The two of them sat face to face but not one of them spoke.

Finally, Melione croaked, "You are the granddaughter of Theodora Clearwater." Her brown eyes expanded in disbelief. "But she—you died in a fire."

"My mother died in a fire, not me." Raspy breaths left Emara's throat.

"You are the promised one. Promised to the House of Air."

Goosebumps spread like a virus over Emara's body as she turned to ice. Emara's blood ran cold. Every muscle in her body stiffened into hard marble. "You are mistaken," Emara quivered.

"I saw what you saw," the Spirit Witch confirmed. "I am not mistaken."

"Emara? Speak to me! Are you okay?" Clear blue eyes penetrated hers.

Melione advised him to give her a second by gesturing to him to step back.

He refused.

The stone, the ancient voice whispered faintly into the back of Emara's mind. And then it was gone, like it had never existed at all. The thread had been severed from the ancient world to hers.

Emara grabbed the stone that lay on the sparkling fabric and pushed to her feet. She felt a little wobbly as she shoved the chair back allowing her to move from where she stood.

Torin was on his feet quicker than she could follow. "Emara, say something," he called in the background, but her head was like ocean waves during a giant storm, droning him out.

Waves of information crashed into the coves of her skull; she couldn't hear properly or even breathe. Leaving the vision and the prophecy behind, she bolted for the exit and headed for anywhere other than here.

CHAPTER TWENTY-THREE

Gideon found Cally alone in the middle of the dance floor, her head tilted back in ecstasy as she moved her body to the beat of the music.

Gideon hated taverns; the crowds, the dancing, the drunken idiots who weren't self-aware as they barged about spilling anything they held—but somehow, he still managed to be in one. He'd only agreed to come to make sure Torin didn't lead the girls astray. Knowing him, Torin would do it deliberately just to piss off his father and they would all be punished for it.

"Cally?" Gideon shouted over the music. "Cally?"

Another reason why he hated taverns like these—you couldn't speak at a normal pitch. Everyone had to shout into the other person's ear, still missing half of the conversation, anyway.

"Cally, why are you alone? Where is Emara?" He couldn't hide his irritation that he would probably have to repeat himself in a few seconds.

Cally lifted her hands into the air and shook her hair around her face before looking up. "Emara was here, she might be at the bar," she shouted over the music.

She wasn't at the bar; he had just checked.

He looked around, trying to see if he could set his sights on Emara or Torin.

He knew he shouldn't have left! But Breighly had caught up with him, asking him to help her shift a crate of sparkling wine, which he couldn't refuse.

Gideon had known Breighly since he was little. She was a shifter,—half human, half wolf—and belonged to the Baxgroll Pack that lived close to the tower in the Ashdale forest. She was the daughter of the pack's Alpha, Murk Baxgroll. Murk and Viktir had meetings at the tower regarding magical politics, so she had been around often.

They were the same age, only two seasons parted their birthdays. Therefore, they were normally left to entertain each other whilst the meetings took place. She had often teased him about being older and he had *tried* to unleash his new-found hunting skills on her, which he quickly found out was useless. Her supernatural instincts were far more superior than his and she always landed him on his ass.

Something Torin had always mocked him for.

As a young boy, he had crushed on Breighly hard. She was funny, bright, and strong. She was a beautifully independent badass. But no matter how he felt about her, she was in the pack and would find her mate within the pack. He had decided early on that there was no point in wasting feelings on someone who would be pulled in a direction—one which she couldn't control.

She knew it, too.

When shifters mate, they mate for life.

And it was normally with another shifter.

Therefore, he hadn't explored the idea of a future with her. Not in the way a relationship mattered, anyway. However, that hadn't stopped them from exploring other *things.*

Just following their eighteenth birthdays, after a few months of kissing and messing around, they'd made an agreement to keep things purely physical. *Nothing more.*

He knew he was in a temporary position and that suited him. And her. She was not his to love and never would be. It didn't help that he found her insanely attractive, and she'd seemed to be into him for a while, too.

But as life moved on and she was given more responsibility with the pack and La Luna— which was owned by the Alpha—the physical relationship had fizzled out, but they'd managed to remain good friends, catching up every now and then.

He scanned the tavern, pushing the thoughts of his first physical encounter to the back of his mind.

Where were Torin and Emara?

He pulled Cally from the dancefloor and ordered her a water at the bar.

"Drink this." He placed the glass in front of her. "You will thank me in the morning," he said.

"Where is Torin?" she mumbled into her glass. "He's such an ass."

"Yeah, my thoughts exactly," Gideon muttered to himself. The fact that both Emara and Torin were missing made him anxious.

Just as he ordered another water for himself, Torin's face moved through the crowd, head and shoulders above everyone else. Relief dispersed over his body, but he kept his face harsh, not showing the reaction to his brother. He pushed weight up into his toes and looked for Emara to be sheltered behind him, but she wasn't.

"Gideon,"—Torin's hand went to Gideon's shoulder—"she's gone." Torin's face was flushed like he had been running for hours. "Emara. I can't find her." He ran a hand over his face.

Cally slammed the glass onto the bar, spilling its contents, and stumbled off the stool to her feet. "What do you mean she's gone? Gone where?"

Gideon knew it was bad news. His father was going to gut the two of them alive.

"What happened, Torin?" he demanded.

Torin worked his way through some bullshit story about Emara freaking out because of the crowd and her disappearing out of the tavern. He then briefly skimmed over that they both, somehow, ended up at a fortune teller, which he thought was odd, and that she had bolted from the stall. As Gideon tried to piece it all together, he knew something was off. It just didn't make sense. If Torin knew more about Emara and why she would run, he neglected to say.

"And you're telling me everything?" Gideon glared at Torin.

"Yes, Gideon. I have just run through the full story, for Thorin's sakes."

Somehow, he doubted that.

Gideon shook his head and downed the last of his water. There was only one way he was going to find out the truth. And that was to *find her*.

Emara had run so fast that her lungs had nearly collapsed in on themselves. She had only slowed as the burning in her legs threatened to trip her, her chest heaving up and down in fiery pain.

She had ducked down an alley to lose Torin and ran until she couldn't hear him calling her name anymore.

She needed a minute. Alone.

In fact, she needed more than a minute to process what she had just seen with the Spirit Witch and she'd known that his stubborn ass wouldn't have granted her that time. So, she'd fled and ducked into a path that he hadn't seen her take. She wouldn't have outrun him otherwise.

She halted, now desperate for her breathing to return to normal. She rested against a brick wall, her head tipping back into the grained texture. The alley was disgusting with waste bags and litter. The smell was repugnant. She heaved as she pushed herself against the wall, steadying her balance and closed her eyes. She ran through the last ten minutes in her mind.

The Spirit Witch. The wave of power. Her grandmother's uncompromising face. Her own mother's eyes, her pleas.

Her mother had loved someone she was forbidden to be with. Is that why her grandmother had never mentioned her father?

Emara struggled with the concept of her grandmother despising her father so much that she would forbid her mother to be with him. There had been no signs of who her father was in the vision, only signs of fire, water, and air. Signs of witchcraft.

Magic.

Her chest raised up and down rapidly. Her grandmother was magical. Her grandmother was a witch and so was her mother? Her grandmother had said that she was the supreme. Head of the Witches. The supreme was the most powerful witch in the covens, according to what she had learned from Gideon.

Her head fell against the brick and her skull vibrated in pain.

This couldn't be true…

Her breathing accelerated instead of slowing. Her mother was destined to be the *Empress of Air*. A fate that she was unwilling to accept for herself.

Empress of Air. Empress of a witching coven. A witching house! Supreme.

Emara pressed her fingers to her lips and swallowed the nausea that churned in her belly. Theodora and Sereia Clearwater had once belonged to The House of Air. She shook her head in disbelief. It had to be a mistake. A vision that had warped reality somehow. There was nothing in her grandmother's house to even indicate that she was a witch —let alone the supreme.

She ran a hand through her hair, pushing herself up from against the wall. She slowed her breathing.

In the vision, Theodora had blackmailed Sereia into not revealing that she was, in fact, a fire bearer—which probably meant that she should have belonged to The House of Fire.

A cold sweat broke over Emara's skin.

Is that what the spirits had wanted her to know? That she came from a line of witches? Powerful witches? Or that her mother and grandmother's relationship was so fractured it was beyond repair? She was never going to get answers now. Gods, if anything, the vision had confused *everything*.

No, not confused—*ruined*. Tarnished!

Her grandmother had lied to her about who she was—*what* she was. And just then, as if everything else in the alleyway suddenly vanished, something occurred to her.

If her grandmother and mother were magic wielders, did that mean she was, too?

"Emara!" Cally's voice screeched down the alley.

Emara looked up.

Her sandy hair was blowing like a golden banner behind her as her best friend ran towards her. Emara quickly noticed that she was flanked by two warriors, dwarfing her in size.

Reaching her, Cally flung her arms around her neck and she returned her embrace. "What the hell Emara, where did you go?" she asked.

Emara's eyes flickered to Gideon as she stepped back, his gaze not faltering from her face. She flung a quick glance at Torin and his eyes told her that he would not say a word.

"I just needed some air," she lied. "The shots made me feel a little sick."

"You never could handle your liquor, Em." Cally slid her arm around Emara's shoulder. "I was worried for a second."

"You don't need to worry about me," she dismissed, looking at the two Blacksteels. "Are we going home—I mean back to the tower?" She started walking without an answer.

"Had enough of the big, bad markets, have you?" Gideon joked. She just nodded, cutting the usual intensity of their stares short.

"I don't know why, I had a great time and I got that beautiful guy's name and address—he invited me to another party later this week," Cally announced, speaking louder.

Her eyes flashed to Torin, but he was uninterested, lost in thought as he stalked on ahead.

Maybe his mind was in the same place that Emara's was?

"How are you feeling now?" Gideon asked, walking beside her.

"I will be fine," she couldn't say it quickly enough as she avoided his eye contact for a second time. Her thoughts turned to the gorgeous barmaid who had been leaning into Gideon, laughing. They looked so comfortable together. A little spark in her chest ignited and then died.

For the first time, she was looking forward to being safe in the infirmary room.

"Remember, you are up at sunrise tomorrow," Gideon's voice was playful with a hint of authority.

She turned to look at him, her eyebrows pulled closer together. "You wanted to learn how to fight. *Fully*. Remember?"

"Oh! Yeah," Emara rubbed her head. "I remember."

"Well, I can categorically tell you I will not be there and will be nursing a potent hangover," Cally interjected. "Hey, do you think I could get a healer to, you know, heal the hangover?" She raised her eyebrows a few times quickly.

"I don't think using them for hangovers would be efficient or practical." Gideon's tone was light, his attention back on Emara. "You know where to find me if you want to train. I will be there regardless." He waited for a few seconds before stalking ahead, giving up on trying her for conversation.

Cally slipped her hand into Emara's. "You should totally let him train you, Em. He's *so* into you."

Emara didn't question what she had said. At this point, she wasn't sure if Gideon was into her or if he was into the blonde girl from the bar. But that was the least of her worries.

"I am not learning how to fight for him. I am learning how to fight for me." She looked forward, her fingers still linked with Cally's.

"Do you know something? I admire you for that, I do. But sometimes, you need to let someone else in. Especially someone who looks at you the way Gideon looks at *you.*"

She turned to her best friend. "Cally—"

"I'm serious, I wish someone would look at me like that—and not just as someone they want to sleep with a few times, or date and then get bored," she concluded.

Emara pulled back, turning Cally to her. "Callyn, men don't look at you like that because they are afraid to. They are intimidated by your beauty. They are scared that *they* are not good enough for you. It's not the other way around. They can't match your fierceness or your independence. And they couldn't possibly match your sex drive." Emara side-eyed Cally and they both burst into laughter. "Besides, it's not you that's the problem. You are great. Your taste in men, however…" Emara ran her tongue along her teeth trying not to laugh. "Not so great."

"My taste in men is not *that* bad," Cally laughed whilst talking. Emara shot her an incredulous look and then gestured to Torin who was marching on in front. Cally rolled her eyes, "Okay, maybe it's not *great*. I do make a lot of shitty choices. I just like a guy who is emotionally unavailable." She sighed. "It's like I want to be with the male version of you." She bumped her shoulder into Emara's and laughed.

"I am not emotionally unavailable," Emara took a breath in and stared ahead. Cally just pouted and raised her eyebrow, not willing to argue about this one.

Emara realised that her heart felt a little lighter already. Cally had always been the best at providing her with a lightness she couldn't explain.

She was the light and Emara, the dark. The best friend balance…

"I know we don't do feelings and stuff because, like, ew! But you really are my rock, Emara." Cally squeezed her hand into Emara's.

"And you are mine." Emara squeezed back.

They said nothing more as they walked behind the Blacksteel Hunters. The moonlight followed them as they made their way through the Huntswood markets and back to the wagon. Emara investigated the sky before getting into the back, but instead of looking at the moon, she turned her attention to the stars that littered the night's sky.

A star—a new symbol that gave her life meaning.

CHAPTER TWENTY-FOUR

Removing the hair that had swept across her face with one hand, Emara rolled from the bed. She hadn't slept much—at the most she'd had two hours—but she was going to train, regardless.

The winter sun had just started to awake in the sky, illuminating the clouds with soft pastel colours of orange, lavender, and yellow. For the first time since she had moved into the tower, she made her bed, running her hand over the blankets to smooth them like she had in her own home. She refreshed herself in the bathing chamber and pulled on her combat gear. She took the stone that had lain underneath her pillow the entire night and cursed. Feeling like the stone was solely to blame for her restless sleep, she whispered a prayer to the ancient Gods to give her a sign, anything that would tell her what it meant. Give her more answers.

Opening her mind, she reached out to hear the ancient voice like she had the night before.

Nothing.

She was alone. In her room in the tower, miles from her home, and truly alone in the world. She had no guidance. No answers. No family.

She hurled the stone and watched as it scattered across the floor, hoping to piss off whatever entity that protected it.

Still *nothing!*

She couldn't stand to look at it for another second, wondering what it meant and why she had it now. But even from across the room, it pulled her in. She got up from the bed and grabbed it with a scowl. Taking a different approach, she placed it on the stand next to the door and whispered, "Sorry."

Still nothing.

With a sigh, she tied her hair into a ponytail and made her way to the east wing to forget all about last night.

As she got there, she entered through the doorway and bowed to the large portrait of Thorin on the wall. Gideon was already halfway through a cardio workout and she wondered how long he had been awake. She watched him as he jumped over a knee-height bench from side to side, never faltering in his pace or agility. Sweat dripped from his brow and his lips pushed shut, concentrating on the circuit.

"You made it," he said without looking up at her. His jumps slowed and he came to a stop before lifting his gaze. "How's the head?" He took a towel and wiped his face and neck.

"Messy," Emara replied without thinking.

He laughed. "I meant do you have a hangover?" He squirted water from his bottle into his mouth.

"Oh." She took in a breath. "Do you not have to actually sleep to get a hangover?" She walked onto the mats.

"Not always." He shot her a quick smile. "It's going to be a rough session today, though. I need to see where your limits are. What your strengths and weaknesses are. I need to see your abilities. Are you ready for it?" He stretched his arm across his chest.

Limits? She had no idea where her limits began and where they ended anymore. But she guessed she was going to find out.

She nodded.

"Okay, we are going to start with obstacles. I have placed out different obstacles around the room." Gideon gestured to the ropes that were tied to the floor, a massive vault, and large metal ladders that went extremely high, almost touching the ceiling. "I need to see how you overcome them and what your strategies are. Then I can coach you and teach you how to manoeuvre them quickly and efficiently."

"I thought I was learning how to fight?" Emara popped her hands onto her hips.

"First lesson of the day, not every situation is fightable. A good hunter will try to fight in every situation, but an excellent hunter is an intelligent hunter, and they know when they can't win. They know when to get out." He walked around her. She followed him, only turning her head. "You need to learn how to be quick and be creative with that. That could be the difference in your survival. Or your death." He moved over to the vault, displaying it like some sort of art piece. "The first thing I want you to do is get over this vault only using your hands. No legs or lower body can touch it."

He took a step back and then sprinted towards the vault with sheer strength, his strides so fast she could only see him take flight into the air and glide over the vault with ease. His hands didn't even touch the base.

Show off, she thought.

He looked towards her, his emerald eyes dazzling with the rush of his activity. "Your turn."

"You expect me to do what you just did? Without help?" She snorted. "Without some sort of harness?" Her eyebrows lifted, making her cheekbones more angled. "I am not powerful enough."

"How do you know you're not powerful enough if you've never tried?" Gideon's chin stuck out confidently. His long, thin nose flared, causing his lips to part. He looked over his thick lashes at her.

She swallowed hard. "Okay, just show me again." Her hands circled over each other, trying to focus on the task and not Gideon's face.

"Come here," he commanded delicately.

Moving towards him, she took a second to look at him as he turned to position himself so that he could help her angle her body correctly. With his leg, he nudged hers to where it should be. Moving her hips, angling them with his large hands, he positioned her stance. Her hip bones tingled underneath his touch.

She concentrated on the vault ahead. Or tried to.

"Okay, now pull your weight onto your back leg and spring yourself forward. Make sure you are pulling your arms back as you run, it helps with the speed." He touched the bottom of her elbow and pulled it back to where it should be. "Flatten your back," he said as he traced a hand down her spine.

Every muscle and bone instantly fell into command, tingling and sparking.

She pulled back on her leg and propelled herself forward into a sprint as instructed. As she neared the vault, she put her hands out, ready to make contact with the vault in order to thrust her legs over.

But it wasn't enough.

She slammed into the hard apparatus and it knocked the air out of her lungs. Rolling off the vault, she hit the ground, a groan escaping her throat.

"Are you okay?" Gideon shouted seriously.

He stalked towards her and offered her a hand. Emara looked up at him, humiliated, and she placed her hand into his before he hauled her up.

"Let's try again, shake it off," he ordered. "You need to use these to pull your legs up over that vault." He put a hand against the muscles of her stomach.

A red-hot heat swarmed her, but she nodded and kept her eyes on the vault. She disregarded the feelings that started sparking all over her skin.

"Not a bad first attempt," he complimented. "Again."

She pulled back and then sprang into action in another attempt. This time, she pounced onto the vault but couldn't haul her body over to the other side.

She jumped down, frustrated.

"That wasn't too bad," Gideon encouraged. "Don't get frustrated. You just need to believe you can do it. More power this time."

"Who are you kidding? It sucked!" a deep voice boomed through the empty space. "I didn't take you as a liar, Gideon." Torin's smile was provoking as he strode closer to them. Another hunter walked beside him; he had one blue eye and one green eye. He was like a mixture of both Torin and Gideon, only he hadn't grown fully into his features yet. "Her technique was off and if you are not going to be man enough to point that out, I will." He looked over Emara, taking in every detail of her face. "If you want her to get better, you will tell her the truth. She needs to lift her knees and chin. She's not going to get over it by looking at the ground."

"Kellen," Gideon dismissed Torin's observations, "I can see that you have the misfortune of training with Torin this morning. You know how he gets when he's hungover." Gideon didn't look at Torin as he spoke, but at Kellen, the *other* Blacksteel brother.

Torin stepped into Gideon's line of vision, demanding eye contact. "Let's just hope he can keep up, even if I am *hungover.*"

Torin made his way across the sparring mats and Kellen followed.

Emara watched as the other Blacksteels walked away, feeling a little strange. The way the lighting that was hitting Kellen was...odd. She looked up to the ceiling. No windows. No beams of light…

Strange. She would have sworn that he had a glow about him.

"Okay, again," Gideon interrupted her thoughts as he waved to the vault and turned his focus back to the training.

She felt a little uncomfortable as she looked to where Torin and Kellen had started a warm-up.

"Don't worry about anyone else." He moved towards her. "You need to zone in on what is important," Gideon said lowly. "And that is getting over that vault. Okay, try this. I want you to focus on something that makes you angry. Something that makes you want to scream. Just as you think of it, spring back on your left foot and let the anger power into your body. Let it drive you forward."

Emara took a deep breath and rolled her neck, shaking her hands. She got into the stance she had been shown for the third time. This time, before she ran, she pictured Taymir Solden standing in her room. The arrogance of his face, the venom in his words as he degraded her. She let the thought of his hand smacking across her face build a picture into her mind and she ran. She took off fast and hard towards the vault, clenching her teeth to keep the anger from forming a scream.

Her arms and legs worked quick and strong as she thundered towards the apparatus. She threw her hands out to feel the material of the vault, but she was above it. She soared into the air and her feet hit the ground. Bending her knees, she wobbled slightly and then stood up tall.

She turned to face Gideon. Pride burst from his face in a brilliant smile, his hands in a clapping position. She couldn't help but laugh in shock.

"That was excellent!" Gideon shouted across the room.

Her eyes flickered to Torin briefly as she walked across the mats and she could have sworn she saw a slight smile form on his lips—but as quickly as it had formed, it was gone.

Gideon threw her a high five and smiled. "Again."

For the rest of the early morning, she let Gideon guide her through the training he had prepared. He coached her in techniques to help her speed and agility. He demonstrated creative methods on how to duck and dive whilst in a small space. He corrected her form and pushed her to challenge her body. She tackled the ladders, her hands and arms burning in pain as he shouted for her to pull herself up and over the top.

Not quite there yet on the upper arm strength, were his words.

For a while, the training had distracted her from the never-ending thoughts and questions that plagued her mind. Emara found it peculiarly satisfying to train like a Hunter.

Of course, these were just the baby steps.

"Can I ask you a question?" she approached Gideon whilst they both drank from their water bottles.

"Sure, what's on your mind?" Gideon replied.

"Women Hunters? Are they not a thing?" She drank from her bottle.

He looked down, considering carefully how to answer her question. "No, they are not. Only males carry the Hunting gene."

"But surely, there are women born into Hunting families who can fight just as well as the men?"

"Yeah, probably."

"But they are not allowed to fight?" she asked.

Gideon shook his head. "Nope, the girls usually take other magic genes—like the Witching gene."

"And witches can't learn how to fight? In this war against the Dark Army, surely you need everyone ready to fight. Can't it be a girl's choice to have both magic and combat in their remit?"

"I guess that's something that you should take up with the prime." He smiled gently whilst looking at the floor.

Well, of course she wasn't going to do that.

"I have another question for you," she said. "Since we are taking a quick break."

He chuckled. "Ask away."

"When the demon attacked us in Mossgrave, it—*he* had a normal face. It was human-like, but he wasn't human. I knew he wasn't human. Why is that?" She tilted her head slightly to look at him.

"Higher demons can take on any form. They can make themselves look as attractive as they want or as terrifying as they want."

"How do you know that it is a demon? You know, the ones that show themselves as human-like, surely they could be walking among us and we wouldn't know." She shuddered.

"There are always tell-tale signs. I have been trained to find them, but some are obvious. It might be that they have different coloured eyes or that they have different shaped teeth. It is only a glamour, after all, hiding their real form with demon magic. Their true form is much more terrifying, but it's how they go through kingdoms undetected, and then they change into a more destructive form if they want to." He looked at Emara and shook the hair from his eyes. "Not all of them can transform themselves. Only powerful demons that are high-bred can do that." He stopped for a second and took another gulp of water. Emara watched as his strong throat bobbed, taking the water down his gullet. "You can normally smell their stench, too," he added. Emara couldn't forget the smell that had violated her nose, almost choking on the revulsion of it. "That's something your body just can't ignore. Your senses are trying to tell you that there is danger, and you should always listen. A hunter's senses can tell almost imme-diately if there is one within our radius."

"When the demon attacked me—well, before he attacked me—he drank my blood." Emara closed her eyes, feeling a cold sweat form on her palms.

Gideon let out a sound of revulsion. "Demons are predators. They tend to drink blood or eat humans and animals. But they don't really need to do any of it. They don't need food to survive." He took a breath be-fore continuing, "No one really understands why they do it."

"Maybe they crave blood?" Emara added.

"Or maybe they are just pure evil," Gideon replied.

A terrible coldness spread a shiver over her skin.

"They want to end this world." Gideon looked at her, his deep green eyes intense. "To create a new one, where the creatures of the underworld roam free, out of their cage without suffering the consequences. That is what the King of the underworld wants most. However, there is a tale, dating back a century or two, that Veles doesn't rule the underworld anymore. Folklore states that there was an uprising and he was too weak to defeat one of his most powerful knights. But that's probably just a bad example of demon mythology."

Emara ran a hand up and down her arm to remove the evidence of her fear as she nodded.

"Are you cold?" Gideon noticed. "Your body temperature must be coming back down from the training." He took his black training shirt that had been on the floor all morning and handed it to her. "Here, put this over you until training commences. I have a briefing in fifteen minutes with my father, but I will see you at breakfast."

He offered her a smile before leaving the sparring room. She pulled the heavy, black material over her head and tugged it down over her legs. The material was soft, warming her fear-pimpled skin.

"Ponytail," Torin's voice commanded the room. And her attention. She turned to see him walking towards her, his chin raised in the air. "Give us a minute, Kellen."

Kellen nodded, grabbed his fighting blade, and ducked out of the room.

Torin Blacksteel stood in front of her with two massive swords strapped across his back, making him look absolutely murderous. As if his face didn't already have that effect. And his massive body, ripped with muscle after muscle tumbling down his torso, showing how destructive he could be…

"What?" Emara gulped, shaking her lingering thoughts of his ripped torso from her mind.

"I was thinking—" Torin started to speak, but she couldn't help but cut him off.

"You think?" Her arms now folded just under her chest as she faked surprise in her tone. "Oh, wow. I didn't realise the air in your head allowed space for you to actually process thoughts."

"Cute!" he dismissed. "Anyway, before you take another verbal stab at my heart"—he pouted—"I wanted to talk to you about last night." His eyes darkened, and all wit was gone from his face. His jawline moved as he turned his head to the side, making it look sharper and more prominent.

"I don't want to talk about last night." She looked at the floor.

She *did* want to talk about it—with anyone who would listen. But not Torin. She didn't want anything else to be awkward between them.

"Well, that's good because I was going to do the talking," Torin moved closer with one step, "That stone, you just so *happen* to have, is an ancient relic from the Gods." His tongue touched the tip of his teeth.

"The stone has been lost for Millennia; The ancestors believed it to be missing. Gone." His face was serious.

"Listen, I have no idea why or when it came into my possession. I just found it in my box, okay?" Emara lifted her gaze. "I clearly didn't think it would be a big deal when I took it to the markets. Did I think it was magical? Yes. But nothing that would cause a scene."

"Well, that pretty, little stone is a massive deal, Emara," he argued. "It's the *Resurrection Stone.* And here you are, just carrying it around with you like it's a coin in your back pocket. Do you have any idea how much this stone is worth? You couldn't put a price on it."

"Yeah, well that means nothing to me." She hissed through her teeth. "All I know is that my grandmother or mother was trying to keep it hidden or something. I don't know why it was concealed in my box. Neither of them ever spoke of it."

Torin stepped closer. He bowed his head down. "I thought I knew what you were before last night, and I can now relish in the fact that I was correct in my assumptions. But we don't want everyone else to know." The comment Torin made threw her off guard, draining the colour from her cheeks. "Due to last night's little escapade to the Spirit Witch, I can piece it all together now. You come from a witching bloodline—and not just any witching bloodline, but an extremely powerful one, too." A smile tugged on Torin's lips. "I told you we all had secrets."

"How did you know?" Her eyes studied his face and she tried to stop her body from shaking "Before last night?"

His icy blue eyes stared back at her with an intensity that turned her veins to frost. His dark hair lay across his face from the workout.

His annoyingly perfect hair.

"Your eyes," was all he said, keeping his face indecipherable. "I knew because of your eyes."

Her heart quickened.

He put one hand against the wall. Leaning in, he said, "Let's keep the stone and who you are a secret. We don't need anyone else knowing about it. And especially not my father. And that goes for lover boy, too. Gideon tells my father everything."

Why didn't he want his father to know?

Her face must have given away her confusion because he added, "It could put you in danger."

Danger?

"I haven't told anyone about what happened last night. Not even Cally." Emara's voice shook. A part of her had wanted to tell Cally about who she really was the minute she had found out, but of course that would lead to explaining about the stone. Of course she wanted to tell her, they never kept secrets from each other, but she wasn't ready to speak about it. Maybe because part of her thought that speaking it out aloud meant that it was real and maybe she wasn't ready to accept that. Maybe she wasn't ready to accept the truth at all.

"You having the stone puts you in a compromising position. You have no idea who would want it or what they would do to get it."

"I haven't spoken of it."

"And no one else has laid eyes on it?"

"No."

"Good." His lips tugged up at the corner, show-ing the hint of a dimple on his cheek. "Look at us...we have our own dirty little secret." He pulled back from where they stood. "I like it." His eyes were gleaming like the sun hitting the ocean. His jawline expanded as he pushed his lips into his cocky smile.

"There's nothing dirty about it," she disagreed, screwing her eyes up as she narrowed them in on Torin's face.

"Whatever you say, ponytail."

She was about to say something utterly un-lady like when footsteps pounded against the floor outside the room.

"Torin!" Kellen ran back into the sparring room. "Father says if you are late for this briefing, he's going to lash you."

An awkward silence broke into the room, caus-ing Emara to shift nervously on her feet. Finally, Torin broke the connection from Emara for a second to look at Kellen and then his eyes found her again. He walked backwards, still burning his gaze into her face, and then he spun on one foot and was jogging out of the room.

She inhaled deeply and then exhaled slowly. Slumping against the brick wall, she slid halfway down. Why did the Blacksteels always have to be so intense? It was like it was a family trait or something.

Our dirty little secret...

She replayed Torin's words over in her mind.

Torin knew that she wasn't human.

"Your eyes," he had said.

She knew her eyes changed colour, but never in a million years did she think her eyes were a trait of a witch. Something that had stared right back at her from a mirror had always been a key to understanding who she truly was. And Torin bloody Blacksteel had worked it out before she had. A strange emotion flipped around in her stomach. But then again, her eyes were like her mother's.

"You know someone is good by the look in their eyes. You will know if you can trust them or not; the bad can never hide the wickedness in their eyes." Her grandmother's voice echoed into her mind and wrapped around her like a comforting blanket. She shrugged her shoulders and closed her eyes, memorising her grandmother's face. Not ferocious like she had seen in the vision, but calm and relaxed, like when she used to paint.

Paint!

Emara stood up straight. *Grandmother's paintings!*

Emara knew exactly where she needed to go to find out if everything the Spirit Witch had said was true. She kicked off the wall and headed straight for Mossgrave.

CHAPTER TWENTY-FIVE

Viktir Blacksteel had finished his briefing to the hunters in record time. Torin knew he had raced through the morning brief for a reason. He could see in his father's face that something was bothering him, but he couldn't work out what.

"Torin, I will see you after breakfast in my office." Viktir's voice was unyielding as well as his stare. Torin nodded as the clan made their way past him.

Gideon threw a look Torin's way and an unseen thread of thought entered Torin's mind, questioning what it could be about. The brothers were never normally separated for individual briefings. Torin shrugged discreetly.

"Gideon, I will see you after lunch," Viktir spoke quickly and then left the room like the others.

Gideon approached Torin. "I assume you have no idea as to why we are being called in separately, then?"

"Nope," Torin dismissed. He, too, was trying to understand why they both had different meetings. But

Torin was more intrigued to know what Gideon's meeting would be about more than his own. What couldn't his father say to Gideon in front of Torin? Viktir couldn't have found out about Emara Clearwater and what had happened at the markets. He had been the only one there, and she had assured him an hour ago that she hadn't told a single soul.

"So, you can't think of why?"

"No, Gideon, I can't think of why Father wants to speak to us separately," he snapped. "Maybe it's because he wants me to monitor how many times you end up around Emara Clearwater when she's not dressed."

Gideon scowled, his face turning a shade of pink. "Maybe he wants to know why you are keeping tabs on me, being around Emara when she's inappropriately dressed," he shot back.

"I didn't say *inappropriately,*" he challenged, flashing his brother a smile. "I like it when beautiful girls turn up in towels around the tower." Torin made sure the plains of his face were smoothed into a casually smug smile.

Gideon's jaw ticked.

Bullseye. He had just hit a nerve. "Maybe Emara would like to wear my towel sometime."

Gideon's jaw ticked again. It was too easy.

"Don't you dare speak about her like that. She's not just some plaything that has turned up on your doorstep for you to toy with. Leave her out of your games, Torin."

Torin thought over the silent threat that was lined in Gideon's words and revelled in the thrill that it gave him. It also staggered him to see his brother so bothered by a female. But the fact remained that Gideon was telling him not to do something…

Torin would do what he wanted, when he wanted, and no one would tell him otherwise. In fact, if he were told not to, he would. He had always been twisted that way. It was a curse. At times he wished he could change it. But after years of fighting it, he decided to embrace the rebellious streak that lived in his soul. Unless it was an order from the commander, of course.

But even then, it was hard for the rebel in him, not to make an appearance every now and then.

"I think Emara Clearwater is *more* than capable of making decisions in how she handles herself." Torin threw a wild smile towards Gideon and his face turned red with rage.

Another bullseye.

"It's a shame you weren't on the dancefloor last night, actually. Good dancer! She knows how to move her body."

Torin knew from the Goddamn minute Gideon had saved Emara from Mossgrave that he would be besotted by her beauty. Torin found it oddly irritating that he had made it so obvious, too. His brother was entirely predictable.

Save the girl, fall in love, have little hunter babies, and live happily ever after, carrying on the Blacksteel legacy.

If the prime allowed it.

Even the thought of that life made him want to shoot rum through his eyeball and taste a thousand different kisses.

Being the first-born Blacksteel, it was inevitable that he would have to settle down in a marriage soon. A marriage that would be without love and warmth, but of course, he would do it for what it could provide for his clan. It would be a marriage ceremony that could make alliances in foreign territories stronger. Not a marriage of love, but a business deal.

The thought of it made him feel like the sky was slowly closing in on him, crushing down on his chest, his head dizzying. The thought of marrying a woman he barely knew chipped away at a little part of his soul every time he thought about it. So, he would have fun whilst he could.

A lot of fun!

Gideon's voice brought him back to the matter at hand. "You didn't tell me that you had danced with her."

"In all honesty, I had forgotten about that part," he lied. He certainly had not forgotten the way she had moved, or her bright smile as she let her body relax. Her hair as she let it flow in abundance around her…

"Convenient."

"I also forgot to mention that I almost kissed her. And I—"

Torin was cut short as a fist crashed into his face so hard, he had to blink twice to make sure it happened.

Yup. It had happened. The pain shot into his jaw and up his cheek. He wiped his mouth to make sure there wasn't blood, because if there was, – Gideon better be on the move, running from this room. Fast!

"I am telling you right now, don't even think about going near her. She's not like the girls you go for," Gideon spat. "She's different," he spoke through his teeth. "She's been through a lot and doesn't deserve to be pulled into another one of your *flings."*

Oh, she's different, alright. But Torin wasn't about to reveal how different she truly was.

"Is that a warning, little brother?" Torin spoke as he took a step towards Gideon. He should put him on his ass for even trying to fling a punch at him, never mind landing one.

"Yeah, actually, it is." Gideon also stepped in, face to face with Torin. Nose to nose.

Interesting...

"It's a rather brave move for someone who actually doesn't know *half* of who she is."

But that's our secret.

"And you do?" Gideon scoffed. "As if you would even take the time to get to know *any* girl."

His brother made a very valid point—one he found difficult to argue with. But he wasn't provoking an argument to converse about his sex life or his lack of strings attached. He was doing it to see what Gideon knew, to see if he would let anything slip of what he knew about Emara. Gideon was a hunter, of course he would have done some digging on her.

Torin stepped back nonchalantly and crossed his arms. "If you must know, I happen to know a thing or two about her."

"The only thing you get to know about a girl is what type of alcoholic drink she prefers and her bralette size."

Torin barked out a laugh. "You don't even know what a bralette is."

His jaw ticked. "Keep her out of your *nonsense*," Gideon warned again, pointing a finger at Torin's face. "I mean it."

"Don't size me up like a snake, thinking you can take me on because I had a little flirt with a girl you *just met*. You and I are not even in the same league when it comes to girls." He offered Gideon a twinkling smile laced with ice.

His brother didn't respond verbally, but the heat of his face did. If Gideon was big enough to poke the beast in the first place, he should be big enough to take the bite.

"I am just saying stay away from her."

"It is ludicrous if you ask me, brother." He walked around Gideon to leave through the threshold of the door. "You have spent a whole two minutes with the girl, and you have already whipped your mind into a frenzy about your feelings for her. Get out of your head and you might have a shot with her." He leaned in, knowing that there was no warmth in his voice, and said, "But what's the point? You are either going to end up in a marriage that Father sees fit enough for the clan, or you are going to spill your blood before that happens."

Gideon stood utterly still for a moment, not responding to Torin, before he began to shake. He closed his eyes and then spoke, "You know, Torin, I used to look at you and I would wish I were you. My big brother—the god. My brother—the *brave*. But now when I look at you, all I see is fear."

Torin froze at Gideon's words.

"Fear that you aren't good enough for my father. Fear that you are not good enough to step into his position once he's gone. Fear that you will love, and it will be taken from you."

Torin's chest tightened as Gideon continued, feeling like the air was being pulled around his lungs like a tornado.

"You *fear* to open your heart and be vulnerable because we were always told it makes you weak. But it doesn't." Gideon shifted his weight between his feet. "It's sad when you fear love and happiness more than you fear death, Torin. It's miserable to think that all the fear that consumes you is going to ruin who you are before death finds you."

Gideon walked past him and slammed the door shut.

Torin didn't move for a few minutes. He was numb. He couldn't move his body or his legs, or even feel his heart in his chest. He couldn't swing a punch or even come up with some snide remark about how his brother was wrong.

He was stunned.

The Blacksteel brothers never showed each other emotion, not since they were small children. Even if one had injured the other during training, they were not allowed to show any remorse, or they would see the back of their father's hand.

It was the commander's method of conditioning.

Would you show your enemies the same empathy? Would you offer your hand to help the enemy?

Torin flinched at his father's words before running a hand through his hair.

"May as well get this over with too," he muttered. He left the briefing room, disregarding breakfast, and headed in the direction of his father's office.

Torin strode into the commander's office, his perfectly trained poker face intact. He had pushed any emotion that had been stirred up by Gideon's words in the briefing room to the back of his mind.

"You really should knock when you enter the commander's office." Viktir Blacksteel looked over his nose at his son, his face unimpressed, as usual. "Or do I need to remind you of your rank?"

Torin flung himself into a brown leather chair that sat opposite of his father. "You told me to be here, so here I am." He offered a fake smile whilst propping his feet up onto the mahogany desk. A few books fell from a pile.

His father paused, but didn't say anything as he dragged his eyes from Torin's face to his boots. Viktir knew that if he gave him any indication of exasperation, it would only spur Torin on to continue. He waited for the flicker of irritation to cross his face. But Viktir was skilled enough to keep himself professional. "We have had word from The House of Air about our alliance."

Torin's heartbeat advanced with every second his father didn't speak.

"The House of Air would like to promise their empress to you in exchange for our protection. Aligning you both in a marriage that would benefit not only the coven, but the clan." He spoke with no emotion, only with authority. "As you know, we have built an extraordinarily strong alliance with the House of Air, and we intend to keep it that way."

That was his father's diplomatic reminder not to screw anything up before the alliance could be forged in matrimony.

"And have you heard from the chief commander and the prime, regarding this?" Torin asked.

The chief commander. The man who had the ability to seal his fate with just one signature. The man who represented the hunting faction in the prime.

"Yes, he agreed to the alliance a few moons past."

Torin's temper boiled. "And you didn't find it relevant to inform me sooner?"

"As advised before, I would tell you when both parties sent word on the matter." Viktir picked up a letter, scribbled with black ink, and began to read, which irritated Torin to the underworld and back.

"So, I guess this is my final warning not to seduce her sister before the wedding of the year?" he taunted.

His father put the letter down and locked eyes with him. Finally, the reaction he had been waiting for. Torin hid his smile beneath his icy exterior.

"Maradia." His father's lips curved into a smile. A smile that dug into Torin's heart as the name of his bride was announced. "She doesn't have a sister." He raised one eyebrow. "She will be at the annual uplift and we believe that it would be of your best interest to make her feel *special.*"

Torin almost growled at the word. He could make any girl feel *special,* that wasn't a problem, but that didn't normally have to involve a Gods-damned wedding.

Viktir smirked, victory sparkling in his eyes. He pulled open the drawer that lay within his mahogany desk and sat a small black box atop it. "Open it," he instructed.

Torin knew what it was. He didn't need to open it, nor did he want to. It was his mother's wedding ring that had been passed down through centuries. Torin swept his feet from the desk and took the box in his hand, quickly removing it from his sight. His father waited for him to open it, but he clamped his fist around it tighter.

"I want you to give her the ring at the uplift as a gesture of your intention," his father instructed. "This is a momentous occasion for the clan and for Maradia's coven." Viktir's gaze fell to the box that was now almost cracking under the constraints of Torin's grip. "Your mother has given her blessing that the ring be used. She looks forward to meeting your future wife at the uplift."

The uplift was an occasion held to bring the magic community together, allowing alliances to form from covens, clans, and packs around the kingdom. Normally, he preferred to use the event to get blindingly drunk and end up in bed with at least two of the witching covens.

Last year, it had been a toss up between the House of Fire and the House of Spirit, and in the end, he had taken both. A glint in his eye twinkled at the memory.

Now *that was* the kind of alliance he needed right now. Not to be giving his mother's precious ring to a woman he had met just once. A woman he wasn't attracted to. She was beautiful, but there was no instant spark.

"Torin, you are promised to the Empress of the House of Air," his father reminded him, as if he could see the clogs of his mind turning. "Do not do anything to ruin this alliance." His father's brows were low. "We need her— the coven—to strengthen us for when the time comes. The witches are more powerful—"

Torin cut his father short, "I understand the importance of the alliances with the witches."

He had heard enough about how crucial it was. He had heard enough on how valuable it was to be aligned with a woman who held magic. He knew any decent witch could create a ward of magic that acted as an invisible shield to protect hunting grounds, such as the tower. An empress of a coven could channel enough power to protect a clan for years. So at least by marrying into a Witching House, the Hunters could rest easy at night.

"Well, then, now that we are clear, you can see yourself out." Viktir's hand gestured a dismissal and Torin felt his fist twitch.

"You have made yourself very clear, *Father,*" Torin said, with dangerous intent. "It's clear you have no issues with the fact that I am being whored out for an alliance that we could have without a marriage proposal." He kept his hand from flinging out in anger. Instead, he tightened it around the box. "I think we need to look at our priorities as a clan instead of playing a game of marriage."

"You always knew that your marriage would be one of political stance." The bitter part of Viktir's personality broke through. "The head of the Blacksteel Clan can't afford to be married in matrimony for *love.*" His father spat the word like it had been created by Veles himself. "The head of the clan requires power which the witches can provide. The most powerful alliances are ones that are established in marriage."

"Just like you and my mother?" he threw in.

Viktir ground his teeth.

Gods, he was hitting everyone's nerves today. He was impressed.

"Can't I focus on strengthening the wards through a treaty with the witches instead of marrying one?"

The wards around the Tower were weakening. Their current Witch too old…

"There is no treaty stronger than a marriage," Viktir snapped. Torin begged to differ. "And as for the wards,"—he paused—"they are not your concern."

"I think you will find it is my concern." Torin leaned forward. "The clan are my men as well as yours."

Viktir Blacksteel shot to his feet. "For as long as I am in command, I will decide what is your concern and what is not." A blue vein protruded from the side of his neck as he leaned across his desk. "When my bones turn to dust, then it will be your concern to decide what you see fit regarding the wards. Until then, you rank under me," he snarled through his teeth.

Torin could feel a rumble in his core, the infernal anger threatening to appear.

"The sooner your idiotic brain registers that I am your commander before I am your father, the clan will be a stronger unit." He stood for a moment more before walking over to a glass unit. He removed a crystal glass and sauntered back over.

Torin tried to control the vicious rising of rage in his chest as Viktir poured from the decanter that always sat on top of his desk. Before taking a sip, he swirled the liquid in his glass and said, "You will not speak of the weakening wards to the clan. Instead, you will focus on what you can do to impress the Empress of Air at the annual uplift." He sipped the liquid and savoured the taste on his tongue before saying, "That, my son, is your concern."

Torin's body trembled with anger.

"Now, see yourself out. There is work to be done here that you cannot even comprehend."

Torin rose slowly from his chair, as the thirst to smack his father in the face almost overcame any sensibility. He crossed the room to the door, thinking about how much he wanted to rip the solid wood from its hinges. Challenging your commander was one of the worst offences you could commit as a hunter. And Torin was the closest he had ever been to it. As he opened the door, he looked over his shoulder. He wondered if his father had been born without a heart, or if he was so conditioned to life as a hunter that his heart had emptied of everything that made him human. Viktir sat at his desk, the ruthless Blacksteel Commander, and Torin saw what his future looked like. Lonely and bleak and resentful.

With the promise of a loveless marriage in front of him, this was what his future looked like, and it was something Torin wanted to run in the opposite direction from.

CHAPTER TWENTY-SIX

It had taken some time for Emara to sneak out of the tower and get to Mossgrave by foot, but when she arrived she headed straight for her grandmother's art gallery. There had been a light flurry of rain, but nothing that her borrowed cloak didn't keep out. Thankful that she had kept a key to the gallery in her personal box, she walked up the cobblestone path with it tightly in her palm. Looking around, the village was eerie in the quiet of winter, but also in the stillness of destruction. Clearly, the Gods had been protecting her grandmother's gallery as no flames or demons had touched the exterior of the brick building. Maybe it was blessed by magic?

Pushing the key into the lock, she felt the weight of the mechanics click and she pushed down on the handle. Before going inside, Emara surveyed the street to make sure no eyes watched.

Her grandmother's art gallery had three rooms. The first room had whitewashed walls splashed with colourful art as you walked in the door. A counter was set up where her customers could pay their coin and have their art packaged.

She felt a pull in her heart knowing that her grandmother would never stand in the main gallery again, welcoming the villagers or the Elite customers who travelled to purchase the paintings. The gallery held another room that was situated in the back, used for storage and supplies. But Emara knew she wasn't headed there, either. She was headed to the gallery's third room. A room she was never allowed to venture into.

Emara walked to the painting of a sunset that loitered behind the trees of a forest and ran her hand down the back. She had witnessed her grandmother do it many times before. Feeling her hand brush over something cool, she gripped it in between two fingers.

"There you are," she murmured.

She pulled the brass key from its safe place and headed to the third room of the gallery.

Her grandmother's private room.

She remembered being rushed through the space as a child, but she had never taken in much of what it held. As she had gotten older, her grandmother had forbidden her to go into that room, saying the natural light would affect the art pieces she had stored in there.

Pushing the brass key into the door, it clicked twice and then the door sprung open. The lighting in the room was a dark crimson, and before any natural light could make its way to the art, she swerved around the door and closed herself inside.

At first, it was overwhelming as the red light filtered into the darkness of the room, casting unnerving shadows onto the wall. She blinked a few times to adjust her eyes to the lighting and it seemed to do the trick.

Emara walked slowly, taking it all in, everything that her grandmother had painted in secret. She couldn't believe the amount of artwork that was collected in this small room, and most of the paintings were of women.

All women of magical origin.

She had painted them bathing in water, dancing naked under a full moon, expressing themselves, owning their bodies. She had painted females who walked through fire, unapologetically. Women who gathered air around themselves as they moved mountains. Girls who grew flowers and were surrounded by wildlife. Women who sat bedecked with cards and crystals.

Emara studied all the paintings in awe.

Witches. The women are witches. They were women who were all beautifully in touch with their own magic. Their element. Women of empowerment.

That was all Emara needed to confirm who her grandmother had been, of the life she had once lived. There was no doubt in her mind that that was who Theodora Clearwater had been once upon a time.

But what happened?

Emara turned to face the middle of the room. A large painting hung as a centrepiece in a golden frame that swirled around a grand portrait of watercolour. Emara's eyes filled with emotion as she took in her grandmother dressed in a black gown with a spectacular crown displayed on her head, of gilded golds, dancing rubies, and stones of onyx black. She looked down to her hands and a platinum ring gleamed, bearing the initial 'S.'

Supreme.

In the painting, Theodora Clearwater looked only a year or two older than Emara was now. She was radiant and sovereign. Looking around, it was the only portrait that didn't have her grandmother's initials engraved on it, which told her she hadn't painted it. Someone else had.

A dark painting caught Emara's eye from the side. A woman who was depicted as her grandmother, taking off her crown and passing it to a beautiful girl as she sat on a starlit throne. As she looked at the painting, she realised that her own mother's eyes stared back, but it was not honey brown hair that flowed down her shoulders. No, the girl's hair was midnight black.

Emara stumbled back as she took in the face on the painting.

It was her.

She looked down to a corner of the painting, and the date was signed five days after her birth. Had this been what her grandmother envisioned? Was this her prophecy? It couldn't be.

Her heartbeat hammered in her chest.

How could she feel such peace and uncertainty all at once? It was like she was supposed to be here at this time, but she wasn't. She looked back at the painting of her grandmother in her hierarchy. A peculiar feeling drifted through her, like her grandmother's eyes almost invited her back over to steal a few more glances.

Trusting the instinct, she walked over to the painting and ran a hand over her grandmother's face. She took a moment to realise it was the only way she was able to say goodbye.

After a few moments of silent tears and staring at the painting, she tilted her head to the side. Engraved on the inside of her grandmother's hand, in the tiniest of writing, was words. So faint, her eyes almost missed it.

"Find me, like you found the other behind the sunset trees."

Emara blinked. What a strange thing to have written on her hand. She stood back and looked over the painting.

She placed a hand to her chin. "'Find me, like you found the other behind the sunset trees.'"

Why in the Gods above did she have that written on her hand?

And then a vivid thought punched into her gut. Emara dove forward and shoved her hand in behind the back of the painting. She ran her hand up and down and side to side.

Her hand hit something softer than brass.

Pulling it down, she held an envelope. Quickly, she opened it, trying her hardest not to tear it in the poor lighting. Squinting at the paper, she read it to herself.

Twice over.

A sob left her throat as she held the letter tight to her chest. Tight to her heart.

In that moment of solitude, she knew she would always remember the words that were written by her grandmother for as long as she lived. But for now, she had to follow her grandmother's instructions.

Before leaving, she placed a hand to her grandmother's portrait. "Thank you," she whispered, her voice cracking, "for making me who I am. For everything you have sacrificed for me," she croaked. "May you find peace on the other side. I know you will be watching over me. I will do you proud, I promise."

She wouldn't be able to walk out the front door after what she was about to do.

Pulling the match—which had been waxed onto the letter—she headed for the back door. She scratched the match against the rough wood of the door, and it lit, the orange flame feeling pleasant against her cold fingers. She took one look up at the gallery and dropped it. Closing the door behind her, she ran into the back alley behind the gallery. Just like her grandmother had instructed, she'd left the letter and the evidence of her grandmother's secret life to turn to ash.

My Dearest Emara,
Given that you have had the curiosity to find this letter, I fear that I am no longer with you and you have learned about the magic that runs in your blood. I want you to know that I have tried to keep you from this world, but only in the efforts to protect you from it. It is not safe for you. Should you find yourself in this position, trust no one. I want you to leave Caledorna and not look back. But not before you burn this place to the

ground. Wipe the memory of us from this village, dear child.

Please know that you are more than you ever thought possible, and that I loved you more than I thought it possible to love someone.

>*Forgive me,*
>*Theodora Clearwater.*

CHAPTER
TWENTY-SEVEN

"E mara," Marcus' voice sounded from the front door of the foyer. "I didn't know you had gone out." His face showed signs of apprehension. "I thought you would have let one of us know that you had gone out. We could have sent someone with you. That's what we are here for."

"I just had to get a few *girl* things," she lied.

Marcus didn't question her on what *girl things* might be. "I see. You didn't happen to witness a fire on your travels?" he asked.

She shot him a look, hoping her face gave nothing away, and shook her head.

"We received word that an old gallery has been burned to the ground in Mossgrave. You didn't happen to travel to Mossgrave, did you?"

Word travelled to the hunters that quickly? How is that possible? Magic?

"I went into the city for supplies that only girls require." She put a hand on her stomach and screwed up her face. "It's not like there are many women who take a monthly cycle around here, Marcus." She gave a small smile. "If you want, you can take me for more supplies tomorrow?" She held up a brown paper bag. He didn't question what was inside.

Marcus cleared his throat, shifting uncomfortably. "That's quite alright." He nodded. "I will see to it that the maids have more female supplies. We didn't think." He coughed. "Dinner will be served in ten minutes," he announced, avoiding any more uncomfortable conversations for himself.

Emara couldn't help a smile forming on her face. "Great, I am starving."

Her stomach groaned at the thought of food. She had been so consumed about getting into her grandmother's gallery that she had forgotten to eat all day.

"Hey, girl," Cally walked towards her in a pastel blue dress that revealed almost ninety percent of her legs and a pair of silver heels. Her hair bounced in curls as she scampered along the hall.

Emara was glad to see her best friend. It eliminated every other thought she had about today.

"Damn, Callyn. You look amazing! Why are you so dressed up? Are you ever out of the markets these days?"

"And that is why you are my best friend. Even with limited resources around this place, you still tell me I look great." She flicked her wavy hair over her shoulder. "And no, they are my new favourite thing. I am basically best friends with the fabric stall owner."

"That's because you do look amazing. What's the occasion? It can't be for dinner with...them." She gestured to the Hunters who had walked by, giving Cally a nod.

Cally laughed and linked her arm with Emara's as they walked through the room. She was fully aware every guy's eyes took in her long legs and she milked it. "It's not for the Hunters. Do you remember *La Luna guy?*"

Not really, Emara thought as she tried to run through the faces of the La Luna crowd. It was all a blur except for dancing, shots, and piercing ocean-blue eyes.

She banished the memory.

Quickly!

"Nope, I can't get a face," Emara said as they entered the line for food.

"Well, *La Luna guy* gave me an address to a *soiree* tonight and invited me to come along." Her eyes dazzled with naughtiness. "It's in the markets. Tell me you're coming, right?" She pressed a silver tray into her chest in excitement.

Emara half laughed as she picked up a tray.

"Well, are you coming?"

"Um…I think I am going to sit this one out. I am super tired, and I've walked all day—"

"Walked all day? To where? How come I wasn't invited?" Cally laughed as she looked at what was on offer to eat.

"I wanted to go and say goodbye to my grandmother, so I walked to Mossgrave—but you can't tell anyone." Emara's mouth tightened as she looked down at her food tray. Cally was missing major information, like the fact that she had set a building on a fire to hide the knowledge that her grandmother was a witch. She swallowed.

"And how do you feel now?"

"I am not sure." Emara chewed her cheek.

"If you want me to stay in tonight—"

"No way, go and enjoy yourself. You deserve to let your hair down."

"Emara, I am here when you want to talk."

"I know. I have some things to fill you in on, but it can wait." Emara faked a smile. "I will talk when I am ready.".

She still hadn't filled Cally in on what happened with Taymir. Although she desperately wanted to keep it locked down in the pits of her soul, she knew she would need to speak to someone about it.

"Emara—"

"Honestly, I am fine," she nipped by accident, letting the frustrations of her thoughts come out wrong.

A little hurt showed on Cally's face and she put down her tray. "Okay, well, you can come and find me when you are ready to talk."

Cally left, flicking her hair over her shoulder, her eyes pooling with something unusual.

Emara rolled her eyes and let out a massive sigh, allowing the air to puff in her cheeks. That's all she needed today. She hadn't meant to snap at Cally or hurt her.

"Rough day?" Messy hair framed Gideon's face, hovering above his green eyes. Emara looked up at him. "I saw from across the dining hall. And heard," he added.

Emara glanced at the door where Cally had exited, questioning if she should have gone to the party with her. But she really wasn't in the mood to and had no idea where it was.

She exhaled and stopped herself from running out the door after her.

"If it makes you feel any better, I think everyone is on edge today." Gideon moved with Emara in the food queue. "It's the moon, it makes people crazy." Gideon gave a gentle smile.

"You seem fine." She looked him over. His chocolate-coloured hair that was brighter at the tips had swept to one side slightly, allowing her to see his full face. He didn't look like himself, but he was handsome. So handsome. The kind of handsome you read about in fairy-tale books as a child.

"Yeah, that's because you didn't see me this morning after we trained..." he trailed off. "I've calmed a bit since then."

"Did I miss something?" she said as she placed potatoes onto her plate from the food trays.

"It doesn't matter, not really." He smiled, but she noticed a darkness spread in his eyes. "Hey, how about this? After dinner, meet me in the gardens out front?" he asked. Emara noticed that she had never seen Gideon look less confident than he did now, and she was convinced that confidence was a Blacksteel trait. Was he nervous for her answer?

He shot her an endearing look. "We can walk together."

Her heart fluttered. "Yeah, sure," She smiled back at him. "Sounds good."

He nodded and left with a smile still on his face as he strode over and sat with Marcus and a few others. They both laughed about something Marcus had said and she found herself smiling at his face as he broke into another fit of laughter. Her damned heart fluttered for a second time.

After she inhaled her food and engaged in regular chit chat with the villagers, Emara politely excused herself from the table of weeping family members. Almost instantly, she found herself wandering through the gardens of the tower, relieved to get away from the heartache. To breathe fresh air. She was glad to have a little bit of alone time, and she had noticed how beautiful the scenery in the gardens was.

Yellow and red roses lined the gardens, meeting the greenest grass she had ever seen. Hedges that were shaped into waves boarded the outside, and they seemed to have been cut into with the finest tools to make intricate details along the shrubbery. Grey-blue stones paved the walkway, weaving a path through the lawns.

"My shirt looks better on you than it does on me," Gideon called as he jogged to catch up with her, his hair bouncing in his strides. She turned, looking down at herself in his fleecy shirt. Clearly today's events had fogged her mind and she had forgotten to change out of the clothing Gideon had lent her at the training session hours ago. She had left her wet cloak in the dining hall by the fire to dry.

"I don't know about that," she said quietly as she looked at the flowers, pulling the oversized fleece down onto her thighs. It bounced back up marginally.

They walked in silence for a few moments before Gideon said, "She will be okay, you know."

"Who, Cally? Oh, no. I know." She let her lip tug up at one corner. "She's *Cally.*" She raised her eyebrows and fun danced across her face. "She will be fine." *She always is.*

"Well, then, if that's not bothering you, then I would pay top coin to know what is running through your head right now."

Emara looked up at him through her lashes.

"What's on your mind?" Gideon asked as he turned, walking backwards to make sure he was maintaining eye contact. His body easily navigated the way like he had eyes on the back of his head.

"It's honestly nothing."

"You don't have to keep everything to yourself, you know? You can trust me."

Something in his voice made her believe that she could. Or maybe it was the way he was looking at her…

She sighed.

She had been planning to tell Cally everything tonight. Everything about who she was. But she supposed it had to wait.

"I just think it's strange," she started, "that people can live a full lifetime and never show you who they really are." Scratching her neck, she looked round to

Gideon, who looked deep in thought. What she said could open a can of worms, and she'd promised she would keep who she was a secret. For Torin. And her safety. "What I mean is, that people can hide themselves, pretending to be someone they are not."

"Has he said something to you? Because he was told to leave you alo—" Gideon pushed his lips together and clapped his hands forward.

"Has who said something to me?" Emara's eyebrows frowned in confusion.

"Torin! I warned him not to play games with you and with what you are saying, I was wondering if he had gotten into your head." He sighed. "You've been through enough. You would think getting punched in the face would be a clear enough warning."

Gideon casually slid past the punching part like it was no big deal. Emara's head snapped towards him.

"Hold on." Emara stopped walking. "You punched Torin?" she asked.

He nodded with a sigh.

"Why?" she gasped. "What did he say?"

What could Torin have said that made Gideon punch him? A crawling feeling spread across her stomach, causing it to flip. She prayed to the Gods that he hadn't mentioned the part in La Luna where they were so close to kissing.

"He said that he almost kissed you." A strange emotion passed through Gideon's tone.

That bastard.

She didn't want Gideon to know any of that. She had let her guard down for a split second and it had been a mistake.

His eyes flickered to hers and then to the ground. "So I punched him in the face."

"Is it weird to tell you that I am envious that you got to punch him in the face?" Right now? She wanted to punch Torin in the face. He had told Gideon about their moment in La Luna to rile him, nothing more.

He let a stiff laugh split his lips. "You are not the first person to want to punch him in the face."

That she could imagine.

"Not everyone can be a gentleman and keep their affairs to themselves."

There was a momentary pause between them, allowing her to hear the music of the birds nesting in the trees. Both gazed ahead as they walked shoulder to shoulder, enjoying the scenic view. His fingers grazed hers, but he didn't move them together or reach for her.

"You didn't have to punch him for me, you know" she joked. "I would have been happy to take on that responsibility."

He laughed warmly. "No, I did. Not only for you, but for every other girl he messes with." He looked ahead. "It's been a long time coming. Someone needs to let him know his behaviour is not okay." Gideon paused, deep in thought. "He knows exactly what to do to get under my skin."

"You are not the only one," Emara muttered lowly.

There was a blissful silence as they bonded over a sneer at Torin's talents for infuriating them. But curiosity overwhelmed her about Breighly, the barmaid from last night, and she had to ask him about her. "Are you and Breighly, um, together?" she coughed out.

"Breighly?" He laughed fondly at her name. "No." A feeling of relief ticked over in her heart as she tried to remain unfazed on the outside. "Breighly is a good friend. I haven't seen her in Gods know how long until last night." He looked at Emara. "We used to be a thing."

Ah! There it was. That sting. The one she had been told about, but never experienced.

"Well, not a *thing,* but you know…" His face told the story well. He didn't have to say anything as the warmth flushed his cheeks. She knew exactly what they had meant to each other by the look on his face. He didn't want to be ungentlemanly in his words.

"A friend who you could…" Emara didn't finish her sentence. She pushed her lips together. "*Be* with."

"*Be with.* I suppose that's a nice way to put it," he laughed awkwardly. "It wasn't supposed to mean anything to either of us. But the second it did, we both agreed to pull back. She would be promised to someone else—a member of her pack."

Emara's head snapped 'round at the word pack. But she didn't want to interrupt and ask questions as Gideon spoke from the heart, so she tucked it away in her mind for another time.

"You loved her, didn't you?" Emara said delicately.

He let out a small laugh, the kind of laugh you let escape when you didn't expect to be questioned about something you found hard to express. "I tried not to. But I did. I fell for her. Sometimes it just happens, even when you don't intend for it to." He looked at Emara and then looked up, the sunset light causing his eyes to shine forever green. "We both agreed to stop before it got incredibly messy. She and I would be pulled in opposite directions eventually. It's not often Shifters and Hunters can make it work. Shifters mate and Hunters don't really want to be in the middle of two mates." He laughed at the thought. "We were happy to at least remain friends."

He had been in love. Was he still in love?

Emara's heart ached selfishly for something she had never had. A chord stuck within her for a longing that, one day, she would feel love or be in love. Wildly in love—like the women in the books she used to sneak from the shelves of her grandmother's library, in the *forbidden* section. Wildly in love like her mother had been—willing to do anything for the person she loved.

They turned the corner of the path and headed under an arch, an array of blooming white and pink winter roses climbed up the framework, causing her breath to hitch. It was beautiful.

"Did you love—"

"No," she cut him off. She knew exactly what he was going to say, and she didn't want to hear his name. Not today.

Or ever, in fact.

A shudder moved up her spine at the thought of him, his hands on her, his lips on her.

She dropped her gaze to the ground, taking in the silvery stones. "I've never been in love," Emara admitted. She looked at his throat as he moved under the arch, tilting his head to the side. He was so strong, in every aspect of his body, yet as gentle as the roses that framed the archway.

"Waiting for the right one?" he offered a friendly smile.

"I can't be sure there is a right one for me. How can anyone?" She brushed her hand along the arch of the hedge, feeling the leaves and the branches scratch against her palm to take her mind off wanting to reach up and grab his neck with two hands. "When I was younger, I always thought I would meet someone nice from the village and get married after a few months of courting. We would probably have children, and I would work in a shop or with my grandmother when the kids were old enough to fend for themselves—the usual path for a woman in Mossgrave." She shook her head and smiled at the sound of her voice, at the unwillingness to accept that life. "As I grew older, none of that satisfied me. The men that courted me, none of them could make me feel the way I wanted them to. I didn't want the small village life or mentality of the males that lived there. So I told myself I wouldn't settle. I wouldn't settle for anything mediocre. I would settle for nothing short of breathtakingly powerful love that awakes your soul and stimulates your mind. I want a purposeful love, and I think that it's more than just settling for the first guy who shows you affection, you know?" She tilted her chin down, feeling a little blush of embarrassment. She had never had a deep conversation with a guy that involved feelings, her inner desires. But something about Gideon allowed her to be honest and open. Calm. Freeing her thoughts from a cage in her mind. "I'm sorry, I totally went off track. I have embarrassed myself."

Gideon closed the gap between them and ran both of his hands down her upper arms to her wrists, sending shock waves through her heart. "Don't apologise for being passionate, it's refreshing. You are refreshing." He slid his hand from her wrist down, brushing his fingertips over the knuckles of her hand as they studied each other. "Don't ever settle for less than what you have just described. It would be a travesty to have a heart like yours owned by someone who isn't worthy of it."

He brought his lips down to her hand and gently placed a kiss on her skin. She inhaled as the embrace of his mouth warmed her hand, pulling her lungs to a tightening squeeze. He flashed a dazzling smile that gleamed as the lowering sun hit his face, then intertwined his fingers with hers. She had to stop herself from pulling his face into hers and kissing him, there and then.

What was wrong with her? She had shocked herself with how forward she wanted to be around him. She wanted to wrap her arms around his neck and feel him pull her in.

"Since you have been so forthcoming, I will let you in on a secret of mine." Gideon lowered his hand but kept his fingers wrapped around hers. "I don't think my father ever loved my mother. Their marriage was an alliance to the Hunters and that's something I would never want. I am lucky that I am the second-born male of the Blacksteel name, or I would have the same fate as Torin. Not being able to marry for love or desire, but only for power and allegiance for the clan. I don't want to imagine it."

Blacksteel, your fate has not changed since the last time we looked through the crystal ball.

The Spirit Witch's voice rang into Emara's mind. Is that what she had been referring to? His fate? Was Torin hoping that he didn't have to go through with it? An arranged marriage? A dull twinge poked in her heart.

Not likely, Emara counterbalanced her feelings. Torin wasn't the marrying for love type. He would marry for an alliance and have a new mistress each month, that would suit him.

"Where is your mother? I don't think I have seen her around the tower," Emara wondered, distracting herself from Torin Blacksteel.

"You won't have. She doesn't live with us." Gideon lowered his head. "After Kellen entered the Hunter Selection and was successful, my father didn't need her at the tower anymore. He was no longer a boy, but considered a man. She lives in our second home. She's happy there."

They walked hand-in-hand as the garden flowers blew in the wind.

Emara shivered as she realised that his mother had been banished from the tower after she birthed and raised the boys for the Blacksteel legacy. Gideon's mother's body had been used as a host to make sure there would be heirs for the clan. Soldiers.

Emara couldn't hide her anguish. "I am sorry, Gideon, that's awful. I can't imagine what that must feel like." Emara searched his face for something that would make her feel like he wasn't upset. "Do you still see her?" she asked. She saw a glimmer of emotion cross his face, but he only allowed it for a second.

"Yes, we all go and see her when training or our duty allows it." He picked a flower from the garden with his free hand. "She would like you." He bowed his head to smell the flower, and his tone suggested that he missed her greatly. "She will be at the annual uplift. Obviously to keep up appearances with the other clans and covens for my father's sake—the united front—but she will be there, nonetheless." His brows lifted, and he offered her the flower he had picked.

"Thank you." Emara blushed as she lifted the flower from Gideon's grasp and studied it. A white rose, of pure delicacy. The buds had just newly begun to open.

"It's nice to have someone to talk to. Or walk with," he said softly.

"I'm sure there are plenty of people in the tower who you could talk to or walk with," she replied with a smile of her own.

"Yeah, but none of them are you." He flashed a charming smile and her stomach somersaulted.

"That is very true," she smirked. "None of them are me, and my grandmother always told me that was my superpower."

He smiled, his full lips curving into a delicious grin. Lips that she couldn't stop exploring with her eyes.

"I hope you can make it to the uplift," Gideon interrupted her thoughts. "Father says he is extending the invite to the humans to show gratitude for how well we are co-existing in the tower and to raise their spirits.

It would make it more bearable if you were there." His tone was as sincere as his face.

"Mhmm," she pouted. "I have heard of this up-lift in the dining hall. It's quite the topic among the villagers. I will see if I can walk there after the training sessions you have been making me do," she teased, lightening the mood. "My body is aching from them."

"I better take the next couple of training sessions easy, then, since you are going to have to do more than walk. You must dance." Gideon's face lit up as anxiety crept its way along Emara's limbs.

"Dance? Oh, no, I don't really dance." Emara couldn't stand the thought of a formal dance.

"No? I heard you were surprisingly good on the dancefloor the other night."

Torin!

Why does he not just keep his stupid mouth shut?

Grudgingly, her mind flashed back to them dancing as she moved her hips to the sound of the beat. The music as intoxicating as his stare, as Torin pulled her in and then spun her out. Her heart, light like the strobes that pulsed down onto her face. The euphoric feeling of the crowd being as one.

"I'm sorry, I didn't mean to embarrass you." Gideon halted.

She realised her face had flushed with heat. A heat that was unnerving and untouched.

"If I offended you, I didn't mean to. It was just a jo—"

"You didn't offend me." She offered him a fake smile. "I just really need to lay down. I am exhausted," she lied, pulling away from him.

Gideon pulled her back gently with one hand and she staggered close—too close to his chest. "You don't have to be embarrassed about what happened in La Luna." His words shocked her. "I know you didn't want anything to happen with Torin. He just got the better of me this morning, so don't feel guilty."

She inhaled, holding her breath.

"You're beautiful," Gideon admitted. "Of course he would try something with you, who wouldn't?" He paused. "He likes a challenge."

"I am not giving him a challenge."

"I know. Don't let him get into your head." He squeezed her hand.

"I won't," she promised.

His gaze dropped down to her mouth. "I am afraid I must tell you another secret of mine."

She laughed. "I am listening."

"I can't stop thinking about you."

"Oh?" was all she could manage as the heat of his stare stilled her.

Neither could she.

She couldn't help but feel inexplicably drawn to him, like she had known him her whole life. Like he had a way of soothing her. The energy between them was so natural, so organic.

"I never *feel* like this," she whispered as a confession.

"Now I am worrying if that is a good thing or a bad thing," he replied in a whisper.

"I don't know yet."

How could she answer that? She had just met him. She barely knew him at all.

How could she feel something inside of her shift in the space of a few days, but twelve new moons had passed with Taymir and she had felt nothing? The inner workings of the heart were the most complex thing to even try and understand.

But if she had learned anything from the demon attack at her home, it was that life was too short. And now? She felt something that she never had before.

A spark. That current of chemistry that flows from one person to another.

"I have wanted to kiss you for a while, and I have stopped myself because..." he paused, running a hand through his hair.

"Then maybe you should just do it." She swallowed hard, waiting for him to make the next move.

Gideon reached up and weaved his hand behind her ear, pushing into the softness of her hair. Emara almost let a small moan slip from her mouth as he lowered his lips to her jawline. Pulling her closer to his mouth, he danced a few kisses along her jaw and down her neck. A roaring heat swept over her, causing her to be conscious of her feminine curves. He wrapped another strong arm around her waist and pulled her into his torso.

Gods, she couldn't breathe as her chest flattened against his. She could feel his thick muscles tighten under his training gear as she moved her hands upwards. And then he found her mouth with his. He slowly parted her lips and gently pressed a kiss to hers.

His lips were soft and warm, the kiss lingering. He pulled back from her and studied her face for a second. Desire burned in his eyes and then his lips slammed into hers. Like before, she embraced it, pushing her hands up over his arms, onto his neck and into his hair. She deepened the kiss, returning the fire as she rolled her tongue into his mouth.

"Emara," he whispered against her open mouth.

"Yes?" she breathed.

"I need to go," he said.

Disappointment soared through her.

"I can't be caught out here. With you…like this." He pressed his head against hers.

"Then go," she whispered back, not really wanting him to.

He exhaled deeply and then pulled back. Discontent stabbed into her chest and she lingered for a moment before finally opening her eyes.

"See you soon, Emara," he said, before taking his leave.

Emara almost swooned like a little girl, but she held it together as she watched him walk away. Her grip tightened on the rose.

Ouch! She looked down at her hand. A droplet of crimson blood fell onto the ground from the thorny white rose Gideon had gifted her. As she looked at it, she couldn't help but wonder if it was a reminder that what she was feeling was too good to be true.

CHAPTER
TWENTY-EIGHT

It was eating into the early hours of the morning and Cally still hadn't returned from wherever in the Gods' land she was. All Emara wanted to do was speak to her about what had happened with her grandmother's gallery, finally telling her everything, or about Gideon in the garden, but timing never seemed to be on her side.

She was exhausted after today. However, the tiredness didn't stop the swirling unanswered questions that gripped at her heart. Although she had gotten *some* answers today, it wasn't enough. In fact, today's events made the swirling madness in her mind even heavier. Once upon a time, her grandmother was the *supreme* of all witches. And she was gone. And she was never coming back.

She sat up abruptly and rubbed at her chest, as if the ache of her breaking heart would go away. Digesting the words in her grandmother's note that had run around her mind since she had read it, she felt a hollowness in her heart. They had been her last words to Emara instead of the blood-filled words she had choked out the night she had died. For that, she was thankful. Emara pulled a frantic hand through her hair, combing its wildness down, and huffed out a sigh.

Although Theodora had insinuated that Emara must not ask questions about who she was or dig into her past, a desire to look into everything she was told not to clawed deep.

I want you to know I have tried to keep you from this world, but only in the efforts to protect you from it. It is not safe for you. Should you find yourself in this position, trust no one. I want you to leave Caledorna and not look back.

She took a deep breath, beginning to feel the sting of tears in her eyes as she thought through the letter. She pulled her knees up to her chest and exhaled slowly, breathing in and out.

After sorting through her thoughts, she knew she wasn't going to run. Running wasn't an option. She was going to search for the truth.

At dinner, Emara had overheard one of the hunters discussing manuscripts which documented every birth here in Huntswood. Similar to how they documented births and deaths in her own village, and Emara couldn't help but wonder what else she could find stored in tower's library.

It was calling to her. That deeply stacked library in the heart of the tower was calling her name as she sat, irritated, in bed. The endless thoughts that ran through her mind about her grandmother's secret life had taken root, and the seeds of curiosity were starting to sprout and grow now that Cally wasn't here to distract her.

Now she understood why Callyn always kept herself busy. Distracted.

Emara knew she would need to deal with her grandmother's death; she knew she would process it in her own time, but what if she could know more about her? Would that help her healing? Would getting to know more about her bring a clarity that could provide closure? Could there be something—anything—documented about her grandmother being the Supreme in the library? Or even her own mother? Her death? Could that be registered here? After all, she hadn't died in Mossgrave, that Emara knew. She had checked all of the documents in the village library endlessly for her name and there was nothing. Maybe she would find a registered marriage certificate detailing who her father was, or maybe a document that told her more about her ancestors. She wanted *anything* that could give her a true reflection of who she really was. Or even where to start searching for that.

Just a snippet…

Emara kicked off the heavy blanket and her toes touched base with the cold floor. Leaving the infirmary behind, she took off in search of the library.

It was chilly to walk around the tower without her full training gear on, especially at night. The cold, ancient stone formed intimidatingly long and winding corridors with fantom breezes that nipped at her skin. It wasn't like her grandmother's cosy home. Her home, with lower ceilings and burning fires. She hadn't removed Gideon's fleece from earlier because it warmed her core and arms so comfortably, keeping in a toasty heat.

Just as she turned the corridor's final curved corner that led to the library doors, Emara's heart had a sudden moment of weakness.

She halted her steps.

Did she *really* want to know everything? What if there was something that destroyed everything she knew to be true? What if what she found wasn't what she *hoped* for? Was it better to remain in the dark about her family's past? Was it all kept secret for a reason? Was she really in as much danger as Torin thought?

All the possibilities about who she was almost knocked her flat on her rear.

In the vision Melione had shown her at the markets, her mother and grandmother seemed to have different views on how a witch should live her life. Especially an *important* witch. One that laid claims to the supremacy title and had a direct line into being an empress of a coven seemed to have a lot of responsibility. An Empress of House Air couldn't just live her own life without restrictions and reprimand. And Emara's mother had paid the price for that.

She had also rebelled against it.

A prickling at her neck stood all hairs to attention. Like it had every time she had thought of the same thing. Did that mean, because she was a direct descendant of the Empress of Air *and the Supreme,* that she should have lived that kind of life, too? A life that her grandmother had lived for so long until she had gone into hiding?

But the real question that ate at her soul was: Did that mean she, too, had magic? And if so, could she access it? Did she even *want* to access it?

Given that you have had the curiosity to find this letter, I fear that I am no longer with you and you have learned about the magic that runs in your blood.

An overwhelming feeling passed through her chest and it forced her jaw to tighten, stopping any vomit that had sneakily climbed up her throat. It was so surreal to even be having these thoughts. Thoughts of magic and new worlds with dangerous possibilities. She would know if she had magic, would she not?

She cursed under her breath.

It was anarchy in her mind. Chaos.

What if being the former Supreme's granddaughter meant something to the magic community and they held her responsible for her grandmother disappearing? Was she ready for that? *Was she responsible?*

The Spirit Witch had said that it was believed that Emara was killed in a fire alongside her mother. So that meant her grandmother had to have hidden the fact that she was alive. Otherwise, Theodora would have gone on to rule over the covens for Gods knows how long. Maybe she would still be ruling, were she still alive. The thought nipped in her chest, even though something truly felt off about her grandmother stepping away from her title and coven. Maybe she had done it because of her mother's death? But she couldn't be sure of that either.

Her grandmother had to be hiding from someone. Was she hiding from *something?* The demon that had invaded her home the night of the attack seemed to think she had something valuable.

Emara let out a heavy groan.

Every part of this agonising guessing game had circulated for hours in her mind—for days! If there was anywhere in the city that held answers to anything, other than the Huntswood Markets, it had to be the tower's library.

Fear was no longer an option, either. She had to know. Taking a deep breath, Emara pushed the solid wooden doors open and stepped inside. It had been lighter when she had first seen it with Marcus, with winter sun breaking through the small windows above. But tonight, only oil lamps lit the walls and sat glowing on small oak tables. Stacks and stacks of uneven shelves housed multicoloured books and unbound manuscripts; the library swept up onto two floors. As Emara walked through each bookish corridor, it was evident which books were new and which ones had been gathering dust in the tower for decades—maybe centuries. She took her time to read over some of the headings which hung above each section, detailing what manuscripts or books could be found there. To be honest, she wasn't even sure what section she was looking for; she was just aimlessly wandering, hoping to stumble across something that stood out to her. Something substantial enough…

At least at the markets she had the Blacksteels to use for navigation purposes. Here? She was on her own. She wasn't going to find any hidden messages from her grandmother behind paintings. There was going to be no guidance. Perhaps, just some luck?

Where does an orphan of secret magical origin who has been hidden from her family's coven for twenty years start looking for answers after burning her only clue about who she was?

She huffed a small laugh at the thought. It was a miracle she found anything funny anymore. Her situation really wasn't funny, but she feared that if she did not laugh, she would cry.

And she would rather laugh. She had done enough crying.

"Looking for something in particular?"

A deep, authoritative tone had Emara swinging around in a sharp second. The air escaped her lungs as she took in the face of Viktir Blacksteel—the commander of the clan—standing at the end of the corridor she was in.

"I—" she couldn't think of a lie. Not quickly enough. "If I shouldn't be in here, I can leave." Her voice was smaller than she wanted it to be and she found her cheeks burning instantly.

Viktir's dark green eyes washed over her, pinning down on her attire. His son's attire.

She sucked in a breath.

Something about him was so compellingly powerful. Even how he stood in the library of his own home was menacing, yet she couldn't tear her gaze away.

"The library is open to any of the humans who are still staying within these walls." He turned and plucked a manuscript from a section she hadn't checked yet. "But none of them have taken up the opportunity for reading. Except you."

"I am an avid reader," she blurted, wishing it had sounded more controlled. Especially since everything that the commander said or did was controlled with excellence. "I didn't bring any books with me from my grandmother's house and I am missing some light reading before bed."

His stare pinned her where she stood once again. "And what books did you hope to find in a hunting library that are suitable for 'some light reading?'"

Something glitched in her chest, igniting a feeling of warning. Did he somehow know she was snooping? He couldn't. She didn't look suspicious, did she?

Let's keep the stone, and who you are, a secret. We don't need anyone else knowing about it. And especially not my father.

Torin's words surged through her mind, causing conflict. Could Viktir not be trusted with who she was? With what Torin knew? Surely, he was the safest person to know. He was the commander of the people who had saved her. He was put on this world to *protect* people.

But again, that little twinge in her chest told her to listen to Torin's instruction.

Begrudgingly.

"An avid reader knows no limits on what they can read, Commander Blacksteel." She pretended to coast her eyes over the books on the shelf next to her.

"I was hoping to find something on the Great War or the Gods, maybe. My grandmother kept some books about their legends. So that might be a comfort to me while I am here."

"She did, did she?" A lazy eyebrow pulled upwards, and the dark glow of the oil lamps lit the sharpest lines of his face. "Any book on the Gods in particular stand out to you? I know each and every one that is listed here in the library."

Somehow, the question felt like a trap that she had to avoid. "I can't remember specific names. Probably just pictures or illustrations."

"Mmm." He turned and plucked another document from the shelf—it looked heavier than Cally. "Most of the humans in these lands know of the Light Gods. But they don't tend to keep records of the ancient Gods they no longer worship."

"My grandmother loved ancient history. It was a passion of hers." Emara's voice did not falter.

Viktir took a moment before speaking again, "You do know you are in the section regarding witches and not in the section where all the lore you could ever read on the Gods is stored, Miss Clearwater?"

Emara tried to fake a laugh, but her throat tightened. "I didn't. Which way is that section?" She swallowed hard, looking around herself.

He moved, his tall frame stalking towards a small wooden desk at the edge of the shelving. He turned to face her again. "I never did give you my condolences on the loss of your grandmother. It must be very difficult for you, being an only child."

A red flag wrapped around her mind. He knew she was an only child. What else did he know about her? Being the commander of the clan, Emara would have assumed he would have done research on every person who had come into his tower. But how much had he learned about her?

"Thank you," she squeezed out. "It has been incredibly difficult. I am just taking each day as it comes."

He nodded, his jaw hard. "Forgive me for asking, but what was the name of your grandmother again?"

Emara could lie, but she had a feeling she was being tested. Again. And she had a horrible feeling that she did not want to fail this test, even if it gave away who she was to him. "Theodora," she answered. "Theodora Clearwater."

If Viktir knew of her grandmother, he didn't show it. "Ahh, yes. That's right. We had to mark down her death. Anyone who is killed at the hand of the Dark Army, we record. Just for our files." He sat the manuscripts that he had collected on the table. If he was pretending not to know who she was, he was doing a splendid job. "Clearwater…that is an old name. It probably dates back to the deities' children."

"Really?" A shiver ran down Emara's spine, snaking its way into her stomach. "I must look into that when I have time."

"You should. We have documents that go back centuries. Of course, the originals lie within the Temple of the Gods, but we do have our copies here." He eyed her, piercing into her skin with those broken-bottle-green eyes. "Did your grandmother ever talk of the origin of the name Clearwater?"

"No, sir." Emara held her chin up. "She didn't. She often spoke of her parents, but nothing of where they came from. I don't imagine they would have been anyone of importance."

Viktir's lips thinned, and she knew she had said too much. "I see." He stalked forward, lifting another manuscript off the shelf. "Did you ever hear your grandmother speak of the magic world? About anything you have learned whilst being here?"

"Never," fell from her mouth quickly. "I mean, no, Commander Blacksteel. My grandmother never spoke of any of it."

"Do you think she knew of it?"

Emara could feel her eyebrows furrow over her face and her body starting to warm. Sweat. "If she did, she never spoke of it to me," she exhaled out the truth. "We lived a very normal life. An incredibly quiet and boring life, sir."

"Until demons invaded your home and killed your only living relative?"

Hearing it so bluntly punched a hole straight through Emara's heart and she had to take a moment to gather herself. "Yes, until that night." She gritted her teeth, trying her best to keep her demeanour as collected as the commander's. "Did you know of my grandmother?" she asked, not sure she wanted him to answer.

"I know many people, Miss Clearwater. But I don't believe I ever came across your grandmother.

Should I have known her? An elderly woman who lived in a village?" he asked in return.

A stark, thick silence swept through the books, almost suffocating Emara where she stood. "No. Like I said, we lived a quiet life." She picked a book from the shelf and her eyes skimmed the title, not really taking in what it was as her hands began to shake.

"Weren't your parents also *killed?*" The Commander stopped for a second before turning so that Emara could see the cold, hard plains of his face again. His features were so like Torin's, yet he wasn't charming or mischievous. Or even warm in any way. He was just…collected. Working. Calm. The Commander.

A small part of her wanted to punch or scream at him for asking such an invasive question. Or maybe she even wanted to cry. How dare he be so insensitive! Viktir knew the answer, or he wouldn't have asked. But she decided that all irrational options were foolish when dealing with a man like the one who stood before her. He was intelligent and precise. And clearly curious about something. And evidently *informed* about her.

"I wasn't aware that I was under investigation, Commander Blacksteel. I was only looking for some light reading that may tire my eyes. As you can imagine, I haven't been sleeping well since the attack." She held his gaze, even though she feared her legs had now begun to shake enough for him to see.

A small, wry smirk finally appeared on his lips. "My apologies again, Miss Clearwater. I have been the commander of this clan for so long that I instantly go into hunting mode, even when in polite conversation. Please forgive me for prying. The books that you are after are two sections along." He moved again, this time to sit at the desk. "Don't mind me. I will not disturb you, take as long as you want. I am just looking into some ancient history of the witching covens." An uneasy smile twitched under his lips, revealing his teeth.

It wasn't a cruel smile, or even one that would be considered passive. But it was one that told Emara Clearwater that the commander of the Blacksteel Clan knew *exactly* who she was. Or at least he was going to find out.

After selecting three books that weren't related to anything she had wished to find, she tinkled back along the corridors to her room, just to quickly escape the intense encounter with the commander. Verging closer to the infirmary, she noticed a brass plaque that she hadn't before, engraved with the word *Rooftop*. The plaque also had an arrow, pointed in a direction she had never ventured before. She hadn't been shown the rooftop on the tour with Marcus.

Walking slowly, she reached an unseen turn in the hallway and she peeked her head around the corner to see a set of dimly lit stairs that were carved from uneven brick rising into the darkness.

Daringly, she placed her books down on the first step and wondered what she would be able to see from the tallest building she had ever stayed in. Curiosity won the battle with exhaustion in her head.

The stairway was dark and cold as the windows from the narrow corridor let the air filter through the broken glass, also permitting moonlight to glow through in beams. The remaining glass from the windows looked weather-worn, and it was evident that no one had bothered to fix them in years. Clearly, this part of the tower wasn't in use, so no one would even know if she went snooping…

She was glad to be in Gideon's fleece, as it proved to be the warmest clothing she had. However, not putting on proper trousers and only wearing nightwear bottoms for bed had been a mistake. The icy breeze groped at her legs as she climbed the final set of stairs before coming across a wooden door. She halted. It looked like it had been removed from an ancient temple, placed here and forgotten centuries ago. As she turned the handle, it moved with ease. She hadn't expected for the door to come close to opening, it had looked so old. Deep down, she was kind of hoping it wouldn't open and that her venture up here would satisfy her prying mind before returning back down the stairs to her own room. To her bed. To read. To sleep.

That would be the sensible option.

Emara pushed the door open, and a vicious blast of cold caught her breath. She rubbed her hands together, tucking them into the sleeves of the fleece before stepping out onto the rooftop terrace.

The cold wasn't the only thing that took her breath away. The dazzling lights of the Huntswood city preserved the backdrop. The small, diamond-like lights of homes, workplaces and even the markets, all glittered in the distance. She couldn't see far past the landscape in the dark, but she noticed different buildings shaped against it, like mini brick towers, and wondered what sort of purpose they gave to the city. She couldn't see this side of the scenery from her room, only greenery, and she smiled as she took in the contrasting view.

It was beautiful. Emancipating.

She took a moment to herself, letting the wind brush against her cheeks and the backdrop absorb in her mind. She felt like she could breathe clearer up here, like the air was purer from above. She opened her eyes with a small smile itching at her lips.

A dark figure moved from the shadows. A squeal escaped from Emara's mouth as she jumped back, trying to see a face on the figure. Sapphire eyes moved from the darkness to where the light of the moon hit them. Layers and layers of darkness hung heavy in those blue eyes as he stepped out further, revealing his face.

Torin Blacksteel stood in front of her. His face that normally gave off a glowing complexion, sat grey against the glint of the moon. His hair was unusually disorderly and his eyes were heavy with the weight of something dark. In his hand, he held a crystal bottle of rusty coloured liquor and it appeared to be half finished.

Emara took in a breath as she studied him, not quite looking like himself as his shirt lay half open on his chest, flapping in the wind. He turned away from her and strode towards the railings that bound the rooftop terrace, unimpressed by her presence. His tall frame sulked over the railing, resting his arms on the metal.

The movement displayed the truly enormous muscles that gave his powerful back definition.

"What is the prim and proper princess doing all the way up here on the roof terrace at this unholy hour?" Torin's words slurred as he took another drink from the bottle, his voice low and raspy.

Drunk! He's drunk.

"Sorry, I didn't know where I was going. I am still getting used to the Tower. I was looking for, um..." She trailed off, her thoughts stumbling over the sight of the warrior.

It was so unlike him to look this...fragile.

"Save it," he dismissed causally. "There is no need for lies...not tonight."

A feeling of concern tightened in her chest.

"Are you okay?" Emara finally spoke.

He scoffed. A bitter laugh left his throat, causing her to flinch. "Of course." Torin turned towards her, his back resting against the railings, his brute mass almost threatening to bend the metal. "Why wouldn't I be?"

She walked towards him slowly, her eyes raking over every part of him. Emara noticed, for the first time, Torin Blacksteel wasn't armed. No knives, no swords.

"You don't look okay. Do you want to—"

"I said I am fine," he spoke through gritted teeth.

She knew he wasn't. He was not fine at all.

Emara had seen him drunk a couple of times, but this was different.

This was...*destructive.*

She grew close enough to rest her arms against the railings, mirroring Torin. She couldn't leave him like this. She wouldn't leave anyone like this.

"I heard you got punched today." She let a smile cross her face to establish a different direction, one that would hopefully bring out that mischievous grin that she loved to hate.

"Getting punched was the best part of my day." He took another sip from the bottle and pulled the alcohol through his teeth.

She wasn't quite sure what had happened today for him to be brooding, but surely it couldn't be worse than being punched in the face.

And then she reminded herself of who he was. A Hunter. A lethal killing machine. Getting punched in the face was probably normal in a day in the life of Torin Blacksteel.

I am lucky that I am born the second male of the Blacksteel name, or I would have the same fate as Torin. Not being able to marry for love or desire, but for power and allegiance for the Clan.

The memory of Gideon's words stirred up some unexpected feelings in her heart.

"Can I have a sip?" she asked assertively, holding out her hand. She had to admit, it was more of a command than a question. And it felt good.

His eyes moved to her quickly, and one eyebrow raised into an arch. He held out the bottle and a small tug pulled up at the corner of his mouth. "Is your halo finally falling off?" he asked, his face showing a snippet of colour. "Because I want to witness that."

Emara noticed that, even when fully intoxicated, Torin Blacksteel still managed to sound seductively smooth.

"Not yet." She took the bottle from his hands and drew a swig. "But I don't think it's far away from falling off." The liquid burned in her throat as she coughed it down. Her grandmother would be cursing her out on the other side for drinking from the bottle. But when in Huntswood…

"Why are you not in bed?" His voice was husky as he studied the lights in the distance.

"Why are *you* not in bed?" she battled back.

His face was tortured by the thoughts in his own head. She winced at the sight of him. "Torin, what happened today?" she asked as she handed the bottle back to him.

"Hunter politics." He drank another glug from the bottle. "Something you won't understand."

"Okay, give me the bottle back." She took it from his hands, tipped it into her mouth, and drank the remainder of its contents. The cold didn't seem so bitter against her skin after she forced down the burning liquid.

He looked at her through his dark lashes. "Since you just finished a bottle of my most expensive rum…" The expression on his face told her that he was more impressed in her abilities to down liquor than he would have liked to show. "Does this mean we're friends now?"

"Not even close."

He let a slither of a smile form on his lips before it vanished. The wind lifted the ends of her hair and it landed on her shoulder. Torin's eyes followed it as it rested on the curves of her chest like it had done something magical. As he stood up straight, angling his body towards her, his shirt blew further open, baring his soul to the city below them. An indescribable feeling made its way through her spine, warming her.

She ignored it.

"I went to my grandmother's art gallery today," she blurted out. Emara paused instantly, acknowledging that she was about to open a wound by taking out the stitches before it was fully healed.

Torin's gaze lifted to her face. A twitch in his dark brows told her he was interested in hearing what she had to say.

"It's true," she croaked. "Everything. All of it."

Torin's face changed as he heard the crack in her voice.

"My grandmother"—she swallowed, finding it hard to breathe—"she belonged to the House of Air, and then she became the Supreme. I saw it in her paintings. She painted it all. Her Coven, her reign, my mother. Even me." She held onto the railing a little tighter. "I have watched her paint since I can remember, never once knowing that she was painting a secret past or future." She paused as she looked up. "Or my future."

Torin looked more awake than he had a couple of minutes ago.

"It's not the shock of her being magical that is unsettling. I always knew she was different. I guess, in a way, I always knew I was different, too. What's un-settling to me is *why* she kept it all a secret. Why did she leave it all behind?"

"Sometimes we don't get the answers we need to heal. Sometimes, we just need to pray that the Gods have a path for us, and we must trust it."

She thought over what Torin said. Something pure and passionate lay amongst his words, but she detected a dash of resentment that anyone would pave his path but him. And that was something Emara could understand.

"I don't even know a thing about magic," she said, her breath swirling out into the air after her sigh. "I don't even know if I can wield magic, and now that I have found out that it runs in my veins, I am curious about it. But I don't have my grandmother here to guide me. Through any of it." She looked down at her hands as she traced her palm with her thumb. "It's killing me."

Torin took the crystal bottle from her hands and placed it on the ground. "That's not what's going to kill you." He stood straight, inching a little closer to her. "Your magic? It will break through when you need it most." He placed one hand on her shoulder, and the weight of it felt heavy on her bones, but oddly comforting. "Trust me."

He brushed her arm with his hand before he turned and walked away from her.

He was leaving…

Did she want him to? She couldn't speak to Gideon or Cally about this yet, and she needed someone to unload all this too. He was her safe option. He was the one who had kept her secret until now.

Weirdly, she came to the realisation that she didn't want him to leave. "I burned her gallery to the ground today."

That would get his attention!

"I burned down my grandmother's gallery." She laughed as she processed the overwhelming emotions pushing their way into the tear ducts of her eyes.

He stilled. Looking over his shoulder, he said, "That was you?" Something darkened in his eyes. Something that pulled her in, beckoned her towards him.

She nodded and swallowed. "It was her only instruction. Well, that, and for me to run and never look back."

For a second, he thought over what she said. "And are you going to run?"

Shaking her head, she said, "I don't want to run."

"Well, then, it's time to admit that it's the second time I have been impressed by you tonight." He turned from her again, taking steps towards the stairs.

She bit her lip.

"I think I know why you are upset tonight," the words rolled from her mouth quicker than she could stop them. His spine froze as his heavy legs came to a halt. "I know it's none of my business—but I think I know. Gideon told me that you are being forced to marry someone you don't love. And I just thought that maybe...maybe you should have someone that you can speak to about it."

He turned to face her, and she felt a heat crawl into her cheeks.

"I don't have anyone to speak to about this—this magic, this new world."

His lips parted, but he shut them tightly.

"And if you're feeling half of what I feel right now, not being able to talk about it to anyone..." Her hands clamped together as she put her words out there. To Torin. "If you are upset..."

His eyes dropped, like he dreaded to look at her after the words spilled from her mouth.

But she continued, "I know what it is like to not feel in control, and I don't have anyone to talk to about that—about who I truly am. And maybe you feel that way too."

"There's nothing to talk about. My fate is sealed, *remember?*"

Emptiness spilled into his eyes; his mouth parted as he tried to say something else but couldn't. Something inside Emara's heart broke as she finally understood that Torin was just as isolated as she was.

If not more.

At least she had Cally to talk to when the time was right. Someone who got her and always would. He was alone in a world where he shouldn't be. He couldn't make decisions about his own heart.

A feeling that sometimes threatened to consume Emara ached in her chest. As she stood in front of the warrior, with her mass of dark hair lashing at her back, she offered him a look of comfort, a plea to talk to her.

Torin hesitated for a long moment before turning his back on the offer, moving faster than she expected, and disappeared into the shadows of the staircase without a single word.

All the night offered Emara in return was the memory of the hauntingly beautiful stare of Torin Blacksteel.

CHAPTER TWENTY-NINE

When Emara had rolled over in bed as the sunrise broke through the night's darkness, a nest of blond hair had stolen her pillow. Happiness filled her heart as Cally slept beside her, still in the same blue dress from the night before. The fact that Cally had nestled her way into Emara's bed meant that there had been a silent peace offering between them, rendering their discord forgotten. Emara had quickly forced herself to get out of bed, get dressed, and head down the stairs to the dining hall. She picked up a few fruits from the kitchen on her way and headed to the sparring room, where she had planned to meet Gideon for another training session. Apparently, he was going to take this one easy on her.

Walking quickly reminded her that her muscles still ached from the training sessions yesterday, and when she arrived at the doors of the sparring room, they were locked.

"Mhm," she pondered. Gideon hadn't told her they would be training elsewhere. Looking around, she found a note pinned against the wall, advising that all training sessions with the Hunters were cancelled due to tonight's circumstances.

A splash of disappointment washed up in her chest. She had found that training was her only release at the moment, and she didn't like the idea of missing a full day of it. A full day of tempest thoughts with no training to take her mind from them... *Oh, Gods.*

"Emara, right?"

Emara swivelled at the sound of her name.

Kellen Blacksteel stood before her. *The youngest Blacksteel.*

"Yeah. It's Kellen, isn't it?" Emara offered a friendly smile.

He gave a gracious nod. "Gideon's tied up with my father. Even though all the general defence sessions are cancelled, he advised me that you would still be looking to train." His face held an impressed stare, like he had never known a girl who wanted to train. "You can join me if you like?"

Something about his demeanour was different from his brother's, but she couldn't put her finger on it. Maybe he didn't have the same confidence that the other Blacksteels did. Or maybe he was nervous for the up-and-coming hunt.

The Blood Moon would reach its full power tonight, meaning the hunt for the Dark Army was on. She had overheard Marcus talking yesterday, in the dining hall, that the Clan would be hunting tonight. It was their duty to make sure they ended the demons before they could spill any human blood.

A shudder ran through Emara's spine at the thought of the demons ploughing their way through more cities or villages. Villages like the one she had once stayed in—helpless, defenceless, and oblivious. She wondered how many more innocent lives would be lost tonight if the Clan didn't hunt them and kill the demons.

"I will join you." She motioned towards Kellen. "I don't mind doing my own thing, though; I know you will probably have something planned out and I am not sure I could keep up."

"It's cool. You will be able to do my session. Marcus usually trains me, but he is currently looking at the plan of action for tonight. Re-evaluating something, I guess." He held up a set of silver keys and dangled them in front of her. Kellen positioned himself in front of the door, opening it, and led the way in.

"I saw you training with Torin," Emara sparked some conversation with Kellen, wishing she could have avoided using Torin as an accessory in their common ground.

"Yeah, he's the toughest trainer we have. He doesn't allow weakness in the training room." Kellen forced a smile. "What can I expect? He was trained by Viktir Blacksteel, after all."

Viktir, not Father. Avoiding the parental terms, Emara noticed. Perhaps it was because his father had shipped his mother off now that he was a fully-fledged Hunter. Surely, the boys felt the adversities of that?

"I can't imagine what that would be like," she added gently. "Being trained by the Commander himself."

There was a true kindness in Kellen's face when he returned a soulful smile, but something else lingered behind his eyes. Immediately, Emara felt a pull on her heart. Kellen was different. He operated differently than his brothers. He couldn't mask his emotions the same way Torin or Gideon could, and his energy was different, radiating a softness that she hadn't seen in the others. Emara knew that Kellen's training would have determined him a lethal solider, to have been successful in Selection—he was a weapon to cause destruction and death—but his true soul still shone through.

Emara blinked as she watched Kellen set up his equipment, laying out weapons. Her eyes twisted as she followed him along the mats. A thin, white glow lifted from his being; a translucent aura that gleamed from his body. She scrunched her eyes shut and reopened them. The aura still leaked out around Kellen.

What in the underworld?

She blinked a few more times, rubbing at her eyes.

"Are you okay?" Kellen looked over at her with one eye of turquoise seas and the other of forest green moss. His eyes represented where the great oceans and land fused together.

She realised, awkwardly, that she had been staring at him. Fully gawking, but she couldn't shift the glow that filmed her eyes.

"I am fine," she lied, slightly embarrassed about being caught. "I am just a little all over the place."

"Okay." He laughed gently before proceeding on with his set up. "I am working on weights too. I saw you using a ten-kilo weight the other day…" Kellen lifted a heavier weight from the floor—it doubled hers. "You can start there, or you can start with a run."

"I think I will start with the weights."

"Good. I will move on to weaponry after weights and a spear, but I suppose you could pick up some agility training."

The word *wield* made her think of the magic that could, unknowingly, run through her veins. She thought of her own mother wielding fire from her palms. Her grandmother wielding the gift of air and water.

Magic wielders.

She shuddered.

As they got started, he instructed her in a warm-up that made each muscle want to remove itself from her body.

It was agonising.

And this was only the warm-up.

She would bathe later and soak each muscle in a roasting pool of rose buds and lavender oil as an apology.

After he was done with the weights, Kellen showed great ability to manipulate the spear around his hands. His feet were always fast and his jabs even faster. She couldn't help but watch him as he took off on his own path around the mats, his pretend opponents hanging weight bags. Opponents, that—come nightfall—would be raised from the depths of the underworld.

She followed him, studying his movements, and then replicating them on her own weight bag. Punching and kicking, without the spear. As his body moved, she swore she saw a blurring sensation pull away from his body like a soul is supposed to leave you in death.

She rubbed her eyes with one hand.

Had she gotten enough sleep last night? She re-focused and the aura was still present, translucent around Kellen's full body.

As if knowing eyes were glaring into his soul, Kellen stood stationary. "Are you sure you're okay? You're looking at me like you have seen a ghost." He walked towards her.

Her mouth struggled to say the words in disbelief, "Kellen, you are glowing."

The colour in his eyes faded, but he seemed to keep his face straight. The way he had been trained too.

"Have you hit your head recently?" he said, putting down his spear. "I saw you go over that vault pretty damn hard yesterday. Maybe we should get a healer to look at you."

"I am fine, thank you," she said, flustered. "I think I will just lie down for a bit. Bathe, maybe. I probably haven't eaten enough, or something."

His soft, adolescent features warmed into a smile. "I will tell Gideon he has been working you too hard."

She offered him a polite smile back, still noticing the glow, and then hurried from the room.

Emara palmed off her odd behaviour with Kellen as she opened the door to the infirmary room, putting it down to hardly obtaining any sleep last night.

"Where have you been?" Cally questioned, sitting up in the bed with her hair wild around her shoulders.

"I could ask you the same question, Miss Greymore, but I fear the answer," Emara joked, removing her training boots and sitting them neatly in the corner.

Cally's face lit up, her smeared-with-lipstick mouth ready to spill all her secrets of the night, "Wait until you hear what I have to say."

She very much doubted that Callyn's secrets would weigh more than her own.

Our dirty little secret.

"You are never going to believe it. Well, you might now that there are demons and the likes running around Mossgrave."

"Oh, Gods, where is this going?" Emara bounced on to the bed, overly eager to hear anything but Torin's self-loving voice in her mind.

"So, get this. *La Luna guy*, is actually *Shifter guy!*" Cally opened her mouth and placed her hands up to her cheeks for dramatic effect. Her eyebrows dropped as she took in Emara's face. "Why aren't you as shocked as I want you to be? Why has your jaw not hit the floor?" Cally's eyes narrowed as disappointment screwed into her features.

Emara took a deep breath and decided that, for her best friend, she would act surprised.

Just for her.

"Oh my—what? I was just processing it in my mind." She tried to line her words with incredulity. "A Shifter?"

"I know, right? I couldn't believe it. And he told me all about the other kind of creatures that walk amongst us in Caledorna. I mean, I don't want to use the word *creature* in case they totally get offended, but you know what I mean—people that are not *human*. I found out so much information last night, you would have been proud." She laughed as her shoulder popped up in delight. "I actually got to know him."

"I am *enormously* proud of you," Emara giggled back. "What other stuff did you find out?" she probed. Emara wondered what information a *Shifter* would be giving to a pretty blonde at a party.

Shifter...

She wondered if he was part of Breighly's pack or something else entirely. Was he another kind of Shifter? What other kinds of Shifters were out there? How dangerous could they be?

She shut the thoughts down before more anxiety tightened in her chest.

"He told me about all different kinds. Wolves, panthers, mountain lions, hawks—I was speechless. And it takes a lot for me to be speechless." Emara nodded in agreement at Cally's words. "He informed me that there are magical Houses of Witches. One of the Houses is basically a house of mermaids." She opened her mouth again and her eyes were wild with knowledge. "Can you believe it, Em? A fucking house of mermaids, is that not mad?!"

They weren't quite *mermaids,* but Emara wasn't going to burst her magical bubble.

Well, at least Callyn was all caught up. Now, all she had to do was tell her that she, too, was a part of that crazy world and her ex-boyfriend wanted to ruin her life. Her stomach flipped.

Tackle one at a time.

"And this is the best part: *Shifter guy* is going to be at this annual party that the Hunters throw to court the mermaids." She tucked a blonde strand of hair behind her ear—formally, like she hadn't just referred to the House of Water witches as mermaids. "And all the other witchy people will be there too. He asked me to go with him!" she squealed.

Emara blinked as she digested Cally's excitement mixed with her own apprehension.

"He is so gorgeous, he puts Torin to shame," she pouted. "Well, I am going to tell myself that; I have no other choice and it's not like *he* cares. Torin hasn't so much as looked at me since we were together." She looked down. "So, I will be there with my new *date.*" A light of thought went into her eyes. "Oh my gods, you should totally ask Gideon!" Her hands were on her face again, with her mouth open as before.

Emara rolled her eyes. "I will not be asking anyone." She paused. "Besides, Gideon already asked me." She gestured over to the singular white rose that stood in a clear vase on the windowsill. Cally's eyes zoomed from Emara to the rose and back again.

"He gave you a rose *and* asked you to go to the uplift?" Cally let the excitement overwhelm her. "This is like true love."

"Alright, calm down! He didn't so much as ask me, but he may have *insinuated* that it would be more bearable if I was there."

"This is massive, Emara!" Cally looked her best friend in the face. "You haven't so much as gagged or made that stupid face you do when you are grossed out. And here you are staring at a rose that Gideon Blacksteel gave you. Gods, Taymir used to get you gigantic bouquets of all different kinds of flowers and you wouldn't even look at them. You would give them to me to put in my room," she snorted.

"Don't mention him." Emara's eyes closed in disgust at his name.

Cally's brows pulled in, and she sat back on the bed. "That's twice you have flinched when I have said his name. What's going on?"

And here it was. The window of opportunity to talk, but somehow her throat closed. Cally, noticing Emara's struggle, moved closer on the bed and grabbed her hand. "You can tell me *anything*. I am here."

And so, she did. She retold every word, every punch, every part of her that felt ashamed and disgusted with what Taymir had done. Every struggle and fear came flooding out. She told her everything. When she was done, they both sat in silence before Cally jumped onto her knees and threw her arms around Emara.

"If I ever see that son of a wealthy bitch again, I will stab him myself," Cally promised.

"He's not worth it. He won't bother me again. Not after what Gideon threatened."

"But still, I promise to make his life hell. Maybe one day, I will get the chance to tailor his formal wear and as I am doing it, I can stab him in the genitals with my sowing needle."

Emara cut a small laugh from her throat and then for a few moments, only her heartbeat could be heard.

Cally, somehow understanding Emara was done with the conversation, took it in a different direction, "I am surprised Gideon didn't end him, anyway. Speaking of the middle Blacksteel..." Cally laughed lightly. Testing the waters, she pointed at the vase. "You clearly have feelings for him, otherwise you would have chucked that rose in the garbage. It's okay to let him in, he's one of the good ones."

"I know he is…"

He might be one of the good ones, but is he the right one? she asked herself. *Would he set my soul on fire?*

Emara continued, "I don't think that's what I need right now."

"It's exactly what you need right now. Guys come with great distractions."

"Somehow, I don't think that's quite how the saying goes, Callyn."

"Well, whatever it is..." Cally flashed a smile. "What are you waiting for? Let's get down to the Markets and get us *amazing* dresses for the uplift. Treat's on me. Picture me in this dress... white and silk, like I am a virgin, but I would totally sleep with you after a few glasses of wine kind of vibe. Do you know what I mean?" Cally traced her hands down her sides and moved her hips.

"I have absolutely no idea what you mean," Emara laughed. "As great as that sounds, the Blood Moon reaches its full strength tonight; we shouldn't be going anywhere," her tone took a more serious approach.

"I can tell you one thing; no moon is coming in between me and a killer dress. Demons are not going to be invading the Markets! It's littered with supernatural people who would kill them." She smirked. "I will be safe. Plus, Waylen might take me before dusk."

"Waylen? Did you actually learn *La Luna guy's real* name?"

Now she *was* shocked.

"Yes, I did, believe it or not. I did tell you I got to know him." She primed her face angelically. "You would be shocked with the new leaf I have turned." Proud of herself, she flicked her hair over her shoulder.

Emara looked at her best friend as a smile formed, lighting up her face. "Who even are you?"

"Callyn *fucking* Greymore, that's who. The same girl who is about to get you *the* most amazing dress from the markets that you have ever worn, and you can thank me later." She bounced up from the bed. "See you when I get back." She curtsied in jest. "Before dusk."

Callyn was out the door in seconds.

No matter what Emara said, Callyn wouldn't stay in tonight, but she had promised Gideon that *she* would. After what happened at her grandmother's house, she wasn't ready to see any more red eyes or blood-drinking freaks any time soon. Maybe Cally found healing in her new-found freedom.

But tonight, the Tower was the safest place to be. And that's where Emara was staying.

CHAPTER THIRTY

Gideon left the final briefing before tonight's hunt with a slight unease. As he walked with Marcus to the dining hall for dinner, he ran over the meeting in his head. Viktir had been truly clear in what was to be done tonight. He always was. But something was off.

Marcus had handed out a detailed map that he had constructed with Murk Baxgroll, the pack's Alpha, for them to study. The clan was going into the Ashdale Forest to hunt and everyone in Caledorna knew that it was Shifter territory.

Wolfen territory.

Murk had also joined the briefing, advising that his pack would be on the lookout for anything that moved in their woods that wasn't supposed to. The pack had noticed a large increase of animal slaughtering in their woods, which was a sign that demons were taking up residence, hiding in the trees waiting to strike. The demons were gathering strength, consuming whatever blood they could get their hands on before they attacked. Murk had advised that he wasn't quite sure how many demons could be lurking within the Ashdale Forest, as the area was vast and deep, expanding for miles each side, so he had pulled his pack together to work with the Hunters to rid Ashdale of them.

A clever move from the Alpha.

It increased the numbers on their side and Gideon was keen to fight with the wolves; it would hopefully make the hunt sleek and quick, plus it had been a long time since they had joined forces.

Not only that, but he seemed to have other things on his mind that didn't involve arrows and gore, but instead, involved full, red lips and a flowing abundance of black hair, mixed up in his hands.

"I think the hunt should be swift tonight," confirmed Marcus. "I know it's a Blood Moon, and it usually causes chaos, but I think the Hunters merging with the wolves will be deadly." A coolness washed over his face. "For the demons."

Marcus lived and breathed for the hunt. A man who had been shunned by his own father for not making the top one in the Selection process, he was dumped on the doorstep of his father's closest cousin—which just so happened to be Viktir Blacksteel.

Marcus' father had sent him with nothing but a note that instructed Viktir to train him, to evolve his skills and make him a warrior fit for the top selection. And he had.

In doing so, Viktir claimed him for his own. If he trained with the Blacksteel Clan, he fought for the Blacksteel Clan; therefore, Marcus never returned to his family in the west.

However, a Hunting clan was a Hunting clan, no matter where they came from. Their sole purpose was to defend this world until they took their last breath.

It wasn't a longshot to say that Viktir was rather fond of Marcus for proving himself worthy. He was a Blacksteel out of blood. Marcus often teased Gideon about the brutality of his training from Viktir as a boy, stating that Gideon's, in comparison, was a walk in the gardens.

But everyone knew that Viktir Blacksteel's training was no walk in the gardens.

"We shouldn't count our chickens before they have hatched—you taught me that. 'Expect the unexpected.'" Gideon quoted Marcus' words back to him in a voice that sounded just like him.

"Boy, you better not be making a fool of me. I taught you how to shoot an arrow exactly through the point you aim it at, don't forget that" He joked as he swaggered down the corridor.

"I won't forget it." Gideon was serious. He wouldn't forget the work Marcus had put in to ensure Gideon would make the top one in Selection. To ensure, he wouldn't suffer the same fate as him.

"I still remember the first time you shot your first bullseye like it was yesterday. And then ripped your hand open on the fighting knife in your belt." Marcus boomed out a hearty laugh that made his brown eyes close. "You got so excited, you forgot your weapon belt was still attached, and when you danced around—"

"I was *eight* years old," Gideon challenged. A laugh came from Marcus before they settled into a walk. "Do you feel like something is off tonight?" He turned to his brother.

"Like I said, it should be an easy win with the wolves helping out. Just keep your mind in check. Keep focus. Don't let *anything* distract you." He moved in front of Gideon and folded his arms, blocking his way.

Gideon ran a hand through his hair, remaining calm. "I am always focused. What are you talking about?"

He let out a laughy breath. "All I am saying is, I've been there before. Every guy has. We all know what it is like to be *distracted.*" He smirked. "You have a couple of hours to get your head straight before we leave for the hunt. If I were you"—Marcus hinted, raising his eyebrows—"I would go and take care of that *situation.*"

"I don't know what you are talking about." Gideon swallowed the lie down his throat. "There is no *situation.*"

"Gideon, I have seen you with her. I saw you in the gardens with her yesterday, in fact. All you need to do is tell her how you feel and then it's gone. Off your chest. Get it out there. Or get it in there, if you know what I mean…" Marcus slapped Gideon's shoulder.

Was Marcus really insinuating that he should have sexual relations to calm his mind?

His face felt a little flushed. "Of course I comprehend what you are trying to *insinuate,* but nothing is going on." He pushed all his weight onto his feet, pulling his toes back in his boots.

Gideon wasn't concerned about his concentration regarding the Blood Moon mission. What Gideon couldn't take his mind off of was his mission under the confidential orders of his commander. And no matter how he felt about it, no matter how much it made his skin prickle with a cold sweat, he would complete the mission without question.

Even if it did involve Emara Clearwater…

"Gideon, I am a man. You are a man."

"Thank you for stating the obvious, Marcus."

"I know what happens when a man comes across a girl like Emara Clearwater and all I am saying is if you take care of it, the *itch* will disappear." A lazy smile spread across his face and Gideon didn't have to guess twice what he was thinking about. "Trust me."

"I am not talking about this with you. Thanks for the advice, Marcus, but no thanks." He pushed his lips into a thin line that allowed his cheeks to dimple and then let the west corridor lead him to the infirmary, in the opposite direction of where his mind told him to go.

Marcus did have a point…

Maybe he could talk to Emara. Maybe that was all he needed to clear his mind.

Gideon placed his hands on the wooden door outside Emara's room and braced himself against it. He knew he shouldn't be here before the hunt, but he had convinced himself it was the best option. Maybe Marcus was right. Maybe he did have to get the bubbling sensation of feelings off his chest. Maybe that would help for now.

Thoughts of what Viktir had instructed him to do haunted him. He had given him a task that was to be completed after the Blood Moon battle. A task that didn't sit well with him. But it was to be done, regardless. It was a mission only Viktir and Gideon knew about. Not even Torin knew.

This was a mistake, he thought as he looked at the door. Conflict boiled underneath his skin. He craved a little bit more of her every time he saw her. But he shouldn't. What he should be doing right now is polishing his fighting knives and readying his leathers or prepping his arrows. Or taking a shower. Or reading a Gods-damned book!

Anything but being here.

He pulled himself up straight and inhaled deeply, air filling his lungs, expanding his chest out.

You are a man. It is normal to feel this way.

It was normal for his blood to thicken every time he thought of her. It was normal to want to get to know her. Be around her. Even if it wasn't part of the mission for him to actually *feel* something real. But he did feel something real…

All you need to do is tell her how you feel.

Really, Marcus? That was his advice?

But he couldn't, could he? It wouldn't be fair for her for him to tell her his real feelings.

He promised himself one last encounter with her before his mission started properly. Then he would promise himself to keep his feelings for her contained. He just needed one last moment that wasn't pretending. He pulled his fist up to knock on the door and it flew open.

"Gideon," she breathed. The melody of her voice glided through his ears as she spoke his name. Surprise lit up her face. Her black lashes framed the curve in her eye so beautifully.

"I was going to knock, I promise." He tilted his head to the side and offered her a boyish grin.

Cool and collected, he reminded himself. *Stay cool and collected.*

"I'm sure you were." Her gaze lifted to his hand that was still clenched into a fist, hovering above her face. He dropped his arm instantly.

"What are you doing here?" she asked.

"Well, um, that I am not sure of." He gulped, knowing he couldn't say what he wanted to as she stared right into his eyes. By Thorin almighty, she was beautiful. He had to say something. "Are you going somewhere? Because I can come back. Well, actually, I can't come back tonight because obviously I will be on the hunt and, um…" He trailed off as he drove his eyes to the ground.

Damn it, Marcus! He had gotten into his head. He couldn't wait to get him into the sparring room tomorrow to show him how to scratch an itch…with his fist.

Her brow pulled down. "Are you okay? You're acting weird. Is it Cally?"

Even in panic, her voice still sung through him, causing the pressure in his chest to loosen slightly.

What was he doing? His control over himself was weakening by the second. This wasn't cool and collected. He was a trained warrior, Gods damn it, and he could tell a girl how he felt.

"I just thought that I would be—I—I was thinking..." He scratched his head, hoping it would reveal the words he needed to find. Words that wouldn't make him come across as idiotic as he did now. He could even envision Torin standing over his left shoulder with a mocking grin as he cheered him on. *Smooth, Gideon, real smooth. Do you want me to do it for you?*

"*No!*" spilled out like word vomit.

Shock sprung into Emara's eyes. All he could do was offer her a sheepish grin and raise his shoulders to his ears as heat sweltered his face.

"Gideon, is this about what happened in the gardens?" Embarrassment swept across her face. "Because if it was too much, it doesn't ever have to happen again." She looked down. "Just spit it out."

"Yes, it is about what happened in the gardens," he blurted out. "Kind of."

She crossed her arms over her chest and popped out a hip.

"But just to clarify, I do want it to happen again. The kiss…I have relived that moment over and over in my head since it happened. When we are together, I get this feeling in my gut." He watched her as he told her the truth, living fully in this moment, "A really good feeling." He watched as her features changed. She smiled back, giving him an encouraging push. "I guess I am here because I want to let you know something. I

know we haven't known each other all that long, but—
"

"But what?"

"I like you." His gaze held hers. "I like you a lot and I know I shouldn't. I know I am not supposed to, but I just feel this pull towards you and I can't explain it. I shouldn't have kissed you in the gardens, but I couldn't stop myself. It's like my body won't listen to my mind and I had to kiss you."

She stood in silence.

He didn't know if it was seconds or hours that had passed by as she watched him before her lips parted, and she spoke.

"I *liked* that we kissed in the gardens." She angled her body towards him. "I also like it when we spend time together. And when you push your hand through my hair…"

I'm in trouble.

He had half expected her to make this easier for him and turn him away. But she felt the same. His body urged to go to her. He closed the gap between them, standing only an inch from her face.

"Like this?" He raised his hand into her hair, cradling her skull, pushing through her silky locks.

She melted her body into his, her soft curves contrasting against his hard frame.

"Yes," she whispered. Her body rested against his, causing him to feel all of her.

He swallowed, trying to control himself.

Why was this harder than one of Viktir's outside endurance sessions in the depths of winter? He shouldn't be doing this, but he couldn't stop.

The guilt of knowing what he needed to do was weighing him down. She didn't deserve this, even if what he was feeling and had said were true.

"I had to tell you how I felt before I leave tonight. That's why I am here."

"Thank you for telling me. But why do I get the feeling that you are saying goodbye?"

His jawline hardened. "Whatever happens tonight, stay in here. There are always Hunters who stay at the Tower to protect it, but don't go walking around."

"I don't go walking around."

"Marcus informed me otherwise," he challenged.

She rolled her eyes, clearly knowing that he knew about her expedition out of the Tower for hours.

"I just don't want to be worrying about you whilst I am out there."

"I understand." She nodded, lowering her head. From this angle, it looked like her cheekbones pushed out from her face more than they usually did and he lifted his hand up to cup her cheek.

"Will you wait up for me?" The deceit of the question lay thick on his heart. He knew what he had to do when he came back. He had to complete the mission for Viktir. Find what he was looking for…

He breathed hard as he took in the details of her face again. Did he have to end it? Maybe once the mission was complete he could tell her everything and she would understand. Or maybe he wouldn't even have to tell her. Hope swelled in his heart. That could be a possibility. No one had to know. Once the mission was done, the deceit could fade into everyday life and be forgotten.

"You want me to wait up tonight?" She inched her face closer, making it even more difficult not to pull her into him completely and kiss her. He could feel himself ducking closer to her lips, but he refrained from brushing them with his.

"Yes, tonight," he confirmed. "We think it will be a quick hunt with the wolves involved. And I want to see you again."

For the longest moment, he wished that the Commander had gotten Torin to do the mission. He would have been so much better at it. He didn't allow himself to get feelings. Ever. Nothing got in his way.

"I will wait for you." She nodded.

Guilt ripped through him, almost splitting him in half. Why did she have to be so Gods-damned beautiful? And not only that, but a lovely person, too. A frown darkened his face. Viktir was testing him, and he knew it.

"What's wrong?" she whispered. "You are acting really strange." A gentle laugh passed her lips.

"I was just nervous about telling you how I felt," he acknowledged the truth in what he said. "That's all."

"Oh," she said, looking at her hand that now held his shoulder. "It is never easy to admit what is in your heart."

He reached out, and pulled her closer. "I meant what I said." Their eyes connected and her beautiful irises, that he noticed often changed colour, appeared a soft pastel blue. *Does that mean she's happy?* "I meant all of it. No matter what happens, okay?" She probably thought he was saying goodbye to her in the chance that he didn't come back from tonight's hunt. "I will see you tonight," he said finally.

He leaned in and kissed her on the forehead. As his lips touched her skin, he knew his mission lay within this very room. A mission that, with every cell in his body, felt immoral.

But he would do it anyway.

Because the command came from Viktir Black-steel.

CHAPTER THIRTY-ONE

I have been expecting you," said a woman in a deep red cloak, standing at the exit of the Solden diamond mines. "You are a little later than requested. Nevertheless, I knew you would come. You wouldn't be foolish enough not to."

Even in the dark mist of the night, she could see that he was wounded. Taymir Solden limped his injured body over to her. Close, but not close enough to touch her. He would never have dared. She would have incinerated him within seconds for even attempting to come closer. He had witnessed what she could do. What power she had.

"I am afraid I have some bad news to deliver," Taymir spoke with utter dread.

She could taste it on her tongue, bitter and potent. She drank in the fear that poured from him and savoured every drop.

"I know about your news, Little Solden." She clicked her tongue. "He's not going to be happy, our Dark King. Is he now?" She walked towards him. Her brittle hand came out from underneath her cloak. With the smallest tilt of her wrist, Taymir's windpipe collapsed in his throat. "I think it is time for our plan B, my little pet. Or maybe your services have run their course?" Although he couldn't see her eyes under the cloak, her smile was malevolent, and she showed him every tooth. "What say you?"

Taymir clawed at his throat, desperately trying to allow any particles of air into his lungs. His face was past the stage of red, almost going purple by the time she tilted her wrist again, giving him the gift of breath. She pouted. It would have been fun to see what colour he went before his lungs gave out. *Shame* she needed him.

Oxygen crashed into Taymir's lungs and he gasped for life. "I'm sorry, I will do better."

"You failed us," she spoke calmly. "Twice now." Walking over to him, his body began to shake, although he tried to fight it. "If the third time is not a charm, little Solden, I will make you regret the day you were born." She ran a hand over his shoulders. "You will cease to exist. What we are promising you, if you succeed, is not to be taken lightly. But you know that." She dug her dark nails into his back and he cried out in pain. "Don't you, my little pet?"

"Yes," he panted. "I will fix this, I promise."

She always did like to see an Elite squirm. Males like the Soldens basically ruled the realm with the only power they had—coin. Those who could take from the earth's materials and turn it into coin were always powerful through wealth.

She allowed a wicked smile to snake onto her lips. But there was one thing human males didn't have over her, and that was her magic. She, too, could draw from the earth, the elements, and crush worlds with her power. Or she used to be able to…

She twisted her wrist again, pulling the air from his lungs, reminding herself of her strength. Taymir choked and spluttered.

"Don't forget who you are dealing with," she reminded him. "The coin that smothers your life in gold and riches won't save you in my world." She released his airway. "Obeying him will."

"I know who and what I am dealing with," he gasped through staggered breath. "Please let me show you my worth. I can do this." He rubbed his neck. "I have a plan."

"You better hope so, my darling Taymir," she purred. "For I can burst your heart with the click of my fingers." She licked her lips at the thought. "And that is something Daddy Solden will never have enough coin to buy you a new one."

"I know what needs to be done. My heart shall remain intact." He paused. "Even when it stops beating." An arrogant smile appeared on his face.

She let out a low laugh. "Your heart remains in your chest...for now."

Stupid mortals, always getting themselves knee-deep in the darkest ventures of immortality.

"Do we have a deal?" He searched for a slither of hope.

"I will be in touch."

And just like that, she dematerialised in front of him and disappeared into the smoke and shadows of the diamond mines.

332

CHAPTER THIRTY-TWO

After he left the infirmary, Gideon organised himself for the hunt, doing anything he could to straighten out his mind for tonight. Reluctantly, he pushed his thoughts of Emara to the back of his mind like he had been trained to do.

No distractions. Not even the secret mission. Nothing! The hunt came first. It always had and it always would.

He pulled his black tunic over his head and tucked it into his leathers, providing a cushion for his weapon belt to sit on. Over this tunic he placed a protective leather gilet. Drawing a set of arrows from the drawer, he stroked one finger along the shafts and lingered at the point.

Sharp enough to cut through anything.

It didn't take much to hype Gideon up for the hunt, natural adrenaline took over. It never had been a problem for any of the Clan. All he had to do was smell that sulfuric, repugnant stink and he wouldn't bat an eyelid as he removed them from the earth, blow by blow to the heart. Or maybe the skull, depending on his angle. He strapped his bow across his chest, feeling the pump of his heart kick through his veins. He kinked his neck from side to side and strapped on his black, leather fighting gloves that allowed the tips of his fingers to peek through. He shoved his feet into his shin-length boots that laced up the front to protect his leg bones from breakage. He handled a few of his weapons before he shoved them into his belt and left the room.

As he made his way to the foyer where every Hunter had been instructed to be standing after dusk, he heard his father's voice coming from an office space that wasn't his own.

He paused.

"Rhea, I want you to ready as many beds as you can for our return. Get the medical supplies now and keep some in the foyer."

He didn't hear Rhea's response, but he predicted that she would have nodded politely and got to work straight away. Gideon flung himself against the wall as his father emerged from the door in his combat gear. He didn't want his father to think that he was listening in on their conversation, so he opted not to be seen. To be a shadow in the Tower. It's a good thing the sun had made its way to the earth, casting shades in the poorly lit corridors, or his father would have caught him eavesdropping.

Why was his father in leathers and strung with weapons? Was he fighting tonight? Viktir Blacksteel hadn't fought in several years. He hadn't been required to. He had done his time in the hunt, therefore he left it to the fresher recruits. Something felt off about his father in fighting gear.

"Father!" Gideon took off into a jog to catch up with him. "Father!"

Viktir didn't turn as he stalked down the corridor. "Gideon, shouldn't you be in the foyer already?" His tone was harsh and impatient. "And you are on duty—therefore, it's Commander to you."

"I had to go back for one of my throwing knives," he lied. "I picked up the wrong one."

"Carelessness will get you killed, Gideon." His father didn't slack on his strides as he powered down the hallway. "Besides, you can never have too many knives on you."

Gideon ignored what he said and asked, "Are you fighting tonight?"

"Yes," the commander snapped.

The pack was supporting the Hunters tonight— a lethal combination. Surely, he wasn't required.

"Why are you fighting, Father?" His features twisted as he tried to process it. "Sorry—Commander Blacksteel."

If he was truly needed, was there something that Gideon didn't know? Something that wasn't covered in the briefing?

His father's solid build came to a halt. "It would suit you better to concentrate on yourself rather than questioning me. That's when you make mistakes, boy. When you have too much going on up here"—he tapped his temple—"you make mistakes." He drew in a breath. "You can't even show up with the right weapons." His father looked him dead in the eye. "Get to the foyer; I will see you in Ashdale."

Gideon tore his eyes away from his father's sharp face and sprinted into a jog. He knew a deflection when he saw one, and that had been a deflection on his father's part. Viktir had trained him in how to do the same thing to avoid capture from an enemy or to withhold any information he didn't want his enemy to know if arrest was inevitable.

However, Viktir was right. Now wasn't the time to get caught up in who should be fighting. He knew where he was supposed to be during the hunt and that's what mattered. He had memorised it for days, looking at the maps and taking the details and coordinates from Murk's inside information.

As he got to the foyer, Marcus and Torin were loading the wagons with spare equipment and weapons. Ten or eleven Hunters remained in the foyer in silence, probably going over the plan in their minds. The others were already waiting in the wagons.

"You're late," Torin shouted as he sheathed his double swords into their holdings on his back. Torin was ready for a war tonight. Gideon noticed twice as many weapons on his belt as usual.

"Well, it makes a change from you." He stepped out from the foyer and closed in on the wagon.

"Sort out the head?" Marcus flung a grin towards him.

Gideon ignored Marcus as he took his seat in the back of the wagon. Torin also flung an unusual stare his way. It wasn't dripping in antagonism, but wonder.

Whatever that meant, Torin didn't get the chance to start his sarcastic questioning, as the last of the brotherhood piled into the back of the wagon.

"I'm driving." Marcus let out a cat-like grin as he slammed the wagon doors shut.

Darkness invaded the space, but Gideon welcomed it. It gave him more time to get into the zone and find the space in his head where he went to hunt. He rested his skull against the frame of the wagon and closed his eyes—not to rest them, but so that he could visualise her one last time before he went to battle.

He wasn't stupid, he knew he put his life in the hands of the Gods every time he entered a hunt. So he thought of something that made him feel normal, made him feel like it was all for *something*.

When the wagon began to move a second later, she was gone, pushed into a secret cave in his mind.

Now, the Blood Moon hunt began.

The Ashdale Forest was deathly quiet as the Hunters worked their way from their base point to their end point, meeting the Shifters at a plain of field suggested by Murk. The only light that was provided through the trees was by the moon herself. An orange-red glow broke through the branches, casting a haunting light over the Clan's faces as they moved as one unit in silence.

Gideon praised the blood that ran through his veins that allowed him to have excellent vision, even in the dark.

Torin came to a standstill at the front of the formation, flanked by Marcus and his father on the other side. A few of the Clan had spread out on an eastern and western circumference, walking sideways to ensure nothing could attack from the side. Kellen had been positioned in the middle of the formation to allow him time to ease into the fight should there be an outbreak of violence.

And there would be.

The other men scattered in between the structure to deepen the protection. Gideon patrolled the back end of the formation, paying close attention to the tail of the Clan and the trees above. They would show themselves one way or another, he just didn't know where or when.

Torin's hand flew up to indicate that the full unit was to cease. Gideon's knees locked in as he braced himself into a fighting position. His bow was already itching to be released. His brother raised one finger which meant Viktir and Marcus were to ready themselves. Bending their legs, they both slid into a position that Gideon had held more times than he could count—a battle stance. He made sure to keep himself alert, even if Torin's signal had turned his stomach into a butter churner.

Gideon's eyes scanned the trees above the Clan. A rustle came from a giant buckthorn bush out in front. Gideon's finger hooked even tighter around the string, his arm pulled back, ready for his arrow to penetrate through flesh.

Dirty blonde hair glistened in the moonlight as a female emerged from the bush.

"Breighly Baxgroll," Viktir gasped as she moved forward and pulled herself up straight. "We could have killed you. What are you doing out here?" His eyes narrowed in on her face.

She glanced over the Clan, her face unreadable. "I have come here tonight to ask that you let me fight alongside you." Her pale blue eyes pleaded with the Commander. "I want you to let me fight with you. I can fight, Commander Blacksteel." She didn't break his gaze. "Murk wouldn't agree that I fight alongside them, so I thought I would come to you. You are the Commander of this hunt."

"*Murk* is your father, the Alpha, and he should be addressed as such." The words lingered in the dark air of the forest. "What he says, goes," Viktir snapped. "You should not be out here."

"With all due respect, Commander Blacksteel, these are my woods just as much as they are his. I know them like the back of my hand. Let me protect them." Her eyes glittered with a security that one didn't always find in a young woman of her age. "My father shouldn't be the one deciding if I can fight. I should be the one to make that decision." Her eyes darted over the Clan. A wealth of passion lingered on her face and Gideon smiled as his father shut his mouth into a pruned line. "You could reason with him on my behalf."

"We are on our way to meet him now." Her eyes met Gideon's as he spoke. "As I am sure you are more than aware."

The love that used to shine in her wolf-like eyes for him was gone. She didn't respond as she trailed her eyes along his face. Giving him a slight nod in thanks, she turned her gaze back to the Commander.

"We can't stand here wasting time, Viktir; we are sitting ducks," Marcus stressed.

Viktir threw a look to Torin as if to say, '*Your call, make the decision.*'

Torin had been leading most of the hunts since Viktir had aged. Not that his father couldn't handle the fight of the hunt, because he could, but as a right of passage for Torin who would one day be the Commander of the Blacksteel Clan. If he made any mistake, his father wanted that to be on his head to learn the importance of leadership. Or the harsh unpleasantries that came with being in charge. Like making split second decisions that could end a Clan member's life or destroy an alliance. He had to learn the ropes of Hunter politics.

"There's no way a girl can fight with the Clan," a Hunter from the mid-section piped up.

"How much coin would you like to bet on that, Hunter?" Breighly pinned him with a brown-gold stare.

"Make the call, Torin," Viktir nipped.

If Torin didn't allow her to fight with them, she would have to make her way back to her home— alone—in a forest filled with the Darkened.

"Get to the back." Torin lowered his voice. "Let's see what the Alpha has to say about this."

She stepped forward with confidence. Her shoulder-length hair was already pulled back for the fight. She had come ready, Gideon realised, like there was no way she was leaving here without getting her way. As she slipped to the back of the formation, she mouthed "Hi" to Gideon and took a place beside him.

"You're crazy," he lowered his voice enough for only Breighly to hear. "You shouldn't be out here."

"You're crazy to think I shouldn't be here."

"I think the pack would be enough without adding their *princess* into the hunt," Gideon teased.

"Princess," she scoffed. "Do you think a princess would have claws like mine?" Her eyes danced with a confidence that told him she knew how dangerous she could be. "Trust me, *you* need me."

"What is that supposed to mean?" Gideon shot her a confused look.

"If I can put you on your ass"—she smiled mockingly—"so can any demon."

She crouched a little lower as they walked through the forest. Torin had commanded to start the unit moving before Gideon spoke. "You haven't fought me since I was fifteen years old," he fired back. "A lot has changed."

"What's that stupid Hunter saying again? 'You're all the man you will ever be as you enter the Selection.'" She laughed. "I bet you a gold coin a stupid man came up with that *stupid* saying."

"It's not stupid," Gideon defended. "It's an honour to be considered a man at the age of fifteen." He paused. "Plus, I always let you win."

She scoffed, "Let me win, my ass."

Gideon threw her a look.

"You're just defensive because we went from fighting to fuc—"

"Shut up and keep your eyes straight ahead," Gideon cut her off. She pushed her tongue along her teeth and a smile formed. "You wolves can't keep your mind out of the gutter and stay focused on the mission," he finished.

"Sure thing, Giddy," she mocked.

"Don't call me that!" he hissed.

A snigger broke from her lips and he knew she so desperately wanted to say that ridiculous nickname again—but she refrained.

As they walked through the woods, Breighly didn't say another word as she kept her attention on the surrounding forest. With her wolf-sight, she would be able to see through the darkness clearer than anyone else here. And that was why it was crucial to fight with the wolves tonight.

As they reached the clearing, they tightened their form, just like they had been shown in the briefing room. As the space was wide open, this reduced the risk of anyone being intercepted. Murk had advised they would be waiting, and they were.

Viktir picked up his pace until he was beside Torin at the front. Marcus kept the distance between them, knowing his rank within the Clan.

"Commander Blacksteel" Murk nodded. "We should let you know we have already killed two on our journey to the clearing. They took the form of—"

And then Murk Baxgroll paused. He stiffened and his eyes darted to the back of the formation.

"Breighly..." His dark eyes changed from shock to anger, causing his features to form into a scowl. "What in the underworld are you doing here?"

She puffed out her shoulders. "If you won't let me fight with you, I will fight with the Hunters."

Gideon had to admit, he had always admired how brave Breighly was, even as a child. No one challenged the Alpha and lived.

Except her.

"That's not how it works. We have been over this," Murk growled. "It is not your place to fight—"

"Because I am a woman?" she interrupted, raising her chin. Fury started to steam off Murk's face, causing the other pack members to shift uncomfortably. "Is it because I am a woman, Father? Is that what you mean to imply?"

Murk's broad shoulders lifted up in anger as he blew out a puff of air, causing it to wander into the night air.

"Answer me," she demanded. "I am capable of fighting, Father, and you Gods-damned know it. You taught me, so..."

Gideon knew that if it weren't his only daughter confronting him like this, her head would have been ripped from her body and left for the pack to snack on by now. But, being his little princess, she could always wrap him around her little paw.

"This is not up for discussion; get yourself home," he snarled.

"What is up for discussion is the fact that you still treat me like I am a little girl and not a woman who could kick any one of these Hunters asses."

A snuff came from the crowd, but no one said anything. A pack member even let out a chuckle at her boldness.

"Let me fight. I know these woods better than most, it is an advantage in this hunt."

"No." Murk ground his teeth together.

Her nose wrinkled, letting a little part of rage slip through her cool exterior. "I am a wolf. A wolf, regardless of my gender." She lifted her gaze. "I am the same as my brothers. The same as you."

A flicker of acknowledgement flamed in the Alpha's eyes, revealing respect, but it was gone before he spoke. "For once in your life, Breighly, do as you are told." His hands started forming into claws at his side. Gideon watched as the Shifter tried to control his anger to stop the transformation. The shift from human to wolf. "Do *not* push me."

The strength in her voice confirmed that she was not backing down, "Pushing the boundaries is the only way a woman can make a path for herself in this world." She raised her chin.

Gideon ran his eyes to where his father stood. For once, there was no challenge in Viktir's eyes.

"It's the only way you will see me as a member of this pack and not your baby girl. You let my brothers fight with no questions asked. Do the same for me."

A pulse formed in the Alpha's neck as he ground his teeth again. Although he wasn't in his wolf form now, Gideon could see the feral behaviours pushing their way to the surface.

Breighly was right, though, it should be her choice to fight. It should be her choice to do whatever the hell she pleased. "She's good enough, Baxgroll," Gideon said. "I know she is."

"That's not your call, Blacksteel," a voice growled from the pack. Waylen Baxgroll walked forward, joining the Alpha—his father.

"No, but it's mine," Torin scowled. "Here's a thought," he spoke, taking centre stage like he always did, swaggering up too close to the pack. "Instead of bitching about who can fight, let's crack on with it. It won't matter in the long run if a female fights tonight or not. If we don't take care of the situation now"—he looked past Breighly's older brother and locked gazes with the Alpha—"demons will swarm these lands and even the *children* will have to fight them off. So, what does it matter if a woman wants to fight?" he challenged.

A shiver spread across Gideon's shoulders at the thought. Untrained children falling to the soulless demons who would drink them dry of their blood if they got the chance.

"I say we let the little wolf fight and get on with it."

He flung a charming grin Breighly's way and she responded with a wink. Her face lit up with promise.

"Let her fight, Father!" another member of the pack shouted from behind the Alpha. Gideon realised it had come from Roman, Breighly's twin brother.

"No chance," Waylen snarled.

"She's a hunter in a different form," another wolf added. "Let her fight."

Gideon's eyes darted to the last of Breighly's brothers, Eli. So, she had *some* support from her brothers in the pack. The Alpha tensed for a second that felt like an hour, turning over his decision.

He ducked his chin in acceptance and flicked his eyes to Torin. "If any blood from my baby girl is spilled, it will be on your hands. And if it does, we will tear you limb from limb." Murk's threat rumbled through the night. Her brothers growled in agreement.

Torin's face geared up into a wicked grin as he looked the pack's Alpha in the eye, the strongest shifter in the Kingdom, and said, "Deal."

A dangerous smile danced across Breighly's face and in that moment, she craned her neck back, tipping her hair all the way down past her shoulder blades, and let out a howl. Members of her pack followed, sending up their signal to the Blood Moon.

The deal was on; Breighly Baxgroll would join her pack in the hunt.

Just then, crunching broke through the howls to the right of the clearing. Every member of the hunt snapped their attention to the trees that now looked like they had come alive in the dark. Before Gideon could even make out what was moving, his legs were on the go and his hand plunged to his belt for a fighting knife.

His blood tingled like it always did when demons were near. It was time to fight.

CHAPTER
THIRTY-THREE

Gideon plummeted to the ground, flinging out his right foot to sweep the demon's legs out from underneath it. The right side of his body slid along the wet grass and collided with bone and rotten flesh. The demon flew into the air and landed right beside him on the ground. Rolling over into a springing position, Gideon drove a blade through the demon's skull. A cracking shuddered all the way up his arm as he withdrew the blade from bone and was on the move again. He drew a throwing knife from his belt, flicked his wrist, and let it go, catapulting the knife through the air. It landed in a demon's chest. The demon fell to the ground, black gunge pouring from its heart.

As he looked around, the pack had shifted to their wolf forms and were pouncing onto anything that moved from the trees, devouring necks. Heads rolled from their demon bodies and wretched limbs scattered. The Alpha, enormous in size, engulfed a full demon. In his beast form, he was frightening. Even Gideon couldn't deny it.

He found Torin, who had unsheathed both swords that were strapped to his back. He sliced through two demons at a time, leaving torsos halved on the ground. Black gore clung to his face already; he had never looked more in his element as he leapt to his next target.

As Gideon swivelled on his right leg, he mobilised his bow, placing an arrow into the nocking point, assessing where to aim. He shut out the screams of the dying and let a calming mist transcend over his muscles. He listened to nothing but his breathing. He raised his arm, scouting for a target. Searching between the combined units, he looked for the creations of the Dark God.

Got it.

A mammoth demon was stalking towards a silver wolf. But he knew the wolf's fur coat well—it was Breighly. The demon's claws were the size of large blades, curling sharply as it prowled towards her. He released the arrow and it sunk into the demon's side. The demon's bear-like head jerked to the side, eyeing the wound before roaring into the night. Its crimson eyes then found Gideon as foam seethed from his jaw; its lip snarled back, revealing a set of sharp teeth.

Just then, Breighly attacked from the side, going straight for the jugular with her fangs, but the demon spun and smacked into the wolf, pulling her to the ground and landing on top.

Gideon drank down a shot of panic.

Taking a deep breath, he lowered to a crouch, trying to follow them as he drew another arrow and strung the bow. He narrowed his eyes as the two feral animals brawled amongst the trees.

"Can't get a clear shot," he muttered in frustration. "Come on, Breighly, move out of the way."

He needed to get closer.

Out of the corner of his eye, he noticed a dark shadow racing towards him; quickly he spun and released another arrow. This time it pierced into the demon's eye and it let out a high-pitched shriek, deafening his eardrums. As many kills as he had made as a Hunter, he would never get used to the sounds they made as they died.

Another demon attacked from behind, the repulsive scent suffocating, and the frantic attack of its movement penetrated into his back. He pulled the heavy body over his shoulder and flung the weight forward. The demon hit the ground and before it could move, Gideon had pulled the fighting knife from his belt and stabbed down hard. He punctured its heart before it could even blink, so he knew it was dead. Correcting his stance, he scoured between the trees for the silver wolf.

Shit! Shit! Shit!

Breighly was surrounded by three demons hungry for her blood. Gideon sprang into action, closing the distance between them. He pushed up off the soft bedding of the forest ground, landed on a tree stump, and withdrew a small sword. Leaping from his podium, he crashed into one of the beasts, penetrating between the shoulder blades with his weapon. The creature bucked in shock and Gideon was flung back. His head smashed against hard oak and it looked like the world was snowing glitter for a second.

Breighly had pounced again, and by the time Gideon had steadied his vision, she had ended another demon, pulling out his throat with her fangs. Stars twinkled around the woods as the last demon stalked towards him, its lip curling back over its razor-sharp teeth, ready to taste his flesh.

As he tried to spring to his feet, putting the dizziness aside, an axe hurled through the air. It cut into the demon's head, embedding itself in the skull. The monster's eyes rolled to the back of their sockets and it slumped to the ground, blood spilling out like hot soup onto the leaves below.

Gideon flashed his gaze to the left and saw Marcus standing nearby, short of breath. He bowed his head as a thank you.

A bright flash broke through the trees. "Gideon, you idiot! I could have taken all three!" Breighly's voice burst throughout the forest.

She put out her hand, and he took it.

Being hauled to his feet, he tried to master the dizziness. "Oh, yeah? Well, it didn't look like it from where I was standing," Gideon growled. "You shouldn't be back in your human form yet." He looked over at her and then averted his eyes. She was practically naked, all but under-garments.

"Keep focused," Marcus barked. It was unusual for Marcus to raise his voice, but he had been known to raise it when need be. "Now is not the time to dispute your kills. Keep moving."

As they moved on, working together, killing their way through the Dark God's army, an order sounded through the woodland.

"Re-group. Clearing field. Now!"

Gideon knew Torin was checking his casualties and hopefully luring what was left of the creatures out into the clearing where they would all be waiting to finish them off.

The last hurdle of the mission. *Finally!*

"Let's go," Gideon commanded Breighly. But she was already on the move.

"I have ears, asshole," she smiled, giving him a friendly punch on the arm.

He grinned.

As they landed in the clearing, much of the pack and the Hunters were also making their way along the open space. Some running, some limping.

"Here," a Shifter approached and offered Breighly a shirt from his back. "I'm proud of you tonight, baby," he said as he leaned over and kissed her forehead. Her eyes fluttered to Gideon uncomfortably, but he looked away.

That was not his business anymore, but he suspected that the dark-haired male wasn't just a friend.

Maybe she has found her mate.

Gideon broke into a run and found Torin as he counted the numbers of who had made it back to the open field. As Gideon observed the warriors, too, no one was missing that he could see—but a lot were hurt and some were bleeding badly.

"I want everyone—and I mean everyone—to show no mercy as we drive these fuckers to dust!"

Torin's booming voice echoed in the clearing, a menacing frost settling into his eyes. Acknowledgements broke from the Hunters and the pack in agreement. The wolves were also at their most powerful under the full moon and healing would be quicker for them.

"I know you have injuries and I know you are tired, but you can think about that later when you are out of the clutches of the Dark Army." Torin turned to the people who were at his back. "Take your mind to another place and fight through the pain and exhaustion. You are warriors. You were created for the fight. You feel no pain, you feel no exhaustion. Let's remind the demon scum who owns these lands before we annihilate every single one of them!"

Torin's prep talk riled up the group.

The Hunters smiled grimly as they knew their next moves, the pack growling with anticipation to kill. The hunt was going the way they had wanted. They had opted to thin most of the demons out throughout the trees, split them up, and kill them off. The remaining numbers would be confirmed when they pulled back into the clearing, luring them out.

"There can't be many of them left," a hunter exclaimed. "I've killed at least twenty. They normally travel in smaller numbers," he said. "Our wards don't normally allow this many through."

"Well, I'm sure Viktir would be happy to answer any questions you have about the wards in the next briefing," Torin sneered.

The Commander's eyes flew to Torin's face. If they hadn't been in the middle of the hunt, his father would have struck him in the mouth and Gideon knew it. He decided that Torin knew something and wasn't sharing it with the rest of the Clan. Maybe they were both on private missions. And Torin's was to royally piss off the Commander more than usual.

A rumbling sound vibrated through the earth, causing everyone who stood in the clearing to turn. Gideon's reflexes acted quickly and he sprinted to the front of the formation to stand next to his brother and father.

However, he wasn't prepared for what he was looking at. Hundreds of red eyes stood in the distance between the trees, staring back.

In the name of Thorin, God of the Sun and War.

Gideon knew instantly they were outnumbered. And they weren't just outnumbered by a few.

I do not feel fear, I do not feel fear. I do not feel fear, he chanted to himself.

Torin walked forward, trying to get a better look, as if not believing the number of crimson lights that he could see. He shot his father a look so fierce that he thought it might strike him dead where he stood. His father's face was solemn.

What is going on between them?

He would figure it out later—if he made it out of the clearing alive.

A sea of red eyes seemed to part to allow something through, like it was somebody of importance.

Gideon flinched.

One demon rode forward, his blood-red eyes glaring at the whole of the hunting opposition as they stood still, frozen in action. The demon was riding atop a Karkadann demon—a ferocious monster that could spit poison from the horn that protruded from its head. A poison fatal to anything but itself. The male figure that sat atop the Karkadann looked like a knight from the underworld with his black armour and brutish body. He grinned violently as the power radiated from him out into the world.

Within a second, Gideon confirmed he *was* a Knight of the underworld. "Order a pull-back, Torin," he said through his teeth.

What was his brother waiting for?

He would have to stay and fight if Torin didn't pull them back. Surely, he wasn't that stupid! They couldn't win this fight. Even with the wolves, they didn't have enough manpower. And with the expression on Viktir's face, he knew it too.

"Pull us back!" Gideon roared this time.

But Torin didn't turn. He stepped forward again.

"Father?" Gideon questioned.

Even the Commander couldn't speak as he watched his first born square his shoulders to the demon at the front.

A challenge.

The pack started to grumble with uncertainty as Torin raised one hand out and coiled his fingers, gesturing for the Dark God's crusader to come ahead.

"What is that mad bastard doing?" a voice spoke from behind Gideon.

"Commander Blacksteel," Gideon barked. "Order a pull back by your rank."

Gideon's stomach flipped as he watched the Knight of Hell step forward too. With his venomous red eyes, he scanned over his prey. Gideon's muscles tightened as the Knight of the underworld turned to him, finally resting his gaze on his face.

Show no fear.

Gideon lifted his chin and remained in eye contact as everything on this earth screamed at him not to. The higher demon pulled a dagger from behind him that reminded Gideon of a sharp icicle and hurled it through the air at a speed even the Hunters couldn't see.

And it soared straight towards Gideon's heart.

CHAPTER THIRTY-FOUR

Thick, grey fog had descended its way into the gardens of the Tower as Emara watched from the window of the infirmary above. It swallowed the small plants and shrubs greedily, mixing around them like hot smoke. She glanced at the moon as it hovered above Huntswood City like a brass coin, swelling in size with every second that passed.

"Don't hurt them," she pleaded to the Blood Moon—or any of the Gods who would listen.

Emara had spent a few hours sifting through books on the Gods as a distraction. Uttara, God of Stars and Dawn, Vanadey of Life and Beauty, and Rhiannon of the Moon and Dreams. And in the end, she prayed to them all that no Hunters lost their lives tonight. She even prayed to Thorin, God of the Sun and War.

A snaking sensation dipped into her stomach, causing her gut to twist. She had felt the same feeling the night of the attack at her home, but never understood why she had those feelings. This time, at least she knew why she felt anxious, knowing what lurked out there and who was fighting them. Lifting a hand to her hair, she felt the texture of the braid between her index finger and thumb. She dragged her finger down, pulling the braid apart, allowing her hair to spill out, untamed, onto her shoulders.

Tonight, everything she did felt wrong. Anything she wore felt heavy. Anywhere she sat, she squirmed impatiently. Anything she ate made its way back up her throat. Every breath she took felt tight in her chest.

Maybe, it was partly because Cally hadn't returned from the Markets yet and Gideon hadn't returned from the hunt, which made her feel all levels of uncomfortable.

Or maybe, just maybe, it was because she had an urge to fight. She wanted to fight—and sitting in this room, waiting, was killing her. She deemed herself no better than the wealth of Mossgrave as they sat in their protected manors the night her grandmother was murdered, the night the village was ransacked. As the Elite sat back and let the creatures from the underworld burn their village, they had watched ignorantly. They had let the people of the village fight a battle they were inescapably going to lose.

Most of them had lost.

And Emara had a sickening feeling that the Elite had known of the evil that lurked and had done nothing to warn the village. That's why there wasn't a single Elite name on the list of the dead. She had checked a document in the library.

If Taymir, of all people, knew about this world, then the most powerful of the Elite definitely knew. How else had so many of them survived? Why else hadn't she heard of any damage to their homes? How else would she explain Taymir's men keeping an eye out for her coming back? Or them having guards who just so happened to be Clan members?

He had known. They all had. As they sat in their affluent homes, they had turned a blind eye to the horror.

Her pulse raced in anger at the thought, and she kicked off from the windowsill to pace around the room. She had always thought the Elite protected her village—when really, they were just the barrier between them and the evil, willing to step aside to protect themselves. All those rooms in their snobby manors and not one of them had offered a member of the village sanctuary. All the food and the wealth, no one offered even a loaf of bread. She grabbed the pillow from the bed and screamed into it. One Elite manor could have taken in everyone from her village, even if it was just for a night.

One night.

With every thought, she grew more enraged. Everything around her angered her. She kicked over a wooden chair and it hit the ground, then splintered.

"Calm," a familiar voice entered her mind. *"Keep calm. Do something that you would do daily."*

It was her grandmother's voice. She knew it instantly. She closed her eyes and listened. She had always kept Emara to a strict routine—one that was quite different from her training schedule now, but it was a routine, nonetheless.

But her old routine was gone. Now she didn't know what was going to happen from one minute to the next. She appreciated the routine of training and mealtimes within the Tower, but the uncertainty of what could happen next dug into the roots of who she was. But then again, the question of who she really was hung heavy in the air.

Maybe she could be someone completely new in this life. Maybe, through all this turmoil, it would allow her to find exhilaration in the uncertainty. She could be whoever she wanted to be. She felt a sudden rush of empowerment coursing through her heart at that thought. She could have the confidence to be anyone she wanted to be in Huntswood City.

Emara's heart leaped into the air as the infirmary door opened. Her chest eased a little as she saw bouncing blonde hair swish through.

"Aw, Em, you didn't have to wait up. It's late." Callyn smiled and scurried into the room holding three brown paper bags and two large, white boxes.

"You would have woken me anyway with all that you are carrying."

Although she *would* have waited until Cally came home to sleep, Emara had made a promise to see someone else…

Callyn spread all her purchases out on the bed and Emara's first thought was that she had bought more lacey underwear from the markets. But then a horrible notion reminded her that there could be worse things to purchase from the Huntswood markets.

She had seen it firsthand.

"What could you possibly have purchased that requires boxing?" she said, hoping that there was no weaponry involved. That's all Callyn Greymore needed—a weapon in one of her temper tantrums.

"Well, I promised my best friend an amazing dress for the uplift." She smiled, causing her eyes to soften. "Even if she was being a big bore and didn't come with me to the Markets. One box is for you and one is for me."

Cally hadn't had much as a child. Growing up she'd promised herself that she would make as much coin as she possibly could. And so, she did.

Taking her passion for fashion and turning it into a career, she had styled the wealthiest Elite wives of Mossgrave, allowing her to earn a good amount of coin. Cally wasn't shy in spending that coin either and, that also included, on Emara.

A sting pinched its way into her chest.

She didn't deserve a friend like Cally. Loyal to the bone, kind-hearted and truthful – even when the truth of her words did hurt.

"Callyn, you better not have spent a lot of coin on this… you know I don't like it when you do that" She made her way over to the box, running a hand over the lid.

"Emara, stop. I have lived with you for almost thirteen years and your grandmother didn't ask for a single thing from me. She fed me, put clothes on my back, and allowed me to share every moment with you. The least I can do is repay you in amazing fashion. It's my treat and I won't hear another word about it."

Cally's nose flared the way it always did when she was being bossy. "Okay?"

"Okay, alright," Emara agreed, not wanting another fight on her hands tonight. "But I am a little scared to look inside the box." Emara pretended to peek through her fingers "It better be…suitable."

"Just open it," she huffed. "Wait!" She flung out her hand as she called out. "Can I show you mine first? Please, please, please?" She clasped her hands up underneath her chin and rolled her bottom lip out into a pout.

Laughing, Emara agreed. "Go on, then. The suspense is killing me."

She flipped the lid off the box with excitement and pulled out a daringly short dress. The material shone white against the candlelight, shimmering like snow. "I told you I was going for a virginal white colour. It's very angelic."

"I am sure with that dress, you will look more like a fallen angel than one that arrived from heaven."

"Perfect," she purred, her leg popping out. "That's exactly the look I am going for. Angelic and divine, yet sensual and seductive." She spread her hands out dramatically and her eyes smouldered into the distance.

"Well, you got it right with that dress. It really is…*something*. Waylen is a lucky man."

Emara had an inkling that it wasn't Waylen she wanted to impress, but she would play along anyway. She did make the effort of learning his name, after all…

"Of course he's lucky; he's going to the uplift with me." Her shoulders danced, and that made Emara laugh. "Okay, now it's your turn—and keep an open mind. I know you like to dress *casually.*"

"Watch it," Emara warned with a laugh. "I dress simply fine."

"You're not supposed to look 'simply fine' at an uplift!" Cally looked horrified. "You're in amongst the supernatural. Hunters, Shifters, Witches—possibly Fae. And whatever else is out there. Do you think they will look mundane? You're not supposed to look regular. You should stand out."

"Yeah, I usually leave that to you…"

"Not this time. I just want you to be confident, Em. I want you to feel amazing; this is like nothing we've ever done before. It might be the last chance we ever get to go to a ball like this. This gown gives you all that you are in one." She pushed the box further in Emara's direction. "It's time to break out of that comfort zone. Tell those voices in your head to shut up— you don't need to downplay how beautiful you are. You can feel feminine and sensual and still be you! It's also time to show off those amazing curves, for once."

"No wonder people pay you top coin to inspire them into dressing better," she laughed as a blush filled her cheeks. "Okay, fine. I'm in." Emara's mouth pulled into a smile, causing her cheekbones to rise. Callyn's encouraging energy couldn't help but make her beam. "You really are the best; do you know that?"

Cally's face shone with vulnerability before she replaced it with the smooth mask she kept intact. "Yes, of course I do. Why do you think I charge over the odds to put people in pretty dresses and corsets to make them look thinner? It's called having a brain and using it against the rich when they feel susceptible." She batted her eyelashes.

Emara snickered at the thought of Cally waltzing about the high homes of the Elite, taking advantage of their willingness to pay excessive amounts of coin to look better than their neighbour.

Abruptly, a ringing sounded throughout the Tower. Emara's eyes shot to Cally's. "They must be back."

Before she could hear Cally's response, Emara pushed herself into a run.

She didn't even know where she was going, only that she had to know if Gideon was okay. If he had come back from the hunt alive.

She had been waiting all night, like she'd promised.

CHAPTER
THIRTY-FIVE

A siren blasted into Emara's ears as she ran through the Tower. She made it to the corridor that would bring her out into the foyer before she heard the noise of a howl in the distance, then a roar. Emara's chest heaved up and down as she tried to control her breathing, pulling back on the fear that now coiled through her whole body.

She skidded to a halt in time to see a rush of Hunters surge through the foyer door. Fear snapped like an elastic band in her heart as she saw the casualties being pulled in makeshift slings. Her legs jumped into action, heaving the heavy glass door open to allow the men to enter without restriction. A man with blood and dirt encrusted onto his face yelled for a healer, his chest pulsing up and down in exhaustion. Another few Hunters made their way into the foyer as the healers arrived, leaping into action straight away. Two men carried in a lifeless body; the face she didn't recognise, the red blood pouring from his neck causing his face to look pale against his black combat gear. Shouting and howling could be heard from outside and Emara didn't know which direction to look in.

The world spun so quickly.

Marcus hauled the body of a Hunter through the front door. The man was crying out in pain. At least she could be sure that this one was alive, but as she took in the severity of his injuries, she didn't know how long that would last. Marcus put a dirt-smeared hand onto the man's face and lowly said *"May all the stars in the Gods' sky guide you back home."*

He pulled himself upright after leaving the body on the cold foyer floor and darted out into the night before she could ask after Gideon.

A coldness spread through Emara's blood as she heard the Commander yell, "Pull back, the wards should hold what's left of them until sunrise."

The demons had followed them back. There were demons directly outside the Tower. Suddenly, the Tower didn't feel so safe anymore. Through all the blood and chaos, Emara couldn't stand by and watch anymore. She swung 'round the door, dragging her legs into a sprint. She pulled her arms back like she did when in training, allowing her to gain a speedy momentum. Her eyes searched for the wagons, but the mist had come into the gardens like a thick paste, allowing her to only see a couple of feet in front of her.

A startling howl came from the right and she pulled her muscles tight, forcing herself to an immediate stop. Clashing sounds of steel and yells were coming from the left direction.

A terrifying thought occurred to her as she stood amongst the thick mist, alone. She was unarmed. She had nothing but her bare hands. Cursing under her breath, regretting her impulsive decision to help anyway she could. She was not going back now.

"Emara, get back into the Tower." Marcus Coldwell grabbed her arm and swung her to face him. "It is not safe for you out here. The battle is still on going outside these walls, there are men still out there—"

She cut him off, "Where is Gideon?" Her voice shook with concern. Her stomach flipped as she saw Marcus' face pale. "Where is he, Marcus?"

"Emara, get back to the foyer and await him coming back. Go! The wards are holding the demons back for now, but that doesn't mean they will be strong enough to last the night."

Understanding she was not getting an answer from the warrior, she pleaded, "Let me help your men. I can help carry the injured back."

"You are unarmed. It is not safe."

"It will not be safe in the Tower if the demons break through the wards and your men lie outside dying. I can help them get to a healer quicker," she argued. "I can help them live, Marcus."

A screeching noise sounded from behind her and Marcus moved. "Help only a few and then get yourself back to your room and lock the door. We will get the rest."

He turned and was gone in a flash.

She couldn't see where Marcus had gone, so she followed the noise of the battle, not knowing where the wards of protection ended and where the fighting began.

"Someone…please," a broken voice wailed out into the night. Emara knew she was no longer on the garden path as the gravel beneath her shoes crunched when she broke into a sprint. "Help me! Send the Gods for me, please!"

Slowing down, she searched for a body in the fog. A man cried out in front of her, but she could barely see him as she wafted away the thick mist. She found him, walking slowly as she neared his body. His face looked ordinary and a bit pale, but as she got closer she could see how mangled his leg was. And that some of his vital organs were visible. Emara gagged down the bile in her gut as it burned up her throat.

What kind of teeth or talons could shred through human flesh and bone in that way?

He had to be of a magical bloodline because no *human* would have ever survived what his body had endured. She ripped the hem from her shirt and wrapped it around his leg. She then ripped another piece of material and looked to see if there was any point in trying to control the blood that spilled from his stomach. There was too much. She gulped down the sick from her stomach.

"Please, heal me," the man cried out in agony.

He thought she was a healer!

Sorrow sank into her heart at the realisation that she would not be able to save this man. She knelt on the ground and tried to tie the shredded material around his wounded leg tighter.

He screamed in pain as Emara spoke, "Did you manage to make it across the wards?" She kept her tone calm and soothing, just like Rhea would. Her hands shook as she tied the material, now turned deep red, around his upper knee. She wasn't convinced that it would even make a difference to the bleeding, but she tried anyway. "What's your name?"

A cry broke from his throat, "Eli."

His whole body started to shake. She knew what was happening. He was losing his life. There was so much blood—too much blood!

Gritting her teeth, she understood that she couldn't move him. He was going to die here on the ground beside her and she couldn't do anything to heal him. For the briefest moment, she wished that she were Rhea. She might have even prayed to the Gods for her to become a healer.

Taking his hand in her own, caked in gore and dirt, she spoke to him, "Eli, I am going to hold your hand, is that okay?"

He nodded, the tears rolling down his face. Even when dying, he still tried to withhold fear.

Her heart lodged into her throat. "I am going to count to ten and you're going to count with me, okay?" He gripped her hand, and she placed her other hand over his.

She closed her eyes and began to count.

"One, two…" She focused on Eli, the man she barely knew, the Hunter who had fought to keep lives safe, as she held his hand and thought of anything but pain and destruction. "Three, four…" He spoke with her through ragged breaths, mirroring her counts. The end was close as the blood from his leg and core now soaked into her clothing, swarming around her knees. "Five…"

"Are you an—an—an angel? Because I don't—I don't…" As he stuttered over his words, Emara realised that she didn't believe in angels anymore. The beings that were supposed to come for you when you were crossing over to the other side, to guide you to that better place. They hadn't come for her grandmother, and they didn't seem to be coming for Eli.

His eyes were wide with astonishment as she shook her head. Emara looked down at him with tears in her eyes as he tried to part his lips to say something else. Placing her hand on his face delicately, she brushed the matted hair from his eyes.

"I am not an angel, but the pain will be over soon and they will come for you." She tried to force a small smile to hide her cruel lie. "I will wait with you until they come for you."

"Miss, I can't feel anything. The pain…it's gone."

Emara presumed the time for him to leave this world was seconds away if he had gone completely numb. He pulled her hand up to his mouth and kissed the back of it.

"Thank you," he muttered, blood forming at the side of his mouth, "for finding me."

"Six, seven…" she breathed. Closing her eyes, she thought of clouds on a summer's day, drifting through blue skies with ease. "Eight…" The voice of the man was no longer counting with her. She felt the grip of his hand loosen around hers and she knew he was gone. She slid her hand from his as she swallowed the tears that mounted in her eyes. Leaning over, she brushed a hand over his eyes to close them forever. "Nine, ten."

A sob broke from her.

The sound of boots running on stones startled Emara and she swung around to see what came through the mist. Before she saw who or what it was, two deadly swords cut their way through the fog, followed by midnight black hair and an angular face. She wiped her eyes as she rose from the ground.

"Are you hurt?" Torin Blacksteel's concern caught her off guard.

"No, it's not my blood. It's Eli's. He's gone."

Torin looked down at the body on the ground and swore. "Emara, you can't be out here. You are across the border of the wards. The demons can attack you here." He looked around himself and Emara. "There were a few complications and they followed us back."

Just then, he flashed in front of her, placing his swords between their bodies and covering her mouth with his large hand. His eyes signalled danger and his other finger pushed against his lips. As stunned as she was at how quickly he had moved in front of her, she nodded in acknowledgement.

He sensed a demon nearby.

His body gently pressed the steel into hers, holding both swords between their torsos. An unearthly breathing sound came from the far right and he pulled one sword free and sheathed it into the scabbard on his back. He then drew the other, manoeuvring his body in front of hers, holding the sword ready to kill.

The noise of fighting around them seemed to have died down and there were fewer cries for help—although Emara wasn't sure if that settled her or not.

"Stay close to me," he breathed. She nodded in response even though he couldn't see her dwarfed behind him. "Do as I command, when I command it."

A noise broke into the night from a creature so foul it had to come from an unworldly dimension. Torin rolled the sword's hilt in the palm of his hand like he was warming up a fifth limb and bent his knees, ready to spring into action at any given moment. His head turned right in anticipation and he took one almighty swing.

He had been right to do so, as a winged creature leaped at them from the fog.

Emara stumbled back in retaliation of the creature's presence, no scream could escape her mouth. The demon was not human-like at all. Not like the one in her grandmother's house. Before that, if Emara had ever conjured up a picture of what a demon looked like, this was what she would have pictured.

The demon must have been at least seven feet tall and had black, bat-like wings. Its legs were like vines that intertwined around strong, black muscles. Its torso looked like it had been turned inside out and it had guts resting in its open cavities. Its rib cage stuck out around its decaying flesh, creating a chest-like area to support its moose-like head. Its antlers grew from its skull, pointing into lethal spikes.

Emara's core shook as she tried to find it in herself to run or even breathe, but she stood behind Torin. She had not heard any commands come from his mouth.

"Are you just going to stand there?" Torin cocked his head to the side, taunting the beast. "What are you waiting for, summer solstice?"

Is he insane? Was he trying to aggravate the demon even more? She saw what had happened to poor Eli's body and she didn't want that for her or Torin.

The demon sprung towards him, but he had already predicted its move. He jumped to the side, pivoting on his back leg, and brought down his sword in a deathly hard swing. His sword connected with one of its long arms, cutting off its bird-like claw. The creature shrieked and gore dripped from its mouth and arm.

"Move to the left," Torin barked his first command.

As he spun to match Emara's movement, he unsheathed his second sword and drove it into the demon's body. Emara braced herself for the massive frame to fall to the ground, but its vine-like legs held their base. The beast roared in the face of Torin Blacksteel, and she saw a tug on his lips as his eyes grew menacing.

He *was,* indeed, taunting the beast.

His cheekbones lifted as the smile pulled across his face. His sharp, angular jaw mocking the demon to dance with death. Even covered in gore and guts, he was strikingly handsome—dangerously handsome as he looked evil incarnate in the eye with a smile.

Wielding two swords, he got to work. The demon struck out with its remaining talon, trying to swipe the weapons from Torin's grip. "Duck!" he shouted to Emara. "And stay down."

The demon clawed at him again as he whirled around it.

"Get on your feet," he barked again.

"You just told me to stay down!" Emara shouted over the frustrated roars of the demon.

"Well, now I am telling you to get on your feet. Keep up!"

Even saving her life, in a battle with a demon, he could be infuriatingly demanding.

"Torin, behind you!"

The demon took its opportunity to pounce as Torin watched Emara. However, he spun with cat-like grace and drove the sword right through the flesh of its other claw. Emara jumped as a maddening roar erupted around the gardens. Reddish-black gore dripped from the demon's hands, but that wasn't enough for Torin. He drew his swords up into a cross above his head and sliced down towards the ground.

For a moment, the world stood still.

Emara could hear her heart hammering against her chest, feel the pulsing in her neck. The panic, the fear, the thrill, all merging into one. The demon separated into two parts and crashed to the ground. The sound felt human enough to make her wince. Torin walked over to the corpse and raised one sword into the air, swinging down with force onto the demon's skull. Emara could not pull her eyes from what Torin had just done. She knew she should look away, but she couldn't.

She wanted it dead. And she realised she didn't care how. She wanted all of them dead. She wished it had been her that had wiped it from the earth.

Torin looked at her and raised one eyebrow as he pushed one sword back into the casing on his back. "Let's go," he commanded. He turned to start walking. "Stay close to me."

"You have already barked that order," she advised, walking behind him. The mist was starting to thin.

She halted, remembering she had forgotten something.

"Why have your little feet stopped moving behind me?"

"I can't leave Eli. I need to go back for him."

He turned to face her, ice crystalising in his eyes. "Emara, we can get the men to retrieve his body when the mist has cleared on the gardens and the sun has risen. Let's go!"

She dug in her heels. "Torin, please!"

He paused for a second, then ran a hand over his jaw. "Emara, Eli is gone," he announced, his voice softer than before. "There are other men in the Tower who need our help. You did all you could for him. He would have been grateful not to die alone." His eyes softened as he looked at her face.

She felt her lip quiver. "I will carry him myself if I have to." She pushed out her chin.

He didn't budge.

She turned her back on him and tried to take a step forward, but his hand reached out, grabbed her elbow, and spun her into him.

"Why do you always have to defy everything I say?" His eyes deepened as they searched for an answer on her face. She felt bare, like she was exposed as he explored her so close up. "I can't make up my mind if I find it extremely irritating or extremely attractive," he admitted.

He didn't seem to be joking.

"Why do you always expect me to do everything you say?" She yanked her arm back. "I don't fall under you." She stood up taller, on her tiptoes—just a little. His jaw ticked. "I am asking you, as a Hunter, to help lift the fallen."

His nostrils flared. "And as a Hunter, I am asking you to get your stubborn ass back into the Tower so that I can sweep the grounds for more demons. My duty is to protect *you!*" His voice was dangerously low as he leaned in closer to her. "How can I do that when you don't follow a single instruction I give to you?"

She shifted. "Torin, I will be sick to my stomach if I am left in that bloody Tower for one more second, thinking that he has to lay out here in the cold as his blood dries into the grounds of this place. I just can't—"

Torin drew the sword from his back, stopping her from talking altogether. Emara's eyes widened as fear drove up her spine. Oh, Gods, she had pushed him too far.

"Hold this with two hands." He placed the weapon into her hands. "If you see a demon, wait until it gets close to you, then swing as hard as you can."

The sword was heavier in her grip than she remembered, but he had just given her a weapon to defend herself.

His weapon…

"Thank you," she said, laced with a little more attitude than she had intended. But she meant it; she was thankful that he hadn't dragged her back to the Tower. Instead, he gave her the option to defend herself.

A wicked grin appeared on Torin's face; his icy eyes raked over her from beneath his dark lashes. "You look good with some steel in between your hands." He drew in his cheeks and one dimple appeared. "I can think of one more thing that would look—"

"I swear to the Gods, I have never used a sword before, but if you finish that sentence, I will bring it down upon your head."

A second dimple appeared on his cheek. "Stop talking dirty to me, Emara; it will only get me going, and we have things to do." His shoulders relaxed casually.

Prick!

She moved the sword so quickly, Torin's shocked expression fulfilled her as he brought up his own to defend himself.

His eyes beamed with delight.

"Are we doing foreplay right now?" he purred, his voice even deeper than before.

Maddened, she swung the sword again, this time shifting to the left. Again, Torin's sword met hers with a clatter. The vibration rang up her arms and shuddered her bones. Instead of wincing, she felt liberated to hold a sword and swing it hard.

Maybe she could get used to carrying a weapon...

"As much as I would like to do *this* and then take our clothes off," he suggested, sending a heatwave across her face, "we have a body to locate and take back to the infirmary, remember?"

She swallowed and released the lock her sword had been in with Torin's.

"Good attempt at the swing, though." A genuine smile pulled at his lips, causing her breath to catch. "Follow me," he commanded.

They made their way back to the foyer with Eli's limp body. Although he was exhausted from the hunt, Torin carried most of the weight. However, Emara had negotiated for him to allow her to take at least half—or so he let her think.

They hadn't come across anyone or any*thing* else in the gardens and, in a way, he was relieved. As much as he loved slaughtering demons, he didn't want to put her in any more danger. He had to get her back inside the Tower.

He allowed himself to glance at her, quickly. Emara had the Shifter's blood all over her; it was on her arms and face, and soaking into her clothes.

A strange sensation passed over him.

He was satisfied that it wasn't hers. When he had found her, she was sobbing against a broken body, covered in blood, and he wasn't sure if it was hers. A pang ached deep in his chest. He brushed it off.

Going soft? His father's voice taunted in his mind.

He brushed that off too.

As she ran up the steps to open the door for Torin, he saw someone through the glass he would normally be happy to see, but not as he was carrying her dead brother in his arms.

Breighly's blonde hair was caked in blood and gore; she didn't notice them coming through the foyer door. Torin angled Eli's body so she couldn't see his face as she helped another casualty. She pulled a lace from her boot and tied it 'round the arm of a Hunter.

There was an object embedded in the arm. It was gushing blood. He knew the arm straight away.

It was Gideon!

He placed the wolf's limp body on the ground and whispered, "May all the stars in the Gods' sky guide you back home."

"Gideon!" Emara screamed.

She had realised who it was, too.

His body lay in a pool of blood as he roared out in pain. Torin held Emara's waist as the sound of Gideon almost took her legs out from under her, his screams ringing through the Tower.

"He won't let me take him to the infirmary!" Breighly roared. "Torin, talk to him!" Her eyes were bulging out of her head.

If only she could see what was behind her…

"Save someone else," Gideon pleaded. His body writhed in agony as he tried to push Breighly's helping hands away. "I can pull it out on my own."

Torin eyed the demon blade that was embedded in Gideon's arm.

Guilt surged through Torin at an overwhelming pace. If he had just walked away…

If he had just ordered a retreat, they might have gotten away in time.

Rhea was beside him in seconds with an elixir. A treatment for the pain that Torin knew Gideon would refuse. He had to step in.

"Like hell you can pull that out yourself," Torin said. There was no way he was getting that demon blade out himself. It would end his life. It was the first time Torin had ever seen one in the flesh and it made him feel sick to his core. *He* had done this. He had allowed this to happen.

"Open your mouth," Rhea demanded. "Gideon! Now!" Her tone was a little harsher than he had ever heard it, as if she had been trying for a while and getting nowhere with him. Torin went to his side to help hold him down. He placed a hand on Gideon's shoulder and grabbed his arm, holding him against the ground.

"Rhea, I beg you, there are men up there taking their final breath. Take their pain," he cried, thrashing against him. "Not mine."

Torin couldn't stand it. He couldn't hear Gideon give up on his life.

"Hey, hey…" He grabbed his brother's face in his hand. "You do as I say. We are not losing you to a demon blade. A Blacksteel will not die at the hands of a demon blade. Do you hear me?"

Gideon clamped down on his teeth and nodded.

For the first time in years, he allowed himself to comfort his brother. Torin cradled Gideon in his arms and held him there.

"I am here. You are not going anywhere, brother."

Emara stood back as tears welled up in her eyes. She clasped a hand over her mouth to hold in the emotional outburst she could feel taking over. She watched as Torin leaned over his brother and held him in his arms. In that moment, she could see the unconditional link between them. Gideon and Torin Blacksteel. Fire and Ice. Both bound by blood and love.

There was no oath in the embrace he had given him. Just love.

Her heart burst into a million different pieces at the sight of them together. Not fighting, not arguing, not sparring, but loving each other—an unbreakable bond. *Brothers.*

"Tor, it hurts so bad!" Gideon's back arched and he gritted his teeth. But Torin was there to hold him down. He was the only one strong enough to do so.

"Help him, please, Rhea," Breighly begged. "Please heal him."

Her beautiful face was devoured by emotion. She, too, looked like something out of a nightmare, with blood splattered all up her face. Emara noticed that she was wounded, but she wouldn't let anyone touch her until they helped Gideon. She genuinely cared about him—and she let herself selfishly wonder how much she *cared* for him. How deeply she cared.

"The demon magic from the blade is acting as a poison in his blood, Rhea. We need to act quickly before it spreads," Torin demanded.

"I cannot remove the blade until we have burned the leaves from the white oak tree, which are burning right now. Before I apply them to the wound, they must turn to ash." Rhea held Torin's stare. "If I pull the blade out without the ash of the leaves, he will die. The wound will never heal. He will bleed out and the poison will spread all over his body." Her words turned Torin's face into a ghastly white colour. "Help me get him to the infirmary."

Torin nodded and Breighly followed, ensuring she helped with lifting his body correctly.

Although Rhea was small, she was clearly respected within the Tower and it was clear throughout that she was to be listened to. Torin lifted the middle part of Gideon's torso into the air and he screamed in reaction to the movement. Breighly winced, but took charge of his legs, to help Torin guide his body through the Tower. Rhea took his head in her delicate hands and led the way.

Passing by, Gideon's eyes locked onto Emara's. She removed the hands from her mouth and took a step forward.

"You waited for me!"

"Of-course I did," she managed in a whisper.

His mouth parted to say something else, but before he could, his eyes rolled to the back of his head and closed.

"Gideon!" Emara screamed.

A sob broke from her, but he was no longer conscious to hear it.

CHAPTER
THIRTY-SIX

A burning flame engulfed Gideon's body, flicking its way across every cell. He could no longer speak. He could no longer hear the world around him. He could no longer feel the demon blade that had struck him, and it was now only a matter of time…

Being hit by a demon blade was something that very rarely happened to Hunters, as demon blades were uncommon in this world. He had read about the blades that were forged in the fires of the underworld in his studies in the Selection. It was something every Hunter had to study. They needed to know every demon and every weapon that could end their lives to be proactive in their hunt.

A demon blade was lethal to any species that had the light Gods' blood running in their veins.

While in the clearing, he had looked the Demon Knight in the eye as he hurled the blade towards his heart. Luckily, he had dove to the side, but he wasn't quick enough to avoid the blade completely, and it drove straight into his upper arm. It was a message from their King about what was to come.

The pain of the blade entering his skin had been like nothing he had ever experienced before. As he fell to the ground in utter agony, he had heard eruptions around him. Knowing Torin, he would never have walked away from that fight. Only Torin could knock Gideon down, no one else. And whoever did didn't live to see another day.

As the anarchy of another fight broke loose, he had been lifted off the ground by the wolves and carried back to the wagon. However, he must have blacked out with the pain, as when he awoke Breighly and the pack had carried him into the foyer. The last thing he remembered was her face.

Emara Clearwater stood in the foyer, watching him die.

Just after that his mind had gone numb and he was no longer in that world, but in a dimension full of demons that were feasting on his flesh.

Or so he thought.

It had been recorded in the ancient manuscripts of the healers that men had gone completely insane just hours after the blade was rooted. They had lived in their own personal hell as the demon magic poisoned their blood, turning them mad before killing them.

Gideon was living in his own personal hell now, even if it was a trick of the mind. He struggled to fight back to the real world. But he knew he had to. And no matter how tired he was, he would get back.

For all he knew, he spent years in that hell before he felt a cool flannel on his face and neck. That was a good sign! His body was fighting the poison and he was managing to feel a stream of consciousness.

"Is he going to make it?"

"If I keep draining the wound and applying the dressings with the oak tree ash, it should draw the poison out. He's weak, but his heart seems steady enough. He just needs to rest and heal. No training for a while, and I mean that."

"Understood."

He could hear the voices of both Rhea and Torin, but the darkness found him again. He tried to scream for help. Scream for it to end. He begged and begged...until he heard his name.

"Gideon," a soft, melodic voice drifted into his ears. *"Please come back to us, Gideon."*

Worry and concern were knotted in her voice and he knew it was Emara's, he just didn't have the strength to open his eyes and see her.

But the pain had stopped. Was the pain listening to her, too?

"You really scared us, but Rhea said she thinks you're going to be okay." Her voice was becoming clearer.

Us.

He knew she was smiling by the tone of her voice. He had to fight to open his eyes and see that smile. He had to fight and awake his body from the nightmares of the demon world that devoured him as he slept. He felt a cold hand brush over his own.

He could feel his hands.

He twitched a finger on his hand to let her know that he heard her. He was fighting.

"Come back to us, Gideon." Her voice sounded like a beautiful song in his ears.

Go towards the melody.

Gideon tried to force his eyes open. His lids felt like they had paper weights on them.

Push! Push!

"Come back to me," she whispered into his ear.

Responding to her command, his body ignited a fire that had been dormant in his mind and he opened his eyes. He flinched when the sunlight hit them and a searing pain ran through his arm.

"Easy," her voice carefully said.

He looked around groggily, but his neck was too weak to hold up his head.

Not a good sign.

He was trained to assess his injuries from the minute he regained consciousness. To assess if his vital organs were still working from head to toe. But he couldn't lift his head. He was weak. How long had he been passed out for?

"Gideon, you're awake." A sound of relief exhaled from her chest. Emara was here with him and that was all that mattered.

"You are here," his dry voice scraped out.

"I told you I would wait for you." Her gentle hand brushed over his fingers.

He looked up to see her standing over him as the winter sun poured through the long windows of the infirmary, framing a glow around her body.

"You look like an angel." His voice sounded rough and unused as it grated against his vocal cords.

Her lips pulled back into a smile and Gideon's breath caught in his chest at the sight of her. He was sure his heart missed a beat. Even though she looked like she hadn't slept in days with dark lavender circles around her eyes and her hair in a messy braid, trailing down the side of her neck to below her breast—she was still the most beautiful thing he had ever laid eyes on.

"You are the second person that has referred to me as an angel." She half-laughed and pushed her lips together.

"Well, the first person was not wrong." He winced trying to move. "Although I wish I had been the first to say it." He tried to lick his lips, his mouth like dry sand. He needed water.

"Don't bother trying to move," a harsh, deep voice sounded through the infirmary room. One he knew extremely well—his older brother. "You need to remain as still as possible until the white oak ash has completely absorbed into your wound."

Gideon trailed his eyes along to his shoulder and down to his arm. No demon blade remained, thank the Gods. White ash and congealed blood took its place; an ancient healing poultice that combated poison.

He looked over to where Torin stood. He, too, looked like he hadn't slept in days. His hair was uncharacteristically dishevelled. If Gideon had been fit enough to make a verbal jab about how messy his brother's hair was, he would have.

Instead, he braced himself to ask Torin the dreaded question. "How many?"

"Five Hunters and a wolf." Torin's voice was firm.

We got lucky. The Gods had been on their side.

"Names?" He stared at the ceiling awaiting to hear the names of those who had fallen in the Blood Moon battle.

Torin ran through the names of the Hunters who had lost their lives. Leime Oxhound, one of their brethren, had been in the same Selection as Gideon. He was a good Hunter, but his family's Clan wasn't big enough to sustain Huntership on their own, so they joined the Blacksteel clan. Soule Leatherback was a year older than Torin and came from one of the biggest Clans in the kingdom; however, he had just married a Witch from the House of Earth—Rhea, his favourite healer.

He sent a prayer up to the Gods to protect Rhea from the pain she must be feeling.

"And the wolf?" he said. Praying it wasn't Breighly—or any Baxgroll, for that matter.

Torin sucked a breath in through his teeth. "Eli Baxgroll."

Gideon swore out loud. Shock replaced the feeling of dread as the name of the dead wolf was announced. Eli Baxgroll was Breighly's older brother. In order, Murk Baxgroll's children were Waylen (who was destined to become alpha), Eli (who was next in line if anything ever happened to Waylen), Roman (who was Breighly's twin brother), and then Breighly herself.

The weight of Eli's death sunk into his chest. He knew that the wolves would have a send-off for their fallen pack member as soon as the moon lit the sky. It would be a devastating blow to lose Eli. It could be something they might never recover from as a pack. Gideon knew they were all physically and mentally tough, but the way the pack loved their own was second to none.

Unconditionally and immensely.

"Has the send-off happened?" he questioned.

"It will take place tonight," Torin confirmed. "Father and I will go to pay our respects to the pack and watch the body set sail down the River of Vanadey." Torin's choice of words let Gideon know there was no chance of him being well enough to go. "Breighly will be fine," Torin finished. "She's tough."

Gideon already knew that, but he just wished he could be there for her.

Emara's voice sounded through the room. "Is there anything I can get you?"

"No, thank you," was all Gideon could manage to say.

"I will leave you two alone," Emara said. "Torin, let me know when you're finished and I will come back and sit with him."

"No problem, *angel,*" Torin mocked.

She flung a look over her shoulder that caught Gideon's breath and she let a warm smile lift into her tired eyes and left, ignoring Torin. Clearly, she was exhausted, or she would have bit back.

As he heard the door shut, a moment passed between the two of them, both Torin and Gideon not knowing where to start in their conversation.

"Gideon, I—"

"You don't have to apologise," Gideon cut in. "I would have done the same."

A large breath escaped Torin. "No, you wouldn't have." He looked down at his hands. A peculiar expression spanned across his face. One that Gideon didn't see too often. "You would have pulled back. You wouldn't have let your pride get in the way of your intellect."

Gideon wished he had the strength to laugh.

"No, brother, but I wouldn't have gone down without a fight if someone had hurled a knife towards you, either." Torin's eyes met Gideon's. "They would be dead."

Torin scoffed a laugh. "Sometimes, I think you would be better in my position than I am."

"Sometimes I wish I were as fearless as you."

"That's not always a good thing." Torin's throat bobbed, and he rubbed a hand over his sharp jaw. "Maybe you should get some rest."

"I think I have had enough." Gideon tried to move his neck, but he was too weak to lift it fully. "What does father have to say about the battle?"

He lifted his eyebrows. "Another appearance of the Dark King's knights has rattled him."

"Viktir Blacksteel has been rattled." Gideon managed to laugh softly through the shock. "I always thought it would take Veles himself to shake the Commander of the Blacksteel Hunting Clan. Even then, he wouldn't back down."

"In many ways, we are alike." Torin's lips turned over into a frown.

"In many ways, you are not."

A few moments of comfortable silence passed between them. He had forgiven Torin for his bold move on the battlefield. A move that ignited round two of the Hunt. A round they had clearly not won.

"Have you an inkling as to what it is that belongs to the Dark King? Two Knights of the underworld seen so close together is never good."

Torin mulled over the question before he spoke. "I suppose it could be many things."

"Another ancient relic, perhaps?"

"If not that, then what else?"

Gideon thought it over. "Then why send a Knight of the underworld? They have been on the same evil crusade for millennia. Two knights being seen in such a short space of time is unusual. Dark Knights don't just turn up without purpose. I think it to be something more, brother."

"These are not the questions you should be asking yourself whilst you try to rest. We need you to make a full recovery. You won't return to full health squandering all night worrying about demons and their hobbies." Torin's eyes glittered softly.

Gideon half-smiled at his attempt to lighten the mood.

"We will get to the bottom of that. But for now, sleep."

After the door closed, sleep rescued him from feeling the guilt and sorrow of the fallen.

His men. His friends. His brothers.

This time there were no demons or other dimensions to plague his dreams. Instead, he dreamt of a beautiful face and what it would be like to dance with her at the uplift—given he was fit enough to make it. He dreamed dreams that made his duty feel worthwhile, her laugh, her voice, her eyes. He dreamt dreams that gave him hope for the future.

CHAPTER THIRTY-SEVEN

It had been five days since the Blood Moon battle and Emara did everything she could not to relive the moments of that night. She had taken up reading, particularly about the supernatural world. It was all she could do whilst Gideon lay healing in the infirmary. She hadn't left his side much at all; only to wash, eat, or train.

Gideon had been sleeping on and off due to Rhea giving him elixirs that soothed his pain, and she had advised it was best to keep him sleeping as much as possible until the magic from the demon blade had left his system. He would heal faster.

Torin had been in and out, tending to Gideon where he could in between his duties, but he was still scouring the city for any remaining demons. To be honest, he looked as exhausted as Emara felt.

The infirmary door creaked open and Cally's curious eyes peered over the door's edge. Emara closed the book in her hands gently and gestured for her to come in.

"When was the last time you slept?" Cally asked as she walked in quietly. "I am worried about you."

"I got a couple of hours this morning after sparring."

She closed the door silently and walked to the nearest seat she could find. "As your loving best friend, I need to tell you that you look dreadful."

"Thank you for always being your *truthful* self." She flashed Cally a sarcastic smile and the blonde flashed one back.

"No, but seriously, Emara, you need to rest! You are not like these *guys*…you are not used to the lifestyle. No sleep, all the training—"

"I won't stop the training," she cut in dryly. "I will continue my sessions every morning with Marcus as I have been." Emara bit into the side of her cheek. "He has kindly taken over from Gideon whilst he heals, and a few of the other Humans—I mean villagers—are also asking to be trained. We are making progress. Maybe you should come along."

"I certainly will not." She flipped her golden hair over her shoulder. "I will not be messing up my perfect face or my beautifully shaped body for anyone."

Emara rolled her eyes and let out a small, puffy laugh.

"If these so-called Gods gave me a gift, I don't intend to mess it up by having it punched." She laughed her hearty laugh. "That would be rude." She paused, her face changing slightly. "You can train, but you don't have to train like a Hunter."

Annoyance rolled over Emara's tongue at the way she said "Hunter."

"I want to do it, Cally. It makes me feel…strong and powerful. It might not be great for my body"—she referenced to the bruises on her arms and the cut on her hand—"but it has been amazing for my mind." She lowered her eyes to the floor. "I am willing to take that sacrifice if it means I have silence in my head for a little while."

"I know how rough these last few weeks have been for you," Cally's voice was softer than before. "So if it's good for you, then keep doing it. I just don't want you to burn yourself out. And be careful; the bruises I can hide with a little makeup, but the cuts? Not so much. We have an uplift to attend."

"You are still thinking about that?" she said as she reopened her book on the fine art of weaponry.

"Of course I am. What else is there to think about?"

Emara could think of more important things than a stupid ball.

"Sometimes you need to focus on the small things that bring joy," Cally advised. "Otherwise, life would be all doom and gloom with demons and death. Is that how you want to live?"

Emara thought over Cally's outlook before answering, "I don't think we get the luxury of choosing that."

"Well, what you have is the luxury of having a best friend who will make things entertaining. No matter how you are feeling." She paused. "Besides, the wolves are still coming to the uplift after everything that happened. Waylen will be there, and you can finally meet him."

"How is he holding up?"

"Just dealing with it the best way he can, I suppose. I saw him last night after he said his farewells to his brother. Said he needed some space from the pack for a little while. He can feel their grief. It's a wolf thing."

Emara pulled her legs up to her chest. "I can't imagine what it must be like to lose a sibling. Especially when the pack can feel each other's grief. It must be unbearable at times." She had seen how Torin had been over Gideon, and they both had the hearts of warriors.

"Waylen will take care of everyone. He's a good guy, Emara. I think you would really like him…" She grinned demurely.

Emara thought for a second that Cally was being coy as a tint of red shimmered into her cheeks.

"He is a good guy," a rough voice sounded from the bed.

At once, Emara was reminded that Gideon was in the infirmary room. Chats with Cally often felt like they were the only two in the world.

"Gideon, how are you?" Cally said softly.

"I have been better, but thank you for asking." He pulled himself up a little.

Emara pushed off her chair and was by his side in two steps to help him move up the bed. "Do you two talk about me when I'm not here?" he jested.

Emara quickly said "No," and Cally said "Of course" at the same time. As Cally and Emara's answers clashed, Emara shot her a glare. *We are supposed to be on the same page.*

But Cally wasn't backing down as she pulled her '*Tell the truth, bitch*' face.

"So, which one is it?" Amusement filled in Gideon's features and it was the first time Emara had seen a lightness in his eyes in days.

"Maybe once or twice, your name might make an appearance," she admitted, trying to forget the flush that appeared in her cheeks.

"All good things, I hope." He smiled gently.

Her lips curled up in amusement as she thought over the conversations that she and Cally had had regarding him. About his hair, about his muscles, his abs and his arms. About his kiss, his touch. What he meant by giving her the rose. What he meant the night of the Blood Moon when he asked her to wait for him. They thought over the possibility of Gideon Blacksteel liking her in a romantic sense and the disbelief that she liked him back in that way.

She more than *liked* him.

She knew she didn't love him, but she felt that *like* was a discredit to her feelings for him. He was different and, for the first time, she felt comfortable with her feelings. They were natural and pure. And slightly terrifying.

"Would you like water?" she asked, changing the subject.

"What about that fresh orange juice that you like from the kitchen?" His request drove a small smile onto his lips.

"Sure, of course." She stood, dragging her eyes to Cally. "Come on now, Callyn, let's not disturb Gideon any longer than we have to."

She lounged back in her chair and tossed Emara a tormenting look. "I think I am just going to sit here and ask our favourite Blacksteel a few questions."

"Callyn—" Emara tried to warn.

"Things that best friends need to know, you know? Like his favourite author, sunset or sunrise? Does he prefer brunettes to blondes? His intentions with you…is he sleeping with anyone else?"

Emara lunged over to the seat that she had relaxed into, getting comfortable to make Gideon squirm. "I don't think that is necessary."

"Oh, I do."

"I don't think he can answer *any* of those questions." She tugged on Cally's arm and narrowed her eyes. "He's rather sick, Callyn."

She flashed her the *'I am going to kill you'* smile.

"He looks okay to me." Cally smiled back. "Don't you, Gideon? You wouldn't mind little old me keeping you company while Emara gets juice?" She looked over at him with false innocence.

"I would be more than happy to answer any questions that you have." His gaze shifted to Emara, his emerald eyes hovering over her face, causing her breath to hitch in her chest.

She pulled her eyes away from his and turned her attention to Cally. "You get until I am back from the kitchen and then question time is over," she warned her best friend, letting go of her arm. "Okay?"

Cally's blue eyes winked in excitement. "I promise I will play nice." And then she smiled like a cat from ear to ear and pushed Emara out the door, slamming it shut in her face.

Emara had returned only a quarter of an hour later with a jug of freshly-squeezed orange juice and ice to see that Cally was gone—and Gideon was sitting up higher than he had been before, a boyish grin on his face, the bandage on his arm still intact.

"Should I be worried?" Emara sat the jug on the unit beside him and poured a glass.

"It depends on what gets you worried." Gideon's hair was even more unruly than normal as the chocolate brown tufts brushed out from his head in waves.

"The fact that my protective best friend is trying to dig around your head—well, that worries me."

Gideon raised his square jaw and a muscle tightened in his face. "Is it the fact that she was digging around my head, or the fact that she was digging 'round in my head to find out how I feel about you?" he asked.

Emara gulped.

"Everything about that is *slightly* scary." She held his gaze as a heat pushed over her full body, swarming her. Ignoring her feelings, she walked over to the bed and sat down on the edge of the mattress.

A hearty laugh broke his lips. "You're not great with your feelings, are you? Aren't humans supposed to be all in touch with their feelings?"

The word human struck her like a chord through her heart. She couldn't lie to him any more about who she was. She had to tell him that she wasn't exactly *human*. It wasn't right to feel the way she did about him and for him not to know her. *Fully* know her.

"Gideon, I—" she started, but couldn't find the words. She tried again, but nothing came out. Nothing sounded real.

"You don't have to explain why you find it difficult." He ran a hand over hers, sending shivers up her arm. "Not everyone likes to communicate their feelings."

Emara knew she should tell Gideon—tell him everything—but a heavy weight pressed onto her chest, stopping her from revealing who she really was. Why couldn't she just be honest with him?

"Have you thought any more about coming to the uplift?" Gideon changed the direction of the conversation. And, suddenly, the weight lifted from her chest.

"Are you sure you are going to even make it to the uplift?"

"I wouldn't miss it if it means I get to spend time with you." His eyes looked over her lips. "Since I am not training you every morning, I haven't had that quality time." He smiled. "Has Marcus been going easy on you?"

"Not as easy as you, but he's been great with introducing weaponry."

Before she could speak any more, she thought of the mist descending around her as she stood in the grounds, swinging a sword for the first time. *You look good with steel in between your hands.* Her stomach flipped at the memory of Torin's words. She had *felt* good with a weapon in her hands. Better than *good.*

She whipped the thought of his ice blue eyes out of her mind as Gideon spoke.

"He's the best at weaponry we have," Gideon smiled. "Other than Torin, of course."

Emara swallowed as she heard his name. "Marcus is a good teacher and an even better friend. He's like a brother to us." He pulled his hand from hers and untangled his fingers as he yawned. "I am going to get a little bit of shut eye. You should, too."

Emara smiled at the thought of sleep. Knowing that Gideon was back in good spirits, she would be able to sleep better tonight.

"Okay, get some rest." She smiled and turned to leave.

Gideon's hand shot out and pulled her back into him. "I would like to know where you think you are going."

"You said you wanted to get some sleep, so I am just going to..." she trailed off as she gestured to the door.

"I didn't say you had to leave *this* bed to sleep." His white teeth gleamed through his full lips. "Stay with me."

Emara's heart felt like it was about to explode at the sight of his face as he lay back lazily, waiting for her to snuggle back in.

"I will stay with you, but only if I get to keep that fleece tunic you gave to me. It's the warmest thing I own."

He raised his eyebrow and delight danced across his face. "I would say that is a fair trade." He waited a second before he pulled her in close, motioning her to rest her head on him.

After a few moments, she relaxed into him, feeling the warmth of his chest as it began to rise and fall, his breathing getting heavier.

With every breath that he took, Emara could feel her eyelids draw down until they were closed too, and she was no longer awake.

CHAPTER
THIRTY-EIGHT

A mellow voice pulled her from a deep sleep. "Emara..."

No! She didn't want to wake up from the comfort of her sleep or the warmth of the fur rug that was tucked in at her sides. Hearing her name again, she blinked her lids open to see Rhea's face.

"It's sunrise; you slept right through until morning," Rhea said, not looking like she had done the same.

Emara's head snapped to the window where beams of light emphasized the specs of lazy dust that lingered in the air.

"Gideon's having his bandage removed downstairs."

She looked behind her to see that Gideon was no longer curled into her back. "Is he okay?" Urgency ran through her voice.

"Yes, my dear. He is going to be simply fine. He has been incredibly lucky," she said as she made her way to the door. "He is going to try a walk this morning to build up his strength. He then muttered something about reminding *you* that you have a training session with Marcus at sunrise. That is why I woke you, or I would have left you sleeping a little longer." Rhea's kind eyes crinkled at the side.

Emara swallowed, knowing that Rhea was now without her husband. He had lost his life fighting in the Blood Moon battle and her heart hurt for the caring woman. She didn't deserve to feel that kind of loss.

"Thank you, Rhea. I do have a training session." She rubbed her neck and swung her feet out of the bed and onto the cold flooring.

Ugh! She would do anything to get back under the covers and have the warmth of Gideon beside her.

"Gideon had clothes brought up from your room so that you didn't have to go down there." She lifted her eyebrows and a curve settled onto her lips, turning them up at the corners. How she still found it in her soul to smile was beyond Emara's imagination. "He didn't want you being late, then muttered something about one hundred press ups if you had been. You'd best make haste."

Emara grabbed a handful of her hair and started to push it up into a high ponytail, as she moved down the corridor. Even with a ponytail high upon her head, the ends of her hair still swished along her back as she made her way to the east wing.

She didn't have time to even eat a small piece of fruit this morning like she always did, so she filled up her water bottle at the fountain outside and pushed the door open. Her legs jerked tightly to a halt as she saw the smug smile of Torin Blacksteel, standing with his arms folded across his chest, waiting. His maddeningly wide grin pulled across his angular face.

"Where is Marcus?" Emara demanded.

"Marcus," he said, walking towards her with a taunting expression, "was given the day off after suffering the trauma from your training session yesterday." He paused. "Given the fact that the knife you threw missed his head by a fraction of a hair." He unfolded his arms and pushed a hand through his neat hair that lay soft on his head.

"It was an accident!" Embarrassment flushed onto Emara's face. "I didn't mean it."

She had tried to throw a knife and it had slipped through her hand. Poor Marcus had just laughed it off when it had missed the target and clipped his ear.

She had felt terrible guilt over it.

However, she opted out of telling Gideon in case he insisted he was fit enough to train her.

Torin raised his eyebrow. "The poor man has been hunting demons since he could walk and he never has come so close to death."

Humiliation burned up Emara's face and down her neck. She knew he was taunting her to get a reaction. Of course Marcus had been in closer proximities to death. He was a Gods-damned Hunter. Trying her best not to give Torin a reaction, she trailed along the mats and put down her water bottle at the opposite end of the room. Then, she faced him with a scowl.

That she was not going to hide.

"So, here I am." Torin swept his arms out like he was the star of a theatrical production, expecting the audience to have a standing ovation for his efforts. "Your new trainer."

"Lucky me."

Emara took the protection tape and tried to strap her hands like Gideon had shown her. Marcus had, too. But she still struggled to get the technique right. The material flapped around her hand loosely. Why could she never get it to strap properly? She shook her head in annoyance as she tried again, fighting back the urge to curse.

Torin's muscular frame sauntered slowly across the mat. "Would you like me to help you with that, princess?" His eyes dazzled her as he pushed a mocking smile onto his face. A smile she would love nothing better than to punch.

"I would rather be eaten by a demon." She tried one more time to strap the material with one hand.

"That can be arranged, sweetheart." The corners of Torin's mouth raised in amusement.

"Stop with the cute names!" She flung her hands out in protest, rolling her eyes. "They make me want to vomit."

"Really?" his eyebrows scrunched together in question.

"Yes," she snapped.

"You see, I have a theory..." He took graceful strides towards her, not taking his eyes from her face.

"Do you, now?"

"Anyone who says they don't like being called pet names secretly like them deep down."

"Oh? And what's your *pet* name?" she scowled. She thought of many names to call him, none of which were considered endearing.

A sensual smile played along his lips. "Maybe you will find out."

"I'd rather die." she threw him a false smile, still flapping around with the tape.

He chuckled as he stepped closer—almost close enough to touch her. He grasped hold of her hands and took over with the wrapping.

"I can do it myself," she demanded, but she didn't struggle with him. Not when his large hands were all over hers, correcting the material.

He flicked a look up through his lashes. "Evidently not. I don't have all day to sit here and watch you fumble about with a piece of material. Apparently, I have knives to dodge." He couldn't hold back his laugh as he saw the rage cross her face. "I am sorry, I shouldn't laugh. But teasing you has become one of my new favourite things."

"No, you damn well shouldn't laugh. Maybe next time I throw a knife, I won't miss." Her eyes met his in a challenging stare.

He let go of her wrists and they swung down to her sides. "I hope that's the case." His thin nose flared in amusement. "Let's see what you can do, ponytail." He turned and made his way to the door. "Follow me. We are not working here today."

What?

They weren't working in the training room?

"Where are we going?" she demanded to know.

"You'll see when we get there," he said. "Stop being so demanding. I am not Gideon, nor am I Marcus. You will train my way today."

Emara trekked behind Torin in silence.

Great! Now she was going to spend half of her day being trained and coached by Torin Blacksteel. Which really meant they would be spending all day taking verbal swipes at each other.

She cursed under her breath.

She couldn't explain the vibrations she felt when she was with Torin, but she knew it was different to anything she had ever felt before. He was so frustratingly handsome and absurdly crude. She would be lying to herself if she said she didn't get a thrill when she purposely defied his orders to see the look on his face. He pushed her buttons, and she his.

But that isn't normal, is it?

But maybe normal didn't really appeal to her.

She cursed again.

"Keep up," Torin called out from in front, using his big, solid legs to march up the hills of the forest.

Roots lined the forest floor, making natural steps to help her climb. However, they were hard to see with all the fallen leaves from the trees sweeping a burnt orange blanket over the ground. Emara's lungs felt like they were eating themselves alive as she struggled with the incline. Nevertheless, she promised herself that she wouldn't let Torin see her struggle. He wanted to push her physically today. That's why she was out in the middle of nowhere, trying to keep pace with a man who was basically twice her size as they climbed terrain, she had never trained in.

Torin shouted again, "Are you asleep back there? Or are you going to get those leg muscles working?"

Ignore the burn in your legs.
Ignore the burn in your lungs.
Ignore Torin Blacksteel.
She chanted repeatedly.
Ignore the burn in your legs.
Ignore the burn in your lungs.
Ignore Torin Blacksteel.

"You are really slow," he yelled, half turning back to see her. "Kinda like one of those small creatures from your world."

Emara gritted her teeth and remembered the old saying her grandmother used to recite to her. *Bite your tongue if whatever you are going to say will make you look foolish.* So, she decided against the un-lady-like comment and pushed her lips into her mouth and bit down with her teeth.

"What do you call them again?" he asked. "Oh, yeah, a snail. Or is it a slug? I can never quite remember which is which,"

Emara imagined all the rude gestures she wished she could give him behind his back.

Maybe she could just do one.

"What's the matter, Clearwater? Demon got your tongue?"

Although he was looking ahead, she didn't need to see his face to know that he was smiling.

Smug ass!

"I didn't realise you could be so mute, or I would have taken this job from Marcus days ago."

The thin line of her patience snapped.

"Will you just shut up already?" she bellowed. "Why are we walking so much? Why are *you* talking so much? What are we actually doing?" She panted.

"Ahh, there she is…"

"Who?" Emara screwed up her face.

"The girl who likes to know everything before she is given a command. That's not how training works." He finally turned to face her, "I make the rules, angel."

"Can one of your ridiculous rules be that all pet names are banned from training?"

"Only from training?" He cocked one eyebrow towards the sky.

"Everywhere!" she almost screamed.

He paused for a second, as if mulling over something, before he returned to his hike. "I like 'angel.'"

"You're infuriating," Emara growled.

He halted and spun around quickly; he was so close to her face before she even had time to blink. "Tell me, why do I get under your skin so much?" His voice was unpredictably calm.

"Because you are exasperating," Emara managed to say fully collected.

"But have you ever thought about why? Why I make you so enraged?" His voice was like sweet honey warmed through chocolate.

"I…I don't know. It's because…" Her eyes traced his face, down his muscular neck, and to his broad shoulders. She swallowed. She then traced her gaze along his arms, strong and sculpted with muscle. A singular blue vein ran from his wrist right up the inside of his forearm. She closed her mouth, unable to find any words that would make sense.

"I will tell you why." His eyes sharpened. "Because ever since you met me, you have found yourself drawn to me, and you can't think for the life of you why. It maddens you to think that someone like *you* would be attracted to someone like *me.*"

Her pulse quickened at his words.

"It scares you to think that you could be involved with someone who has a wild side, someone who doesn't do everything by the book." He allowed his lips to stay parted, not quite forming a smile. "Yet, I think you *crave* the wild."

Although it was a winter's day, Emara could feel nothing but scorching heat. Red hot, scorching heat pounding through her.

But Torin didn't falter. "You get angry when you are around me because you don't want to like that I challenge you—but you *do* like it. You are the kind of girl who needs someone who will challenge you, or you get bored easily."

Emara's full body seized into a tight knot.

"You can't stand the fact that you are *sexually* attracted to me, and it scares you to even think about exploring it, so you shut it down."

She felt like her stomach was rolling around her insides as her heart hammered against her chest.

"I would go as far to say that I bet that you think about me at night…when you're in bed." His eyebrows lifted into a cocky frame to highlight the pleasure in his eyes at his declaration. "Alone."

"That. Is. Preposterous." Emara balled her hands into fists, digging her nails into her palms.

How dare he?

"Absurd!" she yelled at him.

A thin layer of amusement crawled into his stoic frame. "Which part, angel?"

She wasn't sure which part! She wasn't sure if all of what he said was true or if none of it was. Confusion rippled through her, causing a wave of dizziness. She glanced at his lips as she always did when his face broke out in a wicked smile.

There was a part of what he said that might be true…

Maybe all of it.

"There is a part of you that wants the danger. A part of you that strives for it. Why else do you want to be trained?" he asked genuinely.

"I want to be able to protect myself," she blurted out, unable to think of anything else.

His chin dipped in agreeance. "You want to be able to feel alive and liberated. I saw it in your eyes in the courtyard when I gave you my sword. You are like me."

"I am nothing like you!" She shook her head once, her body stilled.

"That's where you are wrong." He smirked. "You'll see."

"I do not have an ego that could burst any minute."

"I will take that as a compliment."

"Of course you will," she sneered. "Even if I punched you in the face, you would take it as a compliment."

He walked towards her slowly; as he neared, she could smell his scent of frozen berries and pine, causing nerves in her skin to spike. His dark brows pulled down to crown his glorious blue eyes and she couldn't predict what he was going to say or do next.

Torin was predictably unpredictable.

Maybe the unpredictability of his character made her feel these—these *strange* things.

He lowered his lashes before speaking in a low, husky voice, "One day you are going to want to kiss me. You are going to want to experiment with your feelings and step outside that bubble you have lived in for too long. You are going to want to explore your deepest and darkest desires."

She couldn't breathe, not when his face was so close to hers. She could see the air from his breath swirl past her.

"And when you do, I will be waiting for you."

Any moment now, Emara felt like her heart was going to explode from her chest. Why did he make her feel like this? She struggled to regain normal breathing.

It felt like the only way to break the tension between them would be to scream. Or punch him. Or kiss him.

No, not kiss him. Absolutely not!

That would be the worst thing she could do.

"I am never going to want to explore *anything* with you," she argued. Straight away, Emara couldn't help but wonder if the lie on her lips had sounded believable.

He was right about one thing, though: She wanted someone who could consume her heart by exploring every desire she had, even if they were her darkest; she wanted someone to share that with. She wanted someone who treasured her and didn't want anyone else. *Only her.* But when she went exploring those darkest desires on her own, she also toyed with the idea of someone who was unpredictable and fierce, but loving and kind. And someone who would be unapologetic about how passionate he was.

Unapologetic about *who* he was.

From the moment she had seen Torin, she had accepted that he was strikingly beautiful, but she had preserved that thought due to who he was.

Would it have been different if Gideon hadn't kissed her first?

Would it be different if Cally hadn't acknowledged a relationship between them? Even though Torin probably didn't see it that way. She thought of the hours that she had spent with Gideon, sleeping in his bed. Torin's brother's bed! She couldn't *feel* these things for him. She had to deny them. Not if what she felt in her heart for Gideon was real.

"Are you going to tell me what is happening in that intriguing little head of yours?" He grinned cheekily.

"No," she said all too quickly.

"Are you thinking about what it would be like to kiss me?" He folded his arms over his broad chest. "Because I would rather just show you."

"I will never kiss you. Do you hear me, Torin Blacksteel? I will *never* want to kiss you!" she hollered. Some birds flew from the trees above them, momentarily taking her attention from the warrior in front of her.

"I am not so sure…" he laughed. His head tilted to the side in amusement. "*Angel.*"

"Do not call me that."

Rage bubbled in her blood. How irresistible did he think he was? How conceited could someone be?

"If I keep calling you angel, what are you going to do about it, Emara?" he challenged with a sensual grin.

"You are the most annoying, most arrogant ass I have ever met in my entire life!" she cursed.

"Now, now, angel, I wouldn't say in your *entire* life—"

"Agrrh, I want to smack you so hard—"

"Then show me." He leaned into her. "Prove you can."

"I am not going to show you anything." She spoke through her teeth as the rage began to boil over.

"Oh, yeah?" he said again, coming closer to her face. "How about I make you show me?"

"You can't make me do *anything!*" she screamed, swinging a fist towards his face.

Okay, maybe I just lost my marbles, she thought. Had she just swung a punch in the direction of a ferocious Hunter?

Torin responded with movement, swinging out with his arm, his hand catching Emara's. She swung again, but missed.

"What a temper you have, little *Witchling.*" He gripped her fist in his hand. "I like it."

Emara ducked quicker than he expected, breaking the hold, and unsheathed a small sword from his weapon belt. She noticed surprise flicker in his eyes, but he didn't show any other emotion to her theft. She pulled herself back and kicked her leg out forcefully, connecting her foot with Torin's abdomen.

Create an opportunity for space if you can.

Gideon's words ran through her mind like a stream of directions. Torin's mass only took one stumble back, and then he was crouching like a predator stalking his prey. He smiled wickedly while drawing out a dagger from his belt.

"You should have said you wanted to play, angel. I would have been more than obliging."

Dangerous excitement edged into his features and he sprung up and dove towards her. She raised her arm to block his blow with her weapon, but it was a trap. He spun under her arm and was behind her before she could react. His firm grip pulled her into his hard body, the dagger pointing to her neck.

"That will be a win for me," Torin breathed, the warmth from his mouth tickling her ear. "Just a heads up, I don't lose."

I would rather go to the underworld than let him win. The steam in her blood sizzled and the rage erupted like lava pouring from the funnel of a volcano. The wind blew through the trees, and the dead leaves from the ground twirled into the air like a swirling pool of colour. One hand slid down her waist and spun her to face him; his large hand lay heavy on the base of her back. Her eyes locked down on Torin's face as his gaze smouldered into hers. Torin didn't even look to see the storm that was brewing around them. He looked at her like she was the only person in the world—the universe.

But she wasn't done.

The air around her brought Emara a new strength and she pounced forward, bringing up her weapon, but Torin anticipated the move and pulled back. Taking a different approach, she swung her elbow like Gideon had shown her and cracked it into the side of his face as he moved towards her. He quickly recovered and ducked around her arm, causing them to be standing face to face. A tiny bead of blood dripped from his lip.

"Torin." She stilled. "I am so sorry." She placed her hands up to his lips. "Are you okay? I didn't mean to hurt you."

The leaves fell around them and the whipping wind that lashed at her hair died instantly.

"Don't apologise." He sucked in his lip, drinking in the blood. "You did exactly what I wanted you to." He wiped one wrist over his mouth, looking down at his hand to see a smear of blood.

"What?" Her nose wrinkled in confusion. "I don't understand what you mean."

"I got you to show me." His face was unreadable, not like before. "Show me what you are made of."

"I still don't—"

Torin cut in, "I provoked you into using your magic." His eyes ignited a fire within them as he wiped his hand on the back of his leathers. "I wanted to see if another of my theories was right. Magic is often connected to feeling and emotion. I want to see what stirred beneath those unusual eyes."

She blinked. "I…I…I used my magic?" She stumbled backwards, but Torin caught her elbow quickly, pulling her upright. "I have magic?"

"Did you not just see the winds wrap around us? Nowhere else in the forest had a gale force breeze ripping at their trees." His face relaxed. "That was the element of Air."

The element of Air.

Her mouth hung open as she looked around herself. "Did I do that?"

"You did." He grinned, somewhat genuinely. "And you threw a mean back elbow." His eyebrow raised in amusement, allowing a dimple to appear in his cheek. "I am slightly impressed."

She raised her chin towards him. "Just slightly?"

A dimple appeared on his other cheek for a second and then flattened out. He turned to begin the trek back up into the forest. "You are going to have to do better than that to completely impress me, ponytail."

Emara stood, stunned.

He provoked her into using her magic.

Magic that she didn't even know she had. She could feel it now, the pulsing in her blood. Or maybe that was from the fight with Torin. She didn't want to mix those two kinds of magics up.

"Wait!" she shouted. "Did you mean any of what you said in the argument?" the words fell from her mouth. She gasped as she realised what she had said, trying everything she could to inhale them back in.

He stopped in his tracks and turned to face her. "Were we arguing? I just thought that's how we communicated."

She took a few steps towards him. "Torin, I asked you a question! Those things you said about me,"—she looked away from his stare—"about wanting to explore my darkness... With you. Was it just a prompt to stir up my emotions, in the effort to get me to use my...my magic?"

Uncertainty crossed her face and she let it. It would have been a clever tactic from him, she had to admit. A very smart move from him. But she didn't know how to feel about it, about what he had said. Had there been any truth to his words?

"Emara, what you feel between us..." He paused. "I feel it too." All vulnerability that had been lingering on his face was now gone. His cheeks drew in. "It's called sexual chemistry."

Her chest tightened around her heart. *Just sexual.* Got it! She felt ridiculous to even think for one second that it could have been anything more.

"I know what *chemistry* is, Torin. I may be less experienced than *you,* but I am not an idiot." Her tone ripped from her mouth harshly.

A muscle ticked under his eye. "Everything I said was...was…" He let out a sigh and rolled his cut lip over his teeth.

"Was what?" she pushed. An emotion that she couldn't place pulled at her heart.

"Was done to see if you could access your magic."

Unbelievable.

That bastard had used her as an experiment.

Emara couldn't imagine toying with anyone's emotions to incite a reaction. But it had worked.

She crossed her arms over her body. "How did you know to make me angry? How did you know it would work?"

"I just know things." He turned to face the incline of the hill and began making his way up.

She fell into step behind him, taking two steps to his one. "Torin, if you know something about my magic, please, tell me." The desperate desire to know overtook her pride. "I have no one else but you to speak of this to."

How could Torin Blacksteel, of all people, know how to stir up any sort of magical energy within her?

"The minute you jumped over the vault in the training room, I knew. No human could learn a skill that quickly without a little *help.*" He craned his neck over his shoulder to see if she was behind him, and she was. "Gideon told you to think of something that enraged you. So, I am guessing you did, because you should have never made that jump. Given the little training you have had, you shouldn't have made that kick to my stomach, either. Or the blow to my face with that feisty little elbow of yours." He allowed a lazy smile to form on his lips. "So I wanted to get you angry and see what happened."

She let out a barking laugh.

She *had* elbowed Torin Blacksteel in the face—and she had enjoyed it. Probably more than she should have. She laughed again.

"I am glad you find that amusing."

She did. But she stilled, holding back her enjoyment. "Do you think the magic within me is helping me in training?" she asked. She was arguably better than most of the villagers that had signed up for the more extreme sessions.

"Of course. Magic pumps through your veins just like your body allows your blood to. Your magic has probably been lying dormant, just under the surface, since you were born." He gave her a look. "It's just never been stimulated."

The way he said it made her blush. She bit into the corner of her cheek. "I am guessing that's why my grandmother always tried to get me to stay in control. 'Never lose focus,' she would say. I was never to lose my temper. Never to lose routine. That's probably why she had my life scheduled down to the very second."

"Probably. She either didn't want you finding out about your magic or for anyone else to find out about you." He tucked his hand down to his weapon belt and pulled out a throwing knife. "Okay, less chatting, more throwing."

But she wasn't done talking.

"For the record"—she looked up at the warrior who towered over her—"I do crave someone who does things differently; someone who makes me feel alive." She took the throwing knife from his hand. "But that person is certainly not you..." She smiled devilishly as she pointed the knife at him. "Torin Blacksteel."

He looked over her body, from head to toe. "For the record, you really need to stop lying to yourself! No one else could make you feel the way I *could* make you feel"—he broke into a lower tone—"*Emara Clearwater.*"

Her heart shook at the sound of her name on his lips. She mentally punched down everything that was stirred within. "Less chat, more instruction, please?" she said, mocking him. Emara waved the throwing knife at him and he had to bite down on his lips to stop himself from smiling.

He controlled his chiselled features well before saying, "Gladly."

As they walked through the forest, she could see wooden targets painted in red. Torin instructed her that when he sounded, she was to try her best to meet the target by throwing her knife.

"Remember your breathing," he coached. "You can't kill a demon if you can't concentrate because you are out of breath. Oxygen must flow through to your muscles."

She did what he said, concentrating on her slow inhale and exhale.

"Left!" Torin yelled so loudly that her heart jumped up her throat.

She took on the command, her eyes searching for the nearest tree on her left. She flicked her wrist back like Marcus had shown her and let her elbow lock as she hurled the knife through the air towards the red target. The blade smacked the tree but didn't stick as it bounced into the long grass that swept up the trunk.

"Also, to kill a demon you need to aim the blade so that it penetrates into the flesh. You only have seconds to do so. You can't make a mistake; that could have been your last blade."

"I managed to sink a few in the target boards in the sparring room." She sounded pleased with herself.

"This is not the sparring room. You don't fight real demons in the sparring room. You fight me and, as ruthless as you think I might be, demons are worse. *Much worse!*" He walked over and stood behind her. He moved her arm and rotated her hips, placing them into a better position. "Bend your leg slightly," he commanded.

She did as she was told.

He took one of his throwing knives from his belt and placed it in her hand. As he rubbed a thumb over her wrist, showing her how it should be angled, a flame of unexplainable tension gripped her stomach.

It shouldn't have felt that good. Oh, Gods above.

He pulled back her wrist and allowed himself to command her arm. To command her full body.

For once, she let him.

He squinted one eye as he jerked her arm forward, projecting the knife straight into the target's centre.

"See, it's always better when you listen to your instructor." He turned with a grin and sauntered up the incline.

He left her to stare at the dagger and, as she did, a tingling swept over her body.

"Left," Torin commanded. And with a smile, she took her aim.

CHAPTER THIRTY-NINE

Emara spent the next few days training twice a day. Once with Marcus in the morning on speed, agility, and endurance, and in the afternoon her sessions with Torin were on weaponry and hand-to-hand combat, which took more focus and precision than she had ever anticipated. Gideon had been letting her off lightly. But Torin certainly wasn't.

After her training sessions, she would take to the infirmary to read, or if Gideon was awake, attend to him, allowing Rhea time to herself—which she reluctantly took. Gideon had been a bit brighter in the last few days, which let the tight band around her heart loosen slightly.

Once back from her daily trip to the library, Emara filled Gideon in on her findings regarding all the ancient manuscripts she had taken. Many of the books that she took were on demons, weaponry, and historical battles, which Gideon informed her he had already read.

She also slipped in a few on witchcraft and the ancient history of the Coven's, but they were in her secret pile, next to her favourite box.

Each night, Gideon had read to her in return for her help, drawing circles on her arm with his fingertips as he did. She nuzzled into his side on the small infirmary mattress and listened to his voice making sense of all the ancient events that had shaped their world. Night after night, they slept together in the infirmary, neither of them going to their own rooms. It was a safe space for them both to spend time together.

Often, she would find that their legs intertwined as Gideon cocooned her from behind in his sleep, stealing kisses when she woke up. And for the first time in a long time, she felt safe again.

Emara knew Gideon was making progress in his recovery when he started to dot kisses all down her neck, sending a warmth across her skin. He was finally putting weight on his arm, and Torin had brought him some weights from the sparring room to work on strengthening his muscle again.

"Good morning," he said, his velvet tone caressing the back of her neck. "How long have you been awake?"

"Long enough to see the sunrise break through the trees," she uttered, trying to downplay the change in her breathing at his mouth on her neck.

Gideon edged his body closer to hers, like he had every morning when he woke. She felt the heat from his skin seeping through her silk nightwear. The silk nightwear that was *another* gift from Cally and her never-ending trips to the Markets.

When Emara had told Cally she would be staying with Gideon in the infirmary again, she had insisted that she wear a strappy, charcoal grey blouse that was made of the finest silk—and the extremely short undergarments to match. Cally had tried to roll up the garment from the waist to show the curve of Emara's buttocks, but Emara had pulled it down in protest.

Have a little fun, Emara. Show off your curves. Embrace them. It will drive him mad. Do you want Gideon to look at you like you are a friend, or girl whom he might want to ravish in the night?

Deciding between the two outcomes, she had rolled the undergarments over once at the waistband.

The sweetness of Gideon's breath tickled into the nape of her neck, distracting her, as he spoke, "I am sorry for nodding off on you so quickly last night." He kissed again and again at her skin. "I wish I didn't need to keep taking those elixirs that make me drowsy, but it's the fastest and least painful way to heal." He ran a hand up her bare leg, tenderly. He rimmed the hem of her undergarment with his index finger.

She tightened the muscles in her legs, forcing them together.

Oh, to the ancient Gods of Caledorna.

"It's quite alright." She collected herself. "I know first-hand how fuzzy Rhea's potions can make you. Plus, it's allowing me to brush up on my knowledge whilst you sleep. I have missed twenty years of learning, you know."

He ran the backs of his knuckles down her arm and kissed into the tip of her spine at the same time.

Her back arched in response.

She fought to keep her breathing steady. "I have enjoyed it. The books, the manuscripts...all very informative."

He laughed softly. "Do you want to know what I have enjoyed?" He pulled himself up and over, rolling her underneath. Her head sunk fully into a feathery pillow. "I have enjoyed waking up to your face every day." He brushed his nose over hers and her heart fluttered.

"I can see that you are feeling a lot better." She smirked back at him as she ran her fingers down his side. "Please don't hurt yourself." Emara felt her brows pull together.

His chocolate brown hair fell over his forehead as he lowered his face to hers. "I had to feel better for the uplift. I promised someone a dance…"

She snorted. "I don't think that *someone* is overly fussed about dancing at the uplift. So you don't have to mend yourself for that reason only. Plus, you said you don't dance." She allowed herself to run her hands down the plains of his back, wishing the shirt he had on wasn't there so that she could feel his skin under her palms.

"That's not the only reason..." He paused. "It was essential to get better for *this* reason, too." He lowered himself slowly down against her body and brought his lips to hers. He gently separated them so that her mouth was wide enough to deepen the kiss. Emara's heart pounded in her chest as he moved his knees closer to her body to stabilise himself, freeing a hand that reached up and cupped her face. Feeling the kiss deepen in her mouth, she pulled his shirt, closing the small gap between their bodies until the curve of her upper frame connected with his.

Moving his hand slowly around her jaw, he traced his lips down her neck and kissed into a soft spot. A moan escaped from her lips and a tingling sensation led directly to her core. "I would dance for you."

She took a breath.

He kissed further down, hovering over her collarbone as he went, causing her body to arch into him. He trailed his tongue further down, to her breastbone, pulling at the skimpy material with his teeth. A breathy moan escaped from her throat and he planted a kiss between her breasts.

She had never done anything like this before, but everything felt so natural. Like her body was automatic to his touch.

He kissed along the top of the material, where the fragile lace met the delicate silk. Emara felt his hot breath seep through to her skin. Her head fell back, and she closed her eyes. Quickly, he lowered his hips and brushed against her, allowing her to feel every inch of him against her.

All of him.

An unfamiliar satisfaction devoured her as she knew in that moment that he was enjoying this as much as she was. Spurred on by Gideon's arousal, Emara lifted her hand to his neck and angled his head, running her teeth along his earlobe. A primal moan purred from his throat, sending sparks all over her body.

And then his mouth was against hers, desperately. The kiss quickened as she ran her fingers through his hair wildly, grinding her hips against his hardness. He moved with her, mirroring her movement, intensifying everything.

She didn't want this to end.

With the taste and touch of Gideon Blacksteel, her body craved more. Her mouth wanted more. It wasn't enough.

His lips twisted with hers as she pushed her tongue back against his, finding a sweet friction between them. She ripped at Gideon's shirt and he sat back on his knees, lifting the material over his head, and flung it to the ground. He winced, for a second, looking at this arm. She stared at him, the perfectly laboured muscle that knitted his torso together, as he leaned over her. His throat bobbed as he looked down at her, watching him. She sat up to meet him, sweeping her hand across his abdomen, and he shuddered in response. Emara traced her index finger down the soft line of hair that swirled into the waistband of his pants and she allowed herself one soft kiss to his stomach.

"I want you so bad," he whispered as his mouth found hers again, pushing her back against the mattress. He thrust his tongue into her mouth, wide and deep. His kiss left her breathless as he pulled away. This time, he skipped her collarbone and, through her shirt, consumed her breast with his mouth. She let out another moan of pleasure.

A sound she hadn't known she could make. She blessed and cursed the material that lay between her bare skin and Gideon's tongue as she flung her head back in gentle ecstasy. The pleasure ran through her spine and in between her legs.

He moved quickly, tucking his arms under her bare legs and yanking her down the bed. Before surprise could set in, he had pushed the silk material of her top up to the lining of her breasts and he trailed his mouth down her torso.

Down and down and down...

Emara inhaled so deeply, her breath caught in her chest.

"Are you okay?" Gideon mouthed against the lining of her waist band.

Emara's hand tugged on his hair as a gesture to keep going, don't stop. She didn't want to talk. She didn't want to listen to anything but the noises he made as he kissed her, as he moved further and further down. Her hips lifted to meet his mouth as he positioned himself between her legs.

This was the furthest she had ever let a man take her, even if she did still have her nightwear on.

It felt right.

The pulse between her legs throbbed as the heat from his mouth kissed against the silk. She hadn't known that she could feel like this. *It* could feel like this.

She tried to stop her body from squirming, feeling the electricity in her cells pound against her blood. Her body writhed against his mouth as he continued to kiss her centre. She had never let a man be this intimate with her—and right now? She didn't care. If he pulled her clothing to the side, she felt like she might implode.

And she would let him do it.

Her knees felt magnetic as they pulled themselves together in pleasure. With one hand, Gideon stopped them. His emerald eyes were a darker shade of lustful green as he looked up at her from between her legs. He pulled one side of the material back and kissed the inner parts of her thigh, grazing her pants as he changed sides.

He kissed the centre of the silk. The centre of her heat.

Oh, Gods.

Flinging her head back, a loud moan escaped her. "Gideon," she breathed, "I want it. I want it all."

He lifted his eyes to hers as surprise flashed across his face. She swallowed down the watery sensation that had appeared in her mouth and her stomach flipped in both anticipation and delight.

"Emara…" he spoke her name with a croaky void in his tone and she knew that meant one thing.

No!

It was a no. He wasn't going any further.

"Gideon, I know what I want. I'm ready."

I want it all.

He hung his head as he dug his hands into the mattress, fighting with himself over something.

Didn't he want to? Did she do something wrong? She tensed as something flickered through her that was so unfamiliar. Blood rushed into her cheeks as she pulled the silk slip down her torso, covering her exposed skin.

He didn't want to!

He didn't want to be with her in that way. Somehow, she had gotten carried away. She had gotten so caught up in the moment.

"It's not that I don't want to," he finally whispered. "Don't think that for one second." He looked up at her, something unspoken torturing him from within. "I want to. I *really* want to. Just not like this." He dipped his head again.

Like what? Things felt perfectly fine to her. She felt a surge of disappointment, confusion, and embarrassment all melting into one sickening cocktail.

"Is it me?" She closed her eyes and awaited his response. "Did I do something wrong?"

"Emara," he croaked her name again and pulled her closer to him. "Look at me."

She slowly lifted her eyes to meet his.

Hurt set around his features. Hurt that she didn't understand. "Trust me when I say I want to. I just can't…not right now."

She bit the corner of her cheek as she stared at the swirling patterns on the ceiling. For the first time since she had awoken from her sleep, she felt a chill in the air. An overwhelming emotion took over, feeling all kinds of stupid, hurt, and reckless.

To even tell him she was ready…

She couldn't stand being in here any longer.

She pushed her legs off the bed only to feel a warm hand on hers. Without meeting Gideon's gaze, she forced a polite smile. "I'd better go." She pulled her hand from underneath his. "Cally will never forgive me if I don't start her pre-uplift preparations early."

"You don't have to go just yet," he begged.

"I do," she replied quickly.

"I will see you tonight," he promised, his tone insistent for a response.

But instead, she pulled up the strap that had fallen down her arm and padded to the door in her bare feet. She closed it without looking back.

When the door clicked into place, she filled her lungs with air, placing her head against the wood. *Breathe.* Emotion choked in her throat. When she closed her eyes, all she could see was Gideon's mouth, as he traced down her naval and kissed into the silk of her night garments. She could still taste his mouth on hers as he whispered, *I want you so bad.*

And she had wanted him too.

She realised in that moment that she wasn't going to stop. She was never going to stop, but he was. Hurt coiled in her gut at the rejection.

If Gideon had taken the opportunity, she would no longer fit into the maiden category in the witches' cycle. The Maiden, the Virgin, the Mother, and the Crone. Was she ready to let someone take something from her that she could never get back?

She knew the answer was yes. She would have given herself to him. She would have let him kiss below the silk, she would have let him—

"That good, huh?" a deep, husky voice taunted.

Emara's eyes snapped open, and she jerked her head off the wooden door.

"Completing the walk of shame? I didn't have you down for that type of girl." Torin Blacksteel stood in the corridor, leaning against the brick with his bulking shoulder, spinning a long, silver knife in the palm of his hands. One by one, he sent it back and forth through his fingers, letting the lethal blade roll over his knuckles.

Heat swarmed her face. "You don't know what type of girl I am," she sneered, crossing her arms over her body.

"Well, I think Gideon's just found out." His dark lashes lowered as his lip curled at the side, causing that infuriatingly cute dimple to appear.

"What I do with Gideon is none of your God-damn business," she scoffed. "You need to remember that!" She turned, ignoring the heat that now flushed down her neck.

"I know you didn't do anything," he called from behind. His voice was quick and snappy, like he didn't want the conversation to be over.

Go straight to your room, the voice of her inner sense roared inside her head. *Ignore him.*

She whirled around.

Of course she wasn't going to ignore him.

Emara strutted up so close to him, she could see his pupils dilate as she neared, but his strong chin pushed up boldly.

"You don't know anything about what just happened." The slow, sensual tone of her voice surprised her.

He repositioned his feet on the ground as he tightened his jaw, revealing a second dimple. "I know that if *anything* had happened, the wet patches on your silk nightwear would have had time to dry." He looked at her through a fan of dark lashes. "It would have been lying on my bedroom floor for a *long* time." He stood up straight, leaving the wall behind. "There would have been *plenty* of drying time." His deep, ocean blue eyes fixed on her face, his nostrils flared. "Plus, I would never have let you leave my bedroom wearing that," he said as he drank her in. He reached out and she gasped as he pulled up the strap of her top that had fallen from her shoulder again. His fingertips slid against her skin, all the way up her arm to her shoulder, and a charge of energy tingled where he touched. "I wouldn't have let you leave, all fucking day." He closed whatever distance was between them. "And I can assure you, you wouldn't have wanted to, either, angel."

With a sensual wink and a carnal smile, he was gone.

Emara stood in silence for what felt like an hour, unable to move or even breathe.

Finding her sanity, she cursed a million swear words under her breath and ran a hand through her hair frantically before heading to her own room—where she was safe from smouldering eyes, sensual smiles, and dangerous taunts.

CHAPTER FORTY

Callyn Greymore stood back and contemplated what was going to be done next to Emara's face. "Let's try a red lip."

She rummaged around her large, leather-bound case for the perfect colour to paint upon them. Cally had spent the good part of two hours turning Emara's straight hair into beautiful waves that cascaded down her frame. Whilst doing that, Emara had filled her in about her morning with Gideon. She left out the odd encounter with Torin, though; she wasn't even going to give that room in her mind to expand.

Cally took a colour palette from her box of trickery, screwed up her eyes, and then flung it back in. "I mean, I can't believe he didn't even try and at least get your pants off."

Emara let out a laugh, but the dull bite in her chest reminded her that the sting of rejection was still present. "I don't know what happened, if I am honest; one minute he was—"

"Between your legs," Cally casually announced as she pulled out another red colour.

Emara pressed her lips together before she began, "Between my…legs, and the next he was just over it. Maybe I misread it," she said, shaking her head.

"Ah, perfect!" Cally drew out another colour, finding the one she had in her mind. "I can assure you, you did not read the situation wrong. I have seen the way he looks at you. Maybe he respects you too much to go there yet. I think that's…sweet."

Emara snorted, "You are a terrible liar."

"If the man that you're going to end up giving yourself to questions himself, he isn't the right one." She brushed a swatch of colour onto the back of her hand. "However, it could just be bad timing. He is still in recovery."

Emara felt a twinge of guilt at Cally's words, but she knew that he had basically made a full recovery.

"Gods, it still happens to me and I lost my virginity years ago. Girls question themselves all the time. It happened to me with Torin the other week. Just because they don't want you, it's like you second guess yourself. I knew he wasn't into me, but I still did it anyway." She shrugged her shoulders. "But you still want to be the one they want, I suppose."

Plus, I would never have let you leave my bedroom wearing that. I wouldn't have let you leave all fucking day. And I can assure you, you wouldn't have wanted to, either, angel.

For the second time today, she clenched her legs tighter together, forcing Torin's words to the back of her mind.

Bloody Blacksteels, she cursed internally.

"I am almost done, and can I just say, you look sensational!" Cally clapped her hands before lining Emara's lips with a full red line and then filled it in with a ruby red gloss. "Dress time," Cally beamed from ear to ear.

Emara couldn't help but gleam back at her. "I can't believe you haven't even looked at it once!"

Grabbing a glass of flush pink wine, Emara made her way to the box that lay waiting in her bathing chamber. In the main room, Cally had started pulling out shoes and accessories from boxes whilst pouring herself a wine with her free hand. The skills Cally had when it came to liquor and fashion were second to none.

Emara sat her glass down on the unit which held the oval, ceramic sink and opened her box. She hadn't seen the dress until now and, as she pulled it out, a black satin slip of material lay heavy in her hands. She held it up, fully taking it in, and she noticed dangling diamond straps that hung all the way down the seams of the dress connecting the material at both sides.

Slipping into the dress, she let the satin embrace and hug her skin like the dress was made exactly for the curves of her body. Looking in the mirror, her breath shoved down into her chest in surprise and awe.

It was *exquisite!*

She brushed her fingertips along the diamond chains that started from her under arm and finished amid her thighs, pulling the gown together. All down her sides, bare skin lay under the diamond chains, exposed.

Callyn Greymore!

Undergarments certainly could not be worn with this dress. *Nothing* but the dress.

She brushed two hands over either hip, flattening the material against her curves. Emara turned to admire the dress from the side, noticing the diamond chains glistening as she moved. The floor-length gown scooped down her back like a falling balcony, revealing the top half of her tanned skin. She looked at herself in the mirror over her shoulder.

Really looked at herself.

The girl staring back had changed since the last time she had picked herself apart in front of a mirror. She wasn't the same girl who had seen her body as too curvy or too tanned. She saw a hint of definition in her physique as she moved around, examining herself in the black, satin gown. The diamonds against her skin tinkled like the Huntswood City lights from below the Tower's rooftop as she swayed her hips from side to side.

She would never have been brave enough to wear a gown so daring before; now she was.

"Oh, my Gods, Emara, you look smoking!" Cally fanned herself as she stood in the threshold of the door. "It's like you could go up in flames any minute. I am proud of my work."

Her white silk dress—that could have been passed off as expensive nightwear— fit her perfectly. Her long legs were met at the bottom with silver-laced heels that tied up her calf. She clutched a silver feather purse that lightly waved as she moved. Her earlobes were decorated with stunning, hanging diamonds that tear-dropped into a point, looking like they could have cost her a silly fortune. Her golden hair, unusually sleek and straight, lay beside the curves of her face.

She was a sight for the Gods. She could be mistaken for one in the company they would keep tonight.

"Wow, Cally. You look unbelievable."

"I know, right?" Her white teeth clashed together in a dazzling smile. "However, I have one more thing for you." She strolled over.

"Callyn, absolutely not. I have enough." Emara pushed out her hand.

"I think you might like it. The minute I saw it, I thought of you." Cally reached into her purse and gripped something in a green velvet pouch and handed it over.

"I am not taking anything else from you." Emara tried to push it back.

"If you don't take it, I will throw the biggest bitch fit you have ever Gods-damned seen."

Emara let out a laugh and took the jade pouch into her hand, scowling at her best friend in jest. She reached in and pulled out a solid gold hair comb. Emara gasped as its beauty lay in the palm of her hand in the shape of a crescent moon. The comb was encrusted with stones that danced in the light, sending out flashes of scarlet, indigo, yellow, and cerise. Its weight was surprising for something so small. Emara couldn't even imagine how much coin this would have cost.

"Callyn..." Emara looked up.

"I know how you look at the moon. You always have! Now you have your own moonlight." Cally's voice wavered slightly. "Even when the clouds are grey, and the moonlight cannot escape through, you have your own." She took a deep breath and then continued, "And, of course, it completed your outfit." She tried her hardest not to let any emotion form.

Emara opened her mouth to speak, but nothing could have prepared her for that.

She tried again. *Nothing.*

"Don't," Cally said, putting out a hand to stop Emara from speaking. "If there is anything in the world that represents who you are, it's the moon. She shines in times of darkness and everyone looks at her to lead us into a better day." Cally's smile was small but it was full of warmth and love. Emara fought against the crushing feeling in her throat and rushed towards her best friend. Her sister, not in blood, but in life. In her own kind of oath. She flung her arms over her.

"And although she herself shines bright, she never dulls the light of the sun," Cally finished. She dug her chin deep into Cally's shoulder and squeezed her tight. "Okay." The blonde pulled back. "We don't do mushy, and my face is too pretty tonight to mess it up with your tears." She laughed and pulled further back from their embrace. She took the crescent moon comb and slid it into Emara's hair. "There, perfect! Now let's see what this uplift is all about."

CHAPTER
FORTY-ONE

Chatter in good spirits floated down the foyer to Emara before she could see anyone. As they rounded the corner, her stomach twisted into an anxious knot and she swallowed down her nerves as she saw humans and Hunters congregating in small circles, laughing and conversing.

At first it was challenging for her to pick out which were human and which were Hunters due to everyone's formal attire, but to her now-trained eye she could see more muscle definition in the males who stood amongst the human crowd.

Marcus Coldwell made his way through the group, advancing towards them in a finely-made suit. One that Emara was used to seeing on Elite males. "Emara, don't you scrub up well." He smiled kindly. "I can see this one has done a great job of hiding the bruises on your arms." He gestured a hand to Cally. "You also look wonderful tonight, Miss Greymore." He bowed his head.

"Well, thank you, Marcus." Cally tucked a strand of her blonde hair behind her ear, revealing her bejewelled earlobes. "You don't look so bad yourself."

"It's not often us Hunters get to dress to impress, but tonight we have our work cut out for us, keeping up with you beautiful ladies." He expressed some Hunter charm and Emara realised she had never seen that side of him. It was nice to see an informal Marcus.

"You are too kind," Emara added. "I do have one question: How do we actually get to the uplift? Surely, we can't be walking." She gestured to the shoes on her feet.

Magic swirled in Marcus' eyes. "We are absolutely not within walking distance. Not even in practical shoes." He looked down at her feet, judging the heel size. "We are going to portal in."

"Portal in?" Cally said, way too loudly.

In the gardens of the Tower, a Witch in a dark green cloak waved her hands in front of her like she was an artist mixing paint on a canvas. Air blew around the shrubbery and the trees groaned in response to the building enchantment. Hunters were now gathering outside, partnering with a few of the villagers. They, too, were looking around, nervous. One woman in a beautiful yet simple gown caught Emara's eye and offered her a smile. She smiled back. She guessed she wasn't the only nervous one.

The Witch worked her arm around in a circle motion and a ring of shimmering air grew. Flashing lights appeared in the middle of the circle, displaying green, dancing flames that merged all the magic together. An iridescent pool of blue-green was in the middle of the whirling vortex of what looked like water but was not. The rippling magic of the portal looked like it could tear out cities from their roots and Emara let out a sharp exhale, taking in its irrefutable power.

"Everything is going to be fine," said Marcus. "It isn't that bad." His boyish grin told her otherwise. "Just don't let go of my arm; you must always keep contact with me. Thorin knows where you would end up if you didn't."

Emara swallowed.

"Will it ruin my hair?" Cally's eyes were wide with fear. Not of the portal, but at the thought of one strand of her sandy hair being out of place.

Emara wanted to scream as she watched Hunters, one by one, lead their dedicated humans through the portal. They hadn't shrieked or panicked; they had simply vanished.

"Our turn." Marcus let out a small laugh and linked Cally's arm with his. He held out another arm for Emara to hold. With a small wish that it was Gideon's, she took hold and walked into the vortex.

Walking through the portal felt like she had been flung into a cauldron of stars, darkness, and infinity. Every inch of her body felt like it had turned to liquid. Every cell tingled in her blood, sparking magic to life. A gust of power knocked the air from her lungs, hitting her from the side. Clutching on for dear life,

Emara dug her fingers into the arm of Marcus' suit jacket, who also had Cally screaming on the other side of him.

Although Emara had closed her eyes and tried to hold back the scream that crawled up her throat, she could not hide her trembling. She could see flashes of colour through her shut lids and swirls of blackness with spots of light, all meshing into one as they spiralled around and around.

A sudden thud onto concrete made the bones in her ankles groan and Emara opened her eyes as she took a breath of fresh air. A sudden slap of cold hit her face and she hurled over, spewing the contents of her stomach onto the path. Trying to steady herself on her heels, she placed a hand on her navel and pulled her hair round to one side. Feeling like she had sea legs, she stood up straight.

"Well, that wasn't too bad, actually." Cally's tone was light and full of amusement.

"Yeah, tell that to the screaming I heard the whole time," Emara snapped as she tried to stabilize her wobbling legs. "My ears are still ringing from the sounds you made."

"Here," Marcus pulled out a silver flask from his dress-jacket pocket. "Take a sip of this and straighten yourself out."

Emara took the flask from Marcus' hands, hoping it was an anti-sickness potion, and instantly felt the cool relief of the metal on her fingertips. She pressed it either side of her cheeks before unscrewing the top and taking a large gulp of its contents.

It was pure alcohol. It burned its way down Emara's throat like hellfire and she fought with her stomach to keep it down.

"What the hell, Marcus?" She put a shaky hand over her mouth.

A hearty laugh escaped his throat. "I thought you were made of stronger stuff, Clearwater," he said, leaning forward in efforts to regain the flask. But Emara held out her hand in protest and flung another mouthful of the liquor to the back of her throat. She needed that one for a little courage for what she was about to walk into.

"Ha! That's what I thought. Now hand over the flask, I need that to get through this night." He gestured to a massive, white mansion that sat on the top of a hill, surrounded by forest. "We are here."

She wondered how far the portal had allowed them to travel. *Are we even in Huntswood?*

Turning to see other Hunters and villagers starting to crowd from where the portal had brought them out, a few of them laughing about their portal experience, she glanced over at Cally; however, she was already strutting up a curving stone path that led to the mansion, her silvery heels clicking as she walked.

"What are you waiting for?" she shouted behind herself. "The alcohol won't drink itself!"

Biting her lip, Emara controlled a smile from entering her face. She looked up to the sky to where the stars sprinkled across the night's darkness. They were so clear; Emara could tell immediately that they were no longer in the city, but somewhere with no light con-tamination. Somewhere that allowed the stars to have such a loud presence. They were beautiful.

Echoing Cally's question, the stars looked upon her and whispered, *What are you waiting for?*

A light melody flowed from an array of string instru-ments that took centre stage at the front of the ballroom. Elegant green paint coated the walls as weaves of solid gold coved around the top. The ceiling of the room was a stained-glass dome of stunning colours. It depicted stories of Angels, Gods, Demons, and Creatures all liv-ing in a realm as one. Flowers, weapons, and relics of all sorts, long forgotten, were painted brightly as the moonlight poured through the tinted glass. Emara looked down from the ceiling and eyed the stunning drapes that hung heavy against the large windows in a champagne colour. Tall tables of bronze stood high as gracefully dressed women and men gathered around them.

A waiter dressed in black arrived in front of her, bowing his head as he placed a flute of pink, bubbling liquid into her hand. Cally's eyes sparkled as she, too, received a flute.

Six opulent chandeliers gave the impression that they floated, illuminating the darkest colours in the stained-glass dome with candlelight. Distant laughs of polite conversation filtered through the air, creating a second melody.

"Have you ever seen anything like this?" Cally whispered with her eyes wide as could be.

"Not in a million lifetimes," Emara whispered back, looking at the porcelain floor tiles that she could see her reflection in. A thought occurred to her and she wondered how many hours it had taken the maids to buff and polish the floor for it to gleam her reflection. Taking in every detail of her surroundings, she noticed how oddly attractive everyone was, from their stunning hair to their impeccable complexions to their expensive attire. She noted the Hunters straight away from the muscles and posture that stood out against the more slender and relaxed individuals. Some Hunters were still carrying weaponry fixed around their waists. Most of their faces were unfamiliar. They were from different clans, she realised.

"Excuse me, girls, I can see an old friend. Make yourself comfortable. Grab some canopies." Marcus smiled before buttoning his suit jacket and spinning on his heels.

"That means he can see an old flame and is in for a chance of getting laid tonight, if he plays his cards right." Cally laughed as she placed her lips to the thin flute and drank. "Oh, my world in heaven, have you tasted the sparkling wine?"

Emara placed the flute to her lips and sipped. The taste of bubbles and exotic fruit exploded onto her tastebuds and danced along her tongue before slowly gliding down her throat.

Oh, wow, even the wine tastes like wealth and luxury.

Beautiful women of all shapes and sizes floated around the room in exquisite gowns of violets, reds, blues, and golds. She wasn't sure what any of them were. They could be Witch, Fae, Shifter…

Maybe even human.

An emerald gown caught her eye as a short-haired woman relaxed into a chaise longue. Two handsome men sat beside her, one holding her drink in a crystal glass. They were both armed, she realised, and it didn't take a magic wielder to know that she was powerful. The energy radiated from where she sat. As the woman reached out with her milky hand to grab her drink, Emara noticed a small triangular mark with a thin line of black though the top, near the point. She had seen the symbol before—many times—in her grandmothers' paintings, in the fortune tellers' tent, and in the manuscripts she had been reading. It was the symbol of House Air.

There was no mistaking who she was; she was the Empress of Air. The most powerful Witch in the coven. Emara wondered about the relationship the Witch would have had with her grandmother. Or even her mother.

Dragging her eyes from the Empress' face, she looked towards Cally and said, "I am not sure what we are supposed to do now."

"Are you serious?" She laughed. "Let's sit on their awfully expensive chairs, drink this fantastic wine, and look fabulous." Cally raised her flute to

Emara's and a clinking sound had them both smiling wildly. "It's like I was born to do this."

Emara bowed her head towards Cally. "Cheers," she saluted.

"To us." Cally's white teeth were prominent in her dazzling smile. "Looking like heaven raised by hell." She winked a dark, sparkling eyelid and sank the contents of the flute.

They spotted a seating area designed for four which had high-backed chairs in a dusky pink velour and moved through the crowd towards them. Cally sat herself into the chair of her choice, resting like royalty against her throne. Emara took the seat opposite her as a waiter approached them with another two flutes.

"I could get used to this," Cally smirked as she took the two drinks from the waiter and passed one to Emara. "Your service is terrific." She dramatically rolled out her hand in a bowing gesture toward the man. "Keep these coming, handsome."

"Thank you." Emara nodded to the waiter and then let her eyes wander, looking around herself. "This place is unbel—"

At once, she stopped speaking. Out of the corner of her eye she spotted what truly was heaven and hell as the Blacksteel brothers strode across the room to where they were seated.

Emara wasn't sure she was breathing at all as she took in the sight of them walking towards her like two Gods of the ancient worlds. Everything else around the room slowed as Gideon strolled towards her wearing a white, fitted shirt that hugged around his sculpted torso. His shirt was buttoned at the top, joined by a long, black tie to match his trousers that sat low on his hips. His face was unreadable. Torin swaggered with one hand in his pocket and the other holding his dress jacket over his shoulder—dressed in all black.

Of course, he's dressed in all black again, Emara snorted internally. *It's the colour of his heart.*

For a moment, Emara allowed her eyes to take in every devastating detail of him too. His hair, jet black, sat perfectly atop his head; his long-sleeved shirt, in the same colour, stretched under his carved-to-perfection body. He wore a cocky grin that told her exactly what he was thinking.

Are you checking me out, angel?

She closed her mouth and tore her eyes away from them, turning to Cally. She, too, looked like she was in a Blacksteel trance.

Who wasn't when they strode straight through the dancefloor, looking like that?

"Ladies," Torin greeted them as he removed his hand from his pocket. The other removed his jacket from his shoulder and swung it over the chair next to Emara, marking it his.

Oh, Gods, help me.

Gideon took the seat next to Cally, smiling graciously at her. He lowered himself into the chair, his eyes flickering to Emara for a second, and then to his brother.

"Callyn, you look stunning, as always." Torin spoke with presence as he adjusted a cufflink on his wrist.

Cally leaned forward and put the flute on the glass table that separated the chairs. "You don't get to call me that." She smiled, baring her teeth; it was not a smile of friendship.

It was a warning.

"That's not what you were saying a few nights ago," he purred back. "You said I could call you anything I wished."

"Shut your mouth, Torin, or I will shut it for you," the words emptied from Emara's mouth before she could even stop them. No one tried to shame her best friend—to protect his own stupid macho pride—and got away with it. Cally would do the same for her. She always had.

He let out a whistle and leaned back in his chair, focused on Emara. His chiselled jaw tightened; his gaze darkened as he took in her face.

"Emara, you look…" he played around with words in his mind. *That feeling* coiled in her stomach, sending heat into all the places she didn't want it. Not for Torin. She pushed her knees together, locking one foot behind the other, and swallowed down her surprise at her body's reaction to him. Torin's gaze followed the flow of her muscles and a small smirk tugged at his lips. "You look *exquisite,*" he finished. The articulation in his words sent a warm shiver up her spine and she took another mouthful of sparkling wine.

Emara stole a glance at Gideon, but his attention was on his brother, his cheeks pulled in tight, his eyes crackling with rage.

"Emara," Callyn's voice broke through the tension. Finally. "I am going to find Waylen; he should be here any moment."

She gave a nod, not sure she was ready to be left alone with the Blacksteels, and said, "Come and find me soon, okay?"

"I will." Cally leaned in and kissed her on the cheek. "Gideon, you look smoking, by the way."

A small smile graced Gideon's lips and she turned on her heels, flicked her hair over her shoulder, and strutted into the crowd.

As she disappeared, a waiter brought over a small crystal glass with a rusty orange liquid in it and handed it to Torin. "As requested, Mr. Blacksteel."

Torin took the glass and nodded a thank you in return.

Both Gideon and Emara watched as he sipped the drink, dragging the liquor between his teeth, savouring every drop. "So, *lovebirds...*" He placed an arm over the back of the chair, casually relaxing. "Shall we talk about this morning?"

Gideon's face almost turned purple at his brother's words. "Emara, can we have a moment to talk?"—he flicked his eyes to her—"alone?"

She was never going to have this conversation in front of Torin, about what had happened between them this morning—or what *hadn't* happened.

Before she could say anything, Torin cut in, "As much as I would love to stay and see Gideon squirm under the pressures of being a man, House Earth has just walked in." He paused. "I must go and see our dearest mother." He stood, hanging his jacket over his arm. "Please excuse me."

"I will be over as soon as I can," Gideon said, dismissing him.

Torin nodded and set his focus towards Emara. "I am sure I will see you later. Have a nice talk."

Emara followed him as Torin mingled into the crowd and was then lost.

Out of the corner of her eye, she noticed Gideon move over to the chair beside her with the grace of a cat and her attention followed.

"Hey," he said sheepishly.

Emara smiled politely but didn't say anything in return. He looked down at the flute in his hand and swirled the stem between his thumb and index finger.

Is he nervous? Emara thought, taking a sip out of her own glass to fill the gap in the silence.

After a few seconds that felt like minutes she said, "You wanted to talk—so, talk!"

He flinched at the shortness in her tone. She had been so embarrassed about what happened this morning, replaying the situation over and over in her mind the entire day, she couldn't help but be short. She didn't understand what was going on between them, and he wasn't exactly clearing it up. He made her feel like she had somehow misunderstood where things were going this morning.

She knew that she wasn't imagining the passion between them, but that didn't explain why he had led her down a path that he had no intention of taking. Hurt stirred in her chest as she studied his face. Was she a fool to think that Gideon had wanted the same moment between them? Had she not read the signals properly?

Kissing down her stomach to her most intimate area certainly wasn't a sign that he *didn't* want it.

"Emara, about this morning…I"—he paused—"it's just hard because I can't tell you everything but—but just know that I wanted to go further with you." His lips thinned into a narrow line. "You expected something more this morning and it wasn't fair for me to do that. Especially when I had no intention of going any further; we were just fooling around." He looked up. "For now."

Fooling around! Just fooling around.

He had no intention of being with her the way she had thought. He had just made himself truly clear that what had happened this morning, to him was just fun.

Emara's heart sank to the bottom of her stomach. She shook her head in anger as the sting in her eyes formed tears.

He had no intentions of being intimate with her and she had almost given up something that was so precious to her for something that was 'fooling around' to him. Why would he do that? Stupidly, she had thought it meant something to both of them.

"No, Gideon, you are right. It wasn't fair. I said things to you that I have never said to another man. Ever!" *I want all of it.* She swallowed the memory of her words. "I let you do—ugh! You should never have done what you did this morning. Especially if you had no intentions of— of—"

"Of making love to you?" He completed her sentence. He ran a hand over the back of his neck and let out a sigh. "I told you I wanted to. I just can't. Not right now, it wouldn't be right."

An exasperated sigh fell from her mouth. "I have no idea what that even means, Gideon, and if you think that for one second that that makes me feel any better about myself, then you are wrong. I told you I am not looking to play some stupid game. In fact, I am fairly sure you punched Torin for the same thing. How is that for irony?" She could have cut him in half with the glare she threw his way.

"I am not playing a game with you. I just can't—"

"Stop being so cryptic." She allowed the annoyance on her face to take full form. "You can't say because you have been *ordered* not to? Am I right?" She raised her eyebrows. "Because, for whatever reason, you are not allowed to say by your *father's orders?*" she spat. "I am not a fucking mission, Gideon." She rose to her feet and his face paled. "Do not treat me like one." She turned to walk away, and Gideon caught her by the elbow. She yanked it back. "Don't!"

She heard her name break from his voice as she walked away and didn't look back. As she worked her way through the socialising crowd, Emara tried to control her anger. She had seen what could happen if she didn't control herself, and she had no idea how to stop or start her magic as she pleased. It was new. Newer than new. Emara understood that she was amongst the supernatural tonight and didn't want to make a complete spectacle of herself on her debut into this world.

If she wanted to be a part of this world.

She spotted Cally, who was touching the chest of a dark blond man who was wearing a taupe suit.

Cally caught her eye and smiled, mouthing *"You okay?"*

Emara nodded and forced a smile as she looked around for a waiter who served those delicious pink flutes.

She had thought about telling Cally everything tonight. So many times, over the last few weeks, she had wanted to burst into conversations and explain everything about her magic, about who she was, but something had held her back. Something that she couldn't explain. She never kept anything from Cally, and the longer it lay unspoken, the heavier it felt on her chest.

Emara made her way over to the waiter, shoving the image of Gideon's face to the back of her mind. She swallowed down the truth about who she was for tonight; she could just enjoy tonight as a normal human. Tomorrow, she would tell Cally everything; maybe if she found out whilst she was hungover, she wouldn't be so angry about her hiding a secret.

Perhaps Cally wouldn't treat her any differently and nothing would change between them.

She hoped…

As she took a step closer, someone caught her arm, swinging her around to face eyes of sapphire blue. "Is your lovers' tiff over, or are we still brooding about Gideon not making sweet, passionate love to you?" He pretended to pout.

"Torin, I am not in the mood to bat back and forth with you over the subject of your brother." She pulled her arm back. "A subject that is none of your concern." She ground her teeth.

"Fine," he said sharply. "Dance with me, then."

Something vulnerable flashed in his eyes for nothing longer than a second. He held out his hand gently, probably the gentlest she had ever seen him move.

Taken aback with the fact that he hadn't pushed her any further, she looked him over. "You know that dancing never ends well between us." She flicked her hair over her shoulder and looked into the crowd of people.

"I don't think it's that kind of scene, Emara. It's a formal dance, not an exotic tavern club." The sound of her name on his lips sent her heart into a frenzy as she snapped her gaze back to his face. "As much as I would like it to be." He leaned in and whispered, "Let's show my brother what he is missing."

Her heart thundered against her chest as she contemplated his offer.

She placed her hand into his and rolled her eyes. "You better behave," she warned.

A primal smile appeared on his face as he turned and led her to the dance floor. "Don't I always?"

There were a few couples dancing on the white, star-lit dance floor. Some of them looked extremely uncomfortable as they tried to force a connection; others looked like they could head to get a room any minute, clearly taking advantage of their schmoozing event. Torin pulled her close to him as one hand slid into hers, holding her arm out. The other hand slid down her back and rested at the base of her spine.

A fluttering in Emara's chest hitched her breathing as he moved her to the music.

There was no mistaking who was leading who.

"I do have one question before I start my course of good behaviour for the evening." He kept his face straight. "I must ask because the topic is eating my rational thoughts alive. Are you wearing any underwear under that dress?"

A laugh burst from Emara's throat. "Are you telling me that *Torin Blacksteel* can't tell if I am wearing underwear or not?" She laughed again as he pivoted her 'round in time to the music, surprising her once more at how well he moved in time with melody. "You seem to be losing your touch."

The sounds that emanated from the composition were slow and steady, smooth and dark. Like Torin's movements.

"If I had to guess, I would say no. But again, I didn't have you down as that kind of girl." He said with a smirk.

"Again," she lowered her tone down to match his, "you have no idea what kind of girl I am." She met his gaze as he pressed his lips together. "Nevertheless, you shouldn't be asking me such questions," she said lightly in amusement.

"I think it is relevant for me to know such things." He lowered his hand on her back an inch.

"Do you?"

"Absolutely."

"Well, if you must know,"—she swallowed—"my dress doesn't cater to undergarments." She said it so confidently that she surprised herself. "I thought your trained eye would have been able to tell." She took a breath. "And it bothers me that you keep saying, 'I didn't think you were that kind of girl' like it's some sort of shock to you that I am not fluffy and cute and full of rainbows." She exhaled. "That's not me."

He let out a small laugh against the side of her ear that warmed her heart. "Oh, I know it's not. I just find it funny that you often try to be." He spoke lowly, "But I must admit, you do surprise me."

"Stop underestimating me and you won't be surprised," she sparred.

He pressed their hands tighter together. "I am not underestimating you. I just needed some clarification, because you have no idea what kind of undergarments, I am conjuring up in my mind right now. Especially that would allow you to wear them without being seen under that dress."

A giggle found its way from her mouth. "You said you were going to behave…"

"I said I had a question before I *started* to behave."

"Well, now question time is over."

He chuckled again, "The dress is…something else."

She could feel the beating of his heart against her skin. Could he feel hers?

He lowered his voice, "You have every man in this room looking at you and you don't even know it."

Emara didn't dare turn her head to see if anyone was looking at her; she kept the muscles in her body loose as she moved with the movements of Torin Blacksteel.

"Cally picked it for me. The dress, I mean," she said humbly as she processed Torin's words. "And they are only staring because I am dancing with you."

"Are you trying to pay me a compliment or an insult?" His voice sounded light and crisp and she couldn't get the smell of frozen berries and pine out from her nose. "I can never tell these days."

"Take it however you want," she scoffed with a smile.

He paused momentarily and then said, "They are definitely looking at you. Wondering if cutting in to ask you to dance would be worth the risk to their lives."

Emara let out a small giggle. She felt the same smile form on Torin's face. He spun her out and pulled her back in, crushing her body against his.

"Let's give them something to watch, shall we?" He moved the hand that rested on her lower back around to her hip, caressing her bare skin. He ran one long finger up and down the diamond strapping that held the dress together at her side as his face grew closer to hers.

She held her breath for a long moment.

He spun her around as he moved his feet quickly, leading her in and out of a seductive dance. She, too, moved her feet to the tempo that had picked up pace. Running a hand down her back, so close to the curve of her buttocks, he said, "If I know my brother, he will be over here in three, two…"

A cough came from the right of them. "Excuse me for cutting in…"

Her head tilted to the side to see Gideon standing before them. Her pulse didn't know whether to quicken or stop completely.

"One," Torin whispered, pulling back and creating a space between them.

Before allowing Gideon to take his place, he lowered his mouth to her hand and brushed his lips against her skin. "Have a good night, Angel."

She couldn't find the words to speak as she watched him disappear into the crowd. The tingle from his kiss ran up her arm and into her chest. Gideon lifted his brows to wait and see if she would allow him to dance with her.

Emara gathered herself before she held out a ballroom dance pose and Gideon moved into the structure, placing his hand in hers. He slid his arm around her waist, and she took a deep breath in and exhaled, noticeably placing her hand as far away from his wound as possible.

Finally, she could breathe…

"You seem to be enjoying yourself."

"Gideon, I didn't mean to snap at you earlier." She paused. "Well, I did but it came out harsher than anticipated."

"You had every right to." He lowered his head. "I just wish I could show you how I feel."

She pulled back and looked at him, "You can show me how you feel, Gideon." Emara kept her features stern. "You can also tell me…"

"I have told you. You know how I feel about you."

"I am not talking about what you said the other night. I am talking about what happened this morning. Talk to me!" She gripped his hands tighter.

"That's easier said than done when you are bound to a duty that no one else will understand unless they are bound to it. I meant what I said." He looked into her eyes, every part of his face sincere. "It took me all I had to stop this morning. I wanted to be with you like that. But now is not the right time."

She nodded, understanding that she had to trust him. Now was not the right time to have a disagreement, either. Not in the middle of the uplift. They would speak about this in-depth when the time was right.

His voice was soft and deep with meaning as he asked, "Where do we go from here?"

She chewed her lower lip. "I am not going to answer that question right now because I am not sure." Emara dipped her chin. "I will sleep on it."

"When you say sleep on it, will you be sleeping beside me while you sleep on it?" Gideon's lip twitched at the side.

"We shall see how the night evolves." She grinned.

She was still hurt from this morning, but whatever reason Gideon had—that he couldn't share—she had to respect that it was his duty. She just had to trust him.

He twirled her under his arm and she laughed, feeling coy.

"You look breathtaking tonight." He gripped her hand tighter. "It almost hurts to look at you." He smiled, his beautiful green eyes finally sparkling again.

"You don't look so bad yourself," she said, smiling back at his contagious grin. "But I think it's time you get me off this dance floor and get me a drink."

He smiled and fell into step behind her as she led the way.

CHAPTER FORTY-TWO

The drinks flowed and so did the laughter as Gideon and Waylen reminisced about growing up together. Cally couldn't stop making eyes between Waylen and Emara as if to say, *'Do you like him?'* However, Emara didn't give anything away; she would chat to her regarding the details of the night at a later point.

As she sat listening to the teenage years of the wolf pack, Emara couldn't help but look around the room for the inky black hair and ocean eyes that had been on her mind recently.

She found him after a few moments. He stood with his hand against the wall, whispering sweet nothing into a beautiful redhead's ear. The girl had a familiar symbol at her collarbone, a circle that represented House Spirit. His black shirt had opened at the neck slightly and the girl tickled a finger against the nape of his throat, tipping her head back in roaring laughter.

He isn't that funny, Emara thought to herself.

"And then, there Gideon was…naked in the barn, lying on the haybale!" Waylen barked out a thunderous laugh, showing his canine-like teeth. Cally also laughed with the boys; she had clearly taken in every single word of the story whilst Emara's mind had trailed off somewhere a little more dangerous.

"I will never play that drinking game with you and your brothers again." Gideon laughed and then silence followed quickly.

Brothers. Eli.

Cally went still against Waylen as he, too, paused in laughter for a second. The uncomfortable atmosphere snapped Emara's attention back to the room.

"I'm sorry, I didn't mean to—"

"Don't worry about it." Waylen placed his drink on the table. "They are good memories of Eli and that is how we will remember him." Cally brushed her hand against Waylen's shoulder in a soothing motion and Emara studied them as Waylen looked at Cally. They did have good chemistry, she would give them that.

"I am so sorry for your loss," Emara managed to say.

The wolf nodded in gratitude.

"Shall we go and get some drinks?" Cally asked, making a gesture with her head.

"Actually, I was going to nip out for some air." Emara crinkled her nose.

"Do you want me to come with?" Gideon started to get up from his chair.

"If you don't mind, I will just go to the ladies' room and then head out," she protested. "I won't be long. You stay, chat and reminisce with Waylen; I'm sure he is finding comfort in the memories you have together." She masked a smile onto her face and lost herself in the crowd before Gideon could protest.

The corridors were long and winding and the doors were all the same white wood as she looked in each one for a bathroom. Emara opened a hefty door on the left of the corridor and noticed a master suite with a four-poster bed, wrapped in red and cream sheets. Looking around, she noticed another door that was slightly open and prayed for a bathing chamber. In a manor this size, they had to install bathing suites in each room to save the residents running around looking for a bathroom in the middle of the night.

And she was right.

Praise the Gods.

After washing her hands, she left, turning off the oil lamp that lit the room. As Emara walked along the corridor, she passed a door that was now open that had definitely been closed on the way up.

Stopping before she passed, she peered through the crack in the open doorway. The room was poorly lit by oil lamps, but she noticed a familiar face. Kellen Blacksteel stood against one of the posters on the bed. His perfectly crisp, white shirt lay open at the chest, and he had taken off his formal tie, his brown hair ruffled slightly against his face.

Emara gulped when she realised he was not alone.

"I can't be gone long," a husky voice sounded from inside the room, one that Emara didn't recognise.

Kellen's lips pulled into a gentle smile, which told her that he wasn't quite smiling on the inside.

Had he been a few years older, he would have been astonishingly beautiful. He just needed time to grow into his youthful features.

"I am really glad we can steal a few moments to ourselves," Kellen said as he took a hand from his pocket and ran a thumb along his lips. "I haven't saw you since—"

"Selection," the unfamiliar voice finished for him. "It's been a few moons since. I thought you might have forgotten…"

"I will never forget." Kellen's shoulders tensed, and his eyes glazed over with something Emara couldn't pinpoint. "It's not something one forgets quickly."

"No, it is not," the mystery voice sounded stern and low. "But we must never make that mistake again."

"Mistake?" Kellen's voice broke. "It was not a *mistake*. You can't give someone a hundred kisses and call it a mistake."

Emara pressed her body against the wall.

A hundred kisses.

This felt wrong.

So wrong!

Her ears should not be party to this conversation. How was she going to get past the door without Kellen seeing her?

Oh, Gods.

"I must go, Kellen. Two young men cannot be seen together like this. If we are found in this compromising position…"

Two men? Kellen was in the room with another boy. Not that it mattered to Emara what gender he had been kissing; it made no difference to her, but clearly, it did to *them*.

It mattered to Hunting families.

She had to find a way to leave.

"I know what would happen if we were found. There is no need for you to remind me," Kellen advised with despondency.

Oh, Gods, what would their families do to them? Emara's stomach flipped and twisted. She was truly intruding on a private conversation. Maybe she could go back into the other room until they were done?

"Can't a hundred and one kisses be enough for us to stop?" The other man in the room spoke with a hint of sadness.

When Kellen didn't respond, the male walked forward, making himself visible in the threshold of the door. He had dark red hair, a little longer than Gideon's. His skin was a couple of shades lighter than Kellen's, whose tanned skin looked darker in the lighting of the room. The red-haired boy reached up and cupped Kellen's face.

"Emara?"

Emara's head snapped around.

Gideon stood at the bottom of the corridor; he tilted his head to the side, confused by her standing against the wall. She sprang up—she couldn't let Kellen and the other boy be seen.

Making the decision in a second, she knew she would rather let herself be seen by the boys in the room than let *them* be seen by Gideon.

She stepped into the line in which Kellen could clearly see her, revealing that she was there.

She coughed loudly. "Gideon, I couldn't find the bathroom. I—I—" She had to think quickly.

He started walking towards her.

No, no, no! She heard a curse coming from the room and a slight scuffle.

"Are you okay?" He walked farther down the corridor, his brows pulled in confusion.

Now! She had to move now.

She ran towards Gideon and threw her arms around his neck, smacking her lips against his. He draped his arms around her waist, embracing her as he kissed her back. It felt so wrong to kiss him like this, but she had to get him out of the corridor for Kellen to walk safely out of the room. Unseen.

Pulling at his shirt, she ran her hands through his hair as she deepened the kiss.

"I am so sorry," he breathed into her mouth. "I wish I could tell you everything."

"Don't apologise, just kiss me."

He ran his hands through her hair and moved his mouth against hers. She hated the fact that she couldn't even enjoy this moment between them. She hated that the kiss was a beneficial distraction. But she couldn't see another way…

She pulled back and seized his tie in her hand and directed him towards the door across the hall from the room Kellen was in. She flung open the door and pulled Gideon towards her; his eyes wild with hunger, he complied.

Guilt ripped through her, tearing her conscience apart, but she didn't know what would happen if Gideon saw Kellen—with a boy, in a room, alone. And that wasn't a risk she was going to take. If Kellen was scared to tell anyone, then it wasn't her place to make anyone aware of his situation.

As she pulled Gideon into the room, his back faced the door that one blue eye and one green eye glared from. She reached up, running her hands down Gideon's neck. He bowed his head and kissed into her neck as she made her way along his shoulders with her fingers. She gave a small command to go with her index finger and closed the door, shutting them behind it. Just as the door clicked behind them, Emara pushed herself back.

Confusion coasted across Gideon's face as they stood in silence, panting. She hadn't been sure she even wanted to kiss Gideon after this morning—she had wanted to take it slow, so that there were no mixed signals.

Well, that worked well!

"Emara?" Gideon questioned, his voice low and bewildered.

Emara's lips parted to form an answer—

Smashing and screaming shook through the manor and before she could speak, they were both running into the corridor.

Another crash and screams could be heard as both Gideon and Emara ran towards the shrieks of pain and destruction.

CHAPTER
FORTY-THREE

As Emara and Gideon entered the threshold of the ballroom, she could smell the sulphur and death. Which meant one thing—they had come again. The screams and screeches of the people within the room pierced her ears and another crash exploded as one of the great chandeliers smashed against the ballroom floor.

Emara recoiled back, bile rising in her throat as she looked up at the open roof where once a domed, colourful stained-glass story had hung overhead. Its ancient stories now lay shattered amongst the bodies on the floor. People were scurrying, screaming, and running in every direction, desperate to evade the destruction. She tried not to look down at the bodies that lay lifeless amongst the wreckage as she moved forward, blood seeping onto the polished tiles.

It was anarchy.

The ballroom had descended into utter chaos. Trying to stop her legs from shaking, she took a step forward, her chest heaving. Before she could take another step, Gideon yanked her back by the arm. "Go! Get out of here!" he ordered. "Run and don't stop!"

But Emara's legs felt like cement as she stood and watched the crowd fighting against their greatest fear. Suddenly a wave of people parted to reveal a woman, pinned against the wall by a golden spear. Her throat was ripped, shredded, as the blood gushed down the neckline of her emerald gown.

Emara's legs almost gave in to the pull of the floor as she took in what she saw. No matter how disturbing, she couldn't tear her eyes away from the woman's impaled body.

She knew that gown. Emara had admired it from across the room earlier this evening.

It was the Empress of Air.

"Emara, move! Go!" Gideon shouted over the screaming.

People flew past her in desperation to escape, but Emara couldn't move. Screams broke through the air in the left-hand corner of the ballroom. Another woman, in a baby-blue gown, was speared to the wall, like the first. Her body was hanging limp as her head dangled down enough that she couldn't see her face. Emara had no doubt that the woman was dead; she didn't have to see her face to know that. The golden spear was stuck through her abdomen.

Out of the corner of her eye, she saw it.
The demon.
The creature took the same form as when she had been in the gardens with Torin, the night of the Blood Moon. It was a disgusting, winged beast with

teeth like large needles and talons as sharp as blades. Its spine bulged out of its vile hunched back as it stalked towards a man, locating its next victim. The blonde-haired Hunter pulled a weapon from his belt and dove into action, to kill.

Another smash of a window on her right-hand side pulled Emara from watching the fight as another winged creature protruded through the glass.

Smash!

Another winged creature cannonballed through another window.

Clatter.

And another.

They just kept on coming. Emara almost hurled at the smell that oozed from them, but terror had taken grip of her body. Gideon sprang into action, running like a flash of lightning towards them, and then he was lost to the madness. Another woman's scream sounded and Emara spun around, seeing yet another woman impaled onto the wall with a spear. This time the spear was directly through her throat. The woman's dark eyes went wide with shock as she took her final breath; the blood from her neck and mouth ran down her chest and into the sweetheart neckline of her silver gown.

The horror that filled Emara's veins was unimaginable as she took in the sight of everything around her.

Seconds later, the House of Fire Witches made themselves known as they congregated together. Seething hot fire erupted around the room, aiming at any demon that tried to enter from the windows. Emara forced herself into a run, not exactly sure what she was supposed to do to help, but she would do anything she could to save lives.

You can use anything as a weapon.

She scanned the room for a weapon—her training hadn't been for nothing.

Crash!

Another chandelier hit the floor in front of her and she skidded to a halt. A winged demon soared in from the open dome and landed directly in front of her. The room shook from its powerful roar. It pulled back one wing and batted Emara across the room. The force knocked the air from her lungs and she landed on the hard floor, her bones crunching as they took the impact of the fall. Emara let out a cry in pain, but there was no time to waste; the creature stalked towards her with leg muscles like boulders and skin so deathly grey. She did all she could to scramble to her feet, but her head was dizzy from the impact of the first blow. Speckles and stars floated around in her vison. She felt a warm trickle of blood slide down her face, and she let it run.

With a vile snarl, the creature's hand dove for her neck, but she was quicker; she ducked to the side, its talons missing her jugular vein by the split of a hair.

A deep growl came from behind her and Emara turned, shocked, to see a massive grey wolf prowling towards her—its teeth bared and covered in dark blood.

Demon Blood.

The demon let out a roar that shattered into her ears and the wolf attacked instantly.

Strong hands hauled her up from behind and straight away Emara tensed her body to fight.

"Get those shoes off," Torin Blacksteel barked. "Here." He shoved a golden spear into her hand. "You gravitated towards a spear in the sparring room, didn't you?"

She blinked and nodded. "How did you remember?"

"It's my duty to notice the small things." He reached out, eyes dark with fire, and wiped the blood on her forehead. "Stay by my side. Always look around you, even above you. Be ready for anything."

He had blood and ick all over him, his blade already dripping with gore from Gods know how many of the things he had killed already. His face was no longer full of mischief and sarcasm; it was cold and focused.

A true warrior in battle.

"The wards are down!" Marcus shouted from the left. "The Covens are trying to raise them, but without the Empress or Supreme, they are finding it difficult." His shirt had been ripped from the bottom to show his stomach, giving off signs of a struggle. He, too, had found a weapon; one of the spears that had been used to strike the women who were still impaled to the walls.

Emara looked down at the weapon in her hand. She held the same kind of spear. A sick sensation flowed into her mouth. As she fought it down, she scanned the walls; on the far back wall, she spied an array of display spears with several missing.

That's where they had come from.

"How can the fucking wards be down?" Torin seethed. "I understand them weakening, but to be completely down? That's impossible!"

Marcus panted, "Maybe the spell that holds them up has been severed. But I can't find the Witches I need to answer that question."

"That's because they are pinned against the walls like grotesque art," Torin spat, a vein bulging from his forehead and neck. "Where the fuck are the Empress' guards?"

Emara knew exactly what Torin was referring to; she had read about the old tradition of dedicated Hunters who were guards to the Empress of a House. Gideon had advised that they rarely used them, only on special outings like tonight.

"They seem to have been the first ones killed," confirmed Marcus. "The element of surprise hasn't boded well for them."

"Fuck the element of surprise, Marcus. These men are trained guards, they should be expecting an element of surprise every time they step out bedside their empress." He cursed again, running a hand over his face. "Find my father!" Torin shouted towards Marcus. "Ask him if he knows where the Supreme is. I didn't see her making her grand entrance as normal. She is the only one who has enough power to raise the wards again without the empresses. These are strategic killings. They are hunting the Witches. Find my father, Marcus."

"I'm on it." Marcus left without looking at Emara.

"Were you with Gideon?" Torin asked, scanning the room as they moved amongst the anarchy, his hand reaching out for Emara's arm.

"Yes," she nodded, reaching out to place her hand in his.

Before she could, a demon swooped down in front of them and clawed a man's throat out, splashing blood everywhere. In a flash, Torin drove a lethal knife through its head, and it crumpled to the ground.

Emara choked on a scream.

"And he came back into the ballroom with you?" Torin continued.

Emara's voice refused to work after what she saw. The smell of iron still hung strongly in the air.

"Stay focused and answer my question," Torin demanded.

"Yes, he came here with me, but I don't know where he is now..." She trailed off as she stalked behind Torin, barely managing to put one foot in front of the other.

"He will be fine; I know my brother. We just need to get you out of here." He surveyed the room to find the best route.

Just then, a booming voice sounded over the room, stopping them in their tracks. Rising through the screams and death, she heard, "Can I have your attention, please?" The voice was cold, but contrastingly upbeat. *Familiar.*

A young man took centre stage where the musicians had been; they, too, were now lying in pools of their own blood.

All of them.

Emara wanted to scream, but not at the people who were now lying dead on the floor, but at the man who stood over them; proud to have massacred his prey.

She wanted to scream, loud, because it was *Taymir Solden*.

CHAPTER FORTY-FOUR

Emara felt her knees buckle below her, but she pulled her muscles in tight. Taymir's fierce eyes scanned the crowd as he couldn't find who he was looking for. He was looking for her and she knew it—but why, she had no idea.

Was he responsible for all of this?

She had to go to him. She had to stop this.

She took a step forward, but Torin grabbed her arm. "What are you doing?" His eyes were wild with disbelief.

"Ending this chaos." She yanked away from Torin's solid grip. "He's here because of me."

Torin called her name again, but the whizzing sound in her head was too loud as she pushed her way through the crowd.

"Anyone that has sight of a pretty, dark-haired dream that goes by the name of Emara Clearwater, please, speak up. There will be a grand reward for the one who finds her first."

The crowd watched him in shock.

"Come out, come out wherever you are," Taymir mocked.

The violence stood still around them.

Only whimpers and crying could be heard. And the choking of the dying. Even the Hunters had stopped in the destruction of the demons to watch the Elite male. The dark army, too, didn't dare to move, like he had commanded them to remain dormant.

Emara's heartbeat thudded into her eardrums as she made her way to the front. It thundered so loudly that she couldn't hear herself think.

"I am going to count to three. If you haven't emerged"—a vile chuckle broke from Taymir's mouth—"I will initiate the killing again."

"You don't have to do that." The words escaped Emara's mouth forcefully, and the crowd parted. "You know I am here, or else you wouldn't be."

Emara moved to the front of the crowd and stood strong, straightening her spine as she centred her weight on both feet. She dug the gold spear into the ground beside her, tightening her grip on it.

"Ah! There is my gorgeous wife-to-be." A muscle ticked under Taymir's eye as he gestured behind her. "And her overprotective bodyguards, I see."

Emara hadn't heard or felt Torin or Gideon behind her, but both brothers flanked her on either side. Torin was on the left and Gideon on the right. She didn't know where Gideon had been in the ballroom, but he must have made his way to her as quickly as he could to stand by her side. She stole a quick glance at his face; he wasn't hurt.

The relief was short-lived as Taymir spoke again, "You know, Emara, if you had been a good girl and just obeyed me the first time, this would never have happened." He gestured to the destruction of the ballroom. "All the blood spilled here tonight? That's on your hands."

Emara shook her head and ground the spear into the floor. This was not on her, was it? This couldn't be about their relationship. There had to be more to it; more that she didn't understand.

The Blacksteel brothers growled behind her.

"Didn't you learn your lesson the last time? I told you that the next time I saw you—" Gideon tried to finish but was cut short.

"Does it look like I listened to you, Hunter? Am I not standing here in the middle of your annual uplift, murdering the hierarchy of the magic community?" The arrogance glowed from Taymir as he flung his hands out ostentatiously and laughed.

"Listen to me, dick!" Torin barked from behind her. "We know you didn't come here—an insufferable, *insignificant* human—to slaughter magic wielders at their annual uplift because a girl rejected your proposal." Clearly, Gideon had filled Torin in on her past. "So let me make this easy for you. I am going to give you two options. One, you tell us why you are *really* here and *then* I rip your heart out with my bare hands; or two, which is my personal favourite, I just get straight to it and rip your fucking heart out." Torin stepped closer into the challenge with a feral smile and a storm brewing in his eyes. "Choose wisely, human."

"Emara, I am talking to you, not to your pet dogs." Taymir shot a look over the Blacksteels. "Tell them to play nice or I will tear another hole through this room with my new friends here." He gestured to the demons that had now lined up like a military unit.

There was no way Taymir could be controlling the demons. He was human. Wasn't he? How did he have the power to control these creatures? Unless someone else in this room was controlling them for him? Was he alone?

"Taymir, what do you want? This is not about us, so don't dare say it is." She winced at the sound of her own voice. "Innocent people have been murdered because of you."

"No, my darling. That is where you have it *all* wrong. I am here for *you.* The Witches had to die so that they couldn't reinstate the wards that were shattered. Call it collateral damage. It allowed my little friends to come in and start this party properly."

The demons in the room stirred with impatience. Impatience to devour everything in this room and in this world. If Taymir snapped his fingers, they would show no mercy and begin the slaughter of innocents.

"Why are you here?" she roared, her full body trembling, her hand tightening around the spear. She couldn't stand these games any longer. Enough was enough.

"Because I was sent for you." He walked around his stage, over the people he had slaughtered, glorified.

"None of what you are saying is even making any sense, Taymir." As she looked at him, she couldn't place what was different about him. The young man she had entertained and had known most of her life, was no longer present. "Please, if you ever loved or cared for me, please stop this and go. *Please* go."

"Emara." He let a patronising grin form on his face. "I never loved you. It was never about love. It was about me. It was about what I could gain from you." His cruel laugh barked into the air. "It was about who you truly are."

Torin moved forward again, but Emara pushed out her hand to command him to stand down.

"That's a good boy, do what she tells you." Taymir winked, and she heard a growl from behind her.

"Stop the riddles," she seethed. "If you were sent for me, then why not tell me who sent you?"

She didn't care that the room was full of eyes watching her desperately trying to make sense of it all. Surely no one else was following this outrageous outburst of insanity.

He was insane. He had to be.

"I think the crowd is growing bored of you, my darling," he sneered. "We must go. Put the spear down and come with me and no one else will be hurt." Taymir unfolded his hand melodramatically.

She had to give it to him, in a room full of magic wielders and people who killed for a living, Taymir Solden was commanding the room like he owned it.

"Who sent you?" Emara demanded to know. Still, nothing made any sense; he hadn't given her anything to work with. "Go with you *where?*" she said again through her teeth.

It was about who you truly are.

She took a step forward.

"No." Gideon moved his body towards her so that his gaze was solely focused on her. She could feel his heartbeat from his chest pressed against her shoulder. "Don't you dare." His voice was desperate.

Emara closed her eyes. She couldn't think.

She needed to think.

What would cause the least damage?

"We can work something out," Gideon begged.

"You will see where we are going when we get there," Taymir provoked, unfazed by his audience. "I am not going to harm you. The king's instructions."

He wasn't going to harm her? She still remembered the sting of his hand on her face as he attempted to take her virginity without consent.

At that moment, Emara's blood ran cold at a memory of what the demon had said to her grandmother before he had killed her.

You know we can't touch her, on the king's orders, but we can rip out the living from this kingdom until we find what we have come for.

The King.

The Dark King. The only king Emara knew of was the King of the underworld. The King of the Fae would have nothing to do with this. The dark one was the only creature who could tie this madness together.

Emara's blood boiled and bubbled under her skin. "Tell me, Taymir, does your *king* know that you struck me and then tried to rape me? Is that his idea of protection?"

"He did what?" Torin stepped in front of Emara, fully blocking her behind his monstrous physique. "She's going nowhere with you. You are going to have to kill me first."

"Ahh, the infamous Blacksteel Brothers." Taymir's eyes glistened. "Are you really going to let one girl's life come before that of hundreds?" His lip curled up at the side as he gestured to the crowd.

An unsettling wave swarmed around the room. Muffles from the crowd let Emara know that everyone was asking themselves the same thing.

"This is not just about one girl's life," Torin said. "Maybe the question is why do you want *one girl* over hundreds? That tells me you believe she is valuable. Why would I hand her over to you?" Torin's hand twitched on his knife.

"That's enough," Viktir Blacksteel's voice boomed from the back of the ballroom as he walked forward. His face set into a hard stare. "Stand down, boys."

Torin let another growl rip from his throat, but he didn't move from his stance in front of Emara, nor did he take his eyes from Taymir's face. He was ready to annihilate Taymir Solden from this world. And Emara had the feeling that she could give him one small signal and he would do it.

"I know who you are working for." The Commander stalked towards Taymir. "And if I am right, I have something that could prove to be more valuable than you can imagine. Gideon?" The Commander held out his hand. "The stone"

"What stone?" Emara caught his stare as she studied his face.

"I'm so sorry, Emara," was all he whispered.

"What stone, Gideon?"

"Your stone," he confirmed slowly. Something in his voice broke as he lowered his head. "Your stone," he repeated.

Emara stilled as Gideon pulled out a white cloth from a hidden pocket in his jacket and gave it to his father. Viktir walked up to the front of the ballroom deliberately slowly as he unravelled the material that revealed a small stone.

It was her grandmother's stone.

The resurrection stone.

"Forgive me," Gideon uttered.

"You took my grandmother's stone?" Emara spoke quietly as the betrayal sunk into her heart. "Why would you do that?"

Gideon did not lift his head to look at her. "I had to. I was…"

Why would he steal from her? How did he know about it?

"It was your mission." Emara pulled her lips over her teeth, gathering herself. "You were instructed to?" She looked at him. "Am I right?" Betrayal smacked into her heart harder than a punch. She felt it break as soon as she spoke, "How could you take that from me?"

A thousand thoughts swirled in Emara's head. He was his father's thief, she realised. His mission must have been to get close to her, in order to see if he could find something of importance. She knew Viktir had been suspicious in the library, but he had never confirmed if he had connected the dots.

Not until now.

Emara flicked her gaze to Torin, but he appeared to be as rigid as her. He didn't know about what Gideon had done.

"I am glad you finally completed your mission." She sneered at Gideon. "When did you take it?"

"That does not matter."

"When did you *steal* it from me, Gideon?"

He flinched. "When you were asleep in my infirmary bed," he confirmed.

Gideon had clothes brought up from your room, so you didn't have to go down there.

Rhea's words slammed into her mind. He must have taken it, then. Every cuddle, every kiss, every moment shared between them, was to lead him to the stone. His mission. One singular tear rolled down her cheek and she tore her eyes from him.

Viktir spoke, "I knew the Dark Army would come looking for the ancient artifacts. They are said to be the only objects that can break Veles free from his cage in the underworld. His crusaders have burned villages, savaged cities, and destroyed worlds to find the powerful relics." Viktir threw a glance at Taymir and held up the stone. "And I have one right here."

Taymir's eyes widened.

The Commander continued, "We have tried to obtain the stone for some time; we weren't even sure that it was in this world until *you* showed up with it— and at the Tower of all places." He glanced over Emara. "It has been said that the stone, once locked with the others—the ones that the light Gods created—will free him from the binding spell. A magical loophole, if you will."

Viktir stepped closer to Taymir. "We don't know how many of the relics the Dark God has, but I know he does not have them all if I have one in my hand."

Taymir shifted on his feet.

"Whoever you are working for—be it the Dark God or someone else—what do you think they would want more? The stone or the girl?"

He chucked the stone into the air and caught it. "The decision is yours, Solden."

CHAPTER FORTY-FIVE

The Commander's question hung heavier in the air than the smell of destruction. But Taymir didn't speak. He shifted uncomfortably on his feet.

It was now clear that he was well and truly out of his depth. What was also clear was that who he was working for hadn't informed him about the stone, or its abilities. The whole room watched Taymir as he contemplated the options bestowed to him by the Commander of the Blacksteel Hunting Clan.

A cold wave of terror washed over Emara's body. Her spine tightened and her breathing crashed as she watched him ponder over the question. Her eyes trailed back to the Commander, who was stony-faced and positioned like granite in front of her. Emara dreaded to wonder, was Viktir Blacksteel using negotiation tactics to protect her, or the stone?

"How did you know about the stone?" Torin asked Gideon impatiently.

But Gideon didn't answer. Instead, he dipped his chin with something like shame crossing his features.

Viktir circled round to the front of Torin, who still hadn't moved, and said, "You knew about the stone for a while, and yet I have given you countless opportunities to tell me about it." Torin tensed. "It is not only you, my son, who will find pretty females who can be your eyes and ears in Huntswood, especially in the markets. We will deal with that matter separately, but for now let's get back to the main topic at hand, shall we?" Viktir swung around to the front of the room. "Mr. Solden, I know your grandfather well and he will not be best pleased to find his heir running around in demon business, nor would the Minister of Coin. He might find your crimes unforgivable—cut your inheritance. If I were you, I would realise I was out my depth here and leave before anything else happens."

Like your death.

Emara knew that's what Viktir Blacksteel implied silently.

"I don't think you understand, Commander Blacksteel." Taymir's chin lifted. "I don't work for my grandfather, and I never will—he made that clear. I severed my ties with the Elite. I work for a unique employer, even more powerful than the Minister of Coin. In fact, some of you might have heard of him," Taymir still played out to the crowd. "Veles—King of the underworld."

Every Hunter in the room stood to attention like something had ignited in their blood, telling them to attack. Emara's skin was sent into a frenzy of goose-bumps as he confirmed her earlier thoughts. Thoughts that she had thought were radical and crazy. A few hisses and gasps floated out from the watching crowd.

"And why would the King of the underworld recruit a worm like you?" Torin spat. "He is Veles, the God of Darkness. He doesn't need a shunned Elite ass-hole to do his bidding."

"Through me, he saw a path to Emara." Taymir smiled so cruelly.

Emara's blood turned thin. So, the King of the underworld wanted a path to Emara. She pushed down the swarming vomit.

"That is utter bullshit, Commander." Torin glanced at his father. "Surely, you cannot buy that he is working for Veles."

The Commander thought over whatever dark-ness was starting to unfold in his mind.

"Father, he is lying." Torin spoke through grit-ted teeth again, "If Veles wanted Emara, his knights would have taken her the night of the attack, but they didn't. They wanted something else."

Viktir's jaw moved slightly, acknowledging Torin's point. "And have you spoken with the Dark God himself?" he asked Taymir.

"No, but—"

"Then who have you spoken with?" the Com-mander questioned.

Taymir's eyes darkened. "He wants her. That's all I was instructed to do." He looked over at Emara. "As do I. She's mine until I say she isn't."

Torin leapt forward. He lifted the blade to strike Taymir in the heart.

"Stop!" Emara screamed. "Stop!"

Torin ceased rigidly, as if it was taking all of his strength not to shove the blade through Taymir's heart.

She looked at Taymir—really looked at him. "Your eyes…" She noticed that the rims of Taymir's eyes glowed red. "What have you done?"

A shocking smile graced his lips. "Emara, you don't get to dance with the devil and remain human. The Dark King made a promise to me that my grandfather never could. After delivering you to him, my heart will beat for a million moons."

"I wouldn't be so sure about that." Torin held his gaze.

Taymir ignored Torin and focused on Emara. "Come with me; let's not prolong the inevitable. No one else needs to get hurt…for now." He glared around the room. "He has plans for you. I will not trade you for a stone that I am not even sure is credible. If he wants it, trust me, he will receive it in time."

Emara shook her head in disbelief, struggling to understand. She fought hard to breathe against the pains that constricted her chest.

Viktir Blacksteel spoke, "It looks like he has made his choice. He doesn't want the stone. He wants you." His gaze burned into Emara's face as if he was trying to piece together what was happening. So there was a piece of the puzzle that wasn't clear to him, too.

"She is going nowhere," Torin spoke through his teeth. He shifted. "Emara is soon to be bound to me and, therefore, she will not be leaving my side."

Bound to me?

Emara knew that Hunters would say anything to stall, delay, or trick their opponent. But something in Torin's voice was sincere.

He continued, "In case your little performance here tonight has fogged your brain"—he looked at Taymir with repugnant disgust—"the last time I checked, the late Empress of Air is pinned to a wall over there with a spear through her heart. As is the Empress of House Water and Fire. Your Dark God evidently hasn't given you *all* the information. Therefore, at the next Witching Moon, Emara will ascend to be the Empress of House Air." Torin's hard jawline lifted into a dangerous smile. "Oh, did I forget to mention that Emara Clearwater is the lost Empress of Air, and the *rightful* Empress of House Air?"

A look of frustration finally revealed itself on Taymir's face. "You Hunting lot don't miss a trick, do you?"

"She is the lost grandchild of Theodora Clearwater, thought to be dead. And as you can clearly see, she isn't dead; Emara survives as the only true heir to the title." Torin pointed to the woman in the emerald gown. "The woman who is speared against that wall *was* the Empress of Air, but did not belong to the Clearwater bloodline. She was a mere stand-in until Emara emerged, and if she never did, then the Clearwater bloodline would have been lost to the Witching world."

Viktir's lips pursed. "If you are correct, Torin, Emara cannot leave this room." The Commander threw a glance at the Elite and Emara wasn't sure if Vikir was playing into Torin's words or if he was serious.

"It was confirmed by a trusted Witch and by Emara herself. Her grandmother was Theodora Clearwater," Torin announced. "Previously known as Theodora of House Air—and the Supreme."

Another bustle of noise broke through the room. Viktir dipped his chin before turning to Taymir. "Emara is bound to Torin, and we do not let what is ours be stolen from us without a fight."

The warning was delivered.

Torin smiled and Emara didn't know if it was because there was a mention of a fight or that his father had acknowledged he was right with his facts, but her heart squeezed in her chest.

Gideon moved uneasily. "What do you mean she is soon to be bound to you?" He glanced at Torin, his face grave.

"The Empress of Air is bound in an engagement to the Blacksteel Hunting Clan—to the first born. The House of Air offered their Empress to forge an alliance with us for protection," Viktir informed. "Therefore, she is bound under our oath to protect."

Emara's heart almost gave way.

It was all too much.

Torin softened his approach, "As you know brother, my marriage was always going to be set in stone." He turned his gaze to Taymir. "So, dick, she's going nowhere with you. Unless you kill me first."

"The Darkness does not bargain with Hunters," Taymir's voice barked with ferocity. "Come with me now, Emara."

She hesitated. His eyes maddened by the second. "I thought that would be the case," Taymir huffed. "Therefore, I arranged a little bit of motivation for you. Bring her in." Taymir gestured to the threshold of the door. A winged creature entered, holding onto a weft of golden hair.

As he dragged her, the girl yelped out in pain.

It was Cally.

Cally.

Emara's head spun, and dizziness almost took out her legs from underneath her.

"Shit," Gideon whispered.

Torin's hand tightened around the blade that he now held up, ready to fight.

What Taymir had just done was a declaration of war. This was never going to end in peace.

The demon bolted Cally upright with one clawed hand and the other grabbed her by the neck.

Before Emara knew it, she was running, the spear still in her hand. Strong hands formed around her waist and dragged her into a solid torso, but she didn't care who it was. She battered her elbows behind her to try and get them to release her.

"Cally! No, no, no," she cried as she struggled against whoever held her. "Get off!"

"Your choice, Emara," Taymir's said. "You either choose to come with me, or I get my demon to rip his claw straight through her heart."

An incoherent cry escaped her mouth.

"Listen to me, Emara, we can kill him. We can take him out. He's messing with power that he doesn't understand," a voice sounded from behind her, but she couldn't think straight or see.

It was *Cally.*

Cally's life or hers.

"I will come with you!" she roared at Taymir. "I can't let any more people die. That's enough!" she sobbed. "Let Cally go. Let her go and I will walk with you out of this place freely. No one else has to die."

"Tell your guard dogs to stand down, to allow you to come without a fight, and I will let her go."

"Please let go of me," She wriggled free from the strong grip, like the person behind her was in shock.

"Emara, no," Cally choked. "It's okay. Let me go." Cally tried to appear strong, but her beautiful eyes were filled with emotion and fear. Cally would sacrifice herself for Emara and she knew it. "I know who you are," Cally breathed. "I know *what* you are. I love you."

"I am sorry," Emara cried out. "I am so sorry for dragging you into this!"

Tears blinded her eyes. She couldn't waste any more time, not when it came down to Cally's life. "Thank you for everything." She looked at Gideon and then Torin, her lips pushed into a straight line. "But you must let me walk out of here. There is no other option."

They stood together like two brutes with the strangest expressions etched into their faces.

She really was grateful for everything that they had done for her, but she was never going to let Callyn Greymore die. She was never going to allow her to be harmed. There was no question.

She would die before she let that happen.

Emara walked over to Taymir; the smile that crossed his face was sickening.

He had won!

Emara closed her eyes and took a breath. He held out his hand and she slowly placed hers in his. His grip tightened around her fingers and she winced in pain as he tugged sharply, crushing her bones.

"Kill her," he ordered the demon.

The demon lifted a clawed hand and plunged his talons right into the centre of Cally's chest.

CHAPTER
FORTY-SIX

The sound that ripped from Emara Clearwater's throat smashed the remaining intact windows of the manor. It could have been heard anywhere in the entire Kingdom.

The demon dropped Cally's lifeless body onto the ground like trash and let her heart roll out of his claw.

"Callyn!" she screeched. "Callyn!"

She thrashed against Taymir's grip, breaking free in time to feel a surge of power burning down her arm. Taymir reached out to grab Emara again, but instead she turned and stabbed the spear right through his abdomen.

She rammed it in again.

Shocked, he stumbled back. His eyes were wide as he looked from her to the golden spear that now pierced through his torso. A gust of wind picked up and swirled around Emara, her hair wild in the magical current. Another scream breached from her throat as she turned and walked towards Callyn, whose body lay lifeless on the ground.

"You won't escape what's coming."

Her head whipped back to look at Taymir, her lip curled back, baring her teeth as her features set into a feral and ferocious setting. Her whole body shook as she took him in, the blood pouring from his abdomen. She felt nothing but an unyieldingly powerful rage. Burning rage.

He realised the change in her, fear finally creeping into his eyes. Not of his impending death, she realised, but of her. Of how she looked. Her hands flew out towards him, and with a shriek, piping hot fire soared from her palms. She tipped her head back and roared into the broken sky. The fire rushed towards Taymir, licking his body all over with flames, flames that were devouring him fully.

Incinerating him.

Burning him alive.

His screams penetrated the night. Around her, the room erupted into chaos as Hunters and Witches fought the demons that burst into action.

Pulling away, she ran to Cally's side and dropped to her knees. "No, no, no!" As she screamed out again, the wind gathered around them, creating a tornado of air. The magic vortexed around her and she was in the eye of her own storm.

"Cally, Callyn!" She brushed her golden hair, now caked in rusty red blood. Her pale face, unmoving.

So pale.

"Oh, Gods, Callyn." She tapped her face gently. "Callyn Agnes Greymore, do not leave this world. Don't leave me!" she begged, buckling over her best friend. Her hands touched the hole in her chest where her heart should be.

Another shriek broke from somewhere inside her, somewhere deep and dark, somewhere she had never ventured before. "No!" Emara cried, looking down at Cally's face. Still and emotionless. Her blue eyes that once sparkled, now empty.

She was gone.

Gone from this world.

Beating her fists into the ground, Emara howled uncontrollably. Feeling an unusual heat, she looked up through blinding tears. A ring of fire now danced around her, burning like a high wall. Was she doing this? Was this her magic?

Yes! It was. She could feel it channelling from her core. She was losing control. Emara's body didn't feel like her own as she gripped onto Cally's hand and lay down beside her. "Please, please, please," she whispered over and over as she let the magic burn from the darkest place in her soul. She let it soar out from her, not knowing how to stop it, not caring if it did. As she cried out unanswered prayers to anyone who would listen, the wall of fire burned around them higher, reaching dangerous heights.

Through her bawling, she heard someone calling her name, but she prayed for nothing other than the fire to take her.

"Emara, you must stop! Girl, you are going to burn yourself out!" The desperation in the person's voice reminded her of her own.

She was desperate. Desperate for all of this to be a terrible, horrendous dream. She was desperate for the rising in her best friend's chest to show that she still took breath. Desperate for the fallen to rise. For the death of Taymir Solden to make her feel liberated and justified. She was desperate for the screams of Taymir to stop lingering in her mind as the visions of his melting skin peeled from his bones and engraved into her memory.

Desperate to feel anything but this pain.

"Emara, honey," a sweet, soothing voice echoed through the flames. "Honey, you are in control. You need to stop the flames, my love. This level of magic is dangerous for a new Witch. Can you hear me? If you can hear me, please sit up. I am Naya Blacksteel, and I am going to help you."

Emara could hear the smooth tones of her voice caress against the darkness of her soul.

Naya Blacksteel.

"Please lower your flames. I am going to help you, my love. I can stop your pain," her voice pleaded.

Stop her pain?

Emara sat up slowly. "Nothing can stop my pain," she said through muffled cries.

"I promise, I can help you."

As Emara rose to her feet, the flames blew up around her into the air like red and orange banners.

"Careful! Easy, honey. Take a deep breath. I am going to help you," the sweet voice said. "Place your palms onto your chest and close your eyes."

Emara felt the air whip through the room, fuelling the fires. Her brain was pounding into her skull, but she managed to steady her feet. Her skin felt like ice and lava had combined to burn against her in a rarest torture.

"Make it stop," she begged. "Make it stop!"

The wind still swirled around the room, pushing the fires to burn against the expensive fabrics and furniture. Screams could be heard to stop her and through the gaps in the flickering flames, Emara saw a tanned face, with caramel brown hair that lay around her shoulders in a natural wave of curls.

Naya Blacksteel.

She concentrated on her face and nothing else.

"That's it. Calm your mind. Place your palms on your chest and feel your heartbeat."

Emara could feel her heartbeat slam against her palm at an unhealthy rate. "I feel it".

"Good girl, now repeat after me," Naya said. "Here and now, I call forth the elemental power of water."

Emara repeated after Naya, trembling as she spoke.

"I call you forth to heal the fire."

She could hear another voice begin the chant.

"I call to the ocean waves. I call to the purest streams."

And another joined. "I call forth from the trickling rain. I call you here to infuse my intention."

Women around the room joined in her chant. "Carry my purpose to your current and wash out the flame in my magic."

Emara felt cold drizzling on her skin, but she dared to open her eyes.

"Again," Naya Blacksteel called. "Here and now, I call forth the elemental power of water."

Every witch in the room continued to chant until Emara's hair was drenched by heavy rain. Her gown, weighty with water, threatened to pull her shaking legs down. She opened her eyes and droplets of water clung to her long, black lashes.

As Emara looked around, she noticed the full destruction of the room. Ashes from her flame now filtered to the floor, mixing in the water. The champagne drapes no longer hung against the windows. Shattered glass glistened on the floor, bathing in dark red blood. Bodies lay lifeless and broken among the wreckage. She could see Hunters in the background trying to aid the wounded. The ballroom was fully destroyed and so was her heart.

"We need to go, honey; we must get you out of here," Naya Blacksteel's voice broke her focus. Naya's eyes were a soft blue and solely focused on her. She held out her hand.

"I can't leave her," Emara whispered.

"You are not leaving her. She will be with you, always."

"I can't leave her body here. I won't." Emara's voice scratched against her throat and a gust of wind blew through the room again.

"You don't have to, my love." Naya didn't lower her hand or her gaze. "I will see to it that the boys bring her home to you. Wherever that will be, they will bring her body to rest. I promise you that." A kindness in her eyes allowed Emara to believe that she wouldn't break her promise. "But we must get you out of here. You have drained yourself of magic and you are in shock. It's a dangerous and vulnerable time for a Witch. We must leave. Hold my hand."

She slowly dragged her feet towards her, raising her shaking hand. The minute Emara touched Naya's hand, a calming energy released over her body, spreading as quickly as the fire had.

"You're a Witch," she stuttered. "A healer."

"Did the chanting give me away?" she smiled warmly. Emara's body swayed, but she held on to Naya's hand. "Gideon!" Naya shouted.

In a flash, Gideon was by her side. She gave him one curt nod. Gideon placed his hand around Emara's back and swept underneath her legs to embrace her in a hold against his chest. Pain pounded in Emara's head and the world shifted around her, changing shape.

"What is happening?" Emara tried to speak. "Put me down. Get off me! You betrayed me!" Emara tried to thrash in Gideon's arms but her limbs were heavy. She didn't have much left to give as she struggled to keep her lids from closing.

"You are drained, my love. We are going to get you to safety. Just let Gideon carry you."

"Mother, please give her something. Ease her pain," Gideon begged.

"You don't make decisions for me." Emara's tongue felt like it was too big for her mouth.

"Mother!" Gideon's voice was short.

"Get her back to our cottage, in the Fairlands. The wards will still be up around the cottage, they are my own. She will be safe there for now." She paused and placed a hand on his shoulder. "They will come looking again." She looked at Emara. Gideon's face was subdued. "I must find Kellen and Torin, then we will be right behind you. Take this." Emara couldn't see what Naya had given Gideon. "Place it at the back of her neck and she will rest. Stay safe, my boy." She kissed his cheek and disappeared into the crowd.

Emara felt something cold press into the back of her neck. She tried to call out for Gideon, but she instantly fell into darkness.

CHAPTER FORTY-SEVEN

Two days ago, Gideon Blacksteel had walked through a portal to his mother's cottage in the Fairlands. He had laid Emara on the small bed his mother always had made up in case her boys would visit. He had sat with her in the spare room of his second home, her body not moving, just keeping a close eye on her chest to see if she kept breathing.

An hour later, his mother and brothers had arrived together, also by portal. His mother had closed off the portal by herself when the boys had given her the all clear to.

Emara had slept through the full night and the following day before awakening, thrashing and screaming on the bed. Gideon had moved to aid or comfort her, but Torin had shifted quicker. A tightening had pulled in Gideon's heart as he watched them together, but Naya had removed Torin from the space and comforted Emara herself, gesturing for all of her boys to leave.

The cottage was small enough for them to hear her sobs for three hours before she fell asleep again. He knew his mother would not heal her broken heart with magic. She had refused when Gideon had begged. She had warned that it was not natural to tamper with emotional pain. His mother had once been a talented Witch, bearing the powers of earth and water—predominately earth—healing Hunters from all around the kingdom. But she would not heal what was not physically broken.

Kellen had volunteered himself and Gideon to run around the perimeter of the grounds to make sure nothing had come through the portal or tracked them here. They had found nothing but a deer and a few rabbits.

When getting back from the sweep, Torin was still awake, making all efforts to avoid any conversation by collecting firewood or hunting for food. But as sure as the sunrise, all three brothers fell asleep on the two sofas in the living area and awoke at dusk to their mother's cooking.

Kellen had made sure he was the first to run a hot bath for himself to soak in and Gideon wished he could feel the warmth of the tub water. Perhaps a roasting bath would wash away the cold, hard guilt that was currently eating him alive.

"She is still asleep," Gideon's mothers soft voice startled him as he sat in the chair in front of the fireplace. "I have sent Torin for a run to burn off whatever warrior energy he had left after what happened. Maybe you should do the same." Although his mother's voice was soothing and gentle, it was lined with authority. "I know how you boys get when you need to burn off some steam. I don't want any broken noses. Not here, not under my roof."

Not in her sanctuary of peace, is what Gideon knew she meant. The one thing that she could control in her life was her home, her beautiful cottage filled with flowers, crystals, and books of her choice.

Gideon watched the flames dance amongst the logs as the events of the uplift plagued his mind like a spinning wheel. The first time he took in Emara as she appeared, stunning, in her black satin gown. The fact that he had wanted to kiss her there and then but couldn't. When he saw Torin dancing with her, the rage that doubled over jealousy as she laughed with him, as he touched her. When he had found her in the corridor, lost. And she had kissed him. She had kissed him hard and desperately, only for that to be short-lived as the massacre took place at the hands of a *human* who had gotten himself mixed up in darkness.

Darkness he didn't understand.

And Cally.

Poor Callyn Greymore.

He shook his head as his jaw locked. It wasn't only the Witching covens that had lost people that night, it was Fae, Shifters, and Hunters too. Even the humans. He hadn't spoken to Torin, or Kellen, or anyone.

About any of it.

He knew Torin would be livid about his confidential mission to gauge if Emara did, indeed, have the resurrection stone—whispers that had come from the Huntswood markets. And the fact that his father had undermined Torin, his second-in-command, and gone to Gideon for the mission—he would be outraged.

But Torin had known about Emara being in possession of the resurrection stone and hadn't informed Viktir. There would be serious consequences for that.

"My love," Naya's voice sounded again, "staring at the flames wishing for an answer to all this madness isn't going to happen tonight." She folded a blanket that had fallen onto the ground and draped it around his shoulders. "If you are not going to run, maybe you should try some sleep."

"I am okay," Gideon's voice came out rougher than he expected.

"You did what you thought was the right thing to do for your father, your Commander." She patted the blanket like he was a babe. "What's done is done."

"I could have asked her, I could—" Gideon couldn't look up from the flames as they thrived together. "She would have probably given me the stone had I asked her for it. But I didn't. I snuck, like a thief in the night, into her room whilst she slept beside me, and I betrayed her. She won't forgive me; it wasn't mine to take." He tried to gather himself before emotion poured from him like a fountain. "Mother, I have fallen in love with her and now I am not sure she will never look at me again." He scratched his thumb over his forehead. "The stone has ties to her family, a family she is just beginning to understand, and I took it from her."

"Gideon, son, look at me."

He looked up at her immediately.

Her nose wrinkled as she tried hard not to frown. "I don't know what the Gods hold for Emara Clearwater and her heart, but I do know that they hold greatness and love for you. However, certain greatness comes with integrity and responsibility, so if you care for her, be honest with her. If you keep her out of the biggest part of your life, she will never fully *be* in your life."

Gideon knew his mother spoke of his fate, about being a Hunter and how she feared it would consume him, like it had with Viktir. If being a Hunter was all he was, and that's all he did, it was all he would ever be. He would be nothing more. Feel nothing more. Live for nothing more.

Naya gently combed a hand through his hair and placed another hand on his shoulder. "I do not know what your father would want with the resurrection stone, but I am sure it is to make sure it stays out of the hands of evil. We both know that Emara Clearwater could never protect that stone. Your father can. You did the right thing."

His mother was right; Emara would never have been able to protect the stone on her own, but that didn't make what he had done right. He didn't need to lie and scheme about it. He could have been open and honest. He could have done things differently.

"If it was the right thing to do, tell me why it felt so wrong to look into her eyes when I told her I took it?"

His mother slid onto the arm of the chair. "Because you *feel,* Gideon. It's okay to feel. I am tired of reminding you boys that. And I am sure it was another test of your father's, to prove your loyalty to him. Which terrifies me—"

"For Torin," Gideon finished his mother's sentence.

He, too, feared what awaited Torin for his betrayal. Viktir Blacksteel would punish his eldest son in one of two ways: Quick and fast which normally meant physical pain—a whipping, lashing, or some sort of brutal physical exercise for a day or two.

Or he would punish him mentally.

A shudder ran through Gideon's core at the latter.

The cottage door swung open and Torin stood in the doorway. It had been the best part of two days and they still hadn't spoken. They hadn't uttered a word about the mission, they hadn't discussed the fact that Torin knew about the resurrection stone, and about the fact that Emara was promised to him in a marriage alliance from a stupid tradition to protect the Witches and strengthen the Clan. Even looking at Torin made anger stir up from within him.

He felt his fists tighten.

Emara was promised to him.

"Torin, my dear, come in quick and shut the door behind you. It's freezing out and I already warmed the wood around the cottage to keep in the heat." Naya stood and made her way behind Gideon. Torin did as he was told, knowing how much magic it took to warm up a full cottage in the dead of winter, given his mother wasn't a Fire Witch. His shirt lay wet against his skin, soaking from his run in the rain.

"I have placed a towel by the chair for you to get dried and changed. I will go into the kitchen and make sure we all eat well. It's stew." She paused. "And when I set out the plates on the table to eat, I want this energy between you two to have dispersed. *Peacefully.*" Naya Blacksteel looked at both of her boys. "You are brothers by blood, not just by duty or oath." She threw a glance between them before leaving for the kitchen. Her sanctuary of home-grown plants, fruits, and vegetables, where herbs hung overhead, jars of everything imaginable cluttered wooden shelves, and something was always cooking—whether it be edible or enchanted.

Torin removed his shirt and rubbed the white, fluffy towel over his body before putting on the dry one laid out by his mother. He flung a look over at Gideon and took a seat. He leaned forward in his chair, towards the flames of the fire, and clasped his hands together, blowing hot air through them with his mouth. The light of the flames flickered across his face, making his features unreadable. He opened his mouth to speak, but Gideon had already started,

"Did you know she had the royal bloodline of Air running through her veins before you agreed to the marriage?" He still didn't look over at him.

"Would it matter if I did?" Torin said coolly.

He snapped his head towards his brother. "Answer the damn question, Torin." Gideon tried to remain calm in respect of his mother, but his legs started to tremble.

"No, I didn't! I would never have said a word had the Empress of Air not been murdered. It was the only way I knew how to save her without starting another war," his brother said lowly.

"But, like I said, would it matter if I did?" Torin looked him dead in the eye. "I don't really get a say in the topic of my own marriage to whatever house is providing the best alliance for us at the time." He paused. "In case you forgot, only a few nights ago I was promised to a woman who now has a spear through her heart."

Gideon dragged his eyes from Torin's face and focused on the crackling sound of the fire.

He shook his head. How did this happen? How could this be his path?

"I am in love with her, Torin." The silence that followed his statement almost swallowed the cottage whole. Gideon felt a stinging in his nose as he fought back the emotion of what he just admitted.

"I know," was all Torin said back.

"I have never told her that. I don't know how she feels about me, but I love her." He sat forward on the edge of the sofa. "I have fallen in love with someone who I have betrayed and lost to my brother, all in one night."

Torin thought over his words carefully. "I can't help you with how she feels, Gid. Only she can tell you that."

Gideon, for a second, thought that Torin had a softness form over his face.

"My only fear is that she tells me that she feels something for you too," he finished.

Torin's eyes flew open.

"Oh, come on, brother," Gideon sighed, exasperated. I have seen you with her in training; the exchange of looks when you were dancing together. At first I thought you were doing it to mess with me, but now I can see that there is something between you." Gideon swallowed the weight of his own words. "She might not know it yet, but I think she feels for me just as much as she feels for you."

Torin stood abruptly and strode to his mother's cabinet. He opened the glass door and searched around for something amongst the enchanted elixirs. Torin pulled out a bottle of liquor that looked home-brewed and divided the remaining liquid into two chalices. One for him and one for Gideon. He placed one into Gideon's hand and then took his seat in front of the fire.

"She might hate us both now," he said, taking a full gulp of alcohol. His eyes hid something behind them, something Gideon wasn't sure of.

"But the question remains, how do you feel about her?" Gideon dared to ask.

"It doesn't matter," Torin replied, placing the glass to his lips. He opened his mouth wide enough to inhale the full content of the glass.

"It matters and you know it," Gideon pushed.

"Why, Gideon? Why does it matter? My fate lies with the blood that runs through my veins and the position of my birth, not with what is in my heart. It doesn't matter if I feel anything in my *heart* for her. The Gods have created a path for me with no choice. So what's the point? It is an alliance. A duty. Just like Mother and Father."

"I know you don't believe that," Gideon scoffed. "I saw the way you looked at her as she walked through the ballroom. I saw the pulse in your neck quicken for her as another woman tried to cling to your neck, but you still watched Emara." Gideon's voice cracked. "I saw the way you stood in front of her like she was your prized possession, threatened that a *human* would take her from you. Protecting her life with your own. I know you want it to matter, so therefore, *it matters*. I just need you to admit it."

"Someone's been a very observant boy." Torin titled his head to the side and watched him. His gaze burned right through him. Gideon had always hated how Torin's stare could make you feel like you were pinned to the very spot. "If you are so sure of your findings, then why do you need to hear me say it?" he said nonchalantly.

"Because you are my brother!" Gideon yelled. "And because I am in love with her." He shook his head. "Because I need to know that you can lie next to her every single night for the rest of your life and give her your whole heart. Because I can. If you can, brother, I will walk away. But if you can't promise me to give her everything, then *I* will fight for her. I will stand up to Father and beg for him to dissolve the alliance between you. We can arrange another one for you—anyone but her." A flash of thought took over. "I could be the alliance; I could take on the marriage." Gideon stood, his legs almost failing him to stand. "It could be me instead of you."

"Gideon." Torin mirrored him, standing a few inches above him.

He looked him in the eye, unfalteringly. "I am serious, Torin. That is how I feel about her."

His brother shifted on his feet. "Did you ever stop for one second and think about what she wants? About what *Emara* wants? Because if I know her like I think I do, she won't want *any* of it. She will want choice and freedom. She will want time and space. She won't want something as substantial as a wedding slapped in her face for the sake of her people— who, by the way, haven't known her for more than five minutes. She needs time. Especially after what just happened to her."

"I know exactly what happened to her, I was there!" Gideon slapped his chest in frustration, stifling a growl.

"Then you should know that she is not going to just accept this," Torin gave a responding growl. "Unless you want to take her up the wedding aisle kicking and screaming as your bride, I would suggest you slow down and give her time to process…all of it."

"Is that what *you* need, Torin? Time? To process all of it? To process the fact that your heart feels? Because I don't need time to work out how I feel." Gideon looked at Torin. His eyes narrowed in on his face. He clenched his teeth together and then shot him a dangerous look. "I know that already."

"I am done with this conversation. You know where I stand on this. Don't push me." A small growl bubbled in Torin's throat.

Only inches from each other's faces, their stares locked—one fire and one ice—both unyielding against the other.

Suddenly, the cottage felt too small for them both.

"Boys, stew is on the table," their mother's voice drifted from the kitchen.

A firm hand fell upon Gideon's shoulder. He had been too busy to notice that Kellen had reappeared from the bathing room, his hair still wet, smelling of clean linen.

"What are you guys waiting for?" Kellen's upbeat voice was higher than the other Blacksteels'. It pulled Gideon from Torin's gaze. "If you guys aren't hungry, I'll have your share." He smiled, his youthful features unaware of the tension.

"Oh, I am not so sure, Kellen." Naya appeared from the threshold of the kitchen door. "I think they both look starving to me."

Naya paused, looking at them. Her stare was intentional. It—their fight—was done. "Come, boys. It's time to eat."

The debate over Emara's heart would no longer continue tonight. Torin broke away first, followed by Kellen. Gideon took a few moments to himself and pondered several outcomes of how this could have gone, but only the Gods knew what his future held.

All he knew right now was that if he didn't eat soon, his stomach would soon eat itself. Before heading into the kitchen, he glanced at the door which denied his eyes access of Emara. His heart told him to go in and check on her, just to make sure she was still there.

Safe.

But his head fought back with his feet and he sauntered through to greet his family. As he sat down

to warm food, he realised the only thing that was missing at the table was her—Emara Clearwater.
   The lost Empress of Air.

EPILOGUE

Her dark red cloak battered in the wind as she stood on the mountains of the North. At the amethyst palace. As she stood at the highest peak in the kingdom, a drop of crimson blood trickled from her nose.

She was bleeding.

Again.

Just like she had been for two days.

She was undoubtedly weakening. Her body, wilting and willingly giving up, to allow another to take her place.

She refused this fate. A fate that she once knew would come, but not as quickly as it had. This was a fate that she didn't get to take from the last reigning Supreme.

Why should it be her? She should be granted more time. She needed more time.

However, it was a fate that the Gods had aligned for her. She sneered, as she wiped the droplets with her hand and smiled at the kingdom below.

But she didn't align her allegiances with the light Gods.

No, no. A carnal cackle escaped her throat. She didn't side with those Gods like the rest of the Witching world did. She did not favour Rhiannon, Uttara, Thorin, and Vanadey. They had abandoned her a long time ago.

Or maybe she had abandoned them.

They were no longer her Gods.

Her loyalties were with a Darker God. Some may call him the devil. Others called him the Dark One.

The Darkened.

The King.

And soon, this world would know it.

Thank you for reading!

I hope you enjoyed reading my debut novel and would be forever grateful to you if you left a short review on any book website. Reviews for an author are absolutely integral for us. A few words can make a massive difference to someone's life.

Acknowledgements

Wow, the fact that I actually made it to this part is astounding. Writing my debut novel has been an unforgettable experience and there are a few people that I would like to thank for helping me on this crazy-wild journey.

Firstly, I would like to thank my mamma. Without you, nothing would have been possible. You have taught me how to be strong and have shown me the most unconditional love which has allowed me to know what I will always be okay. Thanks for all the crazy bedtime stories, I am almost certain they have led me here.

To the real Hunter—my father—he wanted me to acknowledge *something* about his humanity that made no sense…So how about something real? Thank you for teaching me that silence is not a bad thing, that my shoes don't always have to be 'clicky' and that twins are not made up of three things. And most importantly, you taught me that its okay to be different and not follow a crowd, the crowd that are meant to be around you will find you when you are unapologetically yourself.

To my sisters, in oath and maybe not so much blood—Chanley and Jorja—without you two, my first ever beta reader and my mini PA, I would not have had the courage to do this. Thank you, thank you.

A massive thank you to my actual beta-readers, who gave me faith that my writing was worth reading.

To Melissa Hawkes—had I not found you—I probably wouldn't be writing my acknowledgements, still stuck in a formatting rage somewhere. Our paths were meant to cross, I am sure of it. You have helped me more than you know.

A huge congratulations to the beyond talented Natasha, who designed my book cover and put up with how technically *unadvanced* I am.

To my editor—RaeAnne—Please forgive me for my terrible grammar and punctuation. You are the best, and I am so glad to have found you.

A note to all the teachers who thought it was a good idea for me to leave school at fifteen—no thank you. Just because I learn in a different way doesn't mean I am stupid or incapable of great things. So, thank you to the drama department who made me feel like I was important and that I mattered at school. You saved me in more ways than one.

And to my soulmate—Scott—without my heart finding yours, I would have never been able to write about intensity, sacrifice or real love.

"So I told myself I wouldn't settle. I wouldn't settle for anything mediocre. I would settle for nothing short of breathtakingly powerful love that awakes your soul and stimulates your mind. I want a purposeful love" - Emara

And I didn't settle.

I found everything in you.

About the Author

Noelle Rayne is the debut author of An Empress of Air and Chaos. This is book one in her debut fantasy series. She has an Honours Degree in Drama and lives in Ayrshire, Scotland. When she is not writing, she is binge watching supernatural TV shows, cuddling her fur baby or curling up with a good fantasy book under fairy-lights. *Or possibly doing all three at once.* She is obsessed with storms, glitter and all things witchy. If you like any of these things, I have a feeling you might like her books…